This One's on Me

Books by Donald Jack

The Bandy Papers

Three Cheers for Me

That's Me in the Middle

It's Me Again

Me Bandy, You Cissie

Me Too

This One's on Me

Prologue

I had now been hiding in the wardrobe for more than an hour, obtaining a surprisingly comprehensive view, considering that the wardrobe door was open only a few millimeters, of the blonde beauty on the bedsitter bed. And the worst of it was, she was now starting to undress.

It was not even 10:00 P.M. and she was already preparing to retire. As she started to strip, I did not dare to remove my eye from the crack in the door in case the movement gave me away. I had already gone to great pains—the great pains of cramp—to ensure that a raw elbow or other osseous projection did not collide with a mahogany panel, or that a coat hanger did not jangle. Though perhaps she would have been too tired to notice even if I had panted. Her posture, after twelve hours in Pathology, was one of bone weariness.

At first she had seemed disinclined even to stir. She had brought home a parcel of laundry and had studied the laundry bill for at least ten minutes, as if it were a code that she was trying to crack. Then she had stared at the wall, on and off, for a further half hour. Then, suddenly, a whirlwind of action, relatively speaking; i.e., she raised her elbows to remove the jacket of her tweed suit. It was a new suit. I had not seen it before. Under the hairy jacket was an ivory blouse. It was surprisingly frilly. Usually she wore the plainest of clothes, the kind of garments that did the least for her statuesque form. Except that statues were usually chunky objects, while this woman in her mid-twenties was a geometry exercise in conic sections: broad shoulders tapering to a narrow waist, then out again to perfectly idyllic haunches, while in front, nicely balancing the buttocks to produce an exquisite equilibrium, breasts that might have served as fenders for an ocean liner. As she unbuttoned her blouse, I could plainly see them rebelling under the oppressive regime of her brassiere.

I closed my eyes, but a cleavage like the Cheddar Gorge hung in the air, sharing the confined space of the wardrobe for a few seconds before slowly fading like the Cheshire cat.

Honestly, how did I get into these terrible predicaments? It was disgraceful that at my age I had not yet learned from experience. I mean, Good Lord, look how often it had happened before. Like the time I was visiting the wife of my brigade commander in France. What was the name again? Arthur Soames. No, no, not *his* name, *her* name. Marguerite. Come to think of it, she had been built in the same yards as this girl, except that Marguerite was ten years older and softer to the touch. "I have no intention of letting you sleep with me," she had said those half dozen years ago in Paris. "I have always been faithful to Arthur, even though we have been married since more than a year." Whereupon, inflamed by my protestations that I had no intentions at all, honorable or dishonorable, as I had just come from the dentist and was feeling poorly, she had seized me by the hand and was in the process of leading me into a room that I sincerely hoped was the bathroom when, from downstairs, we heard the front door opening and closing. We froze like two pillars of salt as the closing of the front door was followed by a thump that sounded either like the body of a recently despatched lover being deposited in the cellar . . . or like Arthur's suitcase being set down in the hall. "It *can't* be your husband," I'd whispered. "It only happens in plays." But it happened in my memoirs, too.

Marguerite had promptly shoved me into the brigadier's study, and there I had hidden, just as I was doing now, until I heard the two of them declare their love for each other, whereupon, goaded into a fury by her inconstancy, I flung myself and a large batch of the brigadier's private papers out the window. Then there was that time in the governor general's mansion in Ottawa when, apprehensive that I might be recognized by the Prime Minister, with whom I did not get on at all well, I had hidden behind an arras like a flustered Polonius, except that in my case it was to avoid being run through by the sword of the PM's hostility. Of course, I was a trifle squiffy at the time. Even so, the moment I concealed myself behind the curtain, I knew it was a mistake. If I was discovered, no eloquence would suffice to explain the guilty concealment.

It wasn't as if I hadn't remonstrated with myself on many such occasions. Why did I behave in this fashion when I had demonstrated on numerous other occasions that I was quite capable of brazening things out? But then of course my normal behavior was usually deliberate. When it was a matter of making a spontaneous decision in an emergency and the conditions were right—that is, if I was assailed by feelings of insecurity and guilt—all too often I took precisely the kind of action I had taken about an hour ago. While paying a visit to my old boarding house in London, I had been trapped in the passageway downstairs by the unexpected arrival of this blonde beauty who treated the dead so much more respectfully than the living. Merely to avoid being ticked off, I had hurled myself from the ground floor to the second floor, reaching the top of the staircase in one bound. Then, realizing in mindless panic that she was coming up after me, I had hidden in the wardrobe in an unoccupied bedroom, only to discover that she was still going my way—that she lived in that room.

So now I was trapped in the cupboard, and there I was to remain for the next six months.

PART I

Reykjavik, '24

Right from the start, Sigridur got into the habit of coming to my aid, as if that hefty Icelander were a boy scout and I some palsied duffer who didn't know any better than to step out into life's whizzing traffic without looking right or left. After I had splashed down into the fiord between Reykjavik and the mountain that sheltered it from the Atlantic, I had no trouble steering the floatplane between the wide-spaced beacons at the harbor mouth despite the rainstorm that had been laid on for my arrival instead of a brass band. It was only when I reached safety that my difficulties began. Inside the sheltered waters of the harbor I had trouble maneuvering the airplane through the lines of anchored fishing boats, partly because of the wind that was billowing Neptune's silver raiments across the fishy scenery and buffeting the yellow fuselage into whichever direction I did not wish to go, and partly because the floats had no rudders. I hadn't thought of adding rudders when I designed the cabin monoplane three years previously, so I could steer only by fanning the tail with the engine; but I didn't dare open the throttle too widely in case I ran smack into a smack, and converted the propeller into a brace and bit. Several times, just as I managed to point the nose toward the only uncrowded jetty in that damned, jammed harbor, the wind put its shoulder to the wheel and swung the high-winged monoplane in the opposite direction. If anyone had been able to see me through the lashing rain, which was drumming on the wing like the boots of a thousand brats in a tantrum, it would have looked as if I were searching a small area of harbor for something valuable dropped overboard. Actually somebody did see me. After I had been blatting helplessly this way and that for several minutes, semi-anesthetized by cold and fatigue after nearly a dozen hours in the air, an oilskinned, sou'westered chap in a rowing boat suddenly appeared, wrapped in sheets of rain, and, with enquiring mime, asked if I'd care for a tow. Upon receiving a waterlogged affirmative, the bulky fisherman ordered me to shut down the power plant, then skilfully ran a rope through the mooring rings in the front of the floats, secured the ends to the stern of his boat, and proceeded, with powerful, steady strokes of the oars, to tug me to a landing stage near the stony, inner shore of the harbor.

As I climbed down from the open cockpit, looking like a defective toy soldier, my rescuer briskly secured the amphibian fore and aft to a couple of the iron staples that stuck out every few feet along the landing stage, then stood waiting with arms patiently folded as, with half-paralyzed limbs, I stilted cautiously over the wet boards, which were pasted with fish guts, and joined him. Whereupon I perceived that despite his bulk, the face deep within the shiny waterproofing was . . . well, embarrassed as I am to describe a chap in such terms, there was no avoiding it—he was lovely. Physiognomically at least, Icelanders appeared to have softened a bit since the days of Eric the Red.

"Spika the English?" I enquired, through a lockjaw caused by meteorology.

"Yes," the other replied. "Do you?"

Cheeky cod, I thought. I would have given him one of my superior looks if I'd had one to spare. But my face was immobilized by coolth. So instead, I turned up the collar of my flying coat against the downpour and tried to think of an appropriate rejoinder; but the best I could manage was a witty sneeze. Anyway, my rescuer had turned away, either to avoid being slapped in the kisser by the rude elements or to watch several children, saturated whippersnappers, who had come pelting out of nowhere and were now gaping at the big yellow monoplane as it drummed and wallowed alongside the landing stage.

"Thanks for the help, by the way," I mumbled through lips that were finally starting to thaw in the warmer air at sea level. "I was getting a bit seasick out there."

"Where have you come from?" the boatman asked in a pleasantly low voice.

"Canada."

The other considered this for a moment, obviously wondering how, after that example of my navigating skill in the harbor, I had managed to get this far. He looked even more dubious when I added, "I believe I'm on my way to England."

"But you're not sure?"

"It's a long story," I muttered, stretching cautiously and taking a deep breath of ozone, or rotting fish.

He continued to regard me curiously from deep inside his oilskins before asking abruptly, "Do you have anywhere to stay in Reykjavik?"

"No."

"You look half dead. Perhaps you would like to come up to the house and thaw yourself out?"

"Shouldn't I check in with customs or somebody?"

"Oh, don't worry about Mr. Magnusson. He can drop in tomorrow and ask if you've anything to declare."

He was obviously inviting me to stay the night. I wondered uneasily if he had taken a fancy to me.

"I think I'd better put up at a hotel," I said. "If you have one in Iceland, that is," I added politely.

"Suit yourself," the fisherman said, removing his sou'wester and shaking a head of tousled blonde hair almost girlishly.

It was only then that I realized that the downpour had ended as abruptly as it had begun, and that the sun was shining. The landing stage was already steaming. As the boards were plastered with piscatorial entrails, an odor of steamed fish immediately arose.

"On second thoughts, I accept," I said. "If you're sure it's no trouble, miss. By the way, my name is Bandy."

"Sigridur Jonsdottir," she said, and shook hands firmly with one stroke, as if pulling the chain of an old toilet.

"Just a minute, I'll get my luggage," I said, and, stepping onto the float, opened the cabin door under the high wing of the amphibian and brought out four bottles of gin.

My first impression of Reykjavik was of a rather dreary settlement of wet stone walls, a scattering of gloomy public buildings surrounded by gray shacks and an excess of waste ground. But now that the sun was out, all sixty degrees of it, the Icelandic capital looked rather more prepossessing. Some of the larger houses proved to be a good deal more solidly constructed than most Canadian abodes; fine, white concrete edifices with bright red or green roofs. Even a few of the smaller houses glowed in the sun, though of course they knew their place in the social color scheme. Primary colors were for the wealthier citizens, and browns and grays, or at best, pastel shades, for the humbler citizens.

As it dried out under a bland sun, the town looked still more attractive. There was none of the hideous North American tangle of wires, poles and petrol pumps, and the sounds were peaceful: the rhythmic crunch of pedestrian feet in the rough streets and a gurgle of water in the storm-chiseled gullies, the creaking of occasional carts drawn by shaggy Icelandic ponies, the distant plaint of gulls and children. The place had the sea-scrubbed appearance of fishing towns everywhere.

"Iceland looks very clean and neat when the sun comes out," I observed, as I trudged up the rough stone streets behind Sigridur.

"Thank you," Sigridur replied, as if she had tidied the place herself.

"You speak very good English. I thought I would have to use sign language, or rub noses, or something."

"You have to know English in medical school," she replied shortly. "And German. And Greek and Latin."

"You're studying medicine?"

"I passed my finals just this month," Sigridur said, trying to sound offhand about it.

"Gee whiz. I suppose you went abroad to study."

"Certainly not. We have a very fine medical school right here. In the Parliament building."

This One's on Me

The Sixth Volume of The Bandy Papers

Donald Jack

PaperJacks LTD.

TORONTO NEW YORK

PaperJacks

THIS ONE'S ON ME

PaperJacks LTD

330 STEELCASE RD. E., MARKHAM, ONT. L3R 2M1
210 FIFTH AVE., NEW YORK, N.Y. 10010

Doubleday & Company, Inc. edition published 1987
PaperJacks edition published July 1988

This is a work of fiction in its entirety. Any resemblance to actual people, places or events is purely coincidental.

ISBN 0-7701-0975-6

Printed in Canada

Contents

"Parliament? And where do the politicians work? In the mortuary?"

"You are cheeky. And I don't like your attitude," she said sharply. "Rubbing noses indeed. You'll be accusing us next of eating whale blubber. I'll have you know we Icelanders were writing great epics when you illiterate Anglo-Saxons were still living in filth with your relatives and pigs—assuming you could tell them apart."

"We still have trouble."

She stopped in the middle of the road, forcing a pony and cart to maneuver round her. "You are a very annoying as well as a very disorganized person, aren't you?" she snapped.

"I'll probably improve when I've had a hot meal."

"I doubt it. Besides, I'm not sure I want to take you home with me after all."

"By the way, I was a medical student myself once," I said, making an effort to be friendly.

"Who cares?" she snapped and dropped my valise in a puddle. "And you can carry your own bag from now on."

As we continued up the street, I gave her a couple of minutes to recover—she seemed to have rather a surly disposition—before commenting, "So you're a brand-new doctor, eh, Sigridur? Congratulations."

"Thank you," she replied curtly.

"Do they require graduates to intern here?"

"No," she said. Then, a few seconds later: "I'm establishing a practice right away. Here, in Reykjavik."

We moved aside to let a pony and cart get past. The young driver called out to Sigridur in the soft, tongue-curling language. Sigridur replied by holding up her hand like a traffic policeman, which I later discovered was a typical gesture of hers to acknowledge a greeting.

By and by we reached the Tjornin, a small lake in the center of town. "Our house is over there," she said, pointing across the water. "And that," she added, indicating a large stone building at the far end of the lake, "is the old Parliament building. Our first Parliament was founded a thousand years ago, incidentally, at the foot of the Almaunagja chasm."

"Oh, yeah?"

Sigridur's house, situated on a slope overlooking the lake, proved to be a two-story frame structure covered in corrugated iron. It was painted a soft shade of yellow and, though unpretentious, was proudly maintained. The front windows sparkled in the sun.

As we drew close, I hung back, regretting now that I had agreed to come home with her. I would have much preferred to put up at a hotel—we had passed one on the way up, the two-story clapboard Hotel Alexandra—where I could have had a nice hot bath and gone to bed early, say at four in the afternoon.

"Look," I said, "are you sure your folks won't mind? I mean, a perfect stranger barging in on them?"

"They are used to people dropping in unexpectedly," she said. "Sometimes relatives come with a quarter barrel of salted lamb and expect to stay all winter."

"And your parents don't mind?"

"Oh, yes. They get pretty fed up by spring. But it's a tradition, you see. Everybody, relative or stranger, is entitled to stay at least three nights. We call them 'guest nights.' Anyone's entitled to them, even someone like you."

"But I don't have any salted lamb on me."

"You have four bottles of gin. That's even better."

We entered via the kitchen, which, with its adjoining scullery, was at the back of the house. Its homey appearance suggested that it also served as the family living room. The floor was of polished planks, with cheery rugs scattered here and there. In the middle of the floor a dining table stood squarely, daring anyone to move it. Obsequious chairs surrounded it. Against the inside wall stood the heating plant for the whole house, a seven-foot stove in yellow enamel. And against the far wall there was an old oak sideboard on which stood a pair of old oak shoe trees. The sideboard also supported a sepia photo of a sailing ship, a glass jar filled with assorted buttons, a fancy sea shell, a heap of knitting and a chipped bowl containing a solitary wrinkled apple.

The room also contained Sigridur's parents. Though sturdy and muscular, Mr. Jonsson was inches shorter than Sigridur and a good deal older. I estimated that he must have been at least fifty when he sired his big, blonde offspring. A bushy gray beard embroidered with silver strands flourished above his waistcoat and collarless shirt. The facial decor was so dense, extending even to his cheeks and obscuring much of his nose, that the only visible features were his ice-blue eyes, which seemed to be focused on the horizon, presumably a habit developed during his years at sea as captain of a trawler.

As he was a bit tight-lipped, it was difficult to determine exactly where his mouth was located, without cutting a way through to it with a pair of scissors. As I had left my scissors in the amphibian, I had to wait until he addressed me again. Even then the words issued from no discernible opening, crevice or fissure.

"You have flown across Greenland and the Strait as well?" he asked. "That must have taken much skill and courage."

"I was scared stiff all the way," I replied with a modest smile designed to suggest the opposite of what I was saying and obscure the fact that it was the truth.

When his wife arose, I saw where Sigridur had got her height, if not her solidity. The mistress of the house, much younger than her husband, was as long as a drainpipe, and in her long black dress she looked like one, too, with clamps at neck and waist. She had a face that in its sternness seemed to be typical of older Icelandic women. Even her hair was severe. It was so tightly drawn back in a bun that it stretched the skin of her face, producing the effect of an instant facelift.

Owning such a face, it was hard to tell whether she was pleased to have me as a guest or not, though she accepted my gift readily enough and wasted no time in plonking four whiskey glasses onto the kitchen table.

As they had nothing to go with the gin except cod-liver oil, which I didn't fancy as a mixer, we took it straight. I started off by sipping mine, but Jonsson and his wife and even Sigridur tossed theirs back in one gulp, so I felt obliged to follow the swallows in the same manner. Whereupon Jonsson topped up the glasses the moment they hit the table, and the first bottle of gin was well on its way to perdition by the time the two youngest members of the family returned from school.

These were a boy of sixteen and a plump girl of eighteen or so. After a polite greeting for the guest, they turned excitedly to their mother and started telling her something, presumably to do with the airplane in the harbor, for their mother said something in reply and nodded in my direction. Whereupon the boy, Bjarni, looked as impressed as if I were some mythological creature—a centaur, perhaps, given the equine lineaments of my face.

"It is your airplane?" he asked, wide-eyed. Then: "I am an expert on aviation. It is a British airplane. I can tell because of the letter 'G' on the tailplane. It is, of course, a Martinsyde Seaplane, powered by a 270-horsepower Falcon engine with a top speed of 110 miles an hour."

I looked really impressed, which greatly pleased him. He was right, of course; except that he had the power plant wrong, and it was a Bandy, not a Martinsyde.

His sister, Thorunn, soon lost interest in the technical conversation that followed and went off to talk to Sigridur, who had gone upstairs to change for dinner. I hoped that dinner would soon be on the table. I had already absorbed several cocktails of gin and gastric juice, and this, added to my fatigue, semi-deafness and numb feet, was likely to prove too much for me if I didn't pack a few victuals into the abdominal larder.

Perhaps it was already too late, for when several visitors came clumping into the house, I got quite confused. Though most of them appeared to be married couples, judging by the way they ignored each other, none of the pairs seemed to share the same name. The woman who was with a Mr. Magnusson, for instance, was a Mrs. Thorvardsdottir, while the lady with Mr. Thorvardsson was introduced as Mrs. Magnusdottir. Similarly Mr. Krabbe's companion was named Mrs. Petersdottir. The only person I could make sense of was an expensively suited fellow named Agnar, and that only because there was no woman with him.

I concluded that the whole bunch of them were living in sin. A couple of days elapsed before I realized that in this country a woman kept her own name whether she was married or not, and therefore all the women probably *were* married to the men they were with—though according to Mr. Jonsson, in Iceland that was by no means a safe assumption.

I was also puzzled as to who they were. Relatives, perhaps, or neighbors who had dropped in to inspect the owner of the airplane down at the harbor, or maybe they were merely passers-by who had heard the clink of glasses and had rushed in to join the party. For a party it had rapidly become. Faces were flushing, voices rising, gestures expanding. I knew it was a party because I heard myself saying so. "By George, you Icelanders sure know how to throw a party," I heard myself saying. Whereupon Mr. Jonsson explained under his grizzled camouflage that alcohol was expensive in their country, so on the rare occasions when it was available they tended to take uninhibited advantage of it.

I could see that, all right. No delicate imbibing before dinner for this lot. Even Mrs. Jonsson, or whatever her name was, was knocking the stuff back as if competing in the gin Olympics.

Fortunately, when Sigridur, accompanied by a giggling Thorunn, came downstairs, I was not too squiffy to notice that she had taken off her clothes. I noticed this immediately. She had removed her maritime gear and was now enclosed in a dress of some thick, cream-colored material. It was embroidered at the hem, around the short sleeves and at the square neck with traditional Icelandic designs in bright earth colors, while her long smooth legs ended in a pair of matching slippers.

Sigridur seemed to be a bit careless about her attire, and typically the cream dress, though proudly national, was not too flattering. Her figure was bold enough to begin with, and the heavy material emphasized her luxuriously curved but muscular build. Moreover, her broad face was devoid of makeup. She looked disturbingly incomplete to a chap who was used to female visages caked with rouges and powders.

Nevertheless, the moment she reappeared I actually grunted, as if someone had sunk a mailed fist into my midriff. She looked dazzlingly beautiful, with those smoothly carved cheekbones and wide, smiling, sensuous lips the color of grade A salmon. The physical ensemble was topped off with a pair of bright, fiord-blue eyes and an almost blindingly bright crest of curly blonde hair. When, becoming aware of my gawp, she turned to stare back at me challengingly, my heart lurched, to match my legs, which had gone all colly-wobbly. I had to sit down suddenly—forgetting to first make sure that there was furniture available to complement the genuflection.

Fortunately Thorunn, obviously a quick girl in spite of her avoirdupois, shoved a chair against the back of my knees just in time, an action so well timed as to create an uproar of merriment from everybody except the dour-looking fellow named Agnar, who didn't seem to appreciate the way I had been gaping at Sigridur.

Sagging onto a very nearly nonexistent chair broke the ice as well as the Icelanders. Until then, despite a ginspired jollity, I was an unknown quantity, a distinctly bizarre-looking aviator—still an exotic profession in 1924. But now I had evidenced human weakness, notably a susceptibility to alcohol and pretty girls. From then on my host and his friends behaved with less stiffness and formality toward me.

Half an hour later, Sigridur, apparently deciding that I was either in danger of enjoying the spontaneous levee or of making a fool of myself, took me by the arm and said, "Your room is now ready. Come." And she led me gently but firmly out of the kitchen.

My ground-floor room was directly opposite, across the central corridor. It was austere but pleasant enough, with a single window overlooking the fenced backyard. The only disturbing feature was the shiny yellow wall covering, featuring a raised pattern of weals, welts and bruises.

On a small table beside the bed stood a water pitcher in a willow-pattern bowl. "You can wash in there," Sigridur said, pointing at the bowl.

I resisted the obvious repartee, not out of literary fastidiousness but to spare myself the cool, uncomprehending stare that such a remark would almost certainly have provoked. Sigridur did not strike me as having much of a sense of humor.

So instead of a wisecrack, I thanked her politely, meanwhile running a hand curiously over the wallpaper. As my fingers slid over the wounds I started shivering as if I were a fetishist getting a cheap thrill from the masochist wall covering. It was with some relief that I realized I was shivering merely because I was cold. After twelve hours in an open cockpit I felt I would never be warm again.

"There is, of course, no bathtub in the house," Sigridur added, looking at me with her big chin raised imperiously, as if daring me to question her family's good sense in not having a bathtub in the house. "If you wish to bathe indoors, you must do so in a tub in the kitchen."

"Are you saying that the alternative is to have a bath outside?"

"Yes, of course."

"What, in front of the neighbors?"

"Don't be silly. I am referring to the hot springs," she said, looking me over as if unsure about whether I was used to taking baths. "We can try the hot springs tomorrow, if you wish."

"Fine, fine. . . ."

"Here is the soap," she concluded, as briskly as a nanny—I half expected her to remind me to wash behind the ears—"and a towel. Supper will be ready in half an hour."

As soon as she left I finally admitted that I was now thoroughly soused. Alone at last and freed from social restraint, I surrendered to inebriation. I allowed myself the luxury of reeling about, sniggering and saying, "Phew" and things like that, meanwhile holding onto the wall and feeling the lacerations sliding under my fingertips. "Lord God, I'll never last out the evening," I said aloud; then, "Shhh," and another giggle.

I thought I had better lie down, but the effect was even worse. The bed promptly took off and climbed at a dangerous angle. It stalled and spun into the nearest canyon. Fortunately the canyon was several thousand feet deep. Before we hit bottom, I bailed out of bed, said "Phew" again and tried to realign my eyes by standing at the window and admiring the view. But the adjoining corrugated house was heaving and rocking as if I had arrived just in time for the latest earthquake.

How I wished it was time for bed. But there were still hours to go before I could decently retire. Or indecently. God, this was awful. All that gin on top of all that gasoline, and the bellowing

Puma engine, and the rushing, freezing air, and the gnawing dread that my navigation might be off by a single degree and thus plunge me a hundred miles out into the Atlantic.

Half an hour later, washed and brushed and making a tremendous effort to keep my face from collapsing in a heap, I recrossed the passageway to the kitchen and entered, fervently thanking God that we would soon be eating, and I would be spared any further liquid hospitality.

"Oh, Bartholomew," Mr. Jonsson cried, "you've just got time for another drink before dinner."

The kitchen table had grown to manhood since I last saw it. It was now ten feet long, covered with an exquisitely crocheted tablecloth on which the best china and silverware gleamed and glittered. By then the other visitors, apart from Agnar, had departed, so there were a mere seven chairs ranged round the table.

Thorunn was arranging a vase of flowers; her mother was in the scullery surrounded by clouds of steam. Mr. Jonsson was also wreathed in gaseous matter. He was puffing a pipe in his favorite armchair near the big yellow stove, which, this being spring, was stone cold. Sigridur and Agnar were over by the sideboard.

Agnar, who had a gray face and matching personality, was doing most of the talking, while Sigridur, head lowered over the fruit bowl, was idly digging a thumbnail into the senile apple, as if practicing her incisions.

Though my first leap of emotion at the sight of her was rapidly subsiding as I got to know her better, it was hard not to stare at her, she was so lovely. Could she really be a doctor? If so, she must have been a sensation in the dissecting room. That glorious mass of blonde hair, those cheekbones inherited from various Viking rapists and ice maidens, that wonderfully edible lower lip and that aggressively contoured figure—thank God she wasn't my type.

Which was just as well, for by now I had learned that the chap she was talking to was her fiancé. He had told me so the moment he saw me mentally practicing ski jumps off the advanced slopes of Sigridur's chest.

"We are to be married in no time at all," he had informed me.

He was certainly no great catch himself. Agnar was at least a dozen years older than Sigridur and, though smartly dressed, he looked as if he had forgotten to wash that day. His skin looked as if it needed a good scrubbing or bleaching, and his fuzzy brown hair, brushed straight back from a low forehead, was as lackluster as his manner.

While he was still talking, Sigridur gestured for me to join them, much to Agnar's irritation. Even after I arrived, desperately clinging to a brimming gin, he continued to drone on in Icelandic and did not stop until Sigridur interrupted to explain to me that Agnar was discussing his latest housing project.

Somewhat reluctantly, Agnar switched to the English that Icelanders seemed so familiar with. "Yes, I am a qualified engineer and builder," he said, failing as usual to meet my eye, which on this occasion at least was understandable, as the eye in question—and presumably its mate—was reeling about in its alcoholic oyster bed. "I am well known in Reykjavik. I have built many of the houses in the better part of town." He gestured, as if to indicate that this particular neighborhood was not it. "Two years ago I completed a fine concrete home for myself on Tjarnagata. It has a garage, and there is space for medical offices on the ground floor."

"For Sigridur?" I asked inattentively. I was looking around for somewhere to hide the glass of gin I was holding. While I didn't like to disillusion Mr. Jonsson, who seemed to think that North Americans could absorb any amount of alcohol, I felt I had had enough to last me until next leap year. But there was nowhere even to pour the drink, not a single plant pot, just the glass jar full of buttons, and I didn't think Mrs. Jonsson would appreciate having her fasteners swimming in gin.

However, the top drawer of the sideboard was open a few inches. I thought there might be just enough room in there in which to nestle the glass and then cover it with doilies and things.

Sigridur was saying something. "Par'n me?" I asked, focusing on her with difficulty.

"I was saying that it was Agnar who paid my way through medical school," she said, touching her fiancé's sleeve. "I owe him a lot."

"Her father, of course, could not afford the fees," Agnar put in complacently, "but I felt it was only right that I should make such a sacrifice for somebody who is to be my wife. I have been waiting to marry her, you know, for ten years."

"That's very patient of you, Agnes," I whined.

"Agnar," Sigridur corrected me.

"Yes, yes, of course—Agnar."

A moment later, Mr. Jonsson limped over to join us. I sincerely hoped that he wouldn't offer me a fill-up. It was with great difficulty that I had managed to sink the gin in my glass to a depth of a mere three inches.

"Sigridur tells me that you claim to have been a medical student yourself at one time," he said, slipping an arm around his daughter's waist. She responded by laying her head on his shoulder. She and her *pabbi* obviously adored each other.

"M'oh, yes," I babbled, to distract him from my relatively ginless condition. "Until I joined the army. I even served as a doctor once. It was in Moscow, you know, at the university hospital." As I listened to myself, even I didn't think I sounded too convincing. "I was helping them with their thousands of wounded—they were having a civil war at the time, you see. I was kept pretty busy, as you can imagine, cleaning wounds, bandaging, assisting at operations, mopping the lino and so forth."

There was an uncomfortable silence. Mr. Jonsson looked away.

After a moment, he said, "Sigridur was always a good student. All my children are clever. I suppose they must have got their brain from their mother."

"Oh, Pabbi," Sigridur said, hugging his arm to her side. "You're as smart as any of us."

"Me? I am just a fisherman."

Sigridur started to protest, but Agnar, apparently feeling that they had strayed off the subject, namely himself, interrupted. "I have already furnished Sigridur's waiting room in my house," he told me, "and ordered a brass plate for her." And as Mr.

Jonsson lowered his face into the bowl of his pipe, Agnar went on to complain about the cost of brass plates and how much one had to pay nowadays for even the most inferior materials.

The rest of us remained silent, but he seemed to think this was because we had nothing to talk about. So he changed the subject himself.

"You are a professional pilot?" he asked.

"I guess so. Yes."

"There is not much money in that, I don't suppose?"

"Very little."

"I didn't think so," he said and actually looked directly at me for a moment, or rather at my suit, the blue one with the chalk stripe, which was creased after a long trip in a suitcase.

Shortly afterward we sat down at the table and were treated to a delicious meal of *skyr*, a sort of curds and whey, jellied consommé, roast lamb and a volcano-shaped cake with a lava of whipped cream, for all of which I was inordinately grateful, as it helped to reduce my fatigue to mere frazzlement.

Not that the meal went off all that smoothly. For some reason, Mrs. Jonsson seemed to feel that a threat to the welfare of Agnar and her daughter had been introduced. Throughout the meal she remained almost sycophantically attentive to Agnar's wants. As the rest of us ate in expressionless silence, she grew excessively concerned to keep Agnar's plate charged with fodder, and she listened as attentively as a sheepdog to his waterlogged monologues. I suspected that if he had emitted the correct whistle she would have bounded off to the scullery for another leg of lamb.

Far from being overwhelmed by these attentions, Agnar took them for granted, as if it were only right and proper that a representative of a humble family should cater so effusively to an important chap like him.

Mrs. J.'s preoccupation with the man's gastronomic well-being and her rapt interest in his opinions made it difficult for anyone to change the subject to one of rather more general interest. I found this particularly annoying because the alternative subject would probably have been me. Bjarni, for instance, was quite anxious to learn why I was making such a perilous and unprecedented journey across the ocean. He knew that Alcock and Brown had crossed the Atlantic nonstop in a twin-engined Vickers as long ago as 1919, but nobody, so far as he knew, had accomplished what I was attempting to do: fly the great circle route via Greenland and Iceland . . . though perhaps it was just as well that nobody had a chance to question me. I might inadvertently have told the truth, that I was fleeing from almost certain arrest on account of my unwitting part in the Great Booze Robbery.* By now, Sigridur was convinced that I was attempting to bolster my ego with lies of both the white and black variety, but, given her opinion of me, this time she would probably have believed me.

So perhaps it was just as well that Agnar was hogging the conversation. Indeed, in order to gain time in which to sober up, I actually encouraged Agnes.

"Agnar," Sigridur corrected me angrily. Agnar himself did not notice the mispronunciation; he was too busy describing how he was incorporating a surgery for his wife-to-be on the ground floor of his new house. This took so long that I was at least half-sober by the time we arose from the table.

Whereupon Mr. Jonsson handed me the three inches of gin that I had hidden under a heap of knitting. "Drink up," he said. "You're falling behind."

Within five minutes I was pie-eyed all over again.

The next thing I knew, four, or fourteen, or forty-four of us were outside. It was like the transition in a film. One second I was standing in a stupor with a dribbly grin, then, dissolve to: EXT. REYKJAVIK. NIGHT. Except that at 10:00 P.M. the sun was still shining. I couldn't even remember going through the doorway into the open.

If the sun was shining, I certainly wasn't. I felt as if somebody had removed my eyes, shaken pepper into the sockets and then replaced them. Whenever my reflexes remembered to function, I shivered.

---

*As described in *Me Too*, the fifth volume of the Bandy memoirs (Doubleday: 1983).

"You have brought us the first warm weather of the year," somebody informed me.

The rest of the population also seemed to be out perambulating; strolling, chatting, greeting each other with grave formality. At the moment I was being neglected by these hospitable people, thank God. I was lurching along by myself, oblivious of everything except exhaustion, until I became aware that a small hairy horse was following me along the other side of the fence. It kept glancing at me from under its straggly eyebrows as if trying to remember where we had met previously.

I stopped, introduced myself and bowed, but accidentally fell into the fence, startling the little beast and bringing snorts and titters from the others.

Sigridur steadied me, gripping my arm as if her hand was a stretch of steel strapping.

"Sigridur?"

"It's pronounced Sigrithur."

"Sigrid—Sigrithur?"

"Yes?"

"Where 'nearth are we going?"

"To grandmother's house."

"Oh, really? In the woods? And does she have great big eyes to see you with, my dear?"

"They are not especially large. We asked if you would like to visit her, don't you remember?"

"Of course I remember. I was just testing you. Sigridur?"

"Yes?"

"I hope nobody's going to give me any more to drink. Your hospitality's killing me."

"It's your own fault," she said, holding me upright with humiliating ease. "You shouldn't have brought the gin."

Grandmother's house appeared to be at the far side of the lake. It was made of mud, with a flourishing grass roof.

"This is how the Vikings built their houses," Bjarni explained. He thought I was taking a close interest in the construction materials because I had my face pressed against an inside wall. "There is a layer of stone, then of turf, which, as you can see, sets like cement."

"Listen, Bjarni—have I met your grandmother yet?"

"Ha? Of course. You met her in her house."

"You mean this isn't her house?"

"No. We moved on an hour ago."

"Oh."

"This is Snorri Petersson's house."

"I see. Is he the one who keeps plying me with some sort of viscous liquor?"

It was after midnight when I finally flopped into bed. With what little brainpower I had left, I wondered how I had managed to survive the Nordic binge. Eight solid hours of it, with an intermission for *skyr* and sheep. I suspected that half the population of Iceland had been flocking in from outlying parts to toast me in shifts.

It took hours to get to sleep. That was a mistake. I was whirled through a maelstrom of dreams so vivid that sleep seemed like reality and consciousness a fantasy. I was flying again over the Atlantic, in a reprise of fear that the engine might fail. In one gossamer scenario it did. The Puma ceased its snarl. I was drifting down in ghastly silence to the great gray wash of the ocean, an ocean with white whiskers sprouting from the wind-lashed ridges of the waves. The surface drifting inexorably closer. I wanted to land, or rather, felt compelled to do so. Useless hands fumbling, unable to switch to a reserve tank, feet embedded in liquid dope. Now I had a passenger. It was the mechanic in Maine who, in return for six cases of genuine London-type gin—a valuable payment in Prohibition America—had installed extra fuel tanks in the Gander's passenger cabin. I was telling him that he had only a few seconds left to tear out the bench seats and put in fuel tanks and a pump. But the mechanic—it was Agnar—was too busy scooping whipped cream off a passing mountaintop and loudly licking his fingers.

In the morning, after a breakfast of spring water, I was down at the harbor, feeling gritty as a sandcastle and with a headache like the pounding of the waves. I was trying to clean and overhaul the engine of the amphibian, but I was so feeblefisted that it was well into the afternoon before I had finished cleaning even a few metal nooks and crannies of the Puma. Then I was ready for the refueling. Mr. Jonsson had kindly arranged for a number of forty-gallon drums of gasoline to be delivered to the landing stage on a large cart owned by a friend of his.

Using a hand pump, it took me more than two hours to fill the wing and fuselage tanks and the extra tanks in the cabin, partly because every pint had to be filtered in the usual way through chamois, and partly because the cart driver mutinied after pumping a hundred and sixty gallons by hand and refused to exert himself further. Still feeling like death painted on a wall, as the Icelandic metaphor has it, I pumped the rest, while Mr. Jonsson, who wandered down in the middle of the afternoon, did the filtering. It was five-thirty in the afternoon before the Gander, noticeably lower in the water, was ready to go. But first the weather had to clear. With heavy cloud and intermittent showers, it did not look promising.

An obliging fisherman in a boat shaped like a Newfoundland dory had just finished towing the amphibian farther out into the harbor to discourage small boys from clambering over it, when Sigridur came bouncing onto the beach, driving a brand-new Citroën.

She braked to a halt almost in the lapping waters of the harbor, burst out of the driver's door and came swinging along the landing stage, causing it to rock and vibrate. She was wearing a close-fitting pink hat that did not go at all well with her oatmeal tweed coat. One of her stockings was wrinkled.

"As you have been working hard for a change," she said, "I have decided to give you a lift home."

"I don't think I have the strength to climb in."

"My goodness, Bandy, you are a weakling," she cried gaily. "Maybe I should tow you, then, like a wrecked motorcar. What about you, Pabbi?"

Mr. Jonsson regarded us thoughtfully for a moment before replying that he would prefer to walk back.

The Citroën jounced off the beach and along a stone street, between a corrugated iron store named "Thomsens Magasin" and a large wooden building with the national flag fluttering above it in the wet air.

"Father doesn't seem to object to you too much," Sigridur said after a while. She was looking bright and happy this evening. "Or he would have come with us to spoil the fun."

"How d'you mean, spoil the fun?" I mumbled, putting up a pair of hands to hold my headache together. After a day spent in a chill, blustery wind inhaling fish soup and gasoline fumes, I was feeling worse than ever.

"Well, you know, two's company, three's a crowd—isn't that how it goes? He always comes with Agnar and me if he gets the chance, to make sure Agnar doesn't get up to any funny business."

"But you're engaged—Agnes is *supposed* to get up to funny business."

"Agnar," Sigridur corrected me automatically. "This is his new car, you know. It's a beauty, isn't it? He lent it to me for the whole afternoon. I had to promise not to drive it at more than ten miles an hour, to save the springs.

"Talking about springs," she continued, chattering nonstop, "you can't visit our country without trying the hot springs."

"Can't I?"

"I am sure you could do with a bath."

I plucked exhaustedly at my vest, which was sweat soaked after a day of toil. My skin felt as if it had been basted with glue. "Does that mean I'm reeking a bit?" I asked.

"Luckily I cannot smell you, as this is an open car. Well?"

"What?"

"Do you want to try the hot springs? It's only a few minutes out of town."

"You mean now?"

"Why not? There is plenty of time before supper." Then, when I hesitated: "I'm just being hospitable, you know," she said tartly. "You don't have to see the sights and try new experiences if you don't want to."

"I don't have a bathing suit."

"Oh, don't worry about that," she cried, altering our course by ninety degrees at full speed.

A moment later she ran over a boulder at forty miles an hour. The steering wheel was wrenched from her hands. "Good car, this," she said, regaining control after a while.

Now we were hurtling out of town along a dirt road, across an apparently featureless landscape of grass. After a few minutes we reached a rough wooden hut with an iron roof. It was on the end of a pier built out into a large pool of water.

Sigridur braked to a halt with a wincing squeal of brakes and sprang out. "Here it is," she cried and, tearing off her pink hat, flung it onto the driver's seat. Then shaking her hair free, she scampered carefree as a puffball along the pier. "Come on," she shouted joyfully. "Last one in is a rotten egg." And she disappeared round the far side of the hut.

I followed along the boards, reached the platform that ran around the hut and stared dubiously at the so-called water. Though I was desperate for a long, relaxing shower after a day of flying, a day of bingeing and a day of toil, the pool looked most uninviting. It was a vile brown color with a distinctly oily sort of swell. It was also malodorous.

Hot springs, indeed. From the air I had seen acres of steam drifting over the volcanic tableland, but here there wasn't even a wisp of steam.

"But it's such a chilly day," I whined, addressing the hut.

"It's lovely and warm when you get in."

"Maybe I'll just swim around the washbasin when we get home."

"Don't be such a softy. Come on, it's wonderful," she shouted, and a second later there was a flash of skin and an extremely bouncy form hurtled from the hut and flung itself into the khaki fluid with a cry to chill the blood of a Boadicea. The form smacked the water with sadistic force.

For a moment there was nothing but filthy brown foam. Then her head appeared. She shouted out, gargled playfully, spat and laughed.

As she gargled and gurgled, I goggled, not at her nakedness—there was nothing to see anyway but the occasional flash of smooth white shoulders—but because it had not occurred to me that she had intended going in herself.

"Oh, it's wonderful," she sighed and closed her eyes as she trod water a dozen feet from the platform in front of the hut. "Like warm silk gloves." Then: "Well, come on. What are you waiting for, the ice-cream man?"

"I suppose mixed bathing is traditional in liberated, broad-minded Iceland?" I enquired in a spirit of sociological enquiry.

"Course it isn't. Boys and girls bathe separately."

"Ah."

"But there is nobody around, so. . . . Well, come on, slowcoach. Jump in." And when I continued to shift about, pre-occupied with various sociological enquiries: "Well, suit your-self," she said, splashing away contemptuously.

A moment later: "Well, all I can say is, nobody could ever call you an intrepid birdman. I don't believe a word of what you told Bjarni."

"I've forgotten what I did tell him."

"That you flew fighting planes in the war. Camels and Porpoises."

"Dolphins, actually."

"You're obviously much too timid to have been a fighter pilot."

"I don't think anyone's ever called me timid before."

"I suppose it's because you're getting old."

"Who's old?"

"Or maybe you're ashamed. But you don't have to feel ashamed, you know. I've seen plenty of naked men in my time. Mind you, most of them were dead."

I raised a boot and kicked at the planking underfoot.

"Or perhaps it is your inadequate equipment you are worried about."

"Who's inadequate? I'm just not in the mood, that's all."

"I promise not to giggle, you know—however much I'm tempted to do so. Well, are you coming in or not?"

"Well. . . ."

"You're cowardly," she snorted, and started to swim away. "Quite cowardly."

"Oh, yeah? Well, we'll just see about that," I shouted, and turning, pounded purposefully through the open doorway of the hut, undressed and hurled my clothes onto the bench along the wall.

However, I emerged rather less aggressively, covering myself with a pair of large, knobby hands. Which was just as well, for she was treading water only five feet away and grinning at me mischievously.

Running a gauntlet of taunts, I dipped a cautious toe into the water. Unfortunately it was at least twelve inches from the edge of the platform to the surface of the water, and because my hands were occupied other than in maintaining equilibrium, I overbalanced. So I was forced to jump in.

Instead of the shock of icy water I found myself enveloped in a medium that was not merely warm but positively hot; or at least it seemed so in contrast to the chill air above it.

It was the first time I had been warm since leaving home, and I was so carried away by the pleasurable sensation that I started to sing and holler and thrash about, and even took in a mouthful and spouted it like a whale. I was just having a spot of childish fun, singing away tunelessly and splashing about joyfully and kicking my legs to see how high I could toss the warm water, delighted to feel the muscular tension dissipating already, enjoying the first skinny-dip I had experienced since the earliest days in Beamington—when suddenly a pair of powerful hands clamped themselves to both sides of my head, and I felt myself being drawn backward, and, it seemed to me, downward as well.

I opened my mouth to utter a cry of alarm, just as a warm wave washed over my face. I shot high in the air, spluttering, and started to lash out, rather ineffectively, given the resistance of the water. "It's all right, don't panic," Sigridur bellowed in my earhole over the warm brown tumult; an order to which I paid not the slightest attention. I was convinced that she was attempting to kill me. Well, that was not as unlikely as it might sound—quite a few people had tried to kill me in my time, not excluding close relatives.

"What d'you think you're gargh?" I enquired.

"Keep still," she yelled. "Can't you bubloom a moomoo blub?" At least that's what it sounded like from underwater.

When I surfaced days later, gasping and blowing, she frightened and disoriented me still further by shrieking right into yet another earhole, "Relax, you fool, how can I save you if you're trying to fight me off?"

That was precisely what I was doing, fighting her off. She believed that I had jumped in out of my usual bravado and that my aquatic merrymaking was the thrashings of a drowning braggart. That was her misunderstanding. Mine was that I thought her patience had snapped and that she was resorting to physical violence. Unless it was my nakedness that had inflamed her passions. So I took action. Forgetting that it might not be quite so effective against a woman as against a man, I kneed her in the groin; or attempted to, but she was now taking even more drastic measures to save me. Despairing of my ever cooperating like a reasonably drowning victim, she carried out Step Five of the lifesaving drill, and deliberately forced my head underwater and held it there for an hour or so.

This indubitably had the desired effect, from her point of view at least, of reducing my resistance to a feeble tussle. In fact the next thing I knew I was being dragged backward, the warm water doing a thorough earwax lavage in the process, toward the soft brown muck that bordered the pool. Finally she was hauling me, partly by my hair, which was loose enough as it was, onto the grassy bank.

And there we both lay panting, attired in warm, oozy mud and strands of slimy reed.

"It's a good job I had my savings certificate," Sigridur said, leaving me wondering, in the slow-witted state that her overwhelming physical efforts had created, why she should be bringing up her financial affairs at a time like this.

By eight o'clock the next morning, I was looking forward with rather more enthusiasm than usual to continuing my journey. I was beginning to find Sigridur's attitude distinctly unsettling, not least because I wasn't used to being protected. Usually people felt they had to be protected from me. Also, my welcome in the Jonsson household had cooled noticeably, after Mrs. J. learned that we had gone hotspringing together. She was anxious to marry off Sigridur, or Sigga as the family called her, to one of the richest men in Iceland, and she seemed to think that I was getting in the way. Actually I was now wholeheartedly on Mrs. J.'s side. I also urgently desired Sigga to marry Agnar—preferably before lunch. I don't know, but somehow I didn't feel safe otherwise.

Not unnaturally, I suppose, Agnar shared his prospective mother-in-law's suspicions; though his first concern seemed to have been for his new car. He had been hanging around for two hours the previous evening waiting for his fiancée to return, but when she did he barely glanced at her. Instead, he rushed out to inspect his Citroën for bumps and bruises, and when he followed her into the front room he made the further mistake of reproaching her. A furious altercation broke out. As we sat in the kitchen in tense silence we could hear Sigridur giving the poor man absolute hell, storming at him as if it were his fault for lending her the car in the first place.

When they finally came in through the front door, it was Agnar who looked guilty and defensive. As for Sigridur, she was in a thoroughly bad temper for the rest of the evening.

It was all very embarrassing. I could have done with a stiff drink, but not a drop had survived the previous day's binge.

It was with considerable relief that I awoke the next morning to blue skies and the gentlest of breezes—the only conditions I dared to fly in, given the hundreds of miles of empty sea that still faced me. But when I consulted Mr. Jonsson, he stood outside the front door, studied the flawless sky, sniffed the balmy breeze and announced that there would be heavy rain and high wind by noon.

"But the weather's beautiful."

"We will have a mackerel sky by the time you have finished breakfast," he said, then added that the earliest moment for a calm flight would be early on Friday morning.

"Oh, no."

"You are not enjoying your stay in Iceland?"

"You are being very hospitable, Mr. Jonsson, but if I don't continue the journey soon I'll lose my nerve and be forced to stay here for the rest of my life."

"That would be a disaster."

"God, yes," I said, before realizing that he had spoken sarcastically.

He stared for a moment at the flawless horizon. "There is plenty to see here, you know," he said, as his wife emerged from the house. "I'm sure Sigga would enjoy showing you the—"

He stopped when his wife raised a yellow duster as if it were a signal flag; which it plainly was, for Mr. Jonsson immediately refrained from telling me what Sigga could show me.

I had the impression that Mr. Jonsson was not entirely displeased at my apparent friendship with his *dottir*. He had it wrong if he thought that there was anything between us, but he was certainly right about the weather. Soon after I had finished breakfast, mare's tails came twitching over the horizon, and within half an hour the front was upon us. By midday it was pelting with rain and blowing like buggery.

That day I saw little of Sigridur, as she was spending most of the time with her fiancé, inspecting her new surgery on the ground floor of his new house. I did, however, see her at night or, to be exact, at 2:00 A.M. the next morning.

"What? What is it? Is the house on fire?" I asked, shooting up in bed. Almost immediately I dismissed that as the cause of the emergency. I didn't think that corrugated iron was likely to burn all that well.

"Shhh."

"What is it, what's wrong?"

"Nothing. It's just that we haven't had much chance to talk today."

"Oh, fine. Well, now we've had a chance to talk, off you go to bed, eh?"

"Don't worry, Bandy," she murmured, sitting on my pillow—on the *pillow*, if you please—"nobody can hear us down here."

"I can hear us. Go back to bed."

"Don't be silly. You know you're really pleased to see me."

"I yam not."

"Move over," she said. "I haven't enough room."

"For God's sake," I hissed, "what about your mother?"

"Why, are you expecting her too?"

"I—"

"Go on, move over," she said, far too loudly. "It's cold out here." And when I failed to make room for her, she accomplished this task herself by using her hip as a bulldozer.

"There now," she said, contentedly rearranging the bedclothes over our limbs. "Now we can have a nice talk."

"Do you usually hop into bed with strange men?" I asked incredulously, now thoroughly wide awake.

"In what way are you strange?" she asked, looking interested. "Sexually?"

"I'm not strange at all. I pride myself on being absolutely average."

"Good," she said, leaning back complacently against the headboard. "Now I know I'm safe with you."

I glared sideways. "First you disturb a chap's slumbers," I hissed, "then you proceed to insult him by calling him safe. It's obvious you think I'm totally incompetent, Miss Jonsdotty—"

"Jonsdottir," she corrected, stifling a yawn. And it wasn't even a nervous yawn, either.

"I know perfectly well what I'm up to," I said shortly at length. "I don't need your protection, maternal instincts, rescue efforts or any help at all. If I've been acting a trifle dazed since my arrival—"

"Dazed? You're so half-dead I keep looking for vampire marks in your neck."

"It's lack of sleep, that's all, and worrying about crossing very large bodies of water. And on top of that," I added accusingly, "being forced to consume large quantities of gin on an empty stomach."

"And who brought the gin?"

"All the same, I'm not as dozy as you seem to think. I'll have you know I'm a man of considerable accomplishments."

"Shhh."

"Well, I am."

"Accomplishments?" she whispered in amused scorn. "At the age of thirty-one you have no money, is that not so? You have no job, no prospects, no possessions other than that peculiar-looking airplane, and no wife, no family, no talent, not even any drinking capacity. You don't even know for certain where you're going. That's accomplishments?"

"Well, I. . . . Well, I. . . ."

"You go around in a dream, Bandy."

"I told you, that was—"

"You need looking after, all right. I mean, look how long it took me even to get you to take a bath."

"Look here, Miss Jonsdottir," I said, agitatedly smoothing the bedclothes, "you can't judge a fellow on just a couple of days acquaintance—"

"Yes, I can. I'm good at judging people quickly." Then, giving me a superior smile, she added, "All right then, Bandy, tell me. What *have* you done since you were supposed to be such a brave knight of the air?"

"Well, briefly, I ended the war as a major general, before being captured by the Bolsheviks on Armistice Day. Then after being given the freedom of the city of Moscow, I escaped from the Red Army and the secret police and made my way through the hostile Red, White and Green forces down to the Black Sea. Then when I got home I became a well-known film actor in America. After that, I . . . I was in the Air Mail Service," I said, beginning to falter a bit. It was her face's fault. "Until I became a . . . well—a member of Parliament. . . ."

After a moment, Sigridur slipped out of bed. "Yes," she said gently, being careful not to look at me as she tucked me in. "Well, I suppose I had better be getting back to my own room." And so saying, and wearing rather a sad expression, she crossed the room and tiptoed out, leaving me with the suspicion that once again she had not believed a word I'd said, though in fact I had told her nothing but the truth, so help me Ripley.

As Mr. Jonsson had said, there was plenty to see in Iceland. On the Wednesday morning, they took me to see a local geyser. We watched it for an hour as it puffed and blew like porridge. Then after lunch I toured the port facilities—an activity that Sigridur characterized as "moping around the harbor." On Thursday, the high point of the day was a visit to Agnar's partially completed house. He showed us his fiancée's new surgery on the ground floor. We all stood around on the concrete floor admiring the bare walls of the waiting room, then the bare walls of the dispensary and finally the bare walls of the consulting room. Agnar told us where every single piece of furniture was to go, right down to the jar of tongue depressors. Over there, he said, he would place the padded benches, which he had gotten cheap from an undertaker. Against that wall would go the roll-top desk that he had inherited from his father. Opposite it, a brand-new examination table would stand. He had paid two hundred and thirty crowns for it.

And here in the dispensary, Agnar's carpenter would, in his spare time, build shelves for Sigga's jars of ointments and powders and green poison bottles.

Mrs. Jonsson was most impressed.

"And now I will show you our bedroom," Agnar said, smirking.

"Is that empty, too?" Bjarni asked, and received a cuff from his mother.

As Sigridur had been following us around in a gloomy silence, I thought I had better give her a word of encouragement. "I'm sure it'll be very nice when it's all furnished," I said, "with a nice double bed and a bedside table and a nice bedcover."

She looked more sullen than ever.

"And with your certificates and eye charts on the walls, and everything."

"Yes," she said, looking away again. "Agnes is lending me the money for my equipment."

"Agnar," I corrected her.

"An interest-free loan, of course," Agnar said, while Mrs. J. basted her future son-in-law with admiring looks.

There was a puddle on the concrete floor. "Mind your feet, Bandy," Sigga said listlessly. "You don't want to get your feet wet and catch your death of cold."

The water had leaked through an unfinished window. And no wonder. It was pelting down outside. Obviously, Mr. Jonsson's forecast had not been a show of maritime swank. If anything, it had been over-optimistic. I couldn't see it clearing in time for a takeoff on Friday. I was doomed to spend the rest of my life in Iceland. Or for as long as my cash, thirty-eight dollars, held out. That was all I had left after paying an exorbitant price for the fuel I'd taken aboard. It had cost four times as much as in Maine.

But, lo and behold, when I looked out the window early next morning, I was just in time to see the last of the cloud cover sailing through. Ten minutes later the sky was an unsullied blue.

After unemotional farewells, I was airborne at seven o'clock, having departed in such a hurry that I left my underwear behind. Sigridur had carried it off the previous evening to be laundered.

A Seascape

Being forced to ditch the Gander seemed like a filthy piece of luck at the time, as well as a most keenly felt loss. That it happened right at the end of the three-thousand-mile journey when I was only a few minutes short of my destination made it all the more upsetting.

It was my damned eyesight that was to blame. I might have degenerated in other respects; my hair might be receding like a reservoir in a heat wave, leaving an inordinate expanse of cracked brow, and my long, deadpan face might be withering under the action of one emergency after another—it had been putting up with rushes of adrenaline now for nine years—but my eagle eye was as efficient as ever. I picked out the tiny dot of color in the gray seas the instant I glanced in the direction of France.

Really, I should have been psychologically prepared for disaster after several dummy runs at it. Six hours out of Iceland I had run into freezing rain and had been driven to within fifty feet of the sea before the ice on the wings started to crack off, enabling me to claw my way back to altitude and to a conviction that I was still alive. Then in Scotland I had made not just one but two forced landings, carburetor, oil pressure and fuel-flow problems being the causes of the first, getting hopelessly lost the cause of the second, over a coastline that turned out to belong to Inverness-shire, a frightening edge of darkness, all precipice and wind, with an ocean whipping the cliffs until they foamed at the mouth. Yet on landing I had done no more damage than to hole the port float.

Funny. If I had remained in Scotland to have the float repaired I would never have sighted the wreck and been forced to sacrifice my only asset. But then I would not have met the prince, and if I hadn't met the prince. . . .

However, I'm getting ahead of myself. The point is that near the end of the journey I found myself off course again, though I was fairly certain that I was not all that far from London. I descended through cloud toward the end of the long flight from Scotland to find that I was flying over sea instead of over land.

That gave me a fright, until I saw that the coastline was only a few miles to starboard. I was further reassured by being able to identify first the Felixstowe lighthouse, and then, a few minutes later, Clacton-on-Sea, as it smudged past under the right wing.

It was fortunate for at least one person that I continued to drone onward over the water while working out a rough heading that would take me to the new aerodrome at Croydon. I was still a few miles out in the Thames Estuary when I glimpsed the red dot. A patch of misty cloud momentarily obscured it. I kept watch, though I assumed it was a small fishing boat. A few seconds later I saw it again, a point of red several miles farther out to sea.

I pushed the high-winged monoplane into a bank, hoping it wasn't what I thought it was, an airplane, crimson and cruciform, doing an ostrich act in the North Sea. But that's what it was, a biplane, appearing and disappearing in the deep, oily waves. Worse, as I glided toward it, I saw that the pilot had survived the crash. Which meant that I would have to attempt a rescue.

He was sitting backward on the top wing of what looked like an Avro trainer, his feet dangling into the front cockpit. His posture was one of resignation, as if he had concluded that what was happening to him was God's will and that there was nothing to be done about it. It wasn't until I swished overhead that he became aware of my presence. He started to wave.

He desisted almost immediately and clutched for support as the aircraft lurched up an aquatic hill and rolled down the far side. Water was already sluicing into the cockpits. I hoped he could swim. I reckoned that he had about half a minute to go before the airplane guggled to the bottom.

Life is fairly simple for a pilot while he is aloft. The decisions he must make are usually as clear-cut as they are urgent. No time for cogitation, rumination, ponderation or any other sort of ation, including, in this case, prevarication in the hope that the pilot would sink and therefore make it unnecessary for me to rescue him. So: which way was the wind? Blowing inland. But the waves were rolling in the same direction, and they were steep, so I would have to put down parallel to them, crosswind. Very well, turn crosswind and aim along a trough heading in the direction of the wreck. Sideslip steeply, keep enough speed in reserve to avoid landing on the peak of a wave. Wheels up? Yes. Now flaps and continue the sideslip to get down faster. Not good for the flaps, that, but one more strain on the spruce and tubular steel structure wouldn't make much difference. Level out, fighting to keep the wing level in the wind. Now skim over the heaving, undulating surface and pretend there was a chance that I might be able to take off again.

I snatched off the goggles for a clear view ahead and was just in time to see the airplane go under, the crimson tail rising to the vertical, then sliding down, quite slowly. No sign of the pilot. I aimed for the tail, hoping I wouldn't clobber him with the floats; but I had to head straight toward his last known position, otherwise in this marine turmoil he could be out of sight at a distance of twenty feet.

It was a peculiar sensation, using the waves as a toboggan run, seeing the runway rolling sideways. A touch of throttle to clear the side of a wave. An oily trough stretched ahead. Now I was flying inside the aquatic ravine. A hollow thump as the floats whacked down. Five seconds later the view tilted as the airplane gushed along a rising slope, then there was a ghastly sinking sensation as it tilted the other way and banked down the far side of the slope. Then somebody flung a bucket of saline solution into my eyes, temporarily blinding me.

The floatplane drifted to a stop, and the engine died before I had a chance to close up shop. Not that it mattered. Subconsciously I already knew that I'd never be able to take off from this corrugated medium even if I managed to start the engine again.

Unbuckling the safety harness, I stood up in the cockpit, clutching the coaming, and stared around. I had calculated the distance well. There was a patch of oil drifting past only a few feet away, rainbow-colored on the gray-green surface. But no sign of the pilot. Surely I hadn't sacrificed my only remaining asset to no purpose.

As the Gander lurched, I had to crouch for a moment to avoid being pitched out. As I stood upright again with feet braced apart, the machine rose to the crest of a wave, and I caught a glimpse of him. He disappeared, then reappeared as another wave went by. He was thrashing about ten feet behind the Gander, his flying coat spread over the surface like a leather tutu.

I threw off my own coat, snatched off my boots and jumped overboard, as far out from the side as possible, to clear the float. I reached the pilot quickly enough and managed to grab onto his coattails just before he sank. Hauling him up again was like laundering blankets in a copper. (Not that I had ever tried that. Mother had always done the laundry.)

As his smooth, boyish face reached the surface again, I saw that it was an awful color, a brownish gray. When it bobbed up just inches away it gave me such a fright I nearly let go and said, "Erch," as if I'd scooped up some sewage. But it was hardly surprising that his face was that color. The water was disgustingly cold, considering that it was nearly June.

Fortunately the boy—he was hardly more than that—had absorbed enough sea water to discourage him from struggling. Shades of my experience at the hot springs. I overlapped a pair of hands under his chin and towed him backwards toward the Gander. Or I thought that was what I was doing, but whenever I glanced back over my shoulder the amphibian seemed no closer. It was drifting at the same speed as we were. After a few minutes I decided to panic. I considered letting go of the lad. After all, there was no point in our both drowning. I was too old to die. But somehow I failed to let go. I think it was because I couldn't unlock my fingers, it was so cold. Instead I used the panic to redouble my efforts. The amphibian remained as distant as a diplomat's wife.

Finally I decided to risk using up the bodily fuel in one desperate burst rather than eke it out for another three minutes at lower revs; and I just managed to reach the machine and grab one of the floats before we both sank.

Another several minutes wallowed by before I managed to haul the unconscious pilot across the float and work off his flying coat, which was causing an impossible drag. Another age went by before I could get him up to the flying cockpit, where he promptly brought up most of the sea water he had swallowed, thus restoring the North Sea to its proper level.

After that I hadn't the strength to get up there myself and turn him the right way up—he was standing on his head in the cockpit with his feet in the air. So instead I climbed into the cabin, which was easier to reach, and collapsed over one of the fuel tanks. It was only when I realized that if I didn't keep moving I would soon be paralyzed with cold that I made another effort, as much mental as physical, to reach for the suitcase that was jammed between one of the tanks and the cabin wall, drag out a bottle and some clothing and outfit myself in gin and dry underwear and my best suit; and then a topcoat of more gin.

Thus warmed inside and out and carrying a bundle of dry clothing, I backed out of the cabin, teetered along the float in the pitching sea and managed at long last to get up to the flying cockpit, upend the pilot and get him out of his wet clothes and into a suit. It wasn't until he was half-dressed that I realized I was outfitting him in my tuxedo. I'd snatched up whatever garments were closest to hand.

I had a terrible job getting him into the boiled shirt. As he was still looking horribly cold, I also togged him out in my leather flying coat.

By then it was growing dark. I had passed the Felixstowe lighthouse at about seven o'clock. Surely it should not have been growing dark this early? But when I peered at the seven-day clock in the instrument panel, I found that we had been wallowing about on the briny for more than two and a half hours. I was staggered.

I wondered if I should have attempted to taxi to the shore instead of flouncing about in the cockpit, dressing up in pin-stripe suits and formal wear. After all, the land was only a few miles away. But no—getting into dry togs was the first priority. Besides, I could never have started the engine in this sea without help from the other pilot, and he was only now beginning to revive and take an interest in the proceedings.

All the same, we had better get moving now, thought I, or we might end up miles out to sea by midnight and be run down by a herring boat or a battle cruiser. So I gave the slender, crumpled figure on my right a good shake.

"Say, bo."

It was the first time I'd looked properly at his face. Underneath that dreadful color he was a handsome lad, with an almost feminine refinement of feature, dainty chin, finely formed nose and sculpted cheekbone, the whole marred only by a certain prominence of eye—unless it was near drowning that was making his big black eyes bulge that way; though even the eyes were decorated with a pretty set of spiky black eyelashes.

"Listen, can I leave it to you to rev up, if I climb out and crank the engine?"

Apparently he was not as alert as he had seemed. His liver-colored lips moved as if he were repeating the words to make sense of them. Evidently he failed to do so.

"Revs?"

"Catch the engine with pump, throttle and fine adjustment," I said, clutching the coaming as the floatplane lurched backward down a wave. "You know, to help start up."

"I don't understand."

"Help me get the engine going."

He shook his head helplessly.

"Heavens, man, it's simple enough," I shouted. "You must have done it dozens of times."

"No. . . ."

"Whatjamean, no? You're a pilot, aren't you?"

"Somebody else always starts the engine for me, you see."

"I don't mean hauling on the propeller, man," I said exasperatedly. "I mean running the engine from the cockpit. You must have done that many times."

"Oh, no, I leave that sort of thing to other people," he replied, as if he were talking about blackleading the grate.

I gaped at him, wondering if he had concussion. He appeared normal enough. His eyes were brightening every minute.

"Just how many hours have you done?" I asked. "How much flying time?"

"Oh, sir, I am getting on extremely well," he said. "I have done twenty hours—counting this one hour in the sea. I soloed after only eighteen hours, you know. My instructor said I am one of the best pupils he has ever had."

I looked at him. But there was no time for incredulity. I'd no wish to spend the night bouncing about on the briny. It was essential that we get the engine started at once. There was little hope of taking off in these conditions, but at least we might be able to taxi ashore if the engine was prepared to put up with all the salts and minerals.

This decision was arrived at all the more briskly when I noticed that the land was rapidly receding from sight. Whether it was vanishing because of the growing darkness or because we were drifting farther out to sea was a question that didn't seem worth answering just at the moment. So after changing places with the boy and quickly showing him what to do the moment he saw the airscrew turning, I switched on for him, then once again removed my flying boots and jacket and climbed down onto the starboard float, inserting my socks into whatever toeholds were available. A cascade of water promptly soaked me from bum to bunions.

Starting up in that unruly medium proved to be impossible. The Gander, swung this way and that by the wind and waves, was lurching so violently that I couldn't balance properly on the float for long enough to bring the generator up to speed. By the time the starter handle was halfway round I was being flung sideways by the pitching, or slammed against the cowling, or being wrenched backward by the yawing effect. After several minutes of bruising effort, I was forced to desist. Then it took another ten minutes to get back into the cockpit. By which time I was drenched all over again.

"Sir, I did what you told me," the boy said apologetically, "but the propeller did not move."

Panting away, I glared at him as if the pounding sea was all his fault, which of course it was.

However, my temper rapidly faded when I perceived that his color had not improved. The shock of the crash landing, immersion in the cold sea and the experience of near drowning had gravely affected him.

Fortunately I had brought up one of the last bottles of gin, only about three bottles remaining out of the six cases I had started out with. I unscrewed the top and proffered it. "You'd better have some of this," I said.

"What is it?"

"Gin. Drink up."

"Oh, no. I couldn't."

"You must. You look terrible."

"Oh, dear, and I was beginning to feel so comfortable and cozy in this lovely warm clothing. But you see, sir, we Hindus do not drink alcohol."

"Hindus? Oh, I see, you're related to Maurice Hindus, author of *Russian Peasant and Revolution*. But my dear boy, even if your family are temperance people, this is no time to—"

"No, no, you are misunderstanding. I am Indian, you see."

It was now my turn to move my lips stupidly, as if repeating the words to make sense of them.

"Good Lord. You're an Indian."

"That is what I am saying, yes."

"But, but, what on earth are you doing in this neck of the woods?"

"Woods?" he asked, looking around at the black waters as they hissed and frothed around the floats.

"This part of the world."

"Oh. Well, I have come to England to learn to fly, you see. It is my father's wish."

"I see. How old are you?"

"I will be nineteen years old in only ten months," he said vaguely, looking around at the smudgy dusk. The cold wind fluttered his salt-tangled black hair.

A terrible thought now occured to him. "I say," he said with a look of fright. "We have not been introduced."

"No."

"We must rectify the situation immediately."

"Yes."

"How d'you do? My name is Khooshie Avtar Prakash of Jhamjarh," he said.

"Bartholomew Wolfe Bandy of . . . of Beamington," I said faintly, shaking his slim brown hand and feeling all at sea.

"Beamington? That is in Wiltshire, is it not?"

"Canada."

"I say," he cried, "a fellow colonial!"

"Mm."

"Nevertheless, I am in your debt for ever and ever," he said, clasping my hand warmly in both of his and holding it soulfully to his boiled shirt. "You have saved my life."

"Oh, it's nothing. . . ."

Even in the near darkness I saw his expression grow dim. He released my hand. "My life is nothing?" he asked, sounding deeply hurt.

"No, no," I said. "That's just an expression, Khooshie. All I meant was, you mustn't feel you're in my debt."

"But I am in your debt. How can it be otherwise?"

"I was just being modest, see?"

"How is it modest to say that rescuing me from certain death is nothing?"

"I didn't really mean it was nothing."

"Then why did you say it?"

"It's just an *expression*."

"It is a very silly expression," the boy said resentfully. "Is it nothing that you have put your life in such danger to rescue me? Is it nothing that you have sacrificed your aeroplane and you are nearly joining me in Davy Jones's cupboard by diving into the turbulent waters of the North Sea to—"

"All right, all right! I rescued you! I saved your life. You're deeply in my debt."

"There is no need to harp on it," he said offendedly.

He sat there sulking for so long that I had ample time to consider our predicament. Perhaps another attempt to crank the engine? But one look over the side at the heaving black water and the frenzied phosphorescent foam dissuaded me. The prospect of being washed overboard and drowning in daylight was bad enough, but subjecting myself to that boiling cauldron in darkness was far more frightening. So I decided to drown my sorrows instead and promptly upended the bottle and poured gin into my neck. Were I vouchsafed another few years of life I could get to like the stuff. No . . . no . . . the engine would never start again anyway. It had quit of its own accord during the slap-down. It looked as if we were going to be here all night.

At first I wasn't too worried. Though there was a heavy sea, there was no reason, I thought, why the Gander shouldn't remain afloat, especially with the extra buoyancy from the almost empty fuel tanks in the passenger cabin. And though we might now be drifting out to sea, the North Sea was a heavily traveled body of water. Sooner or later a vessel was bound to sight us, come daylight.

It was around one in the morning, during a lull in the marine proceedings, when the Gander was lying steady for several seconds, that I became aware that the Indian lad was pushing me harder and harder against the coaming on my left. At first I thought he had fallen asleep and had slumped against me. As I didn't see why he should sleep when I couldn't, I gave him a shove and said, "Stop leaning on me."

"I am not leaning on you."

"Yes, you are, you're leaning on me."

"No, I'm not, you're leaning on me."

"How can I be leaning on you? I'm jammed into the corner," I snapped; and elbowed him again. "I hate being leaned on."

He elbowed back. "I am not leaning," he said loudly.

"Yes, you are, and you pushed me again just then."

"Only because you pushed me," he said; though with an obvious effort, he drew away and hunched in the right-hand corner of the open cockpit.

A couple of minutes later, though, he was jammed against me once more. Whereupon it occurred to me that it was the aircraft that was doing the leaning.

With a cardiac convulsion, I suddenly remembered the port float. The after end had been damaged during that landing in Scotland.

I hadn't done anything about it before taking off again, because I had been expecting to use the wheels at Croydon. Not for a second had I anticipated that a water landing might be necessary. And now the float was leaking, I suspected.

The suspicion was confirmed about an hour later when the moon, though still skulking behind a cloud, turned up the power and illuminated the aquatic wastes quite comprehensively. Looking over the side at the long, slender shape of the float surrounded by hissing foam, I perceived that it was nearly submerged.

"What are you looking at, please?" Khooshie asked suddenly.

"Oh, nothing."

"There you go again," he said, "saying it is nothing, when you are looking over the side all the time, and muttering to yourself. Or is that another expression?"

"Yes."

Now that the expression actually did have some significance he showed no interest in pursuing its meaning. "I will never understand English," he said with a sigh. "But never mind," he added brightly, "you are not intending to offend me, I think, so I will forgive you, Bartholomew. It is etiquette to call you Bartholomew?"

Now that he had gotten over his deplorable childishness, pushing, shoving, being peevish and all that, he was all warmth and friendliness again. He started to chat away as unworriedly as if we had plonked into the Serpentine rather than into a particularly treacherous body of water that might soon be gulping us down for ever and ever. He seemed convinced that the authorities would make a special effort to rescue him. This touching delusion also explained his rather annoying lack of fear over our predicament.

"They will be greatly concerned to rescue me, you wait and see," he said with infuriating complacency. "In India, of course, the English would not care one hoot whether one drowned or died peacefully in one's bed at the ripe old age of fifty. A very disappointing race, the English are, in India. But in their own country they recover nearly all of their humanitarian impulses, you see, and are most concerned to make us natives feel at home. My father was most kindly treated at his public school, you know. In his last will and testament, the Latin master left my father his entire collection of old railway timetables. As for me, since I am arriving in the old country, Bartholomew, I have been most decently treated. Except," he added, his voice darkening, "by a certain barrow boy on Greek Street, who sold me a pound of pomegranates and charged me sixpence, even though the price was quite plainly marked as threepence per pound. And when I pointed this out, he addressed me in a most impertinent fashion. 'Use your bleeding eyes, Abdul,' he replied, and pointed to the miniature 'one half' in front of his very large pound sign. I then informed him that I had not perceived it, as I did not happen to have a microscope on my person. This led to a very unpleasant altercation, I can tell you."

"By the way, Khooshie," I said, only too glad to chat to distract myself from the dangers of coherent thought, "how did you happen to come down into the sea?"

"It is quite simple, Bartholomew. You see, the engine stopped."

"I mean, how did you come to be over the sea in the first place, when you had so little flying experience?"

"My instructor said I was to fly to Dunkirk and back. It would be good practice for me," Khooshie explained.

I shook my head in disbelief; but then realized that he must have misunderstood. A flying instructor would never send a student out to sea, especially one who had taken all of eighteen hours to solo. No, the boy had gotten it wrong. His instructor had probably told him to go to Dungeness, not Dunkirk, or to Clacton-on-Sea, not out to sea.

I was about to say so, but then decided against it. There were other things to worry about. As a moonlit cloud glowed brighter I peered over the side again and saw that the waves were now washing continuously over the float. It was leaking all right, and even though the machine was pitching and tossing, a heavy list was now thoroughly evident.

I tried to imagine what would happen when it filled up, but I was too distracted by cold, hunger and, increasingly, seasickness, to work it out. Anyway, we would find out soon enough. I took another swig of gin to cheer myself up a bit.

"You are looking over the side and muttering to yourself again," Khooshie observed. "What is the reason, please?"

"Oh, it's noth—" I began; then: "Well, if you must know, the float on this side is filling up with water."

"Oh. Then we are sinking?"

"Yes."

"So we are quite likely to drown before we are rescued?"

"Yes."

"There now!" Khooshie cried triumphantly. "That wasn't so hard to say, now was it?" he said, sounding really pleased with my progress.

A moment later the float filled to the brim and, wearily, the wing tilted over and slapped into the drink, and the airplane began to heave and pitch about worse than ever, at a disorienting angle of thirty degrees.

By four in the morning we were both wretchedly sick; but not as sick as the Gander. Though the sea had moderated somewhat during the night, its battering had thoroughly twisted the frame, and the fuselage was becoming waterlogged even though the sea water appeared to be sluicing from every gap and crevice as fast as it entered, and the tubular steel of the center section was buckling, increasing the wing's dihedral to a ridiculous extent. Also the port wing strut had torn loose under the relentless bashing of the waves. As the first glimmer of dawn highlighted the waves, we were so low in the water that spray was lashing continuously over the cockpit.

By now, Khooshie was tilted onto his paltry left buttock and was practically lying on me, absorbing what little warmth I had left. He was still fairly dry, while I, hatless, coatless and hopeless, was soaked through and through. I couldn't understand why I had been so stupid as to give him my flying coat.

Worst of all, as death approached, he became more and more cheerful.

"How long will it be before we sink?" he asked, making an effort to haul himself up the slope of the cockpit bench and turning to look at my dim, dawn face.

"About half an hour, I'm afraid."

"You are afraid? You must not be afraid, Bartholomew."

"That was just an expression."

"Oh, goodness me, another expression," he cried gaily. Then, more soberly, "Remember that all of this is evanescent and illusory."

"What is?"

"All of this," he said, waving his hand around at the earth, the sea and the firmament, and gasping as a bucketful of brine lashed him in the kisser. "But it is important that we do not sink into aloneness, but maintain our human continuity by talking together. Tell me all about yourself, Bartholomew, honestly and truthfully, and with divine humility in the near presence of Vishnu."

"Okay. Well, to begin with, I'm one of the greatest men of the entire twentieth century."

But a few lines further on, Khooshie said disconsolately, "Somehow it is not working. We are talking but it is not bringing us closer together."

"If we were any closer," I wheezed, my ribs bending under the pressure of his wet leather shoulder, "there'd be only one of us."

"Nevertheless I have confidence in you, Bartholomew. There is something about you that inspires optimism and absolute certainty."

"Right. I'm absolutely certain we're going to drown."

"No, you will not allow us to perish. It is obvious that you have survived much greater danger than this," he said, just as the airplane sank a foot lower. The propeller ahead of us disappeared completely into the water, and other samples of the North Sea were sloshing about in the cockpit.

"If we were goners, I would know it, Bartholomew," Khooshie concluded, "as I have a fifth sense about such things."

There was a crunch, then a scraping sound, as still more of the fuselage disintegrated. The impact was so sharp that the machine actually vibrated, almost as if we had struck an iceberg. "I am convinced that your efforts will bear fruits," Khooshie said, just as a wave lifted us to its breaking crest and deposited us with a rending crash on the rocks, and the light of dawn revealed that we had been wallowing only fifty yards from shore for half the night.

Me, Somewhat Travel Stained

From the outside, the residence with the "Room to Let" sign in the window looked far too good for the likes of me in my present penurious state. Located in the Paddington area, it faced a pleasant public garden of the type usually filled with dank shrubbery and statues of Cecil Rhodes and other imperial real-estate developers. This one merely contained grass and plane trees, which set off the boarding house very nicely: a handsome three-story Georgian edifice painted an impeccable white.

The white paint, however, was a front. The interior was as neglected as a loony. The ceiling of the passageway that tunneled far to the rear was flaking, and the runner underfoot was so threadbare that it could have been relaid upside down without anyone's noticing the difference. I didn't think a place like this could be too expensive.

"Didn't you see the sign?" asked the woman who appeared in the hall. Presumably the landlady, a severe-faced woman in a purple cardigan. "No hawkers, circulars or canvassers."

"I'm not a hawker or a circular, madam," quoth I. "I'm looking for a room."

"We don't take just anyone, you know," she said, inspecting my crumpled suit, salt-rimed flying boots and soggy flying coat.

"Doubtless you're wondering why I look like this," I said. "Well, you see, I've been in the sea."

"Most people take off their clothes to go swimming."

"I came down in the sea in my airplane—or aeroplane as you

call it over here," I explained, making an attempt to sound solvent. "I got ashore only this morning."

"You've no luggage?"

"Just a valise. I left it at the station."

"I see," she said, looking me over critically, though she herself was no *Vogue* model. She was attired in the regulation landlady costume, a bleached frock, lisle stockings wrinkled at one ankle and a cardigan with a missing button. All that was needed to complete the ensemble was a mobcap. She had probably left it in the other room with her Woodbines and her Cockney accent.

Actually her accent was an educated one, and she had a cool, wary, middle-class air.

"Twenty-two and six," she said suddenly, issuing a spray of saliva, possibly to lay the dust.

"A week? Yes, that will be satisfactory," I said.

"Shouldn't you see the room first?"

"Yes, I guess I should."

"Well, you can't. I have to go out. But in the meantime you could be fetching your luggage, if you like.

"I shan't be long," she added, moderating her tone to the mere sharpness of a razor.

When I returned from the railway station half an hour later she was still out. So I dumped my salt-stained valise next to the hat and coat stand, and stood metronoming in her mildewed hallway for several minutes, feeling neither impatient nor passive, merely numb; partially anesthetized, I suppose, against a full realization of the enormity of the disaster in losing the Gander.

When the landlady had not returned after a further quarter of an hour, I shrugged and was just about to set off in search of other lodgings when a door opened halfway along the dark passage and a gargoyle peered out.

Britain is jammed with distinctive faces, as if genetics were compensating for an excess of conformity in other areas, and this one was surely the most distinctive face of all. In his late thirties, the man had a long, sharp nose with razor-edged nostrils violently protruding from a physiognomy that in all other respects regressed. His brow swept backward into tufts of hair that themselves leaned backward, like gorse in an endless wind. His cheeks swept more to the rear that to the side, and his chin melted unobtrusively into his throat, as if his forebears were aristocratic and his chin had been worn to nothing by centuries of familial near-incest.

The overall impression was of a face that had been streamlined for speed, with the sharp nose as the forward edge. High winds would meet with almost no resistance as they swept across the rest of his features. Even his eyes, huddled close to the arrowhead of the nose, were streamlined, set back at such an acute angle as surely to deny their owner stereoscopic vision. It was like looking at a face in a convex mirror.

When he gestured me over and the rest of him came into view, his figure proved to be almost as distorted as his head. The shoulders inside his long, black jacket were so narrow as to give him an even more malformed appearance.

Only the voice was fairly normal, though light and lacking in resonance, like most English voices, as it informed me that Mrs. Wignall, the landlady, would be back shortly, and that I was welcome to wait in his room if I wished.

I peered at him suspiciously. Denizens of boarding houses were not usually hospitable, especially to newcomers, who might be thieves, prostitutes, perverts, anarchists or dog lovers. As if guessing my thoughts, he explained that he was a long-term boarder, and that he often did little things for Mrs. Wignall, taking messages, accepting letters or parcels on her behalf, massaging her breasts and so forth. "You are Mr. Bandy, aren't you? The gentleman who's renting the upstairs room?"

Reassured, but not much—had he really spoken those words about Mrs. Wignall's bosom, or had the North Sea unhinged me?—I agreed that I was indeed Bandy.

"Well, she said you could wait in my room if you wished," he repeated, and gestured courteously for me to enter.

Which I did, looking around cautiously. But apart from a shortage of light, explained by the smallness of the window, the room was ordinary enough: a typically seedy bedsitter, with a few items of scarred furniture, including a small electric stove on top of a rickety table. The wallpaper behind the stove had an interesting embossed design. For something to say, I complimented him on it. "That's not an embossed design," he said, "that's grease."

After inviting me to seat myself on one of the two small armchairs that were huddled over the unlit gas fire: "Drane is the name, Archibald Rupert Drane," he said, sitting in the chair opposite. He had obviously been having a quiet drink just before I came in. A small table had been drawn up alongside his armchair and on it stood a fancy cocktail glass. "The room you're renting is more or less above here by the way. Mrs. Wignall will take you up there the minute she gets back."

"Fine."

"She won't be long. She's just gone to the Outpatients for her VD treatment."

"Ah," I nodded. But then I stopped nodding. "What?"

"You know—venereal disease. She goes every Thursday at this time."

"Oh."

"You're from Dorset, aren't you, Mr. Bandy?"

"What? Yes. No."

"Recognized the West Country accent. And you're an airman, Vera tells me."

"Who?"

"You. You're an airman."

"I meant, who's Vera?"

"The landlady, course. Mrs. Wignall. Didn't she tell you her first name? She usually does. She's very friendly, you know."

"Is she?"

He then went on to talk about the upstairs bathroom for some reason, and informed me that my use of it would not exactly inspire transports of delight among the other boarders. His remarks would probably have puzzled me had I been listening. But my attention was otherwise engaged. For I found myself staring at a detached human eye. And what was worse, it was staring back at me.

As I think I've mentioned, an unfinished cocktail in its conical glass stood on the small table beside his armchair. Which was normal enough. A fellow was entitled to a drink in the privacy of his own home after a hard day's work draining and embalming bodies, and so forth. Except for that one thing. There was a human eye at the bottom of the cocktail glass, looking straight at me.

It even had a couple of blood vessels attached to it. Unless one of them was the optic nerve. I remembered that nerve from medical school. Actually it was a bundle of fibers rather than a single strand. It joined inside the skull to form the optic chiasma. It was also the only part of the nervous system that could actually be seen from without, so to speak, using the ophthal—

What on earth was he doing with a human eye in his cocktail? Was it to give it flavor? Was an eye tastier than an olive? Could that be it?

Surely it was a false eye. I leaned closer, trying to make the movement look casual. After all, I didn't want him to think I was staring rudely at his drink—even if his drink was staring rudely at me. Yes, of course it was false. He'd dropped it in there as a joke. But it was not like any false eye I had ever seen, and I'd seen one or two false eyes in my time. This one still had the aforementioned attachments. And on closer inspection it turned out to be bloodshot. Who ever heard of a manufacturer making an artificial eye bloodshot? My God. It was real. Drane was one of those dreadful murderers who crop up quite frequently in Britain, people like Crippen. And just listen to him now, droning on about boarders, bath nights and boarding houses as if nothing were wrong. There was also a live worm in the fruit bowl.

There was a *what*? I looked again. It was true. There was a five-inch worm in his bowl of fruit. It was moving.

It was actually wriggling, though with an obscene slowness, as if it were on its last legs, if it had any to be on.

Through a high-pitched humming sound I heard Mr. Drane asking a question. His voice seemed to be coming from behind several thousand bales of cotton wool.

"What?"

"I said, would you care for a drink, Mr. Bandy?"

"What?"

"As a matter of fact, I've still got a little gin and vermouth left—"

"No!"

"I beg your pardon?"

"I mean—no thanks. No, I'd rather not. Thanks," I said, my eyes darting frenziedly between the substitute cocktail olive and his infested produce, before they froze on the fruit, as if hypnotized. A snake was said to be capable of hypnotizing you. Could a plump green worm do it as well? For that was what it was, a five-inch, fat green worm with tiny black eyes, wriggling slowly among the bruised bananas.

"Well, I'm afraid I must be. . . ." I said firmly, putting my hands decisively on the arms of the chair in order to press myself into a standing position. But my arms had gone all mushy and feeble.

". . . little place on Tottenham Court Road," Mr. Drane was saying, as calmly as if it were perfectly natural for one's room to be filled with human eyes, glistening poison-green worms and a giant hairy spider descending from the ceiling by its silken ladder—

GIANT SPIDER? That, at least, enabled me to rise without further ado. To a height of at least eight feet, I estimate, judging by the mark made by my head in the ceiling. At the same time as I was ascending, I was uttering hoarse cries and flailing at the giant spider—which must have been descending slowly toward me for the past few minutes. I tell you. I could put up with human eyes in cocktail glasses without going into hysterics, what with my medical experience and all, and even the sight of a fat, segmented worm slowly sliding out of sight into a decaying apple was tolerable, if distinctly nauseating; but a spider, that was different. I was really scared of spiders.

". . . also kits of various sizes and degrees of sophistication," Mr. Drane was saying in his light, normal voice, as if nothing untoward had happened; as if I were still sitting there, listening raptly to his discourse, instead of where I was now, standing flattened against the far wall, panting rapidly enough to induce hyperventilation. "Marked cards, wands, Chinese links, vanishing coins and so forth."

"What? I'm sorry, I. . . . What were you . . . ?"

"Kits for budding magicians," Mr. Drane said. "From seven and six up to three pounds. We sell quite a few, especially at Christmas. But as I say, most of our trade is in novelties."

"Novelties."

"Nails that look like they've been driven through your palm, invisible ink, sneezing powder, rubber chocolates, exploding pens and the like. By all means drop in some time, Mr. Bandy," Drane said. "It's near the corner of Tottenham Court Road and Grafton."

"Yes, thank you. I certainly will, Mr. Drane," I replied.

"If you're the sort of person who obtains amusement from that sort of thing," Drane said somewhat distastefully, "my stock is quite extensive. My Horrible Hairy Spiders, for instance, are only one and eleven pence for the giant economy size."

"That's very reasonable," I said. "Extremely reasonable. Very reasonable indeed, I must say. By Jove, yes, quite extraordinarily reasonable." And I was still telling him how reasonable it was five minutes later when the landlady returned and took me up to my bedroom.

Mrs. Wignall had been out shopping, of course, not visiting the clinic—Mr. Drane would get into serious trouble one of these days with his practical and verbal pranks—and she proceeded to provide me with a great many details about the boarding-house routine; that the rent included breakfast, which was to be taken in the room set aside for that purpose downstairs; that there was to be no cooking in the rooms under any circumstances; that the sheets were changed every Sunday morning; and so forth. Unfortunately she failed to mention the bathing arrangements. Perhaps she assumed that Mr. Drane had told me—maybe he had—or perhaps she thought I wouldn't need a bath for quite a while after having had one in the North Sea only that morning. At any rate, she withdrew without informing me that the antiquated water-heating system was capable of providing only one boilerful of hot water every twelve hours, and that as Mrs. Wignall herself was in the habit of bathing every morning in her downstairs bathroom, this meant that only one boarder per day could take a bath, in the evening. Consequently a strict schedule had to be adhered to. With seven boarders in the house, there could be no room for error. The schedule was as follows: old Mrs. Delisle, who as the one with the longest term of residence bathed on the most favored occasion, Saturday night (much to the annoyance of the two youngest boarders, Ian and Betty, who felt that this privilege was wasted on somebody who was far too old to benefit from it, Mrs. Delisle having long since given up Saturday-night dances and other bodily contacts that required fragrant crevices).

On Sunday, the Intensely Private Lady on the top floor had the use of the tub. Monday nights were reserved for Mr. Drane, Tuesdays for a beefy salesman named Frank Ribble and Wednesdays and Fridays for the two students, Ian and Betty, respectively.

That left only Thursday nights, made available by the recent departure of a cook who had been ousted for stinking the place out with his doggie bags of filthy foreign leftovers. It was a mark of the hydraulic discipline that prevailed in the boarding house that nobody had yet attempted to plant themselves in Thursday's fallow tub—though it was suspected that Ian the student was violating an unspoken agreement: stealing Thursday's hot water by taking a stand-up bath at the marble washbasin. The evidence on which this grave suspicion was based was that on two successive Thursdays he had forced open the bathroom window—and why would he have done that if not to dissipate guilty steam and culpable condensation?

Over breakfast one morning in the "breakfast room" next to Drane's quarters, I asked Betty what would happen if another boarder came along in addition to me. "Would two of you have to double up?" I asked.

Betty chortled. She was a plumpish, jolly girl, a student at the Royal Academy of Music farther along the Marylebone Road. Though neglectful of her appearance—she wore the drabbest clothing seen outside the Good Shepherd Refuge—she owned a rich, upper-class accent. "Oh, Mrs. Wig would never take on an eighth boarder," she shouted. "It would be just too direful."

"I wouldn't fancy doubling up with Mrs. Delisle," Ian murmured. "She's so thin I'd have to keep rescuing her before she slipped down the plug hole."

"And I wouldn't fancy doubling up with Mr. Ribble," Betty cried. "I'd be so busy defending myself I'd have no time to wash."

"How about Mr. Drane?" I suggested. "Would he do?"

"Oh, gosh," Betty bellowed. "He'd probably slip me a bar of soap that turned my face black. I'd come out of the tub looking like a chimneysweep."

"It's not a bad idea, all the same," Ian began, looking at Betty.

"Somehow it doesn't seem fair, Mrs. Wignall having seven baths a week and the rest of us just one," I said, but they were too busy blushing, for some reason, to listen.

However, I knew nothing of these arrangements when I arrived, and I made a dreadful mistake that Tuesday evening, my first day in residence. After sitting on my bed until eight o'clock, munching an apple and counting my entire fortune of four pounds five shillings, and hoping I'd be able to hold out until a friend liquidated my assets in Canada—an Avro biplane and a Pierce-Arrow auto—and sent me the proceeds, I gathered up towel, soap, shampoo and loofah and mooched across to the decaying facilities on the far side of the house.

I'd had a lot of experience of British bathrooms in my time, so I wasn't particularly alarmed at the one I now entered, though it was eccentric enough, God knows. To begin with, it was unnaturally long, but so narrow that I could not have flung up my arms in surrender without fracturing a few knuckles on the white tiles. Tiles edged in black, incidentally, which I thought a nice decorative touch, until I realized that the grout had originally been white.

The tiles ran all round the room, except, naturally, where they were most needed, adjoining the fixtures. These included the toilet, which crouched on a dais, as if something worth watching were likely to happen up there. Like most British toilets it had a name embossed in the bowl above the waterline. Frequently these names were of a stern or inspirational character, as if an attempt were being made to distract one from an activity that was shameful because it was natural. I had read such toilets up and down the land, toilets of all shapes and sizes, named "New Windsor," "Morning Glory," "Defiant," "Croesus" and "Sublime"; and other flighty appellations, such as "Canute," "Pallas Athene," "Charity," "Cabbage White," "Blue Orchid" and "Green Goddess." This one, however, was rather more pedestrian, or perhaps one should say sedentary. "Improved Torcade," it was called. If this was the improved version, I thought, withdrawing my head from the bowl, God knows what the original version must have been like. When you pulled the chain, producing a sound like a railway freight yard, the rush of water from the overhead tank was enough to wash out Westminster Bridge.

Despite the ample space available, the toilet dais had been placed only a few inches from the washbasin, as if the fixtures were huddling together for warmth and comfort. The basin was stained yellow from the dripping taps. Worse than that was the looking glass on the wall above it. I couldn't help recoiling when I looked into it, thinking I had suddenly contracted mumps. A moment later, though, I realized that the mirror was distorted because it had been screwed too tightly to the wall, rendering the surface concave. (When Mr. Drane looked into it, I wondered, did his face come out normal?)

The rest of the wall all the way to the window was taken up with warped shelving that sagged still further under the weight of a pharmaceutical warehouseful of toiletries and cleansing materials.

But the truly eccentric feature was the bathtub at the opposite end of the room. It had been driven into the wall as if the brakes had failed—jammed endwise into a space hardly wider than the tub itself. The walls pressed on it from three sides. The only way into it was by stepping over the end that just barely protruded from the wall. Which meant that you had to route march to reach the faucets at the far end.

I couldn't understand why the tub had been inserted into the wall in this fashion, until I heard somebody—it proved to be old Mrs. Delisle—talking to herself. I could hear her angry mutters through the wall on the right side of the tub. I guessed then that the fixture had originally stood in the open until the adjoining bedroom had been expanded partway into this room, thus entombing the tub.

However, I supposed that I would get used to it in time, so, convinced that I was about to learn what claustrophobia was, I undressed, clambered over the cast-iron sill, walked along to the far end and turned on the faucets, expecting the usual British trickle. The flow into some bathtubs I could name took so long that the water was stone cold by the time it had covered the bunions. To my surprise, the water in this one was not only under reasonable pressure, it was adequately hot. My apprehension began to diminish; to such an extent that I could not resist the temptation to gaze at the wall in simulated terror and whisper, "For God's sake, Montresor." You know, as in Poe's story, where the fellow is being walled up.

A pleasing touch of literary playfulness, I thought; until I received a muffled response through the wall: "What? Who's that? Is that you, Mr. Ribble?" That was when I realized that Mrs. Delisle lived just the other side of the wall.

Which was a further sample of the bad luck that seemed to be dogging me these days. While I was bathing she must have listened carefully to my sloshings, grunts and scrubbings. By the time I reached my feet she must have determined that dirty work was afoot. Apparently able to distinguish my detergent activity from that of at least one other boarder, she left her room—I heard the door squeak open—and about five minutes later the tramp of several feet was heard.

For a moment there was silence; then a whispered conference was held in the hallway. Then came an aggressive knocking, and a loud, hoarse voice demanded to know who was in there.

"You're not having a bath, are you?" said the same voice, which was so loud and heavy that I assumed, correctly as it turned out, that it belonged to the steel salesman.

"Is that somebody in the bath? It is, I can hear you," he shouted, simultaneously pounding on the door so angrily that I thought he must be using his case of samples as a battering ram.

"What's the matter?" I cried in alarm. "Is the house on fire?" My voice reverberated in the confined space in the wall.

Ribble's violent protestations and incomprehensible claims that I was using his bath—surely he hadn't installed his own tub when he first arrived?—were so persistent that finally I was forced to cut short my ablutions. When I wrapped a towel round myself and opened the door, I found in the passageway not only Ribble but practically every other boarder in the house as well. They were all looking exceedingly censorious.

Ribble, a beefy chap with a rough, red face, barged past me so forcefully that he dislodged the towel. I clutched at it and managed to resecure it before my usurpation of somebody's sacred rights was compounded by nudity. For usurpation was what I had done, as I now discovered when Ribble barged over to the cavity in the far wall and, pointing at the frothy evidence, accused me of barefaced theft.

Meanwhile the rest of the boarders had crowded into the bathroom as well, to examine the damning evidence, and it took me several minutes to convince them that I had known nothing about Mrs. Wignall's matutinal cleaning operation and their own nocturnal equivalent. "Anyway, you can have my bath night," I told Ribble, "if you want."

"That won't be until Thursday," he shouted. "I needed one tonight—I'm off to Manchester tomorrow, and I won't be back till Friday. You boogger, you've mooked oop my schedule."

"He ought to be horsewhipped," croaked dear old Mrs. Delisle, studying my terrycloth sarong with an eye disgracefully prurient for one of her age.

"Well, never mind, Mr. Ribble," said Ian the student. "You'll get a good bath in Manchester—they say it's always raining there."

"And surely your hotel will have a tub?" I pointed out.

"That's got nowt to do with it. This is my bath night. I've always had my bath on Tuesdays."

I suddenly realized that old Mrs. Delisle had moved to the rear and was now staring in a shocked way at an exposed buttock. And not just any buttock either, but mine, revealed in all its glory where the ends of the towel didn't quite meet. I hurriedly backed away until the buttock in question came into contact with the far wall. At least I assumed it was the far wall, as it was so cold and wet.

"Shameless, that's what he is," Mrs. Delisle quavered.

"He's from Dorset," said Mr. Drane, glancing at the others as if to say, Well, what else could you expect?

Finally I managed to convince Mr. Ribble that it had been a mistake. "Yes, well," he grumbled, "don't forget. You still owe me a bath night when I get back."

"Ar, that's roight, lad," I said in what I thought might be a Dorset accent. I didn't wish to correct Mr. Drane's mistake, so as not to give them a poor opinion of Canada. "Any toim yew say, me hearty," I cried. And, to the rest of them: "Now if yew will pardon me, gaffers, oi—"

"He might at least cover himself decently," said Mrs. Delisle, taking a seat on the dais.

"Is something the matter?" came a new voice from the corridor. This belonged to the Intensely Private Lady on the top floor.

"He stole Mr. Ribble's bath," Betty explained, "and filled it half-up," she added, pointing into the gray suds. "And you took too much hot water, too. You're only supposed to fill up to this yellow tidemark here."

"Oh, dear," said the Private Lady, her tones suffused with tragedy.

"That means that Mrs. Wignall's water won't be hot enough tomorrow," Drane said, looking at me as if to say, Ooh, now you're for it.

Further analysis of the situation ensued, lasting long enough to allow my hair to dry. Then came a loud rapping at the back door, and a couple of minutes later, Mrs. Wignall ascended, followed by a policeman.

They, too, entered the bathroom. Whereupon the bobby demanded to know what was going on here. He had received a complaint from a neighbor that somebody up here was halleged to be hexposing himself. At which point I realized that I had backed my gluteal region not against an opaque wall but against a far from opaque bathroom window.

Looking Highly Dubious

Though the loss of the Gander was a decidedly glum-making experience after all the work, money and ambition that had gone into it, I remained nauseatingly optimistic. I'd had a foot in the gutter before and had always managed to regain the sidewalks of fame and fortune. I reminded myself that I had an almost embarrassing surfeit of virtues: an exceptional memory, lightning reactions to emergency situations (except those involving people), a gift for languages, a grasp of aeronautical engineering, some medical training, experience in administration, and also in politics, from which I had learned that absolutely nobody in authority was worthy of respect except me. And last but not least I had a noble character and an indomitable personality that was none the less suffused with modesty. With such assets how could I possibly fail?

The only trouble was that this illustrious inventory added up to only one marketable skill.

Accordingly, attired in the only respectable outerwear that had survived the dunking, my blazer and gray bags, I went looking for a job in aviation, leaving my name and address with every flying outfit—commercial, training and manufacturing—within a day's public transport range of Paddington.

My optimism quickly proved to be thoroughly unjustified. The aviation business was as down in the dumps in England as it was everywhere else. Great companies that had supplied the world with most of its aircraft were reduced to manufacturing pots, pans and motorbikes, or had gone out of business altogether. Pilots were two a penny, with a packet of sherbet thrown in.

I couldn't even get a ground job in the industry, though I was willing to do anything that might enable me ultimately to stuff my head in the clouds again. At one point I thought I'd aroused interest, at the H.G. Hawker Engineering Company works in Kingston. Hearing my name, one of the directors, Fred Sigrist, came out and, after a few questions said, "I don't suppose you're the one who pinched the Fokker from the Jerries and brought it back over the lines?"

"That's me."

"The D7? By George! You were flying our Dolphins at the time, I remember. Tom Sopwith will be interested in meeting you. Come along," he said, taking my arm. "Let's see if he's in."

My hopes took off and climbed several feet. Sopwith, now a director with Hawker, was the man who had built many of the war's most successful aircraft. I was bound to make an impression on him. Maybe even a good one. I'd had my greatest successes with two of his designs.

Unfortunately he was not to be found. "And I'm afraid it wouldn't have helped anyway, Mr. Bandy," Sigrist said regretfully. "You're obviously in Harry Hawker's class as a pilot, but he does all our test flying."

Sigrist seemed to consider me overqualified, or something. I tried to overrule this judgment. "No, no, I'm not all that good," I said.

"Yes, you are. I remember you now."

"I'd be willing to do anything, Mr. Sigrist."

"No, you wouldn't."

"I would, honest."

"You're much too experienced."

"I'm not."

"You were one of the most brilliant pilots of the war. We couldn't give you just any lowly job—it would reflect badly on us."

"Yes, you could; no, it wouldn't," I said, then added hopefully, "Once I crashed three airplanes inside two weeks."

"I'm sure it was accidental."

I felt even more frustrated when we detoured through the works and I remarked on the machinery, observing that metal presses, millers and lathes seemed to be replacing the woodworking machinery of aviation's yesteryear; whereupon Mr. Sigrist asked if I had experience in aircraft design and, being assured that I had, offered to recommend me to a rival firm if I could prove it.

That was the frustrating part. Over three years of intermittent trial and error I had succeeded in putting quite an advanced design of aircraft into the air; but every single drawing and blueprint, every scrap of proof that the Gander had ever existed, had gone down with the ship. Not even photographs of the unique amphibian had survived.

Still, even by the middle of June, I was not discouraged, though I was down to one and a half meals a day and was losing the battle to keep the crease in my trousers. But I'd had ups and downs aplenty in my life, right up to the political sniper fire that had led to my present plight. Yet even now I had not lost my ideals, my dream that one day I would finally be able to experience the cozy numbness of being a Canadian, with his history dedicated to security rather than achievement, to collectivism rather than individualism, to tradition rather than innovation—the ideals that kept so many of my countrymen out of mischief.

My ambitions were modest enough, God knows. I merely wished to be rich, influential and have a good head of hair; and in the fullness of time settle down with a wife who was keen on sex, but not too keen, so as not to upset the neighbors.

All the same, I was in something of a financial pickle. I didn't realize how badly off I was until I received a substantial sum from home: well over four hundred dollars; about a hundred pounds. This was the proceeds from the sale of my Canadian assets. The trouble was that, anticipating a much larger sum, I had already reduced this largesse to smallesse. I had ordered a new wardrobe—dinner jacket and trousers, white tie and tails and even a topper, two Savile Row suits essential for impressing doormen, quantities of shirts and a new pair of shoes, stinting only on underwear, as no prospective employer was likely to see my undies. The result was that four days after receiving the money, I was left with just seven quid. But even that did not cause inordinate dismay. If I ended up with nothing to eat, I could always swallow my pride. I told myself that I could always sidle up to my late wife's family, the Lewises, and demand the return of the articles I had left with them six years previously: an antique motorcar, a modern painting and a valuable samovar. I ought to be able to realize a few pounds on these items. That's what I told myself. Actually I was lying. I couldn't bring myself to go begging in that quarter. Mr. and Mrs. Lewis had forecast a sunlit future for me. I couldn't possibly turn up in an eclipse. It would be just too embarrassing for them. And besides, I had my pride. Anyway, I didn't know where they lived. They had long since abandoned their London residence and disappeared into the depths of the countryside.

Day after day I trudged in and out of works, plants and offices, briefing rooms, boardrooms and duty pilots' huts, and over acres of dispersal cinders and oily grass. To no avail. In the evenings I sat in my room, munching apples and drinking tap water, feeling sure that something would turn up.

It did. One morning I came down late as usual for breakfast, expecting to find the place deserted. I had discovered that if I arrived in the breakfast room after the other boarders had left, there were often usable pickings from their plates, leftovers that might serve as lunch or, on particularly good days, provide lunch *and* supper. Mrs. Wignall might be stingy with the hot water, but she did a cooked breakfast substantial enough and badly enough prepared to ensure that there was always a bit of bacon or sausage left. Of course, timing was important. I had to arrive after the last boarder had left for work, but before Mrs. Wignall came in to clear the tables.

On this particular morning, my timing was fine, but the schedule was out. Just as I was wrapping some cold fried potatoes in some newspaper (a packaging error, as I later discovered when I found part of a headline about a mass poisoner printed across one of the potato slices), Ian stuck his head into the room, saw me and followed with the rest of his body.

When he stared at the little packets of food in my hand, I had to make some sort of explanation. So: "Just taking them for forensic examination," I said loftily.

"Yes, I know what you mean," he said hesitantly. "Mrs. Wignall's cooking is pretty suspicious. . . ."

He stared at me curiously as I lowered my head over my own breakfast. "I was hoping I'd run into you," he said after a moment. "I hope you won't take it wrong, Mr. Bandy, but I gather you're still looking for a job. Well, what I was wondering was whether you'd be interested in helping me out with a letter. It would only be worth two or three quid, but. . . . Well, I thought you might just possibly be interested, that's all."

"What sort of letter, Ian?"

"It's a composition exercise, actually. We have to make up a letter purporting to come from some Russian bigwig or other, to some organization or other in this country. Well, I remember you telling Betty about your Russian experiences, and I gathered you spoke the language."

"Not well enough to write a convincing letter in Russian, though."

"No, it has to be in English anyway," Ian went on, more enthusiastically. "That's logical, isn't it? The Russkie, whoever he is—say a member of the Communist International—if he was writing to, say, the Communist Party over here, would have it translated at his end rather than expect people at this end to do it."

"I guess so. But I don't. . . ."

"First of all, you know something of the Soviet setup, don't you? I remember you telling us about their committees and things, so you might be a bit of help there. But to make it really sound convincing, I need your help in getting the rhythm right, so that it really looks like a translation from the Russian and not like a letter that was originally composed in English. Do you see what I mean?"

"It sounds a peculiar sort of exercise for the Royal Academy of Music."

"Pardon?"

"It's for the academy, isn't it? You and Betty are students there, aren't you?"

"Yes. Betty. . . . Yes, of course," Ian muttered. "Anyway, will you do it?"

"Well, seeing as you're offering five pounds."

"Oh, er—I did say two or three. Oh, all right, five it is—if you'll help me write the whole thing, and get the salutations right, and the titles, and especially the tone. For instance, suppose it was from, say, the President of the Third International. How would he sign off in a letter to his British equivalent?"

"Oh, something like, 'With Communist Greetings,' I suppose."

"That's good, terrific," Ian cried. "But what I meant was, how would he title himself? 'President of the Communist International,' or what?"

"I'll need to think about things like that, but I'd say . . . let me see. . . . The abbreviation for the International in Russian would be IKKI . . . so I think he'd sign himself 'President of the Presidium of the IKKI.' Is that the kind of thing you want?"

"Perfect," Ian said, leaning back euphorically in the kitchen chair.

But the fee was not to be paid until he was completely satisfied, and he proved to be much more demanding, much more insistent on simulated authenticity, than I'd expected. So in the meantime I was back on iron rations; or rather, greasy rations; and I started to lose weight, and as the weather deteriorated—for the English summer was nigh—a depression settled over the Atlantic, the Faroes, the Dogger Bank and me. Increasingly it required an effort of will to rise in the morning and face the trudging day. As I shaved, the goitrous reflection in the bathroom mirror seemed to look increasingly faithful to the original. And when I would finally drive myself out into the rain—1924 was to have the wettest summer since King Canute—I couldn't resist a few stabs of concern over what had happened to my life. How could somebody as formidable as me, a leader of men with a drawerful of medals, crosses and orders, who had hobnobbed with kings, prime ministers and rumrunners, have sunk to such depths? My land, I even went to a film studio with the idea of taking up movie acting again; I had sunk that low. But not a single film was being made in Britain that year. I was beginning to suspect that I wasn't quite as indispensable to civilization as I had thought.

One day, my schedule called for a visit to a scrap-metal merchant at an airfield near Basildon. The merchant was said to have a flourishing business restoring and flight testing war-surplus aircraft. Unfortunately he had gone bankrupt by the time I arrived, and I was waiting to board the train back to London when I noticed a signboard on the opposite platform pointing to Southend-on-Sea.

That Indian lad, Khooshie, had operated from an airfield near Southend. It occurred to me that it might be worth following that up. The flying outfit that had been training him obviously needed a good instructor, judging by their behavior in sending the boy to sea when he was quite plainly not ready for it.

An enquiry at the ticket office assured me that it would cost only another eightpence to travel onward to Southend. And, after all, it was only midafternoon, and it had stopped raining. I thought I might as well have a go. So I hopped onto the opposite platform and caught the next train.

Southend-on-Sea proved to be a holiday place. Later, on the way back while waiting for the train to London, I had time to stroll around it and note that in many of its features it was identical to every other English seaside resort I had known, in that it had an esplanade usually called the Marine Parade, a rose garden, a bowling green, a putting green, cricket grounds, a boating lake, a lifeboat station, one church of architectural interest and a tub of geraniums filled with toffee wrappers and Woodbine butts. I half expected to see the shoreline divided up into areas named the Reaches, the Levels, the Rocks, the Flats, the Shingles and the Crumbles, according to whether they were inaccessible, flat, rocky, featureless, pebbly or eroded. But in Southend there seemed to be no demarcation between the land and the sea. Both were brown, so that it was hard to tell where the one ended and the other began. The pier was said to be the world's longest. It stuck out to sea for one and a half miles, as if pointing the way longingly toward an immaculate vasty deep, as distant as possible from the defiled Thames and the dreadful sucking mud between the pier supports and the greasy amusements; a one-and-a-half-mile-long signpost for the dads with raw red necks above collarless white shirts, mums in striped deckchairs and pallid infants with bright tin pails solemnly absorbed behind battlements of sand, their grown-up sisters promenading arm-in-arm along the esplanade, eyes slyly swiveled toward clusters of spotty youths, the boys snorting over racks of rib-nudging postcards. ("Grandad, is there anything worn under your kilt?" "Not as much as there used to be.")

Thankfully leaving the town, I took a twenty-minute ride in a noisy single-decker bus and was deposited unceremoniously outside the Southend "Aerodrome." At first I thought the bus driver had been exercising a sense of humor. As I stood by the side of the narrow country road, all I could see were open fields and a five-barred gate. As the grinding of the bus faded into the distance, I listened carefully, but not so much as the blat of a rotary modulated the mild, damp air. There was no sound at all except for the discouraged cheeping of a piddletit or great-crested wickdipper.

At the far end of the field stood a group of three hangars. So I climbed over the gate—catching the lining of my jacket on a nail—and headed in that direction through the unshaven grass at the side of the field.

After I had finished swearing over the torn lining of my only good jacket, I thought briefly about Khooshie and wondered where he was now. I had lost contact with him soon after we attained the isolated Thames shore. While I had remained behind to salvage what I could from the Gander, he had proceeded inland to see if he could get help in saving the amphibian. Two hours later, long after the Gander had sunk, he had still not returned, and I'd set off after him; or rather set off in the same direction, over the marshland, though after losing the Gander I had no real desire to see him again; and didn't.

I should never have dunked the Gander, I realized now. I

should have continued on, and dropped a note to the Lifeboat Society at Burnham-on-Crouch, or somewhere, giving his position. Damn it to hell, it would have been entirely his own fault if he had drowned. He should not have been flying over the sea in the first place, given his lack of experience and even greater lack of common sense. The more I thought about it as I trod through the rough wet grass beside the airfield (and the more I thought about my torn jacket) the more annoyed I got at his stupidity. And even though it was I who had sent him off to look for help, I felt resentful at the way he had left without so much as a word of thanks.

By the time I reached the hangars, my morale was at shoelace level all over again; and a comprehensive view of Southend Aerodrome did nothing to raise it. It appeared to comprise only the hangars, a stack of rusty fuel drums, a padlocked duty hut and a detumescent windsock. Two of the hangars were wartime Bessoneau structures, open and deserted. The third was a wooden affair with a crudely painted sign above the sliding door: "BEE-HIVE AVIATION," it read. Another sign on the side wall read, "Aircraft Available for Travel, Training, Joyrides. Reasonable Rates. B. Hive, Prop."

There was no sign of B. Hive, Prop., however, or indeed of any personnel, and the hangar was locked tight. So that was that. Another failed enterprise. I had journeyed to Southend for nothing.

As I regained the five-barred gate and stood waiting for the bus—assuming, perhaps foolishly, that it returned along the same route—I remembered that the bus had passed a small pub just up the road. Perhaps because of the salty air, I was exceptionally thirsty. Though come to think of it, I'd had nothing to drink since breakfast. I fished for and counted out the remainder of that day's allowance, to see if I could afford a pint. There were a threepenny bit, two pennies and a farthing.

Fivepence farthing. Perhaps it was enough for a pint. The problem was that if I succumbed to the temptation there would not be enough money for the bus fare back to Southend. Quenching my thirst meant that I would have to walk all the way back to Southend, thus building up another thirst that could not be quenched. Gad, there was classical irony for you.

Whilst considering the classical irony, I started walking up the road, and by the time I had reached the pub I had also reached a decision. The sensible course was to walk back the three miles to Southend and *then* have a drink. The resulting quench would keep me quiet all the way back to London. This decision was reinforced as I approached the hostelry. The words "country pub" usually inspired a vision of a half-timbered, stuccoed, rose-bricked, flintstoned, wrought-ironed, pantiled, whitewashed or creeper-clad establishment of almost improbable charm, the very picture of postcard allurement, an optical week's holiday compressed into the duration of a stare. There would also be a side garden flaring with azaleas and, at the rear, a topiary violation of nature's unruly composition, apportioned into artfully artless subgardens by ancient, crumbling walls from which excess flora oozed. A brook would be gossiping nearby, its banks trailing reedy fingers in the sun-sequined stream, while within, the barmaid's chest would match the setting's superabundance. Cor love a duck. But the country pub now being passed on my left had about as much charm as a toenail. It was a mean little edifice of patched brick and modern, leaded windows, opposite a row of whitewashed cottages that, judging by their drunken appearance, were regular patrons of the pub. So onward I strode, stepping fastidiously around a grimy urchin with snot on its cheek.

However, I soon slowed as it occurred to me that fivepence farthing might not be enough for a pint. Last time I'd had a jar it had cost threepence, but that was six years ago. Given today's appalling inflation the price had probably soared. What if I walked to Southend and discovered that beer was sixpence a pint there? Here it was likely to be cheaper. No, better to check here first, so that if it cost more than fivepence I would still be able to take the bus, assuming it returned this way.

The interior of the pub neatly matched its exterior. There was just one parlor, a long, narrowish space crowded with tables. The bar counter on the right had been formed out of bakelite.

A few bottles of liquor were ranged on the shelves behind the counter, most with their seals unbroken, except for the empty bottles, which had presumably been retained in order to present a more imposing array. It was the drabbest pub I had ever seen. The odors of stale beer, mildew and cheap tobacco fought for ascendancy. All seemed to be winning.

There wasn't even a buxom barmaid. Mine host was a puffy chap in a lopsided waistcoat. As I approached he was trying to wipe the flyspecks off a mirror that was advertising somebody's meat pies.

The regulars, mostly farm workers, seemed pleased enough with their tavern, though, and were chuntering away contentedly enough, until I entered. Whereupon every one of them fell silent and stared, as if I were the first stranger to have appeared in these parts since Sir Belvedere de Southend had had his way with a local milkmaid in 1245. As I made for the bar, they continued to gape for a solid minute before the former hubbub gradually reasserted itself.

The landlord was chatting to the other three customers at the scarred bar, and when I tried to catch his eye, he turned and finished cleaning the flyspecks off the mirror with his washcloth before nodding distantly in my direction. "Evening," he informed me.

Hoping to give the impression that I was conducting a survey rather than ascertaining whether or not I had sufficient coin of the realm, I enquired in a hale and stout manner as to how much he charged for his ale and stout.

"Beg your pardon, sir?"

"How much," I surrendered, "for a pint of bitter?"

"Draft? Four and 'alf, sir."

"Ah," quoth I, nodding judiciously, as if comparing this price with that charged by the *Star and Garter* at Richmond. So now I knew where I was.

When my order was not immediately forthcoming, the landlord turned to the young man next to me, who was treating his two companions to a round of drinks. He was a slender young man with lank blond hair and pale blue eyes. He was ordering, in a thin, officer-type voice, an additional drink for himself, a double whiskey.

The landlord hesitated, then turned and milked one of the bottles racked up behind him. As he placed the drink before the young man he leaned over and said as quietly as he could, "I was wondering, sir, if you could see your way clear to settling the rest of your tab."

The other stared at him superciliously.

"Not right at the moment," the landlord added quickly. "But, you know, at your convenience, sir."

"I paid more than half of what I owed," the young man snapped.

"Yes, I know, sir," the landlord said, endeavoring to reduce his height by several inches, "but it's mounting up again, you see, like, and well, I thought. . . ."

His voice guttered as the lank chap continued to stare. Finally the customer heaved a grating sigh and reached for his wallet. Which attracted much interest when its jaws gaped, for it was nine months pregnant with currency.

The blond man's two pals—stable lads judging by the not unpleasant odor of horses and leather that emanated from them—looked impressed as they gazed deep into his leather treasury. Their respect for the man, however, did not appear to match their deference to his wallet, judging by the way they kept nudging each other and exchanging loose grins whenever their blond patron wasn't looking.

After settling his account with surprising reluctance considering that his wallet was so tightly packed with notes that he had difficulty in extracting any of them, the young man rather offensively turned his back on the landlord to talk to his companions; whereupon the landlord turned and glared at me, as if it were my fault that his debtor was treating him like dirt.

"Yes, I'll try a pint," I said hurriedly, and watched, licking my lips, as he filled a dimpled glass to the rim.

After lowering the level of beer by three inches or so, I slowed down with an effort and nursed the rest, to make it last until I was ready to face the three-mile walk. As I nursed, I listened idly to the conversation farther along the counter. Apparently the blond young man had just returned from two weeks in the capital, where he had been living it up in nightclubs and music halls. One evening, two flappers whom he had met in Ma Meyrick's famous drinking establishment had cost him sixty pounds in hardly more than a couple of hours. "Sixty quid," he exclaimed disgustedly. "And the champagne was filthy, too."

"Business seems to be looking up, Mr. Hive," said the crony on his immediate left, the one with the hairy jacket and thin, sly mouth, "now that you're out of business."

Mr. Hive? B. Hive, Prop.? I listened rather more attentively.

"What do you mean?" Hive asked, staring at the lad.

"Oh, nothing."

"What do you mean, nothing? I want to know what you meant," Hive said, making an attempt to keep his voice light, and not quite succeeding.

"I just meant you seem to be doing so well now, Mr. Hive, that's all."

Hive continued to stare haughtily at the lad for a moment before pushing back his lank hair with a sharp movement. "Just because I didn't throw money around doesn't mean I didn't have it," he said dismissively.

"Par'n me."

He started nervously as I discharged air into his earhole.

"What?"

"Pardon me, but are you Beehive Aviation?" I asked.

"What?"

"Mr. Hive, is it?"

"Yes. What about it?"

"Oh, just wondered. I was at the aerodrome just now and saw your name."

"Oh, yes?"

"I was looking for a job."

"Oh, I see. Yes, I'm Bernard Hive."

He looked me over carefully and, as luck would have it, immediately noticed the torn lining of my blazer.

"A job?" he repeated. "Are you a pilot?"

"Yes."

"Fly in the war?" he asked more relaxedly, now that he had ascertained that I was a supplicant and therefore an inferior.

"Yes."

"Never got to the front myself," he said. "Dashed war ended while I was still at Pilot's Pool."

"That's too bad—or too good, maybe."

"I assure you, I was dashed disappointed," he said stiffly.

"I'm sure."

"Anyway, I'm afraid I can't help you, old man. I only had the one machine, and a fool student smashed it up."

"That's too bad," I said, taking another tiny sip. "What happened?"

"Stupid wog student flew it straight into the drink."

"How many hours had he done?"

"Just. . . ." Hive began; but then stopped, the suspicious look returning. "Why? Why do you ask?"

"Just making conversation."

"Anyway, I can't help, old man," Hive said curtly and quickly raised a nail-bitten finger to attract the landlord's attention. "Another," he said, pointing at his whiskey glass.

Seeing that I was about to continue the conversation, Hive turned his back and began to talk to his pals about the Empire Exhibition at Wembley, to which he had taken his two flapper friends; but it had not been too successful as it had rained steadily for the three days he was there, and also the girls had insisted on occupying one of the hotel rooms together, so that he couldn't get at either of them.

I left a couple of minutes later, ignored even by the bewhiskered regulars. As I walked back to Southend, for the first time uncertainty bubbled to the surface and gave off the noxious fumes of anxiety. Not that I was *really* anxious, mind you. I'd crump-holed often enough in the past only to soar to fresh heights. I was certain that sooner or later good fortune would swing the old prop for me. But I must admit . . . I wasn't *absolutely* certain.

A Bit Underexposed

As if things weren't bad enough, a gorgeous blonde joined me in my bedroom one night.

I had been feeling really rotten all day, and not just because of the unseasonably cold, wet spring. I had been overindulging. On the previous day, Ian had finally pronounced himself satisfied with his college exercise, and paid me the five pounds. To celebrate I had gone out and blown five bob of it.

I was quite proud of Ian's composition. I had even taken the trouble to find out from the local party HQ, deviously, the correct phraseology to be used. Hence I knew enough to address the letter to the Central Committee and subhead it to the Executive Committee of the Third Communist International. I was particularly pleased with my first paragraph. I thought it a perfect example of the turgid Soviet style as it might have been translated into English by some other filthy Communist. "Dear Comrades," it began; "The time is approaching for the Parliament of England to consider the Treaty concluded between the Governor of Great Britain and USSR for the purpose of ratification. The fierce campaign raised by the British bourgeoisie around the question shows that the majority of the same, together with reactionary circles, are against the Treaty for the purpose of breaking off an agreement consolidating the ties between the proletariats of the two countries leading to the restoration of normal relations between England and the USSR. . . ." etcetera and so forth.

The only thing I argued about concerned Ian's requirement calling for actual armed agitation by "the masses of the British proletariat." I persuaded him that the president of the Communist International, the person supposed to be writing the letter, would surely not be as blatant as that. We finally settled on the rather more vague and perhaps more convincing, "It is indispensable to stir up the masses of the British proletariat, to bring into movement the army of unemployed proletarians. . . ." which was certainly inflammatory enough.

By the time we were finished, I felt I had more than earned my five quid, so on the previous evening, unable to face another dinner of pork pie at Paddington station or a baked potato from a cast-iron street oven on wheels, I had treated myself to a five-course dinner in the Grand Salon of the Holborn Restaurant. It had cost five shillings, but it was worth it. At least I thought it was until next morning when I found myself suffering from indigestion, heartburn and various other sorts of gastric sedition. Thus in relieving my hunger I had ended up feeling more pegged-out than ever and had been forced to spend the day in bed, eating nothing but my knuckles and admiring the view through the window of rain-lashed brick stuccoed with soot.

All this leisure gave me ample opportunity to worry, and by early evening I had just reached the conclusion that there was no way I could survive unless I went to my in-laws for help, when Mrs. Wignall knocked at the door, thrust her head around it and looked particularly severe.

For a fearful moment I thought she had come to throw me out for nonpayment of rent, until I recollected that immediately upon receiving the five pounds from Ian I had paid not just what I owed but another two weeks in advance, to ensure that when I ran out of dibs next week I would still have a few rafters over my head instead of a leafy bower in Hyde Park.

"Someone to see you," she said grimly, but blocking the doorway to prevent the visitor from actually doing so. "And you know the rules, Mr. Bandy."

"What rules?"

"About entertaining visitors of the opposite sex in your room at night," she said. "You might as well know now, I don't tolerate that sort of thing in my house." And, twitching slightly, she finally moved aside to allow the visitor to enter.

"Sigridur," I cried; for it was indeed the Viking marauder, dressed from head to foot in raindrops.

As Sigridur bounded to the bed and greeted me with assorted cries of pleasure and reproach, Mrs. Wignall remained in the doorway, staring suspiciously at the voluminous blonde in the black oilskin coat and sou'wester.

"You poor thing," Sigridur cried. "You look terrible."

"It's all right," I began. "Just a touch of—"

I stopped with a gasp as she applied a large hand to my cozy forehead. The hand was so wet and chill it naturally caused quite a reaction.

"See, you're not well at all," she cried. "Convulsions." And, turning despairingly to Mrs. Wignall: "I don't know—he just refuses to look after himself properly." She smiled and shook her head at Mrs. Wignall in the manner of one woman sharing with another a common despair over male recklessness.

I opened my mouth to disagree. Sigridur deftly inserted a thermometer.

As she wrestled with her oilskin coat as if it were an opponent, before hurling it over the back of a chair, Mrs. Wignall asked her if she was a nurse. Sigridur replied rather boastfully that she was a doctor, and to prove it she picked up my wrist and felt for a pulse.

"Go on," Mrs. Wignall replied skeptically, looking over Sigridur's spectacular figure. Though Sigga was wearing a bulky suit that looked as if it had been knitted straight from the sheep's back, the contours underneath obviously belonged to the Folies Bergères rather than to Minerva, goddess of medicine. "Now pull the other one."

"The other what, please? Oh, I see, you are expressing skepticism. But it's true, I am a doctor," Sigridur said, frowning and looking preoccupied—possibly because she was timing a twitching muscle in my wrist instead of the artery.

Mrs. Wignall stood uncertainly in the doorway before shifting her gaze reluctantly to my wrinkled pajamas. "Well," she said, "seeing as you're not well, Mr. Bandy, I'll make an exception this time."

I snatched out the thermometer. "No," I said firmly. "I don't think you ought to make any exceptions. A rule is a rule, Mrs. Wignall."

"It's not that I'm a prude, you understand. It's the other boarders, you see."

"I know, I quite understand," I said. "The lady is just leaving."

"She is not. She is staying. She will give you a bath," Sigridur sang out happily. "You are clammy."

"I yam not," I snapped, immediately turning clammy with annoyance. "And you heard Mrs. Wignall. It's time to leave."

"But I have only just arrived."

"Mrs. Wignall can't help that, can you, Mrs. Wignall?"

"Oh, all right, she can stay," Mrs. Wignall said.

"But the other boarders, Mrs. Wignall!"

"They can just mind their own business," she said severely. "There's far too much of this interfering in other people's affairs these days."

"But we're not having an affair, Mrs. Wignall," I protested; but paradoxically it was Sigridur's mischievous landlady-defrosting smile and her words—"As for that, we shall just have to wait and see, won't we?"—that utterly convinced Mrs. Wignall that all was well on the decorum front; and she withdrew before I had a chance to reason with her.

I lay there, glaring at the visitor. It didn't do a bit of good. Sigridur continued to look wonderfully happy at having somebody at her mercy, even somebody she believed wasn't worth her attentions. After examining the thermometer, which seemed to indicate that I had spent the night in a snowdrift, she turned to the bedclothes, which she proceeded to peel back and flap about violently, as if to expel the fetid air underneath. Then she tucked me in again, so tightly that I could scarcely breathe.

"Unhand me, you villain," I wheezed, struggling for dear life.

"Shhh, you must have rest and quiet, Bandy," she said, tidying the bedside table with a great deal of noise.

"You've bound me to the mattress like Andromeda. Who d'you think you are, Perseus?"

"Wrong mythology," Sigga said, rearranging the articles on the table—a comb with missing teeth and pyorrhea, a bunch of purposeless keys, a Nuttall's Mintoe, some magazine advertisements and a ten-shilling note and two coins. "My antecedents are Norse, not Olympian. Besides, it was Cepheus who bound Andromeda, who, of course, was a woman. Perseus—"

"Never mind, never mind," I snapped. Then, scowling like a thunderhead: "How did you find me, anyway?"

"It was easy," she replied, sorting through my chest of drawers and inventorying the contents. "I knew you were a flyer, so I asked people, and finally somebody at the Royal Aero Club on Piccadilly gave me your address."

"Will you stop pawing my undies," I shouted.

"Shhh. Just checking," she said serenely. "Well, at least you have good clothes, that's something. Except for this flying coat."

"Leave it alone."

She turned and regarded me with her hands on her woolly hips. "You don't look at all good," she said.

"I looked lovely until you came," I mumbled.

"But don't worry, I won't abandon you."

"And I wasn't worried until you said that."

"Just because you're down and out. All the same, I just don't understand how even *you* could go downhill so fast in so short a time," she said. She pointed to the cash on the bedside table. "Is that all the money you have?"

"Course not."

"It is. I have felt in all your pockets and read your bankbook. What on earth has happened, Bandy," she exclaimed, "to reduce you to such an abject condition?"

"Well, if you must know, I fell in the sea," I said, wrenching peevishly at the bedclothes.

"Oh," she said, as if that were no more than she had expected.

"Where is the mending basket, please, and I will mend the tear in this blazer."

I took a deep breath, which, because of her bedmaking, caused the mattress at each end to bow upwards. "If I give you a safety pin, will you go back to Iceland?" I asked hopefully.

"Iceland is a backwater," she said, rummaging through the wardrobe on the other side of the room. "I have decided to see the world. It is all your fault."

"Oh, how?"

"You made me see how much fun and excitement I would miss if I settled down."

"But you can't do that! What about your fiancé, what about Agnar? He waited years and years for you."

"Oh, there are many who will be only too pleased to marry Agnes," she replied with a heartless shrug. "He is a rich man, you know. He is so rich that he pays hardly any income tax."

I decided that it was time to straighten her out, get her to see reason, bring her to her senses and establish our relationship on a realistic basis, to wit, that there was no relationship. I would never get away from her otherwise.

So I said, as calmly and reasonably as my straitjacketed condition would permit, "Sigga."

"Yes, Bandy?"

"Sigga, you're a lovely looking woman, brave as a Norse goddess even without your helmet and sword. There isn't a normal male in Asia, Africa, Europe or Syrup who wouldn't be delighted to the point of chuffness to be your, ahem, friend."

"Why thank you, Bandymin," she said with a smile brilliant as burning magnesium.

"Except me. I'm the one exception. Ridiculous, I know, but there you are. I'm not the least interested," I said, with amazing calm. "So you see, there's absolutely no point in your continuing to cultivate me. In fact, if you persist in these unwanted attentions, I could become put-upon. And I should point out that better men than you have gone down like flies when a Bandy has begun to feel put-upon."

"Mm," she said vaguely, as she proceeded to the window and

attempted to force it up in order to admit some nice fresh air into the sickroom.

"And don't bother trying to open the window," I said shortly. "I've been trying to open it for two weeks," I said, just as her muscles bulged, and the window shot up with a crash.

"Poor Bandy," she murmured, taking deep breaths of rain-washed London grit. "You really do need looking after, don't you?"

"Sigga," I said after a moment, "what about your loved ones, back in Iceland? Don't you realize how terribly they must miss you? I mean, my goodness, they must have been heartbroken when you left."

"Actually mother helped me to pack, and Pabbi arranged transport for me. He fixed up a free trip to Hull in Snorri Gustavesson's trawler," she replied, leaving the room. And before I had a chance to tear myself loose and barricade the door with the seven-foot wardrobe, she had returned with a dustpan and brush and a carpet sweeper. "No, I want to see the world before I settle down," she went on, starting to spring clean. "I want to travel to wondrous places, to see the baroque splendor of Austrian palaces and stand at pumice-tortured Herculaneum and visualize the pyroclastic surge; then share El Greco's Toledo vision and the sun-bleached compositions of the east, run my hand over marble chiseled by esthetic gods, sniff exotic scents and feast on Grecian walnuts and on Sicily's frosty *gelati*. Already I have made a start. I have a job in the mortuary at St. Pancreas Hospital here in London."

As she bustled about, clouds of dust arose, threatening me with respiratory as well as digestive complications. I tried to cover my mouth with a damp sheet but she had bound me to the bed too effectively. My fists writhed feebly under the sheets. It struck me that if this ward work of hers was an example of her medical skills it was just as well they had put her in a department whose inmates were not likely to make complaints.

"Tell you what," she said, reaching over to fold down the collar of my pajamas and giving my starboard clavicle a neat pat, "I'll move into the boarding house so I can look after you better."

No, I was wrong. I was capable of movement under the bedclothes. I found that with a supreme effort I could just about manage to clench my fists.

But one morning just a couple of days later it occurred to me—the thought lasting almost a minute before I dismissed it as absurd—that Sigridur had brought me a bit of luck. It was one of the mornings I called at my old club, the Army and Navy, to see if there was anything of interest. I couldn't afford to rejoin, but fortunately the doorman had recognized me from wartime days, and in exchange for the occasional sixpence slipped into his glove he allowed me to check the notice board in the lobby, where employment opportunities in aviation were listed now and again. On this occasion he was not in sight, so I dodged into the reading room to check the aviation magazines. I never bothered with the newspapers these days as they so rarely advertised jobs for flyers. And upon opening a copy of *Flight*, I learned that the newly formed Imperial Airways was looking for pilots with recent experience on the commercial version of the Vickers Vimy.

It was only then that I realized how close I had come to losing heart. I was sloshed by a positive tidal wave of relief. I had to plonk myself suddenly into one of the club's badly chewed leather armchairs. I had not only flown Vimys, I had assembled, tested and owned one of those big, two-engined aircraft for more than three years. I had a quite remarkable two hundred and forty hours in the type. Of course, mine had been the bomber version, but there was no problem there. The commercial variant was pretty much the same airplane, except for a fattened fuselage.

I could hardly believe my luck, and within minutes I had mentally scribbled several pages of interview-type dialogue in which every detail of my experience with Vimys was recounted . . . except that maybe I wouldn't bother to mention that I had crashed my Vimy onto a distillery last fall. I had to be careful, after all, not to overwhelm the selection committee with piddling detail.

The only drawback was that applications had to be made in writing, and the interviews would not be held for some weeks.

Still, I could surely hang on until then. Get a temporary job in some other field, perhaps: ditch digging, or dance partnering. The craze for dancing that had swept the nation during the war was as fierce as ever and, despite my preoccupations, I could not help noticing the thousands of *thé dansant* parlors or night-clubs that dotted the urban landscape. I had learned from the club doorman that many ex-officers were employed as dancing partners in such places. But I tried only one such joint. The manager took one look at me and said, "No, definitely not. The ladies want faceless partners, old boy, not somebody who looks like a stand-in for Lord Curzon."

Perhaps it was just as well that I was dissuaded from pursuing the matter. The only dance I knew was the Dashing White Sergeant.

St. Pancreas

Fortunately, Sigridur's threat to move in came to naught, for there was no spare bath night; even if there had been, Sigridur, as a thoroughly steam-cleaned Scandinavian, would certainly have refused any accommodation that permitted only one tubful of water per week. So she remained in residence at the hospital. However, this did not discourage her from calling on me at every opportunity, to see how I was getting on and to make sure I was eating properly, dressing suitably and remembering to button my flies.

I just couldn't understand why she was wasting her time on me when she could have been playing doctor with her affluent colleagues at the St. Pancreas Hospital. (Surely she'd got the name wrong? Wasn't it more likely to be St. Pancras, like the railway station?) Then why this concern in the face of such peevish resistance?

It is, of course, one's prerogative as a despot of the inkpot or cock of the literary midden to delineate acquaintances in as biased a manner as one chooses. Most people don't deserve any better anyway. Still, one must be fair, occasionally, to one's subjects, if only to allay the reader's doubts that one is a reliable and impartial observer. Thus, one must concede this: that not everyone agreed that Sigga was infuriating, thick-skinned, complacent and inconsiderate. In fact, practically everyone else found her adorable, amusing and quite charming. But then a woman can be forgiven almost any fault provided she is lovely enough.

Sigridur was certainly that, with cheekbones that were not so unladylike as to be prominent but that molded her face with just the right amount of artistry to save it from being ordinarily pretty. As if that weren't enough, her complexion was flawless, her eyes thrillingly blue—though too often coolly critical in my opinion, especially when swiveled in my direction—her lips deliciously plump in the Scandinavian fashion, while overall her figure had been turned by a genetic craftsman.

Yet in my present bromidic state, I wasn't interested in even the most noncommittal carnal adhesion. Her beauty couldn't compensate for her insensitivity to my needs, especially my need to degenerate to my heart's content. Yet my resistance seemed only to encourage her. She seemed convinced that I was a worthless carp, yet she persisted in regarding me as if I were stuffed with caviar. It seemed to me that she lacked insight. For instance, she couldn't even understand why, if I had formerly hobnobbed with prominent Londoners as I claimed, I refused to call on them now for help. "It would place me at too great a disadvantage," I pointed out. But she couldn't see that at all. In Iceland if you were in trouble you called upon others for help. They expected you to sponge off them. She couldn't see that this was not the case universally.

I tried to explain it to her. "Look," I said, "if I appeared before Lord X with enough money to tip his butler and footman, and with the right sort of clothes and with an aura of weary indifference as if I were not particularly concerned whether he helped me or not, he would probably do his best; but if he learned that I had come by bus from the station to save money, and he caught me looking anxious, he would drop me like a brick. It's like a bank loan. The more you show you need it, the less likely you are to get it."

"Who's Lord X?" she enquired.

"Eh?"

"This Lord X, what's his real name?"

"How do I know? He's just a fictitious example."

"Another fiction?" She shook her head. "Oh, Bandy, your whole life seems to be a fiction."

" 'Tis not."

"Very well then, who is Lord X?"

"I told you, he's just an example!"

"Honestly, Bandymin," she said, tying my shoelace, "you will feel better in the long run if you'll just face up to things. Just remind yourself of the truth now and then, that you have never met any lords or generals or prime ministers, or anybody important; and gradually these crippling delusions will fade, and—"

"But I have, I *have* met them!" I screamed, jumping up and down and beating the atmosphere with my fists. "I've even met the King!"

"King X, I suppose."

Because I myself had in the past often goaded people in order to savor their capillary-bursting reactions, I wondered if Sigga was attempting to emulate such provocations, but I finally concluded that she was quite unaware of how infuriating her behavior was. She really believed that she was helping me and was quite exasperated when I failed to respond appropriately. As when she rushed up one evening to announce that she had found me a job.

Yes, yes, she cried, I'd told her that I would soon be flying again, but she would believe that when she saw it; in the meantime I needed gainful occupation, and this was the best she could manage. She'd had a word with the administrator, and he had promised to look favorably on my application if I cared to come to his office at nine o'clock the following morning.

She was quite overjoyed on my behalf that I might soon be restored to reality through gainful employment. I might have been quite touched by her pleasure if the job that she considered to be just right for me was not that of hospital porter, just about the lowest-paid job in the entire United Kingdom.

"Oh, well," I said, not looking the least grateful, much to her annoyance. "I guess it'll lead to better things, when they find out I studied medicine at one time."

"You don't think I told them that, do you?" she snorted.

"Why not?"

"I'm not telling lies for you or anyone."

"But I was a medical student. Christ, don't you believe *anything* I tell you?"

"All right. You say you were a medical student. Show us some proof."

"Damn it, how do you expect me to prove that, after all these years?"

"I see. And about being a war hero?"

"I never claimed to be a war hero. I—"

"You mentioned that your wife kept a scrapbook of your exploits. So, show me some of the newspaper clippings of you as a sergeant major, or whatever you were."

"The Lewises have them," I said shortly. "And I don't know where to find them just at the mo—"

"Photographs of you as a film actor in America?"

"I . . . well, I had to leave the United States in rather a hurry."

"Confirmation of some sort that you were a member of your Parliament?"

"I had to leave Canada in rather a hurry, too."

"Uh-huh. Proof, then, that you designed and built the float-plane that you were flying?"

"It all went down with the ship," I said defiantly with a girlish toss of the head. The gesture was supposed to have been a dignified straightening of the spine, but something went wrong, possibly because of Sigga's expression. Her face was suffused with compassion as she regarded the deluded creature sadly; but not entirely without hope that some day, with her help, he might be able to cope with everyday life.

No doubt she thought that the process of rehabilitation would commence at the hospital, but I rather doubted it myself, especially when I caught sight of the institution. St. Pancreas looked hardly in a position to rehabilitate itself, let alone me. Jammed into a side street off Euston Road, it was a dingy brick complex built around a gritty courtyard, with two clipped wings. The original, central building was so ancient that the year of its construction, chiseled into a loose stone above the main entrance, had long since been nibbled away by grazing acids.

Originally St. Pancreas was an institution for indigents and other poor. By the mid-eighteenth century the standard of care was such as to ensure so ready a supply of corpses that a medical school was established to take advantage of them. Standards had not greatly improved by 1888, when the matron was convicted of smothering a number of her charges who had been disturbing her sleep with their groans and complaints. Though her trial was overshadowed that year by the excitement over Jack the Ripper, a melodrama, entitled *The Mad Matron of Somers Town*, based on her noise-abatement procedures, had a successful run in the provinces. St. Pancreas's chief claim to fame, though, was that Boswell had been treated there for gonorrhea.

Though the main entrance was probably not for the likes of humble job applicants, I went in that way anyway, past pilasters half-buried in crumbling brick and into the mausoleum-like entrance hall. A suitcase-carrying gentleman and a fashionably dressed lady with a flawless English complexion had arrived just ahead of me. They were being greeted by a young registrar and a nurse. "But there's nothing *wrong* with you, Mandy," the gentleman was saying a bit desperately.

"Darling, that's the whole point," the lady said gaily.

"If you'll just come this way, Mrs. Villiers-Wakehampton," the registrar said respectfully.

"I told you, darling," the lady continued. "In the States they say they wouldn't dream of running their motorcars all year without maintaining them, so it would be silly to neglect the rather more important human mechanism, don't you see? They call it an annual checkup, and everybody should have one. Lady Prestwich had it done in New York, and she's recommending it to everyone. She said she felt a new woman afterwards."

"That's all very well, Mandy, but I don't want a new woman, I want you."

"Oh, Cyril, you are the most awful stick-in-the-mud," said the lovely lady, as she was escorted into the depths.

The hall porter, seeing that his services were not required by the lady, had gone back into his glass case. I had to rap three times before he finally flung up a hatch and bawled through it, "Yes?"

When I asked for the administrator's office, he bellowed louder than ever, issuing a stream of rapid and complicated directions, before slamming the hatch shut again and glaring at me defiantly through the glass.

I was to learn that this was his method of bullying the public. He was in the habit of giving visitors a volley of incomprehensible instructions in order to humiliate them when inevitably they trickled back to the front hall for fresh directions.

Not realizing that I was supposed to feign quickness of wit by pretending I'd understood, I gazed back lumpishly through the glass, until he finally shot the hatch up again.

"Yes?"

"I didn't quite catch that," I said in my drawling whine. "More slowly if you please, my good man."

For a moment he looked uncertain, fooled by my pretentious air; but only for a few seconds, until he had taken in my apparel. I was wearing my horrible flying coat. This was not because I preferred to walk around dressed in stains and matted fur, but because I had no other clothing that was appropriate. I could hardly apply for a lowly job shamelessly exposing myself in a Savile Row suit or a Wesbrook blazer. Hence the foul leather, together with a cloth cap obtained just that morning from a flea circus.

"About a job, right?" he asked rudely.

"Yes."

"Outsideturnleftleftagainroundthebackfirstschoolentrance."

"Ah," I said, looking enlightened. "School entrance—I got that bit, Sergeant."

He sighed so heavily that his breath fogged the glass case. Once again he repeated the directions, this time painfully slowly, as if training a parrot. But then, taking another look at me, he stopped and shook his head disgustedly. Emerging from his case, he announced that as I appeared to be a trifle slow on the uptake, he supposed that he had better show me the way himself. Which he did, marching me outside again and round to the rear of the building.

As this was a three- or four-minute walk, which took us round three sides of the east or medical school wing, he had plenty of time for an interrogation.

"Name?"

"Bandy, Sergeant."

"How d'you know I was a sergeant?"

"It must be your kind face, I suppose."

"Officer?"

"A long time ago, yes."

"Job?"

"What job am I applying for? Porter."

He stopped dead and stared at me accusingly. "You trying to be funny?"

"No."

"You know what a porter does, don't you?"

"More or less."

"He gets the dirty jobs. And *you*'d get the dirtiest jobs of all."

"You think they'd save the dirtiest jobs for me, do you?"

"I know they would—because I'd give them to you—*sir*," he added, sneering. "I'm Hodges, see—head porter." He brought his large, fat face close to mine, breathing whiskey. Whiskey, at nine in the morning. "Still want the job?" he demanded, leering.

Actually he himself looked a bit like a bonded whiskey barrel, wrapped in a navy blue uniform and topped by a bullying expression.

"Not particularly," I said. "But I need it."

"Right, don't say I haven't warned you," he said, and continued onward, arms swinging.

By and by, we reached the medical school entrance at the rear of the east wing. The stone steps leading to it were worn to a frazzle by generations of medical students; though at the moment the steps were being given a rest, as the school was closed for the summer.

Finally we marched down a terra-cotta corridor until we reached a door marked "Positively No Admittance." Hodges promptly threw it open without knocking and shouted inside at the top of his voice, "Man about a job—sir!"

The occupant, who was busy reaming out one nostril with the

corner of a handkerchief coiled in such a way as to create a fabric spike, started so violently that he drove the point of the handkerchief into his eye instead. As the porter slammed the door behind me, the administrator's pallid face flushed a dull red, and he clenched his fists and quivered all over. "That . . . that porter," he said through his teeth. "One of these days. . . ."

Rather belatedly he jumped up, rushed from behind his desk and raced out into the corridor, obviously intent on tearing strips off my escort; but by that time the minion was back in his glass bowl, eating ant eggs and blowing bubbles.

The administrator returned, muttering to himself and rubbing his eye. By which time he had apparently forgotten about me, for as he sat down behind his desk again, he started when he saw me standing in front of it.

"Oh. Ah. Yes. The, uh, the, uh, the, uh . . . job, wasn't it? Please—sit down, sit down, my dear chap. Smoke?"

I looked around. "Where?"

"Hm? Let me see, you're the fellow that Dr. . . . our new lady pathologist mentioned. What was the name again?"

"Jonsdottir."

"Ah. Well, do be seated, Mr. Jonsdottir."

"That's the doctor's name."

"Oh, I *see*! You're a *doctor*! My dear chap," he began apologetically.

"No, no, I'm not. I'm Bandy."

"Well, you've come to the right place. We have quite a good orthopedic department here."

"The *name* is Bandy."

"Then why do you call yourself Jonsdottir? That's very confusing, you know," the administrator said reproachfully. "I'm sure we already have somebody here named Jonsdottir."

There was a brief silence broken only by the gurgling of an empty stomach and the faint rasp of a weary hand over a faint beard.

"In that case," I said, "I'd better call myself something else. I know. I'll call myself Bartholomew Bandy."

"If you wish," the administrator said, obviously not overly

impressed with the choice. "Now what is it you want to see me about?"

"The job, sir."

"Yes, of course," he nodded; then looked furtively at my flying coat.

The coat, however, though intended to help me look appropriately seedy, seemed to create an alternative mental sequence, for he suddenly said, "You're an unemployed army officer, I suppose."

"Well, yes."

"Chicken farming."

I sat there trying to work out how he had managed to get from a flying coat to a chicken farm. The aerial connection, could it be?

The explanation, however, was less complicated. "Every unemployed officer I've met went in for chicken farming after the war," he said, blinking his right eye. "And worse, failing at it." He was beginning to look annoyed, for some reason. "Trouble with you gentlemen," he went on resentfully, "is you won't consider an ordinary job. No, it's got to be chicken farming, or something equally. . . . A job in manufacturing or public service—starting anywhere at the bottom and working your way up by dint of the intelligence, initiative and energy you're supposed to have as an officer, that's not good enough for you, is it?" He was looking thoroughly outraged by now. "Oh, no, it has to be something genteel, doesn't it!" he shouted, his face flushing the shade of damson jam. "You come here, spurning an honest job merely because it might require a small sacrifice in social position or prestige. Not good enough for you, is it?" he shouted. "Afraid it might cause your flapper friends to snigger behind your back. 'I say, have you heard—poor old Jonsdottir is actually *working* for a living!' Well, all I can say is, go back to your chicken farm if that's what you want! See if I care!" And he turned away so forcefully that he cracked his elbow on the desk—quite painfully, judging by the way his nostrils flared.

"I'm quite willing to take the job," I said, "if it's offered."

"Pardon?"

"The porter's job. If you could give me an idea if and when you want me to start."

His jaw unhinged itself. "My dear chap—why didn't you say so?" he cried, vigorously massaging his elbow, but pretending to be wiping his palm. "Of course it's offered. You can start tomorrow if you like." His expression had quite changed to one of almost sycophantic eagerness. "You're sure it won't be too difficult or embarrassing for you . . . ? But that's splendid, my dear chap," he cried, and promptly rushed me over to the personnel office himself.

He did so, I suspect, in case I changed my mind en route, with him praising me all the way for my officer-like qualities; though by the time I had been at the hospital for three days I had learned that he would have employed a village idiot provided he was willing to work the excessively long hours for approximately two pounds a week.

The last man to hold down the job had, in fact, been illiterate. "Fact is, he's still with us," said Hodges, who was in charge of the orientation course, i.e., marching me around the complex as if visiting a series of firing squads. "Come on, I'll introduce you."

He led the way along an acrid corridor in the basement of the east wing. "If the man I'm replacing is still here," I said, "why am I needed?"

"Well, he hasn't been hisself lately," Mr. Hodges replied, entering a large room and pointing to one of several metal tables that stuck out from the walls on both sides of the room. A partially dissected cadaver gaped on the second table on the right. "That's him, that's old Tom," Hodges said, "making hisself useful at last."

A New Ward

It didn't take me long to get used to the hospital routine, which was simple enough, God knows. Every Monday, Mr. Hodges gathered his staff together either to confirm them in their current duties or to allocate fresh tasks for the week. Though the orderlies claimed that they were the ones who did most of the hard work because the porters were so skilled at malingery, the porters actually did most of it. Naturally, as the latest recruit, and also because Mr. Hodges was annoyed because he had failed to frighten me with the ugliest sight that the hospital had to offer, I was given the worst job of all.

Having had experience in hospitals in Canada and Russia, I was able to take it in my stride. It involved collecting the trash and the pathological waste from all parts of the building, including the medical school, and consigning the often dripping debris to the incinerator at set times during the day. The waste varied from the occasional cadaver part that was too desiccated to be of further use to the students to armfuls of dressings colorfully stained gentian violet, suppuration yellow, sanguine crimson and draintube green. The only thing that bothered me was that when the wind was blowing from the wrong direction it caused the incinerator chimney to blow back and envelop me in foul smoke.

In the meantime I discovered that, despite its past, St. Pancreas had neither an especially good nor a particularly bad reputation in the profession. On the one hand the octogenarian Professor of Surgery required a periodic reminder not to park his scalpel between his teeth during operations, as he had been wont to do before Lister came along with his antiseptic nonsense; but on the other hand, the Physician-in-Chief was conversant with the very latest and most fashionable diseases, colitis currently being the most popular. As for the medical school, the students might attend it mainly because they couldn't get in anywhere else, but upon qualifying, their level of incompetence was not noticeably higher than the national average. Admittedly the Medical Research Unit had failed to make any useful discoveries during the past twenty years, but there was a good reason for this. They were too busy making wine and distributing it at a tidy profit among the lower echelons of the staff. The winemaking operation had developed quite logically from their studies of fermentation. But generally the hospital needed to cover up no more than the usual number of scandals per year.

Thus St. Pancreas was an average sort of place where tradition—that is, the way things had been done in the nineteenth century—acted as an efficient barrier to medical progress; yet it had somehow contrived during the past few years to become the most fashionable hospital in London. A number of factors had contributed to this reputation, including the charm and handsome appearance of Adolphus Fleete, the Physician-in-Chief, the skill of Sir Philligree Pilchard, the famous hemorrhoids specialist and the fact that a member of the Royal Family had recently been brought to St. Pancreas for treatment after being bitten by a police horse.

But it was the luxury of the private rooms on the top two floors of the west wing that had made St. Pancreas, in the words of the administrator, "The Valhalla of the smart set" (until somebody pointed out that Valhalla meant the Hall of the Slain). Formerly isolation wards, the rooms had been refurbished by a farsighted administration, the costs being met from the proceeds of the campaign that had been designed to raise funds for new X-ray equipment. Some of the private rooms even had mains-operated radio sets, with aerials strung behind specially constructed pelmets, to enable wealthy patients to listen to music from Savoy Hill as they recuperated from the latest pop op—usually an appendectomy, still fashionable years after Edward VII had survived it.

"They got sixteen marble bathrooms up there," said one of my fellow porters as we sat around in the porters' room in the basement. This was a windowless cavern with stone walls, and a brick floor illuminated by a single 150-watt bulb. But the porters liked it because it was warm, being next door to the hospital heating plant.

"And what have they got for us?" the porter continued in his hectoring voice. "I'll tell you, comrades. For the heating men, the morgue attendant, the kitchen staff and all of us porters, they got that one flippin' bog along the corridor there, what backs up into your boots every second flush."

"Bleeding typical, init?"

"Up the revolution."

Ken, another of the porters, tugged at my sleeve so energetically that my mug of tea slopped over my wrist. "There's a really famous actress keeps a suite of rooms on the top floor, permanent, like," he said. "It's for when she feels too tired to go home after a performance, like."

"Is that right? What's her name?"

Ken thought for a moment. "She give me a ten-shilling note once," he offered, "when I brung up the tank for her pet crocodile."

"It's a nalligator."

"Whatever it is, it didn't do Dr. Keats no good. He has to give the anesthetic with one hand, now."

"Talking about doing it with one 'and," said Ernie, " 'ave you seen that new bint in Pathology? Coo. I mean."

"She's a real doctor, too."

"Garn."

"She is. I heard her argy-bargying with Dr. Aigew."

"Legs all the way up to her sternum," someone said, his eyes cataracted with lust.

"Aye," said the oldest porter. "Wouldn't mind clamping me teeth into her glutinous maximum, I wouldn't."

"Well, give me your teeth, Granddad, and I'll see what I can do."

"Cor, what a prow. Imagine getting her to tell you to turn your head and cough."

"She's beau'iful," said the youngest porter romantically. "She seems all lit up from inside . . . like she's got an 'undred-watt bulb up her jacksey."

"She's a foreigner, isn't she?"

"Yerse. She's Dutch."

"Course she isn't," said the oldest porter with a derisive chuckle that turned into a phlegm-lubricated cough.

Everybody waited for him to recover, but he took so long about it that the one with the second-longest service at the hospital jerked a thumb at me. "He'll know," he said, looking at me with a mixture of deference and mistrust, as if he suspected that I was Lord Muck in disguise. "He's a foreigner, too."

"Whatjamean, foreigner?" I asked indignantly. "I'm British to the core."

This assertion was greeted with a lengthy silence while they analyzed it for hidden meanings, errors, omissions, evasions or overall deception; for whatever nationality I claimed, they knew I was not one of them. The business of the white coat had confirmed it. All the other porters wore a rough, navy blue uniform crudely buttoned to the throat; but, after I was taken off the incinerator, which required its own special fatigues, and put on general duties, I had been given an orderly's white jacket and white cotton trousers until they were able to find a serge uniform that would fit my six-foot-one-inch frame. Thus I was not only differently dressed—with a bleeding collar and tie, yet—but I behaved almost as if I felt at home in such la-di-da garb.

They also seemed to think that I was practiced in command. They kept waiting, in a hostile, defensive way, for me to try bossing them around or to demonstrate other forms of presumption, though of course I was in no position to give orders to anybody except the mortuary keeper's dog (a suspiciously well-fed beast). They were also convinced that I had taken the job as a lark and was thus capriciously depriving one of the legion of unemployed of a livelihood.

"It's scabs and dilettantes like you what'll be the first to go when we have a Bolshevik revolution of our own," said the one who dreamed day and night of trotting through the deluxe quarters on the top floors, tossing Mills bombs through every open doorway.

One day the head porter came barreling into the cellar demanding to know why we were all sitting around like bags of bones in a catacomb when there was work to be done.

"You," he bawled, his gaze falling naturally on yours truly. "Yes, you—Clyde S. Dale. I've got just the job for you, my lad."

"Jolly good," I riposted, wondering what ghastly task he had saved for me this time. Yesterday it was several hours of backbreaking work on the infectious diseases floor. Mr. Hodges really enjoyed giving me such jobs, bossing an ex-officer and addressing me in fancy ways to raise a laugh from the others. Clyde S. Dale was just one such designation, presumably inspired by the equine-imity of my face.

"Oh, jolly good, is it?" he sneered. "Oh, I say, isn't he the toff, with his fancy haccent and his laundry whites." Mr. Hodges resented my distinctive garb more than any of them and for days had been chivvying the costume department, or whoever was responsible for porters' uniforms, to get a move on and deliver a uniform, one, porter's for the use of, size extra large, in double quick time. "Well, we'll just see how nice and neat you look after you've finished *this* job, fellow me lad," he said with flushed satisfaction; and informed me that I was to double along to the rear entrance to help unload another couple of "abra cadavers" and dunk them in the formaldehyde tanks, ready for the first-year medical students when they arrived in a couple of months.

I'm afraid I disappointed him again. Having cautious access to Pathology for hurried exchanges with Sigga, I knew where they kept the rubber aprons and other protective gear, so I was able to outfit myself for the job and was as spick and span as ever a couple of hours later when, on my way to the "New Outpatient Department" (1844), I passed a familiar figure in the corridor.

I braked to a halt, slowly identifying the boyish face. It was mustached, well fed and bright with confidence and faith in the future. Below it was a sturdy, lurching body attired in an American-cut pepper-and-salt suit.

"Bandy?"

"Bonehead?"

"Muirhead," he corrected unoffendedly and rushed up with hand extended. "Well, I'll be. Son of a. If it isn't Bart Bandy. Of all the. Gee whillikers," he exclaimed, looking me over admiringly. And indeed, there was much to admire. I looked really nice in my white coat. "Imagine meeting you here after all these years," Muirhead continued, his eyes shining like Whitstable oysters. "After you left med school, we kept hearing things about you. Couldn't believe you'd become, you know, a famous pilot. You never showed any interest in aviation at university, far as anyone could remember. Yet there you were, eh? One moment with stethoscopes stuck in your ears, and the next up there with Colonel Bishop and people like that. And then after the war somebody said they saw you in a filum, but, course, we didn't believe that. Gee whizz, this is," he finished, looking at me with as much respect as if I were Sir Philligree Pilchard himself.

But then Ralph Muirhead was a born hero worshiper, especially of sportsmen. He himself was too heavy and clumsy to shine at sports. Academically, too, he was a plodder. When asked to characterize him, people, after shuffling apathetically through their vocabulary, invariably settled on the word "nice." Worse, Ralph was pleased and flattered by the description. Personally if anybody had called me nice I would have spent sleepless nights inventing ways to injure their reputations. But the word seemed appropriate enough in Ralph's case. He had a nice face, complete with eager blue eyes and a nice smile, nice clothes and nice manners. At school his very inoffensiveness had become offensive.

However, I had since become much more decent, indulgent and benevolent, and could now regard him quite tolerantly.

"What are you doing at St. Pancreas?" I asked, to forestall a similar enquiry from him; and, when he replied that he was in to see a patient: "Good Lord, Muirhead, you don't mean you got through finals? I mean, you were such a dud at school."

"Well, you know, it was 1917, and they needed doctors bad."

"Well, they certainly got a bad doctor in your case."

"Anyway, I'm really pleased to see you made it too, Bart," Ralph said, shining harder than ever. "People said it was an awful waste when you quit only a few months before graduating."

"Who said that?"

"Oh, everyone," Ralph said heartily.

"Who?"

"Well . . . *I* said, for one."

"You? You once put in a good word for Jonathan Wicket," I said, referring to a student at Toronto who had been kicked out of medical school for purloining chops from the dissecting room and slipping them into a dish of gravy at a nearby restaurant. Jonathan had subsequently become resident abortionist in a Chicago bordello.

"Anyway, now we've met again, we must really keep up, eh?" Ralph said, squeezing my arm to see if it was fresh. "It's such a shame, don't you think, the way friends lose touch with each other. Are you on the staff here, Bart?"

"M'oh, yes."

"Say," he cried, his enthusiasm a lamplighter to his eyes, "that's terrific. We must get together some time and compare notes."

"When I say I'm on the staff here," I began, reluctant to confess to occupying the lowest position in the hierarchy, but compelled to do so by my inherent honesty, "I should explain that I'm not *exactly* on the medical side."

"Surgical side, right? Of course—you were specially good at surgery, weren't you! I remember you saying so." He emitted a loud laugh that echoed down the corridor like blasting in a coal mine and caused Sister Drummond to glare at us from the far end. "Remember the operation you did on Derek Crubeen?"

"No, I can't quite. . . ."

"You know, when you were to remove the wart on his . . . ?"

"I don't remember," I said stiffly.

"It's okay," he said, squeezing my arm again. "I know it wasn't your fault when he jumped and you accidentally sliced off his. . . . I mean I was there, it could have happened to anyone," he said placatingly, as he drew a watch from his waistcoat pocket and peered at it shortsightedly.

"But look, old man, I must dash. Appointment with Destinée, you know."

"Appointment with . . . ? Is something tremendous about to happen to you?"

"Tremendous?" Ralph thought for a moment with pursed lips. "No, I wouldn't say meeting Pierre Destinée was all that tremendous—though he's a jolly good chap, of course. He advises me on my investments, you know."

"Ah."

"Well, old man, really must be going," he cried, bringing down another few tons of coal with his laugh; and, after patting me respectfully on the back and presenting his engraved card, he said that he'd come and see me in the surgical staff room next time he was in the hospital. Then he breezed off, looking so busy, well dressed, important and successful that my heart soared on his behalf. And after his poor start in med school, too, where his wits had slowed him almost to a crawl. His progress was really heartening. I felt really happy for him. So much so that even the other porters noticed it, next time we gathered in the 150-watt cellar.

"I met an old school friend," I explained.

"From Canada?"

"Yes. He's gotten on really well since I last saw him. I'm really happy for him."

"Yeh, we could see how happy you was, mate, the way you was kicking bleeding great dents in that fuel tank."

"Just getting rid of an excess of *joie de vivre*, that's all," I mumbled, departing on my next job, which was to deliver a load of rubber sheets to the Bedwetting Department.

On the way I passed Mrs. Villiers-Wakehampton's room. This was the lady who had been admitted on the day of my interview. Though she was sitting up in bed she looked a bit peaked, I thought, as I trundled the last load of rubber sheets to the freight elevator—or goods hoist, as they called it—at the rear of the hospital.

Naturally, Mr. Hodges was waiting for me when I got back to the porters' cave. "Just the man for the job," he said in his stertorous, whiskey-laden voice.

"What job?"

"They want some heavy furniture moving on seven west. Report to S14 on the double, lad."

"I haven't had a break, yet."

"Well, when you have your break, I'll give you a splint," Hodges said; and, after waiting for the guffaws to die down, "But in the meantime, I'd look sharp about it, me lad. He's not the sort of patient you want to keep waiting."

"Who is the bleeder, anyway?" the Bolshie porter asked.

Pleased by the response to his joke, Hodges said, "Some brass hat or other. Admitted yesterday. One of Sir Philligree's patients."

"Oh. In for piles, is he?" said the Bolshie and illustrated the operation that Sir Philligree Pilchard specialized in by grasping an imaginary clump of tissue in midair, hauling it downward then slicing it free with a lateral slashing motion.

Mr. Hodges winced, and bent over slightly. But instead of glaring at the Bolshie, he did so at me. "Well, get moving, Clyde. We're not paying you to graze in the meadow, you know."

Helped on my way by this exhortation and unaware that I was about to be lassoed by another twist of fate, I strolled somewhat faster than usual along the corridor to the goods hoist and pressed the button for the seventh floor, which was where S14 was located.

While I was ascending at the hoist's usual speed of four feet per minute—over the years it had adapted itself to the pace of the British workingman—it occurred to me that encountering Ralph Muirhead need not be an entirely negative experience. Maybe I could use him to elevate Sigridur's opinion of me. Muirhead could certainly confirm that I had attended medical school. Once convinced of that, perhaps she might start to believe in my other accomplishments.

First, though, I would have to clear up the misunderstanding that had developed between Ralph and myself. So I resolved that the very next time I met him, I would try to get the poor sap to understand the situation. "I'm a *porter*, you fool, not a doctor," I would say, seizing him by the shirtfront and giving him a good shake, to increase his ability to absorb information.

Not that I really cared what Sigridur thought of me. I merely wished to set the record straight; so that when posterity finally acknowledged my achievements, there would be no room for doubt that I was a great man. There was always the danger that some future author might dig up some derogatory material about me from sources such as Dr. Jonsdottir. My biographer would surely seize upon any uncertainty that she might create and set his entire argument teetering atop it. Lytton Strachey had already established the fashion of affixing warts to biographical subjects in his *Eminent Victorians*, published half a dozen years previously. I, of course, having made many enemies in all walks of life, had to be specially careful to keep my reputation as pure as dissimulation and evasion would allow, otherwise I'd end up positively covered with such excrescences.

So that was why I was keen on persuading Sigridur, certainly not because I personally cared what she thought of me.

S14 was one of the posh private rooms on the seventh floor of the west wing. Before entering it, however, I checked first at the nurses' station to make sure that the message had been correctly delivered or interpreted. At St. Pancreas, you were quite often given an order only to discover, usually when it was too late, that it was another task entirely that you were supposed to have done. I once spent three hours on my hands and knees polishing a hundred feet of linoleum only to learn that I was supposed to have torn it up and replaced it with a roll of new brown lino. I don't know. It often seemed to me that though humans worshiped efficiency, in fact they had an inherent resistance to attaining it and were happiest when rambling or pottering along life's less efficient byways. It sometimes seemed to me that the only efficient person in the entire northern hemisphere was me.

So: "Did you summon a porter, ma'am?" I asked the nurse on duty. She not only confirmed that I was indeed needed in S14 but told me off for being late. They had called for a porter more than half an hour ago. Apparently the patient wanted the wardrobe moved a few inches, as it was blocking his view through the window.

So I hurried along the corridor to the appropriate ward and

walked in to find an elderly nurse fiddling with the patient's behind.

S14 was one of the renovated rooms overlooking the gardens at the back of the hospital. It was flawlessly painted in white and apple green, with gold curtains at the windows, and was furnished with lamps and heavy mahogany furniture. The only regulation item in the room was the hospital bed. Despite the protests of the more prophylactic-minded among the staff, the decorators had even laid down a carpet, a brand-new floral affair with a pile just perfect for harboring bacteria, crumbs, dust, mites, chicken bones, etc.

The patient was a lengthy man in striped pajamas, with broad shoulders and buttocks like giant toadstools. I knew how the buttocks looked because they were fully exposed. He was lying on his side facing the far wall.

Thus I could see only part of his face, but what I could see of it was quite red. Whether this was a permanent hue or a temporary discoloration resulting from embarrassment could not immediately be confirmed; probably the latter, as he was being given an enema.

The senior staff nurse was holding up the bell-shaped glass jar with its trailing rubber tube, the other end of which was now firmly plugged into the patient. With her spare hand she was trying to reach the trolley, on which stood a tray of stainless steel, rubber and glass effects; but the trolley kept rolling out of reach, much to her annoyance.

As I stood there, morosely examining the tall mahogany wardrobe that stood between the bed and the window, Senior Staff snapped her fingers at me imperiously.

"Well, don't just stand there," she said sharply, pointing an irritable finger at the trolley: "Pass me the Riemann."

The name being familiar from my student days, I hurried to the trolley, picked up a large glass container half-filled with a heavy, slightly yellowish fluid and held it out to her.

"Well, at least *somebody* knows what I'm talking about," said the thin-lipped angel of mercy. Then: "You've given an enema before, I suppose?"

"Yes, ma'am."

"How often?"

"A few times, ma'am," I said, respectfully, assuming that she was enquiring merely out of interest. And again I proffered the enema fluid.

"Thank goodness for that," she said; then pointed at the lower shelf of the trolley, on which stood a stoppered glass jar containing what appeared to be an entire gallon of enema fluid that stood next to a bedpan. "Well, I'll let you get on with it then," she said. "And afterwards use that—understand?"

Thinking she was addressing him, the patient half turned and said in a curt voice, "What?"

"Nothing, sir," the senior nurse said, her voice turning smooth as vaseline. "I was just talking to the orderly. But you must keep still, sir."

"No," I said quickly, waving the yellowish fluid in the air. "I just came," I said, pointing at the wardrobe. But the senior nurse was still addressing the patient. "You won't mind if he takes over, will you, sir?" she asked, with well-lubricated respect. "We're awfully short-staffed at the moment, and I was expected in James Boswell Ward ten minutes ago."

"Yes, yes," said the patient harshly. "Just get on with it. I wouldn't want even Pilchard to see me in this position."

At which I started, nearly dropping the Riemann. The voice had sounded exceedingly familiar.

I was sufficiently distracted by the authoritative growl that several seconds elapsed before I could pull myself together to explain to the senior staff nurse in a hurried undertone that she had mistaken me for somebody competent. But the hesitation appeared to have lost me the continuity of her attention, for she brushed aside my whispered mumblings and merely ordered me to get on with it for heaven's sake. She thrust the bell jar into my remaining hand, and before you could say *cerumen impaction*—as we medical men describe earwax—she had swept from the room.

I didn't even have time to mime my true function by pointing impotently at the wardrobe. And thus it was that I found myself at one end of a tube with an irascible patient at the other.

Normally, as soon as I recovered from the surprise that the

senior nurse could have fallen for that old saw that clothes make the man, I would probably have felt quite proud at being handed such a responsibility. Nor would such pride have been misplaced. Administering an enema was a procedure well within my capabilities. All you had to do, if I remembered rightly, was to keep pouring until the level in the bell jar refused to lower itself any farther, however high the jar was elevated, indicating that the atmospheric pressure was equal to that built up inside the patient.

But I had two surprises to recover from, not one. And the second was not so easily rallied from. I had now had time to sort through the mental filing system under the heading of "Persons Authoritative," and had come up with the most authoritative of the lot: my old Chief at the Air Ministry.

Now that I looked more carefully, I could add a partial visual identification to the aural one. Yes, it was him all right, though I could see only one feature of his face, the end of a beetling eyebrow. It was the Chief of Air Staff, no doubt about it. I'd have known that eyebrow anywhere.

The fact that he had been my superior officer way back in 1918 was not in itself particularly disturbing, though I was still a trifle reluctant to meet anybody who had known me when I was the toast, rather than the dog biscuit, of London. "I say, do you know who I met the other day? Bandy the scout pilot. By Jove, he's sunk low, poor chap," they would say, with a satisfaction directly proportional to the incline of their own social or economic progress. No, the problem was that the big man lying there shamelessly exposing his bum was the formidable air force chief who, with many a bellow over my disloyalty in spilling certain beans to the press back in 1918,* had stripped me of my Air Ministry title and rank and flung me back into the infantry just in time to meet the great German attack of March 21.

Somehow I had the feeling that he had never particularly cared for me even when I was at my most glorious. In fact, it was said that he had subsided into the most awful depression when he

*As detailed in Volume II of the Bandy Papers: *That's Me in the Middle* (Doubleday: 1973).

heard that I had managed to wangle my way back into the air force a few weeks later in 1918. So I was now feeling a trifle apprehensive that he might recognize my voice as readily as I had his.

Fortunately his posture and the critical position of the projecting vulcanized plug ensured that he could not turn and pick me out from his own personal identity parade. Otherwise he would have recognized my face straightaway. He was bound to remember it. Every time he'd met it in the Air Ministry it had stopped him dead. His staff had gotten thoroughly tired of colliding with his broad back every time he encountered my face in the corridor; which was pretty often, as my office was on the same floor as his.

Though visually I was safe enough for the moment, aurally I was in great danger, for it had been said often enough that my whining drawl was almost as distinctive as my face. Luckily I had not really spoken up yet. I think I'd been mumbling a bit when replying to the senior staff nurse. Even so, there already seemed to be a certain tension to his recumbent posture, as if something was disturbing him, but he couldn't quite understand what.

As I hesitated, holding aloft the bell jar as if attempting to emulate the pose of the Statue of Liberty, I reviewed three possible courses of action. The first was to leave forthwith, as the general—or air marshal, as I suppose he was, now that the air force had dropped army ranks—had not yet identified me and was in no position to turn round in bed and do so. But if I sneaked out of the ward it could worsen the situation. It might cause a fuss, or inspire an investigation. Moreover, it would not be easy to discontinue the procedure. The shape of the bell jar made it impossible to set it down without cascading the contents over whatever surface it was placed upon, and I could hardly tap the patient on the shoulder and ask *him* to hold it. Even if he agreed—highly unlikely, given the sort of person he was—the hospital would not take kindly to the idea of a patient conducting his own treatment. It might give others the idea that the medical staff weren't all that necessary. Surgical patients would be expecting to operate on themselves next. So abandoning the CAS to his gurgling fate was out. The second course was to remain speechless, or at most to respond with primeval grunts. But such apparent surliness would attract his attention all the more keenly. I remembered that if there was one thing he hated, it was anything resembling dumb insolence. Which left the third and last course of action: to respond, if he deigned to address me, in either a disguised voice or a foreign accent.

He did deign. "Well, get on with it," he snarled suddenly, sensing, presumably, that nothing had been happening for a while. "I'm not exactly enjoying this, you know."

I realized that the jar was now empty. I hurriedly transferred all the remaining fluid from the Riemann glass. However, I did not fail to sniff the liquid first. This was to make absolutely sure that it was the right stuff. There had been one or two unfortunate incidents in my life resulting from a failure on my part to check such things properly. I had resolved that such embarrassments must never be allowed to occur again. So I tested the fluid with my nose, but it was all right. I recognized the odor right away.

The bell jar gurgled faintly, and the level began to sink once again, as the fluid made its way along the rubber tube. The patient's cheeks twitched as he felt the effect.

After a while: "Is that it, then?" he asked harshly.

To my surprise, I saw that the bell jar was already empty. "Oh, no, sir," I said. Then, remembering, I continued in fluent Irish, "No sore. The norse was afther saying you had to be having all that as well," I said, pointing at the large container of enema fluid on the lower shelf of the trolley, before realizing that, in the circumstances, pointing was somewhat redundant.

"Well, hurry up, then," he shouted. "Do you expect me to lie here all day like this?"

Hurriedly I reached for the gallon container, removed its glass stopper, not without difficulty for I had only one free hand, and poured a quart or so into the graduated bell jar.

As the typically yellowish fluid flowed, the patient started violently. "Christ, that's cold," he gasped. "Where the hell have you been keeping it, the mortuary?"

For some reason, the level was going down even faster than before, as if it were of a lesser density. I poured another quart or so into the jar and, to distract the patient from his discomfort, said conversationally, "You're afther expecting Sir Philligree Pilchard, are you, sore?"

"What?"

"Pilchard, sore? You were afther saying to the norse you would not be wanting Pilchard to be seeing you in this position."

"What? Yes, he's coming along later," he said, sounding as if he were under some sort of strain.

"A foin surgeon, I understand, famous for his hemorrhoids, sore."

"He's got them too, has he?"

"Operations, sore. Hemorrhoid operations. He specializes in them."

"I'm well aware of that."

"Bejabbers, and I guess that's why you're having this lavage of the colon."

"A very thorough one, too, it seems to me."

"So you're facing one of those operations, are yis?" I continued, relaxing a bit. "If the word 'facing' is the right word for it—under the circumstances."

My old Chief failed to answer, possibly because his lips were so compressed.

"Personally, it's not an operation I'd want to go through meself."

With some difficulty he asked why not.

"Well, I watched such an operation once. Personally, I'd rather a lithotomy—rather have the stones crushed in me bladder without benefit of anesthesia—than have one of them hemorrhoid operations."

"But why?"

"Well, it's the way they do it, you see," I said, clicking my tongue in distress and sucking in my breath. I also shook my head, but of course he couldn't see that.

"Why—how is it done?" he asked hoarsely.

"My God."

"What?"

"Nothing, sore. I was just remembering."

"Remembering what, what?"

"Well, it was the way the surgeon did it."

"How, how?"

"He inserted four fingers and wrenched open the pore bastard's sphincter. Sort of hauled it open sideways, as if. . . . Well, you know when you arrive at an elevator—lift, I mean—just as the door is closing and you try to hold the door open so you can slip through? Well, that was just what it looked like, with the surgeon wrenching at the fellow's sphincter. The surgeon, you see, was trying to overcome the reflex action of the sphincter, to combat its natural insistence on remaining closed. He was trying to sneak up on it, take it by surprise, as it were. But, Jesus, it was awful to watch. Which perhaps explains why so few doctors ever have the operation themselves. Are you all right, sore?"

"Get my clothes."

"Pardon, sore?"

"And remove this."

"It's all right, sore, there's only a point or two left in the whole jug."

"Remove it this instant."

"But sore, the senior staff nurse definitely ordered me to use it all," I protested. " 'Use that afterwards,' she said, pointing at the. . . ." I said, before dribbling to a halt, realizing that, in pointing at the lower shelf of the trolley where the gallon flagon had stood, my finger was pointing straight at the bedpan that had stood beside it.

At which point a certain uneasiness began to steal over me like hemlock. Use that afterwards, she had said. Could it be that she had been pointing, not at the extra supply of enema fluid in the gallon jug, but at the bedpan?

But even that wasn't all. As if that first doubt had created a breakthrough to allow others to follow and fan out to the rear, another doubt attacked, as I looked again at the gallon jug, and then up at the graduated bell jar, whose fluid was now flowing down the tube at a very sluggish rate indeed, if it was moving at all. As I looked up at it, it seemed to me that though approximately the right color, the liquid looked slightly clearer than that with which I had started.

I lowered the jar and sniffed cautiously at the contents. And I started slightly.

"Yes," I said breathlessly. "Well, I think that should do the job." I hurriedly pinched the rubber tube between thumb and forefinger and then proceeded, with a somewhat shaky hand, to empty what little was left back into the gallon jug. That done, I leaned over, intending to remove the nozzle from the patient as carefully and tactfully as possible; until he said suddenly, "That voice."

Still bent over, I froze, staring at the Chief's behind as if that was where the words had come from.

"That voice," he said again, speaking with dangerous emphasis, considering that until now he had been making a considerable effort not to emit too many philological plosives. "Where have I heard it before? Where, where?"

"Nowhere," I said quickly, to allay his fears; for on top of all the other indications of distress that he had been exhibiting over the past half hour, he was now sounding almost frightened, as if suspecting that the voice from his past might belong to someone inimical.

"I have, I've heard it before, somewhere. What's your name, orderly?"

"My name?" I asked incredulously, as if astounded that he would consider that the likes of me should have a name.

"Yes, your name, what is it?"

"Just a moment, sir, I'm trying to unplug y—to disconnect the apparatus, sir. No, no, sir, don't turn around!"

"In case I recognize you, is that it?"

"No, sir—the nozzle—your might drive it up your—"

"I insist on knowing your name, orderly. At once!"

"Actually I'm not an orderly at all, sir," I said hesitantly. "I'm a porter. I only came in here to move your wardrobe."

"But what I don't understand," Sigga said that evening as she walked me home in the pouring rain, "is how you are still working at the hospital after such a catastrophe."

"I don't know."

"You said yourself that this man is the kind who would not hesitate to have you dismissed without a reference."

"Maybe I've got him wrong."

"But you must have upset him very much, the way he dashed out of the hospital without even waiting to see Sir Pilchard."

"He was in no condition to dash. In fact he departed very gingerly."

"You know what I mean," Sigga said, stifling her laughter. "I just don't understand why he did not complain about your disgraceful behavior. After all, one word from him and you would have been back in the gutter where you belonged."

"I suspect the reason is that if he'd done anything to get me sacked, the story might have got around. You know, about a porter coming in to shift the wardrobe and ending up prepping the patient instead."

"Yes, perhaps that is it. As the head of your air force, he would not be too anxious for people to know about it."

"Mind you, he might not have been so restrained if he'd known the rest of it."

"What rest? Why, what else happened?"

"Well, you see, I gave him the wrong mixture. It wasn't until I sniffed it that I remembered about the medical research unit and that they distributed their profitable sideline in gallon jugs to the various departments.

"No," I added, "I think it might have been too much for the Chief if he had learned that I'd been giving him an enema of white wine."

Looking a Bit Feverish

Despite such a contretemps, and the insults and humiliations that a new porter was heir to, my morale rose like a butterfly over a bunker as the interview with Imperial Airways approached. I was confident of getting the job, for the qualifications seemed to have been drawn up with me in mind. So I whistled contentedly as I lumbered from one heavy job to another, hummed as I trundled Mrs. Villiers-Wakehampton into the operating theater—she had suffered a seizure after a catheter had explored in the wrong direction—and sang out loud the day the letter arrived from Imperial Airways requesting a medical report and asking me to present it and myself at Croydon Aerodrome one week hence at 11:00 A.M. for a flight demonstration, weather permitting, and at 2:30 for an interview before a selection board.

The warbling, though, lasted for only a few seconds, until I reread the second paragraph. I had to take a medical exam. Worry warts instantly sprang up all over. Aviation medicals were expensive, as much as two guineas. Where was I to find the money for that? I would have enough trouble paying for transport to Croydon Aerodrome without forking out for a medical as well.

There was no way I could scrape together a sum like that in the time available. I would have to borrow the money from Sigga, much as I hated being in debt to her financially as well as gastronomically. (For instance, by now she had paid for dinner on at least a dozen occasions.)

Usually she finished an hour or two before I did, but that night she was working late, microtoming and staining tissue sections. This histological work was the first responsible job the chief pathologist had given her since her arrival. It had not increased her liking for her superior, with whom she was not getting on at all well. Her boss was highly suspicious of an assistant who looked like a Mack Sennett bathing beauty and who could not move a step outside the department without being surrounded by slavering medicos. Worse, his suspicion was conjoined with resentment when he discovered that merely by graduating she was entitled to add the letters "MD" after her name, American style. This infuriated the chief pathologist. In Britain, an MD degree was awarded for an original research thesis. It was a much higher honor than a graduating accolade, and the chief, an MB, ChB, feared that people would think that his assistant was more highly qualified than he, as well as being better looking. So he refused to allow her a share in the post-mortem work except for the weighing of the various organs, and even then he often checked her work by reweighing her lights and livers.

Consequently, Sigga was often in a bad temper by early evening, and tonight she was more upset than usual. She had had an unfortunate experience the previous evening. She had had a date with one of the doctors. He had taken her to the opera. "That was bad enough," she'd told me, "but he didn't even make up for it by trying to seduce me afterwards. Not that I would have allowed it," she added primly, "but at least he might have tried. He had no excuse, either—he had a very nice flat with a view of Regent's Park. What's the matter with these English, anyway? Are they cultivated, or something?"

Anyway, after making sure that there were no witnesses to our meeting—it would never do for a porter to be seen hobnobbing with a doctor, even a foreign one—I popped into the lab to explain about the medical and ask her for a loan.

After she had scrubbed her hands at the sink, she said briskly, "Come with me," and, snatching up her wee black bag, led the way through the tunnel to the outpatients' wing, thence up a flight of stairs and into one of the consulting rooms off the main hall. The department was, of course, closed at that time of night.

"No point in paying a milkman if there's a cow in the back-yard," she said. "I'll give you the medical."

"But of course," I said enthusiastically. "What an excellent idea. You can give me a note just as easily as any other quack."

"Is there a special form to fill out?"

"No, they just require a letter from a qualified physician affirming that I have good health, two eyes and a reflex or two."

"I'll write it on hospital stationery, then," she said, shuffling through the forms in the wall rack in that antiseptic room with its frigid green tiles. "Strip, please."

"Uh?"

"Get undressed."

"Pardon?"

"Take your clothes off," she said, drawing a stethoscope from her bag.

"Oh, that won't be necessary," I said with a smile. "Just write the note, that's all I need."

"I am not attesting to your good health without confirming it for myself," she said. "For all I know, you might have tertiary syphilis."

"I beg your pardon?"

"The spirochetes might be munching away at your brain cells right this minute," she said; then suddenly looked thoughtful. "In fact that might explain one or two things. . . ."

"Forget the whole thing," I said shortly, at length. "Just lend me the money."

"I don't have it."

"Garn."

"I don't. I only earn five pounds a week—and you're getting about half of that already."

"That's right, rub in all the free dinners," I shouted. "I said I'd pay you back, soon as I could."

"You've said a lot of things."

"Oh, go on, Sigga, you can spare a couple of quid."

"I tell you, I can't. I only have a pair of nickers to last me until payday."

"What?"

"Two nickers. Don't you know anything? That is English slang, meaning two pounds. So, off with your clothes."

"Ah," I said, rooted to the spot.

"Come on," she said impatiently. "I want to get home."

"Look," I said with a charming smile, "there's no need, Sigga. I'm in perfect health, take my word for it."

"I should take your word for anything?"

Charm having failed, I resorted to authority. "I see absolutely no need for this, Sigridur," I said coldly.

"You *do* have a disease," she said suddenly.

"I do not."

"Then what are you covering? You're afraid."

"I yam not."

"You are. You're scared."

"A Bandy isn't scared of anything."

"So? Strip."

I was forced to do so in the end. With shaking fingers I removed my shirt. I winced as she applied the frigid stethoscope.

"Mm," she said dubiously, not once but several times. Then: "Drop your pants."

"What? Are you mad?"

"For heaven's sake, I'm a doctor."

"You're a woman."

"A woman doctor."

"A woman friend. Damn it, don't you see how impossible it is?"

"It is not the least impossible. Oh, do get on with it, Bandy," she said, raising her voice, her patience quite plainly at an end.

After a rustling moment: "Underpants too, underpants too," she said, spitting with exasperation. I could tell, the way the saliva was raining on my chest. "Good heavens, Bandy, if your reactions are as sluggish as this, maybe you should think twice about going back to flying."

So I did as I was told, and with cotton-swathed ankles gazed toward the gray window and tried to think beautiful thoughts.

"Your muscle tone isn't what it should be," she said, whacking my abdomen with the flat of her hand.

I thought about very tasty dishes. A delicious meal of roe and shrimp cocktail, blood pudding and jelly, and a nice cup of tea—

"Turn your head and cough. Again."

No, I made it a procession. Stepping out to a brass-necked band. Wistful widows sipping Benedictine, and monks a-loitering in cloisters, papier-mâché lads in fetid closes, housewives mustering feather dusters with apron pockets crammed with carnal reveries, of men in berets kissing jellied eels and voting democratically for dictatorship. Mayfair girls in sheeny dresses, gossiping from frowsiness to jazzy evensong, and on the sidewalks going nowhere the dandies with the bedsprings in their steps, or jumpy tourists undoing the passing flappers with the zippers of their eyes. And so to bedlam. Outside, the light catching the leaves, they are setting for clusters of diamonds of raindrops and everyone that passes, brows pale, serenity on the stave of their lined brows—

"Ever had crabs?" Sigridur enquired.

Though Imperial Airways had quarters of their own at Croydon, the interviews for new pilots were being held on an upper floor of the main terminal. This was the building where the passengers huddled, customs men glowered and the control tower flashed its red and green lights.

When I walked in for the interview that momentous Thursday afternoon, my heart was thumping like a jack rabbit. This was it, I was thinking; maybe the final fulcrum in the mechanics of my life. Somehow, despite my face and superior abilities, I had to make a good impression on the examiners ranged in front of me. I was perfectly suited to the job. I wanted it. I needed it. I had to have it.

The chairman was a neat little man in a suit that was almost as smart as mine. "Ah, Mr. Bandy, is it?" he asked pleasantly; and upon receiving a shaky affirmative, "We're sorry to have kept you waiting, Mr. Bandy. Two of our members have been detained, you see. We were hoping they would turn up in time, but . . . however." And gesturing with an upturned pudgy hand at the chair that was standing to attention in front of him: "Please . . . ?"

The four members of the selection board were seated at a trio of tables that had been ranged in front of a long metal window. The window, which overlooked the aircraft-boarding tarmac, was divided into panes. During the course of the interview I counted them. Several times. There were eighteen panes, including the cracked one in the lower left-hand corner.

One of the examiners was the chief pilot. That was a great relief. He had been impressed by my flying that morning. Better still, he was familiar with my career in the RAF. Best of all, he approved of it. I hoped that he had already put in a good word for me.

The others were certainly looking me over with what appeared to be more than routine interest. Besides the chairman they included a lordship, who had a woolly expression and a voice to match, and an admiral, who had a rude stare. For some reason there was also an experimental biologist from London University. Perhaps they had asked for a psychologist and an experimental biologist was all they were offered.

After I sat down there was a somewhat suspenseful silence. I tried to settle myself more comfortably in the wood and leather chair while the members of the selection board moved papers around with their finger tips. A bluebottle butted its head against one of the eighteen panes, stubbornly buzzing.

"Bandy. Yes," the lord said with a start, as if he had just come to. "Talkin' about you in the club last night."

"Were you, sir?"

"With Rackingham. Mentioned I was seeing you this aft. Sends his regards."

"That's very good of him, sir," I said, taking a deep breath of cigar smoke and furniture polish.

"You worked for him at one time, I believe," the lord said, shuffling vaguely through my dossier.

"Yes, I was his personal aide when he was Air Minister," I whined proudly.

The chairman looked so impressed that I didn't think it would be fair on him to mention that Lord Rackingham and I had both been sacked from our jobs.

"Yes, well," the little chairman said with a little nod. "Perhaps we can start things off, Mr. Bandy, by telling you a little about us, and then you can tell us something about yourself, eh?"

"Fine, sir," I said; whereupon he went on to explain what I already knew, that Imperial Airways had been formed just this year from a merger of four British airlines that had been operating routes to the continent.

"Is that clear so far, Bandy?" the chairman asked, as if he had been trying to explain the Fourier transforms to somebody who was a bit shaky on the times tables.

"Yes, thank you, sir," I said. He had addressed me as Bandy. That was a good sign, omitting the Mr. In Britain when they addressed you by your surname alone, it signified a degree of acceptance.

It was now my turn to say something about myself. What I should like to have told them was that I was a changed man, a reformed character; that they could rely on me to be as cautious as a snail, as regular as a laxative, as reliable as a windsock; that I had come to the end of a turbulent era, that the pattern of my life had finally changed to the most circumspect design. No more soaring to temporary success only to plummet the moment somebody found me out. No more mad alternations between prosperity and penury, no amplitude of fluke or flop. From now on my progress was to be stately. Not one step was I to take from now on until I had made absolutely certain that rose petals rather than banana skins littered the path. I was to be unfailingly respectful to my superiors whether they deserved it or not. Never again would I kick against the pricks—there were too many of them. Never again would I indulge in the pleasures of camouflaged malevolence, of devious retaliation against those who had done me down. In place of bludgeoning people with personality, I would caress them with sentiment. From now on I would be utterly ordinary, not least in the cause of anesthetizing myself against the twinges, stabs and shocks of life.

However, there wasn't much point in telling them that I had reformed when they were unfamiliar with my unreformed state; so I just stuck to the facts about my life—but not too many of them, in case they checked. I managed, for instance, to present my employment at St. Pancreas Hospital as being merely an interesting and challenging stopgap between flying jobs; and when they asked what I was doing there, I managed to suggest, without actually lying about it, that it was an interesting and challenging continuation of my medical education, which had begun at the University of Toronto.

"Toronto? That's where they've just found a cure for diabetes, isn't it?" asked the scientific one. "Insulin, or something."

"Yes, that's right," I said. Actually that was news to me.

Then followed a few other questions, including the highly significant one of how soon I could obtain the appropriate British flying licenses. "I understand I'll be getting the commercial ticket today or tomorrow," I replied, relaxing for the first time and smiling around so charmingly that they all looked quite concerned for a moment.

But, gad, I felt good. The entire day was beginning to turn out splendidly. Even the weather was fine. Nineteen twenty-four was already establishing records for excessive precipitation, but on that Thursday not one spot of rain had moistened the landscape. In fact by the time I had arrived here at the airport, several square inches of blue sky were showing between the clouds. And when I sat down to lunch—paid for by the company, yet—the sun was positively sizzling in the airfield puddles.

Best of all, I'd had no trouble wheeling the big, fat Vimy Commercial through the airport circuit and landing it without breaking anything. And almost as good for my morale was the assurance from the general manager of the new company that I fitted their requirements perfectly as to age, background and experience.

"I'd say that you'll get it if you really want it," the general manager had confided. "There's only one other man in the running, and he's too young. The paying customers don't like being piloted by dashing young fellows," he said, looking wonderingly over my aged face, which would soon be thirty-two years old.

It looked now as if he were right, that the job was in the bag. For the selection board was now talking money. "We can only offer you eight pounds a week to start," the chairman was saying apologetically, shielding the side of his face from the sunlight that was streaming through the long, multipaned window behind him. "Just for the probationary period, of course."

"I guess I could manage that," I said, trying to look as if a raise of 400 percent would be a bit of a sacrifice, but that I was prepared to grin and bear it.

There was a pause. Suddenly conscious that he had not yet contributed to the interview, the admiral said sharply, "Know anything about sailing?"

"Not a thing, sir."

"You've never even pottered about in boats?" he shouted ferociously.

"No, sir."

The admiral nodded, satisfied. He hated people who pottered about in boats and had often tried to run them down with his battleship.

The chief pilot then asked a question, but his voice was absorbed into a growing uproar of aero engines. The members twisted around in their seats to peer out the long window. A huge Handley Page with Imperial Airways markings was just coming into view. Ponderous as a hippo, it was swinging its flat snout slowly parallel to this, the main airport building, bellowing with the effort.

As it was impossible to hear anything over the racket, I took the opportunity to do a spot of daydreaming. I was already seeing myself with gold rings up to my armpits, flying amazing numbers of passengers, as many as nine at a time, to historic Brussels, stately Amsterdam, artistic Paris, romantic Manchester. Utterly circumspect flying would of course be required, but that was all right, I was quite prepared to subordinate my skills to a scrupulous regard for the safety of the public.

Of course, I would have to start out as a co-pilot in their single Vimy Commercial, the *City of London*, but that was all right, it wouldn't be long before I was placed in command. After that, I thought I'd have the chief pilot's job. Ultimately I would aim for the chairmanship—or, no, maybe I'd settle for a vice-presidency, operations, which would enable me to go on flying, and which would also enable the airline to take full advantage of my superb organizational abilities. As for my immediate plans, I would move out of the boarding house this very evening and into a small flat in W2, and then I would start to save up for a house and a wife or two. . . .

The eardrum-banging uproar from the Handley Page just outside the window reached a fortissimo as the aircraft halted, so I didn't hear the newcomer enter the interview room and, as I had my back to the door, I failed to see him either, until the chairman hurriedly rose and proffered a hand and a wheedling smile. So naturally I turned, and saw a tall man with broad, square shoulders, dressed in a black business suit and carrying a bowler, umbrella and briefcase, a fine figure of a man with black, bellicose eyebrows and a face the color and very nearly the composition of granite.

Outside, the engines of the Handley Page were shut down, and the noise drained away almost as rapidly as the blood from my face. I had recognized the Chief of Air Staff. I also recognized, a few seconds later, as the chairman chattered at and fawned on the great man, that he was one of the missing board members.

"Sorry I'm late," he said, his rough, peremptory voice sounding, for once, almost smooth, as he looked at me with eyes like armor-piercing shells. "But I take it I'm not too late to prevent the board from making a grave mistake?"

By skulking like a Balkan assassin, I managed to evade Sigridur that evening, and indeed for most of the following day. I even managed to keep out of her way when Hodges sent me into her territory. I was given the job of wheeling Mrs. Villiers-Wakehampton's body down to Pathology.

Sigga was busy in another room, typing up the chief pathologist's reports. As this was the job she hated most of all, and one that always made her extremely bad tempered, I was particularly glad I didn't have to confess there and then that, after assuring her dozens of times that I was perfectly suited to the Imperial Airways job, I had failed to get it.

Unfortunately she caught up with me in the main corridor of the building when I was only a few yards from the exit to ask how I had gotten on yesterday; and worse still, just as Ralph Muirhead appeared and greeted me like a long-lost friend. Consequently I was forced to introduce him to Dr. Jonsdottir.

"So you're the beautiful cutter everybody's talking about," Ralph said, wearing a particularly fatuous smile.

Sigga smiled back kindly and looked at the sky to see if it was likely to rain.

"And she's as beautiful as they all say, eh, doctor?" he said, nudging me playfully in the ribs.

"Doctor?" Sigga asked alertly.

"Say, listen," I exclaimed. "You'll never guess who I met the other day, Ralph. My old Chief at the Air Ministry. He—"

"Doctor?" Sigga repeated. "Why do you call him doctor? Is it a joke between you, perhaps?"

"Joke?" Ralph replied. "No. I meant, you know, Dr. Bandy."

"Anyway, guess what else?" I continued. "I met him again yesterday," I cried, "and guess what? He turned out to be a member of the interview board. What d'you think of—"

"He isn't a doctor," Sigga interrupted.

"Sure he is."

"Is that what he told you?"

"Well, yes."

"So I'm sure you can guess what happened at the interview, Sigga," I said heartily. "I mean, him being on the Imperial—"

"He isn't a doctor," Sigga said. "He's a porter."

"A porter?"

"In the hospital here. He's a porter in this hospital."

"So anyway, that's what happened," I concluded and gazed down at my nicely polished boots. Except that one of them wasn't as nicely polished as the other. So I stood on one foot and polished it on the back of my trouser leg.

"But he said," Ralph began, turning to me uncomprehendingly; then stopped and started again. "You are, aren't you, Bart? A surgeon?"

"Um. . . ."

There was a really nasty silence.

It was even worse than the nasty silence at Croydon Aerodrome when the CAS, rising up and down on his toes and taking deep, satisfied breaths of stale office air, told the interview board that I was definitely not the kind of man they would want at Imperial Airways. I was the least appropriate person it was possible to appoint to such a responsible post. It was his duty to report his own experience of Bandy, which had taught him that if Bandy went north, he personally would about-turn and head straight south; if this candidate ever assured him that such and such was the truth, he personally would be strongly inclined to assume that it was a pack of lies; if this man ever agreed with him, he, the CAS, would instantly be forced to reexamine his own arguments and opinions to find the flaws in them. They would just have to take his word for it, but putting passengers in the care of this man would be as foolhardy as entrusting a surgical operation to a. . . .

The Chief didn't actually finish that particular sentence, but the interview board had already got the general drift of the Chief's remarks, so it didn't particularly matter anyway.

Mr. Lewis

It was nine at night, raining as usual; I was trudging home from work and had almost reached the front door of the boarding house when I recognized the slender form of my father-in-law. He was questioning Mrs. Wignall, his bowler held respectfully in his kid-gloved hand, exposing his baldness to the chill July air.

As I had been required to provide references when applying for the Imperial Airways job and had given them Mr. Lewis's name and his address as "formerly of the Foreign Office," I should not have been so surprised to find that he had managed to track me down. Nevertheless I was shaken enough to emit a shocked grunt. Instinctively I sidled behind a red pillar-box, bent over to tie another knot in my bootlace and proceeded to spy on him from dog-dirt level.

As soon as Mrs. Wignall invited him to step inside, I turned and scuttled away, cursing something chronic. I had a filthy cold, derived, I suspect, from disappointment. For twelve hours I had been looking forward to peppering myself with aspirins and denting the old mattress. I was shivering and aching all over. Even my hair ached. But I couldn't risk handing the microbes on to Mr. Lewis, so I walked along to the only place nearby that was open at that time of night, Paddington Station, and sat huddled on a bench for an hour or so. The Stoll Cinema nearby was showing a good movie, but the seats had recently gone up to fivepence, so I contented myself with watching the pigeons as they positioned themselves on the girders, ready to spatter the travelers below with happy coos and guano.

Next day, Mr. Lewis attempted to trap me in the hospital, but fortunately he received detailed directions from the head porter, which guaranteed that he would never find me. After that, I expected him to give up and go home. But no, he reported again at the boarding house that same evening. So again I was forced to retreat, and it was ten pip emma before I finally sneezed my way into my boudoir, to find that he had left a note on the dresser, informing me that he had called round and would I get in touch with him at the Conservative Club before noon next day, Saturday.

What a shame. I'd just missed him. When I checked at his lugubrious club two or three days later I discovered that he had left town, presumably for his country place, wherever that was. Oh, well. Perhaps I would be able to catch up with him next December when he returned to do his Christmas shopping.

I was wrong. He braved the metropolis on the following Friday, leaving messages for me as profligately as if engaged in a paper chase. He returned to the attack on the Saturday, and it was only by loitering with intent in the British Museum reading room all that day and by spending three and six for a seaside excursion on the Sunday that I managed to avoid him and thus preserve him from my shocking cold. Really, he ought to have been exceedingly grateful to me for this considerate behavior, especially as, after a nice day at the seaside, basking on the Brighton promenade under a July sky the color of a workhouse bedsheet, my nose was streaming like the sea lashing through the seafront conduits. It would probably have killed the little man if he'd caught my cold.

There was one advantage to these evasive tactics, in that they also served to keep Sigga at bay. This was neatly balanced by the disadvantage that my efforts to avoid them both brought them together. On the Sunday evening as I made my way home in the seaside excursion train, surrounded by vicious holidaymakers—one mother, driven to distraction by her three whining children and a screaming baby, dumped the malodorous infant in my lap without so much as a pleading look and refused to take it back until she had first slapped and cuffed the balance of her brood, then marched to the far end of the corridor to polish off a bottle of Dutton's Green Label Pale Ale, so that I was soon stinking of feces and boiled milk—I faced up to it that I couldn't continue to avoid my dear father-in-law without appearing to insult him. There was also, I thought, as I opened the train window and held the howling baby in the fierce but hygienic blasts, my dignity to consider. These shame-faced evasions of mine were unworthy of one who had risen nearly to the top in three separate professions. Mind you, there was much satisfaction in this self-pity of mine. Poor Bandy, alone, friendless, penniless and hopeless. Gad, it felt good, that churned-up feeling derived from hurting one's friends, the exquisite satisfaction to be gained from despising oneself, the delight of unearned tears pricking at the corner of the eyes. But I had to admit that it wasn't exactly a praiseworthy condition. So I decided to sacrifice myself utterly and abandon this slinking activity. I would relieve their anxiety, allay their concern and hearten them with my presence. So when I caught sight of Sigga and Mr. Lewis worrying themselves sick outside the boarding house that Sunday evening, I marched forward resolutely; and was just in time to see them walking toward a taxi, laughing away and talking animatedly as if they had everything in common—except me.

I hollered and waved and ran after them and just failed to catch up before they boarded the taxi and hurtled off round the corner. And though I waited up for them, sneezing and spraying snot until nearly midnight, they failed to return. I was absolutely furious at their insensitivity.

The reunion, however, was accomplished the next day. I had just emerged from the mortuary entrance at five past eight in the evening, wearing my new blue uniform, the collar of which, buttoned to the throat, had already chafed several layers of skin off my Adam's apple, and I was looking up at the sky, wondering why it wasn't raining, when a large, rough hand shot out of nowhere and clamped itself to my arm. "Come with me," Sigga said, leading me in the general direction of the Grand Union

Canal, as if intent on hurling me into it. But it was only to meet Mr. Lewis at a nearby restaurant.

"Bartholomew, my boy," he murmured huskily, rising from the table and pressing my hand emotionally.

"Father!"

He twitched and seemed to shrink inside his careworn suit. "Oh, God, yes, I remember now," he said. "You always did make your greetings sound like lines from a Whitehall farce."

Then he stepped back to study my uniform—or perhaps recoiled was a better word. "Good God," he murmured, blanching like an almond. "And to think I nearly invited you to my club." Then, after another affectionate squeeze: "Fortunately Sigridur advised me to meet you in the darkest restaurant I could find."

It was, in fact, pretty dark. The paneled dining room appeared to be illuminated mainly by the candles on the tables and by numerous emergency-exit signs, the superfluity of which did not exactly fill one with confidence in the establishment's culinary standards. It was a so-called French restaurant; in England, the worst kind.

"If you think this is dark," I said, "you should see my basement room in the hospital. It's where they used to keep the shrouds."

"Are you sure that's not a shroud you're wearing?"

"Lord, no, I wouldn't be seen dead in one of those."

At which point a shadow appeared at our elbow. Assuming that this was the waiter, we ordered and, in a dismayingly short time considering the elaborateness of that order, he returned with the *cabillaud avec sauce aux huîtres*. Mine tasted like wallpaper from a condemned building boiled down and flavored with goat droppings.

"Well, this is very nice," I said, looking around with satisfaction; then leaning forward as if to see him more clearly: "And I must say you're looking very well, Mr. Lewis."

"I beg your pardon?" said a strange voice.

"That's someone at the next table you're addressing, Bart," Mr. Lewis said. "I'm over here, now."

"Yes, of course. Sorry," I said, taking a sip of the wine. Then, leaning in the right direction: "Say, listen," I whispered, "while Sigridur is away in the ladies' lavatory, I'd better warn you about her. She may look gorgeous, you know, but actually she's a terrible woman. She—"

"I am not in the ladies' lavatory, I am here," Sigridur snapped.

"Good heavens, are you? Where, where?"

"Now stop that."

"Isn't it dark in here?"

"Keep your hands to yourself."

"I was just trying to locate you, Sigga."

"Oh, yeah?" she said, employing what she believed to be an up-to-date Americanism.

"So, Bartholomew," Mr. Lewis said heartily, "You have finally succeeded in reaching bottom."

"I beg your pardon—I wasn't feeling anywhere near there."

"I meant socially."

"Oh, I see. Yes," I said gloomily. "Failure, you know, isn't all it's cracked up to be. When you finally attain it after years of struggle, you discover that there's something missing, somehow."

"The trouble with failure," Mr. Lewis murmured, delighted, I think, to be having serious conversations with me again after the frivolity of the Foreign Office commissions that he was occasionally called upon to undertake, "is that it leads to feelings of guilt. But really, it's success, not failure, that should make you feel guilty."

"How?" Sigga asked scornfully.

"Because man isn't made for success. He's intrinsically inefficient. It's wrong to tamper with his natural incompetence," Mr. Lewis said, as the waiter cleared away various untouched dishes, to make way for something even worse, the *hanche de mouton*.

Half an hour later when Sigridur did actually leave us alone for a few minutes, Mr. Lewis said quietly, "Why didn't you call us when you got to London, Bart? We still think of you as one of the family, you know."

"Ah."

"It's unlike you to be so sensitive."

"Thanks very much."

"How could you harbor any doubts about us?" he went on softly. "We owe you so much for the fun and happiness you brought into Katherine's life. And ours, too."

"Mm."

"Of course," he said carefully, "I'm assuming you still want to see us. We're not being conceited, are we, in thinking that?"

"No."

"Oh, good. It only occurred to me last weekend, when you kept—when I failed to catch up with you, that perhaps you didn't want to be bothered with a couple of old fogies like us."

"Sure I want to be bothered with you."

"I thought that might be the explanation, but Mrs. Lewis said nonsense—of *course* you wished to see us. She said you were merely being your usual awkward self, and she would give you a good talking-to when she saw you again.

"As a matter of fact," Mr. Lewis continued, hunching forward and hovering, mothlike, over the candle, "I believe she is more than half-convinced that you married mainly in order to acquire her as a mother-in-law."

"Dear Mrs. Lewis. How is she?"

"She has not been well this winter. I can tell because ever since Guy Fawkes Day she has not complained once about her health."

"I'd like to see her again," I said wistfully.

"Then come home with me tomorrow and stay for a while. Better still, stay for good—you're still one of our two sons, you know—and give up this job. Apart from anything else, it doesn't seem entirely worthy of your talents, Bart."

"Gee, I wish you could convince Sigga. She thinks the job is perfect for me."

"Are you . . . in love with her, or anything like that?" Mr. Lewis asked carefully.

"Good Lord, no. I've been trying to get away from her for years."

"You've known her that long?"

"Actually, it's only a few weeks."

"A strange young woman," he murmured. "She appears to

have developed a depth of skepticism about you in a remarkably short space of time. It usually takes much longer for people to see through you. Excuse me, will you?"

"She's convinced that I can't tell the difference between fact and fancy," I chortled, leaning forward and lowering my voice confidentially. "She doesn't believe anything I tell her about my life. I wish you'd convince her that I was nearly a qualified doctor like her at one time, and later I went on to glory, with my picture in the *Illustrated London News*, and everything—"

"Are you addressing me, sir?" a voice said, in a sharp, angry tone.

"Eh?"

"This is the second time you've butted in."

"Butted in?"

"I don't know how they do things where you come from, sir, but in this country you do not intrude on other people's conversations, especially without an introduction."

"I was talking to this gentleman, not you," I replied tartly.

"What gentleman? There's nobody at your table—and I'm not surprised."

"Course there is. Tell him, Mr. Lewis. Mr. Lewis?"

"You've been talking to an empty chair," said the man at the next table—as Sigridur came trotting back, just in time to overhear this remark.

"I just can't take him anywhere," she said helplessly, when Mr. Lewis returned to the table a couple of minutes later.

Feeling like plunging a fish knife into her back, I took a deep breath; but then expelled it as being surplus to requirements and took a shallow one instead. It was hopeless trying to remonstrate with Sigga. She was impervious as lead. "You have to admire her determination," I told my father-in-law with a chuckle that was only slightly forced. "She's determined to gaze at me like an adoring mother who sees the worst in her son. She'll never believe anything about me until it's backed up with irrefutable proof, including affidavits," I said, patting her hand indulgently—after moving the candle over to make sure it was her hand and not the man's next door.

"Still, we'll be glad to have you, if you'll come home with me tomorrow," Mr. Lewis said, trying to read the bill by candlelight.

"Come home, all is forgiven," I said jauntily.

"After all, it's ridiculous for you to be working as a hospital porter."

"*Why*?" I asked quickly, hoping he would enlighten Sigga; but the blasted woman interrupted before he could answer.

"Please," she said. "You should not put ideas into his head."

"Quite right," Mr. Lewis said, though he sounded taken aback by this remonstrance. "I forgot that ideas don't belong there. What I meant was—"

"He was penniless and hungry when I got the job for him," she interrupted. Then, as if addressing a presumptuous pupil: "But perhaps you have a better job to offer him, Mr. Lewis?"

"Well, no. But—"

"Then you have no right to tempt him. At least now he is decently employed."

If I had been able to locate Sigga's throat in the dark, I would have throttled her. To my further fury, when Mr. Lewis answered he sounded quite apologetic, as if the reprimand, from a woman far beneath him in years, rank, experience and accomplishment, was quite justified. "Well . . . at least you'll come up to Hampshire for the weekend?" he asked quite timidly.

"I see no objection to that," Sigga said. "Certainly. We shall be glad to come."

"Oh, Er. . . ." Mr. Lewis began. He had obviously not intended to include Sigga in the invitation.

"But Bandy works next Saturday until one o'clock and so cannot come until late that afternoon, if that is satisfactory."

"Oh. Er. . . ."

"Fine. You will now give us directions to your house in Hampshire, please."

"Oh. Er, right," Mr. Lewis said, probably wondering if he dared give us directions that would steer us away from Hampshire . . . towards, say, Scapa Flow.

Back Home Abroad

On the following Saturday we caught a fast train to Winchester; but from that former capital of England progress was sluggish: a slow bus to the village near which the Lewises now lived. It was getting on for six o'clock by the time we reached the foot of Tipple Downs, the estate that an aunt had willed to Mrs. Lewis just the previous year.

Naturally the moment we blundered off the bus it started to drizzle. What with that and the other frustrations of the journey, we were not in a particularly good humor, especially when a very comfortable-looking Daimler followed us into the sodden driveway, and the driver leaned out to inform us that he had been sent to the railway station in Winchester to collect us.

"I've been waiting for hours," the chauffeur said, irritably biting his officer's mustache. "I mean, it's not worth it now, is it?"

"What isn't?" I asked, breathing hard as Sigridur put down the heavy luggage. The August air was muggy as well as saturated. It felt as if most of the oxygen had been extracted.

"Not worth giving you a lift now," he replied. "I mean, you've come all this way without me, so there's no sense in driving the last hundred yards, now, is there?" he said and, clashing the vast vehicle into gear, continued on up the driveway and round to the back of the house.

The Lewises' country place proved to be a large Victorian edifice in gray stone, with a porticoed main entrance. Half a dozen straight-backed automobiles were parked in the gravel clearing in front of it.

The sight of all these cars dismayed me, but Sigridur was quite impressed. "These friends of yours must be even richer than Agnar," she panted, setting down our suitcases. She had insisted on carrying the luggage so that I could take special care of her new evening dress. It was hanging over my arm in its protective wrapping. I had attracted many a curious stare on the bus from Winchester, mainly because Sigga kept drawing attention to me with comments like, "Careful, don't get your dress creased," and things like that. Despite a certain embarrassment I had seen no reason to protest this arrangement. After all, she was stronger than me.

"When I write home, should I refer to this house as a mansion?" she asked; then added impatiently, "but of course you wouldn't know."

"I know all about English houses," I snapped, and to prove it went on to explain how the natives used all kinds of code words to advertise their properties. I wasn't sure about "mansion," but if a house was described as having "character," it meant that it was overpriced. "Offering an unusual opportunity for purchasers to undertake internal fitting" meant that the interior hadn't been painted or decorated for fifty years. A "period" house meant that it was riddled with woodworm, dry rot and possibly death-watch beetle. A "family house" indicated that it was too large to be adequately maintained or heated, a "country house" that it was architecturally indescribable and so forth. If advertised, I told her, the Lewis property might be listed as a "residential estate," meaning that the house wasn't up to much but that there was a lot of ground to look after—though not enough to earn the respect of the local landed gentry.

In the case of the Lewises' latest property, there were about sixty acres, most of it useless hillside.

Assuming that I was talking nonsense, Sigridur paid no attention, but busied herself removing her trusty sou'wester, which was proving to be even more useful in England than in her own rain-swept country, what with the buckets of rain that had been clanging down since spring. She slashed the air with the headgear to dislodge the beads of water. "But I don't understand," she said, looking along the not inconsiderable length of the gray façade. "This is a very big house, but Mr. Lewis is obviously very poor. I mean, that suit he was wearing."

"I didn't see anything wrong with his suit."

"You wouldn't. It was threadbare, for heaven's sake."

"It was a perfectly good suit," I snapped. "I remember it from 1917, when he worked at the Foreign Office."

"Oh, he worked at the Foreign Office, did he?" she replied with a smile that made me look around for the nearest knobkerrie. "And his wife is a duchess, I suppose?"

I made the mistake of answering that one, too; that Mrs. Lewis was, in fact, the daughter of an earl.

"Oh, Lord," she said with a hopeless sigh, plainly convinced that my fantasies were spreading like mumps, and that, not content with delusions of personal grandeur, I was now attempting to elevate my deceased wife's family into positions of importance.

I bunched my fists and measured the distance to her front teeth; but before I could continue the discussion, she had picked up both suitcases as easily as if they weighed a mere ninety pounds each and swung off toward the portico, leaving me to mince along behind with my fancy frock.

The young butler who opened the door started slightly at the sight of the blonde whizbang with the two bags; then started again when he saw her thin-lipped frock carrier. However, he took the unequal weight distribution without further flinching, possibly because he knew me. "Welcome back, Mr. Bandy," he said, cleverly simulating a delighted surprise. "We've been looking forward to seeing you again, sir."

"M'kew. Uh, you were with the Lewises at Burma Park, weren't you?"

"Yes, sir," he said, pleased that I had remembered. "Hobbs, sir. They made me butler when Mr. Burgess retired last year."

"I remember Burgess."

"He still remembers you too, sir," Hobbs replied, as if, once encountered, I was not likely to be forgotten, like a Black and Tan at an IRA reunion.

As Hobbs hung up our damp outerwear, then went off to fetch Mr. Lewis, Sigga paced around, studying the hall. It contained three large oil paintings in elaborate gilt frames and an eight-foot marquetry-inlaid grandfather clock that actually worked. It was striking five-thirty a mere half hour late.

Standing in front of one painting, she read the brass plate on the frame. " 'Edmond Louis, Before the Battle of Valmy, 1792,' " she read out, squinting a little, for at twenty-five she was becoming quite shortsighted; then she added in an equally loud voice, "I wonder what he looked like *after* the battle."

"That's one of Mr. Lewis's forebears," I muttered, gazing anxiously through the double doors to the left of the hall. The doorway led to a lounge where a female servant was collecting a trolleyful of cups, saucers, plates and crumbs; which indicated that a fair number of guests had been taking afternoon tea and had now gone to their rooms to rest before changing for dinner.

My heart had already sunk into my socks at the sight of all those automobiles outside. Here was further evidence that many other guests were staying for the weekend—people whom I might have encountered in the past when I was a man of promise. Such acquaintances, once equal or perhaps even subordinate to me, were probably all ambassadors, magnates or knights of the garter by now. It would be decidedly shame-making if I had to confess that I had broken the promise. And I wouldn't dare to be evasive about it either, or pretend I was still somebody, not with Sigridur in the same building, or even in the same county, ready to refute me and set the record straight.

"Ah, my boy," said a husky voice from the dark passageway under the curved, carved staircase, and Mr. Lewis entered the hall, looking quite relieved to see us, for some reason.

He checked me over quickly as we shook hands and looked even more thankful when he saw my newly pressed blazer and bags. Perhaps he had feared that I would turn up in my porter's uniform.

As he welcomed her, he also inspected Sigga, but there was no need to worry about *her*. In honor of the occasion she had bought some new clothes. She was draped in one of the acquisitions at the moment, an afternoon frock in the latest style, with the waistline so low at the hips that the skirt was shorter than the bodice. As I had said to her on the train from London, "If anyone put an arm round your waist he'd have to marry you."

A couple of minutes later, while we were still chatting to Mr. Lewis, a hermaphroditic voice suddenly blared from the double doorway on the left of the hall. Whirling, I perceived a dowager empress, disguised as one of the common herd. She was wearing a twinset and pearls and an almost democratic expression on her long, lined, haughty face.

Endeavoring not to display pleasure and thus lay myself open to a charge of vulgarity, I loped forward and kissed her hand.

"Bartholomew," said Mrs. Lewis, with a regal nod of acknowledgment. "I thought I heard your unmistakable voice from the far side of the house; the proper distance, I might add, for listening to a vocal organ sounding like a bandsaw cutting through a plank of Burmese teak.

"I happen," she added immediately, as if to forestall the kind of rejoinder she was likely to get from me, "to have verified that simile quite recently, by having George the gardener saw through a spare commode composed of that material."

"Surely my voice is much more muted these days."

"Not in the least, my dear Bartholomew. In fact, to preserve my hearing, I seriously considered greeting you not in person but from the telephone extension in the orangery; until I recollected that you had a habit of raising your voice still further whilst engaged in telephonic communication."

"Oh, I've got over that, dear Mrs. Lewis," I replied. "I'm not the least afraid of telephones anymore."

"They will continue to be afraid of you if they have any sense. Incidentally," she went on, her eyes straying involuntarily to Sigga's lovely, smiling face, "I understand that you have made yet another precipitate descent into debauchery."

"Oh, no, we're just good friends."

"I am not referring to this young woman, Bartholomew, I am talking about your employment," Mrs. Lewis said severely.

"Yes, I'm afraid I've finally been forced to earn a living."

"That is indeed unfortunate, I must agree."

"I have a job as a porter."

"Indeed? Still, that is an acceptable enough occupation, Bartholomew," she conceded. "Porters are quite necessary for helping young ladies onto the train, as well as for blowing whistles, abusing luggage and despatching one to platform twelve when one's train is actually leaving from platform two."

"I'm a hospital rather than a railway porter, Mrs. Lewis."

"I see," she replied severely, glancing again at Sigga, who was standing nearby, smiling uncomprehendingly. "Well, if you *are* a hospital porter—and we have only your word for that—I should have expected you to appear in better health, considering the many hygienic and other facilities available to you. But then I seem to remember that you have always had a habit of looking the worse for wear, regardless of your occupation."

"Well, you see, I haven't been myself lately."

"Then who have you been?" she demanded.

"Oh, some impostor who resembles me, I guess."

"My dear Bartholomew, nobody in their right mind could possibly wish to resemble you," she said; then, seeing that I was about to reply and not wishing to risk being topped, she turned to Sigga and demanded in a peremptory voice to know who she was.

As Mr. Lewis, glancing anxiously at his watch for the third time in five minutes, mumbled introductions, Mrs. Lewis was plainly deciding how to deal with the strapping wench. The old lady set out to discomfit only those strangers whom she suspected of being pretentious or arrogant. As Sigga emanated an air of unassailable self-confidence and massive complacency, I felt certain that our hostess would soon wipe that smile off her mug with the eraser of her wit.

To my surprise, Mrs. Lewis's face underwent the relaxation that was the closest she usually came to smiling, and she actually went on to welcome the fair visitor in terms so conventional as to cause even her husband to stare at her suspiciously, as if he suspected that Mrs. Lewis was disarming the visitor in order to knife her the moment she was rendered defenceless. But no, the lady had actually taken a shine to the flaxen Saxon.

"Are you really a qualified doctor?" Mrs. Lewis asked in almost a naive way. "Looking at you, my dear, one would expect you to be inflicting dreadful wounds with a broadsword rather than healing them with surgical scissors.

"And tell me," she added, lowering her voice confidentially to a level where it could not be heard more than sixty feet away, "what on earth do you see in Bartholomew?"

When Sigga answered, "Not much," Mrs. Lewis actually laughed aloud, the first time I ever remember her doing so; guffawed, in fact, in a way that I had formerly thought to be illustrative of that colorful eccentricity for which the English were famous, but that I now perceived to be symptomatic of their degeneracy.

The two of them were starting to get on so well that I was quite relieved when Mr. Lewis interrupted to ask if we would care for a wash and brush-up before dinner. He made the suggestion with some urgency. It made me wonder if he had caught a whiff of armpit effluvium. Or was he merely in a hurry to get us out of sight, as if we were a pair of Gorgon heads that were likely to turn the other guests to stone?

In fact, as Mr. Lewis personally led us to the remotest reaches of the house, we encountered no other guests, as if they had been warned to keep clear. Moreover, it seemed to me that there was a certain tension in the air, as if something was expected to happen, or war with Turkey was to be declared.

"What's going on?" I asked, as Mr. Lewis ushered Sigga into her room at the back of the house.

"Hm?" Lewis answered, vague as mist. "By the way, you have evening wear, do you, Bart? If not, I could let you have a spare outfit of Robert's."

When I reassured him, he said, "Good," watching Sigga. She was bouncing up and down on the double bed, presumably testing it for resilience. "Before dinner," he went on, wrenching his eyes away, for the bed was not all that was bouncing, "we'll be gathering in the lounge for cocktails or whatever. Perhaps you should come down at around seven-thirty, Bartholomew."

"Uh-huh. But what's going on, William?" I asked, daringly using his Christian name for the first time.

"Going on?"

"Why are you so jittery? Are you expecting a murder or something? Or has it already happened and you're waiting for Inspector Dawdle of the Yard?"

"No, no, nothing like that," he laughed, passing a distracted hand over his unclad pate.

He started for the door, but turned when he realized that I was following.

"Did you want something, Bart?"

"Yes. My room."

"Pardon?"

"I assumed you were leading me to my room."

"What?"

"You know—where I'm supposed to sleep?"

"Oh, but. You mean you. I thought that," Lewis said, looking flustered.

"You were going to put us both in here?"

"Well, I. . . ."

"You thought Sigga and I were cohabiting?"

"Well, I. . . ."

"Certainly not," I said indignantly. "Damn it, when you get right down to it, we're not even good friends."

"But I assumed that . . . she was so familiar that. . . . You see, you both acted as if you were, you know, married, practically."

"Just because she treats me with contempt and contumely," I said with dignity, "doesn't necessarily mean we're married."

"But there's no other bedroom available," he said.

"Well, I'm not sleeping with her," I said. "So there."

"Huh," Sigga said.

"For one thing, if she rolled over, she'd crush me to a pulp."

"You'll have to excuse him," Sigridur said with flushed cheeks and a sweet smile. "He's not used to polite society."

"Of course, there's the maid's bedroom," Lewis suggested.

"Now you're putting me in with the maid?" I cried. "Good Lord, William, is there no end to your depravity?"

"Where the maid used to be—the boxroom in the attic," he replied; and looked more taken aback than ever when Sigridur answered as if he had addressed her.

"That will suit me perfectly," she said, picking up her suitcase and evening dress. "Lead on, Macduff." She was rather proud of her ability to misquote entire sentences from Shakespeare.

"Oh, but . . . you mean *you* . . . I thought," Lewis said.

"Bandy shall have this room," she said firmly, gesturing around contemptuously at the decadently elaborate ceiling, the sybaritic bed, the Epicurean cornucopia in porcelain with its very own jardiniere, the Brussels game park tapestry and the Aubusson verdure. "We Icelanders are a simple and austere people. The boxroom you talk of is good enough for me."

Gritting my teeth, I refused to be blackmailed into masquerading as an errant knight—or knight errant, is it? "The boxroom is probably too good for her," I snapped, as I dumped my suitcase on the bed. "My advice is to put her in the stables."

Well, I was really annoyed at the way she always contrived to show me up and, in this case, at the implication that a luxurious room like this would be a real treat for me, a brief compensation for a life of inconsequentiality.

After they had departed to view the boxroom—Mr. Lewis still looking at me reproachfully, almost as if he thought that I wasn't behaving as a gentleman should—I went for a route march across the decadent chamber and ended up at a large bay window.

There I stood for ages, gazing gloomily at the view. Not that it was worth more than a cursory glance. There were a group of stables and a courtyard, and that was about it. The stables were being used as garages, judging by the absence of horse buns and the presence of oil patches. The oil patches on the flagstone gleamed iridescent in the drizzle.

It reminded me that the Lewises might still be in possession of three articles of mine, a painting, a samovar and a Rolls-Royce. If

I could get them back they might be turned into ready cash. Gosh, I might even finish the weekend a couple of hundred quid richer.

Of course, the samovar wasn't likely to fetch much, nor was the picture, a kindergarten exercise by a French "artist," Matisse—he'd actually had the nerve to sign the canvas. But the car, though sixteen years old, might be worth two hundred. And with two hundred in the bank I could afford to look for a better job.

But how was I to pry these assets from the Lewises with any degree of grace? The trouble was, I had left the three items behind without a hint as to how I wished them disposed of. It was entirely possible that the Lewises had long since convinced themselves that the great brass and copper tea-maker, the Parisian daub and the posh jalopy actually belonged to them. For a moment I was tempted to forget it, until I remembered how well off the Lewises must be to run a house of this size. No, somehow I would have to maneuver Lewis into recollecting that the three items were my sole remaining assets. So: "Guess what?" I would say to him at the first opportunity, "I saw a 1908 Rolls the other day, the only example of that model I've ever seen—apart, of course, from the one I left in your care six years ago until such time as I was able to reclaim it."

"Why, what an amazing coincidence," he would reply. "We were just talking about those items you left in our keeping in the summer of 1918, to be reclaimed at your convenience. I do hope you will forgive me, son, but, aware of your straitened circumstances, we took the liberty of selling the vehicle, and we have obtained a particularly good price for it. Consequently, here is a handsome check, which I hope you will regard as satisfactory recompense."

Oh, Lord. What I could do with two or three hundred pounds. Pay back Sigga, for instance, before she became utterly intolerable in her possessiveness. And obtain some decent tobacco for my pipe, join the Royal Aero Club and buy socks so I'd have a pair for every day of the week. . . .

The thought of imminently acquiring so much money so elated

me that I remained in a good mood right up to the moment that Sigga appeared at seven-thirty. She came into the room, without knocking, to scold me for being late and to retie my bow tie and to brush my hair so as to cover much of the growing expanse of fallow forehead.

This accomplished, she took my arm and we descended, she radiating pleasure at the prospect of showing off her new evening frock, and me wondering for the fiftieth time why I put up with her, the way she was always trampling all over me with her bossy boots.

As we entered the lounge where everybody was gathered, we caused something of a sensation. Naturally I assumed it was Sigga who was responsible for the dramatic silence that greeted us, and the subsequent hiss of excitement. After all, she was built to a scale unusual in polite society. She made even the men seem willowy. Like some of the other women present, her shoulders were bare; beautiful Devonshire-cream shoulders; but hers, though smooth enough, suggested a musculature beneath that was ready for any kind of action from sumo wrestling to hay baling. As for her bosom, it could have served as a model for the prow of HMS *Implausible*.

To these natural features she had added fashionable artifice. After consulting one of the rich patients on the top floor of St. Pancreas Hospital, she had gone out and bought a diaphanous evening frock in light gold, an interesting color, though not one that went too well with her milky complexion and mass of curly blonde hair. Her taste in clothes was still not impeccable. Still, the long wispy skirt was graceful enough. The designer had been exceedingly careless, though, from the waist northward. The top was so scanty looking that at first I thought there was nothing underneath but her personal topography, and her back was quite bare, with only a fold of foamy gold to prevent the eyes from climbing down to her lower vertebrae; the whole suspensefully held up by one thin shoulder strap. No wonder people gaped. She was a sight.

So, as I said, I took it for granted that the attention would be directed exclusively at her, leaving me free to sidle over to the drinks trolley and guzzle as many free drinks as I could manage before Sigga showed me up again. Yet after a good gape at Sigga, almost every set of eyes wrenched themselves away from this beacon among fireflies and swiveled in *my* direction, if you please, as if I were the belle of the ball and Sigga merely a pumpkin. Further, the eyes remained fastened upon me. Further still, they actually shone with anticipation.

Good Lord, even Mr. Lewis was grinning away, as sloppily as if he had been taking daft lessons. And some guests were even elbowing each other for a better view of me, as if I were expected to break into a soft-shoe shuffle, or do magic tricks or something, at any moment.

"Wot?" I enquired defensively; whereupon, after a final smirk, Mr. Lewis stepped aside as if executing a *verónica*, and the movement exposed a slender figure in evening dress; a handsome lad with a beaming beige face beneath a wave of brilliantined black hair.

"*Khooshie*?"

"Bartholomew," replied Khooshie Avtar Prakash, with an attempt at cultivated reserve. "Yes, it is I, Khooshie."

"Well, I'll be hornswoggled. . . ."

This not exactly sparkling exchange yet elicited an explosion of excited laughter from the other guests, as if it were exactly what they had been hoping for, that and my expression. They crowded closer, eager for the next sample of scintillating dialogue.

"Am I as big a surprise as we planned?" Khooshie asked breathlessly. "Am I, am I, Bartholomew?" Then, unable to sustain the pretense of sophisticated reserve, he rushed foward, seized my hand and made a hot beef sandwich of it between his palms and, to my further embarrassment, held it to his starched front. "My goodness," he cried, "we have been waiting with so much impatience all afternoon for this moment, have we not, Mr. Lewis?"

"All week," Lewis murmured with a smile.

"Yes, yes, all week, ever since Mr. Lewis is finding out that you are the one who came down into the drink to save me. And he told my father on you, you see."

"I met Khooshie's father some years ago when I was with the

Foreign Office," Mr. Lewis explained. "Fortunately he still remembered me."

Clasping my hand to his boiled breast, Khooshie suddenly looked at me with eyes swimming in abject apology. "The trouble was, you see, Bartholomew, I could not for the life of me remember your last name, to give to all the journalists, you see."

"Journalists?"

"But then," he went on in mock reproach, "it is also your fault, you naughty fellow, you should have got in touch with us, you see."

"I don't think Bartholomew read any of the accounts of the rescue," Mr. Lewis said.

"Of course he did," Khooshie said, releasing my hand at last in order to brush aside the interjection. "My face was in all the papers."

"However, that is all water under the bridgework," he went on with a shout, spraying my white tie with saliva in his excitement. He was positively quivering with emotion. "Now we have met again, never, never shall we be parted." Then, reproachful again: "But why did you leave me, Bartholomew? After I telephoned my father I am waiting for you to come back from the seaside, but you never did."

"I was trying to save the airplane, Khooshie."

His polished black eyes took on an extra shine. "My father is wanting terrifically to meet you," he shouted joyfully. "He is coming here tomorrow specially to meet you. I am sure he is bursting with pleasure at the prospect, don't you think, Mr. Lewis? Oh, my goodness, yes, excited all over, to be able at last to thank you, because you see I am his favorite son."

"How many sons has he?"

"There is only me. There was also a girl, but I believe he gave her away," Khooshie said; a vague thought that seemed to calm him, because he went on much more quietly, "He is wanting to thank you in person, of course, when he comes tomorrow for afternoon tea."

"And we know how generous he can be," a lady guest exclaimed ecstatically.

"Generous?"

There was no immediate reply. I looked around enquiringly.

"Khooshie's father," began Mr. Lewis, "happens to be visiting the country at the moment."

"In his steam yacht," said a male guest.

"After visiting Monte Carlo."

"He lost millions."

"Did he really?"

"Only francs, of course."

"But still."

"In London," a debutante breathed, "he presented Queen Mary with a jeweled blunderbuss."

"Khooshie's father," Mr. Lewis told my uncomprehending face, "is the Maharajah of Jhamjarh, the second richest man in the world."

The Maharajah

"After realizing, from the little you told him, that you must have been the anonymous flyer who had saved Khooshie's life, William spent the entire week planning last night's encounter. And I must say it came off splendidly, just splendidly," Mrs. Lewis said, nodding approvingly at her husband.

As it was morning, we were sitting in the morning room. (Had it been afternoon we would, of course, have been sitting in the afternoon room.) Mrs. Lewis and I were sipping coffee. Mr. Lewis was rummaging through a folder of press clippings.

"Our guests," Mrs. Lewis went on, "particularly enjoyed your look of petrified incomprehension, Bartholomew. They were not to know that it was your normal expression.

"In fact," she continued, rapping me playfully on the knuckles with an apostle spoon, "I feel eminently satisfied that the story of your reunion will be told and retold throughout the county until the end of time, or the overthrow of Prime Minister Ramsay MacDonald, whichever comes first.

"Indeed, the encounter is almost certain to obliterate the previous record for drawing-room sensationalism held by Mavis Penruddock." Mrs. Lewis looked profoundly satisfied at this triumph over her friend Lady Penruddock who, two years previously, had brought together a couple who had just undergone a rancorous separation. Lady Penruddock's dinner had ended quite spectacularly when one of the former partners attempted to brain the other with a Jacobite decanter filled with an effete Lafite-Rothschild '22. "Our drawing-room scene, though," Mrs. Lewis preened, "is bound to supplant that epic battle, even if it does not become the stuff of legend or material for Rider Haggard. After all, it is not every day that a romantic mystery is solved between the pink ladies and the brown Windsor soup. Incidentally, Bartholomew," she added severely, "how could you possibly have missed the extravagant accounts in the press, or the Maharajah's appeal for the mystery aviator to step forward and receive his just reward? Even *I* was aware of the hydrographic melodrama, and *I* read nothing but back issues of *The Field*."

"I guess I was preoccupied with the employment situation," I whined, still jangling after a night of frantic dreams. My fingertips were numb from impoverished sleep, my voice was a frayed basso from last night's hooch and chatter. Still, my eyes were bright enough now: positively glassy with greed. I couldn't decide whether to receive my reward in bank notes, money orders, precious stones, gold or shares in the Indian subcontinent.

"Ah, here they are," Mr. Lewis exclaimed, holding out a couple of newspaper clippings.

I looked them over, at first eagerly, then with a certain discontent. Dated last May, their account of the rescue seemed to me to be unnecessarily succinct.

"Is this all there is?" I asked. "From what they were saying last night, I had expected handfuls of cuttings and great screaming headlines."

"These are from *The Times*, Bart. You were lucky to be mentioned at all."

"But I'm not—there's no mention of my name anywhere."

"How could your name be mentioned," Mrs. Lewis thundered, "if you were a Mystery Aviator? Next you'll be asking us for the address of the Unknown Soldier."

"What did the other papers say?" I asked. "I expect they wove a thoroughly romantic story about the Indian prince rescued from certain death by a handsome aviator, eh?"

"As a matter of fact, to make this story even more romantic, one of the newspapers turned Khooshie into an Indian princess," Mr. Lewis put in.

"Really?"

"Of course, his being so good looking helped a lot. His photo didn't need much retouching."

"What a sensation it must have caused," I said wistfully. "I wish I'd been there."

"But Bartholomew, you *were* there," Mrs. Lewis said patiently.

"Sigridur is right," she added. "You are very foolish, sometimes."

"Anyway, what about the rest of the papers?" I asked hankeringly. "I expect there were great black headlines about me in the popular press."

"Probably," Mr. Lewis said.

"How big were they?"

"How big were what?"

"The headlines. How big? Two, three inches deep, I expect?"

"I'm afraid I didn't measure them, Bart."

"I don't know," I said discontentedly, waving the cuttings, "why you don't take a decent newspaper instead of this rag. I mean, look at that—they've given more space to a diplomatic *volte-face* in the Cameroons than to my story."

But I wasn't really annoyed. I was too thrilled at the prospect of receiving some tangible expression of the Maharajah's gratitude.

What a reward it was likely to be! He was so rich that he owned several palaces. "I wonder if he'll give me one," I dreamed, eliciting a feverish laugh from a lady guest who seemed almost as excited as I was, as if she had a solid portfolio of preferred shares in my dreams of avarice.

"Maybe he will," she gasped. "He's noted for his generosity."

"Really? Is he really? He's not a skinflint, then, like most rich men?"

"Oh, no," somebody else chimed in, and mentioned the case of the English tutor in India who had helped Khooshie to pass his London University matric. He had supplied the boy with the answers, some of which even turned out to be correct. The Maharajah had rewarded the tutor with—wait for it—a *fistful of precious stones.*

All the accounts of this munificence were consistent as to the manner in which the gift had been bestowed. His Highness had ordered the tutor to hold out his cupped hands. When the tutor, wonderingly, did so, he received a veritable shower of gems. Among the stones there was said to be an emerald the color and very nearly the size of a greengage.

The tutor had promptly abandoned any further attempt to educate Khooshie and had sailed for Bali where he understood that the girls were in the habit of shamelessly exposing their northern hemispheres.

"Khooshie is going absolutely wild since coming to England, spending an absolute fortune on motorcars and flappers and God knows what else," somebody else panted. "And the old man pays up without so much as a glance at the bills, they say."

What with anecdotes such as these and rumors of other splendid gifts, I looked forward to meeting Khooshie's pater with an eagerness in which greed and cupidity wrestled for an ascendant fairback. Both wrestlers had drawn long before the Maharajah finally arrived.

As the Lewises had been informed by India Office that tea on the lawn of an English country house was among the Maharajah's more favorable memories of his school days in England, they had decided to present a garden party in his honor. When I heard about it, I naturally visualized the usual sort of beano, a genteel scene of damask tablecloths, Georgian silverware, cucumber sandwiches and buttered scones set out on an impeccable English sward of the sort that might have been laid down by Egbert the Hardboiled and clipped with manicure scissors ever since. But Tipple Downs, being a hill, had no flat surfaces anywhere except in the billiard room. The only place that a garden party could be held was in the "side garden" as they called it; but the side garden was a burlesque of the English lawn far beyond the bounds of good taste. Slashed from the hillside on the right-hand side of the house, it was a respectable enough size and seemed to have had as much care lavished on it as any ordinary garden, but in quality it was still little better than a cropped field. Its chief eccentricity, though, lay in the way it sloped—quite dangerously, it seemed to me, toward the deep, treed slope at the back of the house.

The truth was it was an utter disgrace of a lawn, and only the Lewises could have gotten away with such vegetational impertinence. Other people in their class would have been hauled up before the county on a charge of agrarian heresy. Yet here was Mrs. Lewis showing it off as complacently as if it were a grassy terrace at Balmoral Castle and saying, "So, how do you like my lawn? I did it all myself."

"Did you, indeed?"

"Except, of course for the physical contribution," she said. "I was never afraid of plain, honest toil, as you know, Bartholomew. Rain or shine, I watched unflinchingly as the men labored to transform this hillside."

"It's true," Lewis said. "When she started, this part of the property was hardly more than rough field."

"And with a bit more work," I said, "it could easily become a meadow."

"What are you talking about?" Mrs. Lewis snorted, striding bravely onto the lawn in question. "It's perfect."

"For mountain goats?"

"If you are referring to the minor gradient," she replied loftily, holding onto my arm to avoid spilling downhill into the valley, "we have taken steps to solve that problem."

I understood what she meant later that afternoon when I saw the staff setting up the tea tables. Despite the pronounced slope, the tables remained amazingly level. Or perhaps not so amazingly: Mrs. Lewis had had the legs cut short on the upslope side.

Sigga noticed it too. "Two of the four legs of each table are shorter than the opposite two," she pointed out.

"Yes, of course."

"But why?"

"Well, it's obvious. You need shorter legs on one side because the ground is higher on that side."

"But that is stupid."

"What's stupid about it?" I said loyally. "It makes the tables nice and level, doesn't it?"

"But why didn't they just level the ground?" she hissed angrily. "Or make terraces?"

"Oh, do be sensible, Sigga," I said, but with an indulgent smile and a pat on the shoulder. "You and your ideas." My tone suggested that I was quite used to her impracticalities. And I was happier than ever when she scowled and clenched her fists in frustration. It wasn't often that I got a chance to get my own back.

Though the Maharajah was expected at two o'clock, an hour later he had still not arrived. By three-thirty the guests were starting to fidget, including Khooshie; though his restlessness had a different cause. "I say, Bartholomew," he said, "do you know that girl over there?"

"The one with Robert Lewis's party? No, I don't."

"She came over to talk to me. She was standing so close I could not think of a thing to say," Khooshie said discontentedly. "Her name is Bubba Carruthers."

"Really?"

"She kept talking to me for ages, and I could not think of anything at all to say. How I hate myself on those occasions. I could claw at my face," he said, his voice trembling with self-loathing. "She was being so nice and friendly—and warm—she has such tremendous warmth, Bartholomew—and all I could do was stand there like an idiot.

"But of course, it could have been her perfume," he added, looking at me resentfully, as if I were arguing about it. "It was making me quite dizzy. That is why I couldn't think of anything to say."

But a few seconds later he was admitting in despair that he had been as tongue-tied then as he was now in bondage. Three and a half seconds later the despair had turned to elation. "Oh,

Bartholomew," he said, gripping my shoulder—I could feel him trembling—"is she not splendid? I have never met anyone like her."

Then, a minute later, he was whispering shyly, "She caressed me."

"Caressed you? Whereabouts?"

"Here, in the garden. She caressed my pullover," he said, indicating his white cricket sweater with the green-and-black border. "And she said she adored my throat."

"Your throat."

"Yes," he said, touching his smooth brown throat between the open collar of his cream shirt. "Never have I met anyone so . . . so. . . ."

I looked across at the girl, who was seated at Robert's table talking animatedly to the others. She looked ordinary enough to me: a short, sturdy girl with light brown hair and a loud laugh. Like the other girls in Robert Lewis's party, her lips had been doubled in size by the application of an excessive amount of bright red lipstick. She was waving a cigarette in a twelve-inch ebony holder, oblivious of the disapproving looks of a couple of older women nearby.

"What should I do, Bartholomew?" he asked, despairing again. "She tried to make friends, and I just stood there like a schoolboy. I feel like throwing myself at her feet and kissing them, but it is too late, I have lost the chance. Do you think it is too late, Bartholomew?"

It was at that moment that the Maharajah arrived.

As I had visualized him in curly slippers and fluorescent silks, busily showering gold coins from atop a crimson howdah, at the head of a convoy of elephants, all loaded with frankincense and myrrh, escorted by a bodyguard of scimitar-twirling Pathans and with a van of dusky concubines, his appearance that Sunday afternoon was something of an anticlimax. He turned up in a Ford convertible, carrying a Woolworth fly whisk.

Even more disappointing was that there were only three servants with him: a damp Hindu whose sole responsibility was to hold a large black umbrella over the Maharajah's head, a private secretary incongruously attired in a dhoti and mackintosh and a chauffeur who was so diminutive as to be unable to see the road ahead without the aid of several cushions.

"I requested a chauffeur," said the Maharajah in a squeaky voice, pointing his fly whisk at the driver, "and that is what I am given, believe it or not. I am having to sit beside him all the way from Southampton and lend him my foot, because he cannot reach the pedals himself. Very many times I am called upon to do this. I am most put out, I can tell you. And to make matters worse, sometimes when this man here is not satisfied with the alertness of my foot, he is, believe it or not, he is ducking down underneath the, the board-with-all-the-instruments thing, in order to reach the pedals himself, thus leaving me in complete charge of the steering wheel. I mean, is he the chauffeur or am I? If he is, then he should get on with it. Oh, yes, I assure you, I am most put out, most," the Maharajah concluded; and as a coda to this singsong passage, he suddenly leaned over and cuffed the offending driver. "There," he said breathlessly, "let that be a lesson to you."

As this outburst, delivered in a high voice that badly needed lubricating, was unanswerable, nobody answered. Besides, we were all too busy studying the Maharajah with a variety of stupid looks on our faces.

He certainly warranted the silent awe. Apart from a pair of fine eyes, His Highness was spectacularly ugly. His face, pitted with smallpox or shotgun pellets, was quite concave. It sloped toward his orange lips as if the principal purpose of his mouth was to act as a rainwater drain. Below a forehead that seemed to be not so much a brow as a dike, it curved inward from his prominent cheekbones and from the chisel edge of his jutting chin, past a nose that offered little obstruction. I just couldn't help visualizing him in a prone position during a thunderstorm, with the rain sluicing down the washbasin of his face and emptying itself into his mouth in a veritable torrent.

I could only assume that something remarkable had happened to him as a child; that a log had fallen on his face and been allowed to remain there for several months, or that the cook, mistaking him for some dough, had rolled his face with a rolling pin while it was still pliable, and continued to roll it backward and forward, endlessly, from jutting chin to bulging forehead.

The rest of his appearance was almost as noteworthy. His skinny, five-foot frame was encased in a ghastly purple coat and matching trousers, the coat abrading his knees at one end and compressing his Adam's apple at the other. For decoration, there were many more rings on his fingers than there were fingers. On the left breast of his long purple coat was a gold medal suspended from a green ribbon. Dangling from his ears were a pair of diamond earrings, while a single emerald had been sewn into the gold brocade at the front of his maroon velvet cap. Below the edge of that little round hat, which seemed at least one size too small for him, wisps of fuzzy gray hair escaped, like steam from a double-boiler. He appeared to be wearing orange lipstick.

His peevishness over having to act as assistant to his chauffeur vanished the moment he caught sight of his son among the guests. His rather beautiful eyes went all misty, and his knees, as he hastened forward to embrace the boy, went all weak with desire. He held his son with enormous tenderness, as if years rather than hours separated them from their last meeting.

There was certainly no doubt about his love for the boy, even if it wasn't reciprocated quite so obviously. Khooshie accepted his father's devotion and responded to the eager parental enquiries with the offhand manner of youth, as if the Maharajah's effusions and compliments were so thoroughly warranted as scarcely to require a verbal framework. However, when dad gave way to overwhelming impulse, and stood on tiptoe to kiss him on the cheek, Khooshie's neat brown features twitched in embarrassed annoyance. Throughly disconcerted, he drew out an embroidered handkerchief and scrubbed his cheek vigorously. He looked more revolted than ever when he saw the orange stain on the hanky.

"Really, Father," he snapped. "That's not done, you know."

"What isn't, dear son?"

"This kissing business."

"But I am so overjoyed to see you again, Khooshie," the Maharajah said, bathing the lad with his liquid eyes.

"Yes, but dash it all, Pater, they don't do that sort of thing here. In England a curt nod is considered quite adequate."

"Even when a father is not seeing his only son for hours and hours?"

"My dear Father," Khooshie said with a disdainful laugh, "allow me to tell you about Rude Yard Kipling, the great author."

"Yes, please do, dear son, I am most anxious to learn."

"Rude Yard Kipling," the handsome lad said loftily, "was left behind by his father in a boarding house in Southsea when he was only six years old. And when his father came back from India five years later, all they did, he and his father, was to shake hands."

"He was separated from his son from the age of six for five long years? How can this happen?"

"It is the way things must be in England, Father. Rude Yard had to go to school. Kipling senior had to go to work in India."

"Could not the son have gone to school in India, dear son?"

"That is not the point, Father," Khooshie said, treating the rest of us to a patient smile. "It was for Rude Yard's sake that they did this. It is a tradition in England to put as many miles as possible between a child and his parents. He must go away to school at an early age and must never again see his mother and father excepting in the Christmas holidays, and so forth, until he has grown up and can be fending for himself."

The Maharajah nodded meekly, as if to indicate that Khooshie had explained it all beautifully, and he continued to gaze at his neat brown son as if he were the incarnation of Krishna; though actually the Maharajah knew far more about it than did Khooshie, as he had experienced the same situation in reverse. At the age of seven he had been wrested from his Anglophile family in India and placed in an English preparatory school for five years. It was this experience that had convinced him never to send his own son away from home until he was old enough to defend himself at least as effectively as Krishna defended himself against the demon Agni.

"Is he not the most handsome son ever born?" the Maharajah sighed, optically caressing the lad's refined, almost dainty features. "As well as being the best-dressed man in the whole of the British Empire," he added, gazing yearningly at Khooshie in his cricket pullover with the black-and-green border, the open-necked cream shirt that so nicely complemented his light brown skin and the gray trousers with their razor-edge crease.

It did not occur to the Maharajah, even though Khooshie kept glancing at dad's attire in cringing embarrassment, that if his son was the best-dressed, he himself could easily be elected the worst-dressed man in the empire, and that his purple suit, his embroidered maroon cap and his constellation of precious stones were not entirely appropriate to afternoon tea on the lawn of an English country house, even a lawn as peculiar as this one.

Meanwhile, Mr. Lewis was dying to complete the introductions, with me as the climax. Sensing that this moment was nigh, the rest of the guests crowded around, eager to find out how much I was to receive in the way of mazúma. Even Khooshie watched suspensefully as I was led up to his august pappy. Would dear old dads take me in his arms and embrace me, too? Break down and weep with gratitude? Trundle up a steamer trunk filled with negotiable bonds? Make out his will in my favor?

Not a bit of it. It appeared that his attitude was to be one of instant hostility.

This was not an unfamiliar reaction to my ill-done-to face, but in the circumstances it was quite unexpected; and I had Sigridur to thank for it. After we were both introduced—with Khooshie, bless him, eagerly putting in, "This is the one, Father, this is him!"—Sigridur proceeded to climb over the wall before the Maharajah had a chance to open the gates. She started to monopolize the conversation, quite ruining Mr. Lewis's carefully prepared climax and distracting the Maharajah, too, especially when he made the mistake of mentioning that he had a yacht.

"Oh, yes," she replied. "What type?"

"Type?" the Maharajah said, plainly overawed by the size of this Nordic beauty.

"Lugger, yawl, ketch, what?"

"I am not quite. . . ." he faltered, staring up at her, wide-eyed.

"Well, does it have a spit sail? Standing lug? Bermuda rig? What?" she asked impatiently.

"Ah!" The Maharajah exclaimed as if she had not until this moment been communicating too clearly, but that now all was clear. "Yes, that is so," he said.

"Well, which?" she demanded.

He was back at sea again. "Uh. . . ."

"Look," she said, with long-suffering patience, "how many masts does it have?"

"Ah. I believe it has . . . two. Two!"

"You *believe*? Don't you know?"

"Well, I . . . I haven't looked lately, you see," the Maharajah mumbled; and promptly contracted another foot or two with mortification as he became aware that she was smiling around at the rest of us as if to say, "Another braggart. His yacht is probably no more than a dinghy—assuming he has any kind of boat at all."

Well, *I* had certainly had a boat, until then. My ship had been just about to come in. And she had sunk it, right at the harbor mouth.

I looked at her. I tried to imagine what she would look like being slowly turned on a spit over roaring fire, with me occasionally basting her with boiling fat until it ran down her hide and sputtered wildly in the white-hot flames.

She had certainly managed to turn the potentate into an impotentate, judging by the way he was now twitching and glancing around in a hunted way. And now he was patting himself to make sure that he was all there.

But when he spoke, it was obvious that he was at least as furious as he was humiliated. He looked up at me and asked sharply, "You are the pilot they are telling me about?" Then, turning away: "Take my arm, take my arm," he snapped; and I very nearly took it, until I saw that he was pointing his fly whisk at the mackintoshed secretary—who was hovering around looking at me as offendedly as if *I* were the one who had made a fool of his master.

As they lurched off across the canting meadowland, I could almost hear the syllogism burning through the Maharajah's mind. Sigridur had made him look foolish. I was with Sigridur. Therefore I had made him look foolish. He was probably disinheriting me at this very moment.

I turned to Sigridur. "You . . . you . . . ," I announced, through my teeth.

"What? What's the matter?" she asked, with quite genuine innocence.

But perhaps all was not lost, for the august visitor, who was heading toward the far end of the inclined plain, suddenly turned and said to me irascibly, "Well, are you not coming?"

Reaching an ornamental iron bench that had been freshly painted in honor of the occasion, he sank down with a grunt of relief. Then, after mopping his bulging forehead with a rather grubby handkerchief, he gestured impatiently for me to sit by him. The secretary, Rahat, prepared to sit down on the other side, until a look from his master—a look that told me the Maharajah was not entirely lacking in authority—caused Rahat to rise again. He walked away a few steps, trying to look casual, as if he had not really intended to sit on such an uncomfortable piece of garden furniture anyway.

It was uncomfortable, all right. I knew because we sat there in silence for at least five minutes, before the little man asked abruptly in his high, poorly lubricated voice, "What do you think of my son?"

"A fine lad, Your Highness."

"He behaved with credit when he was in the sea?"

"M'oh, yes, very bravely."

"Very bravely," he repeated, and his orange mouth moved silently, as if he were repeating the words and turning them over and over to view them from different angles. Then: "He is a handsome boy, too, is he not?"

"Yes."

"Not like his father," the Maharajah said with a smile. He seemed to have recovered his spirits. "And it is your impression that he is intelligent?"

"Certainly."

"A thoroughly all-round decent boy, you think?"

"Yes, sir."

"Cool, calm and collected?"

"Definitely."

"An affectionate, loving son, too?"

"No doubt about that, sir."

"And responsible—chock-full of common sense?"

I hestitated. "Uh," I said.

The Maharajah looked at me sideways, slyly. "You say, 'Ah,' " he said, hiding his mouth with his hand. "What does that mean exactly, please?"

"Um. . . ."

"You don't think, then, that he is reliable—ready for much responsibility?"

"I'm, uh, still thinking about it, sir," I said; and I was. I was thinking that there must be a reason for these questions, but that I hadn't a clue what the reason was.

The ugly, likable little man glanced at me several times in silence before giggling faintly to himself.

A couple of chaffinches came hopping across the grass. One of them flew onto the iron bench only inches away from the Indian. After looking at the purple figure with its head to one side, the chaffinch wiped its beak on the bench then flew off. The Maharajah, sitting with his head bowed, did not even appear to have noticed.

Two or three minutes elapsed before he raised his head, complete with its embroidered maroon comforter and wisps of gray hair. "As for what you did for dear son, words cannot say how I feel," he said; and he appeared to be illustrating this remark by holding out his thumb, forefinger and middle finger. I assumed that this was an Indian-type gesture to indicate that words could not express the way he felt, until I saw that the fingers were poised over a flat tin box that he had drawn from some recess of his person. On the lid of the box were the words "Farrah's Original Harrogate Toffee." The Maharajah was trying to decide which of several identical squares of toffee to select.

After agonizing thought he picked the corner lump and popped it into his orange drain. As his lips parted, two or three ruined teeth appeared. "You risked your life to save my son," he said.

My heart leaped. At last we were getting down to brass tacks.

"I don't know how I am ever going to repay you," he said in a toffee-sucking mumble.

Now for it, I thought. At last, I was about to get my just deserts.

"I understand that as a result of your so very, very brave action," he added, slavering a trickle of caramel juice, "you have lost everything."

Any moment now—a shower of baubles. My hands were already cupped in anticipation. "Well, mainly the aircraft," I said, to impress him with my admirable moderation.

"It was very expensive, this aeroplane?"

"I had it made specially to my design," I replied, squinting modestly at the high white sky. There was no need to exaggerate the loss. He'd understand. He'd be able to read between my modest lines and comprehend the very considerable expense of producing a prototype. He would understand the magnitude of the sacrifice I had made to save his son.

"It was just a homemade aeroplane, then?"

She-it! I was carrying the modest trumpery too far. Quick, enlighten him before he settles for five quid and a lump of toffee.

"Homemade only in the sense—" I began portentously.

"Ah, good, good," he said, thinking, because of an imperfect grasp of the language, that I had finished the sentence. "I am most relieved, Mr. Bandy, that it was not such a loss. I was fearing that it was a real aeroplane costing thousands and thousands. But just a homemade contraption, was it? That is a great relief, a great relief."

"Actually," I said agitatedly, hauling out my pipe before remembering that I had no tobacco for it, "a prototype is a good deal more cost—"

"Give Mr. Bandy a cigarette," the Maharajah said to Rahat.

"Very much more costly than—"

"Well, light it for him, light it," he said testily to his secretary, who had proffered a tin filled with fat Turkish cigarettes.

A minute later the Maharajah turned away, beckoning Rahat over for a quick conference in Hindi.

Meanwhile I examined the heavens. At the moment they were high, moist and featureless, but usually they were well worth examining. The sky was one of the first things that had excited me about the British Isles, the beauty and drama of the cloudscape, constantly rearranging itself into new compositions, sometimes every few minutes; sometimes great banks of cloud flew overhead at amazing speeds, sometimes the dawn and dusk air turned into a glory of indescribably beautiful color that no professional artist would dare reproduce on canvas. I was never tired of looking at the sky, whether I was on the ground or in an aircraft. It was the one phenomenon that reconciled me to the concomitant British rains.

After a while, when the Indians continued to behave as if I were not there, it seemed only logical not to be there. So I got up heavily and moved back to the others, who were now nibbling genteelly as they sat at the amputated tables. I looked around to see where Sigridur was, and was not at all displeased to see that she was fully occupied in talking to a party of young men in blazers and celluloid collars. They were watching her open-mouthed as she polished off entire platefuls of moist sandwiches and scones inches deep in butter, cream and strawberry jam. She was helping it all down with drafts of tea and gestures.

I was glad there was no room at her table. The only spare place was with Robert Lewis and his disreputable friends. So, in spite of the lack of a warm welcome, or indeed a welcome of any temperature, I sat there and nibbled genteelly as well.

Robert, the Lewises' thirty-two-year-old son, had not actually been invited for the weekend but had turned up nonetheless, late the previous evening. Worse, he had brought with him two shameless young men and two girls; one of them a strange-looking creature with pop eyes and an Eton crop, and the other, Bubba Carruthers.

The rowdy quintet had been accommodated with some difficulty, but Mrs. Lewis had looked worried rather than upset at having her arrangements disarranged. "Robert has been a trifle out of sorts for the past six years," she explained. "You will find him somewhat changed, Bartholomew, and not everyone agrees that it is for the better."

As he had arrived late and had only just risen, this was the first time I had seen Robert. I was shocked at his dissipated appearance. He looked even more haggard than me. His eyeballs were yellow, and his lips, formerly those of a man of effortless authority, were loose and roiled with bitterness, exposing a set of teeth that had once been clean and perfect. Deep lines had formed parentheses round the digression of his mouth.

"He's really very bitter," Mr. Lewis had confided unhappily the night before, "against the church, government, army—against rules, regulations, good manners—" He stopped, realizing that he was in danger of showing emotion.

"A belated war casualty."

"Yes, obviously." Mr. Lewis cleared his throat. "I might have known, Bart, that you'd understand right away. Not many people do. I'm afraid his mother doesn't. He, ah, he's going in for some pretty outrageous behavior these days. I wish . . . well, I wish he were more like you, Bart."

"I can't begin to tell you how closely I share his feelings."

"Really? Really?"

As I sat down at the table, Robert regarded me with yellow-eyed distaste. "I hear you're still flying," he said.

"Hello, Robert. Yes, when there's an airplane under me. Are you?"

He ignored the question. Instead he looked around contemptuously at the other guests as they clung desperately to the hillside. Then: "Well, at least you haven't amounted to anything," he said. "Thank God for small mercies."

"How do you mean, darling?" Bubba asked loudly.

"Bandy becomes lordly when he's doing well."

"I say," Bubba said, laying a quintet of cobalt nails on my arm, "you're the one who rescued that absolutely gorgeous Indian boy, aren't you?"

"Yes."

"You must tell me all about it, darling. It's the most utterly dramatic story I've ever heard outside the nursery. Confidentially, *I* couldn't have done such a thing to save my own life, let alone anyone else's, but then one is quite powerless, my dear, in the grip of forces utterly beyond one's control, as Freud tells us. Have you read Freud? Oh, you must. Too, too revealing, you know. Do you mind if I hold onto you while I straighten this damned chair? I wonder if gripping your thigh this way is significant. . . . Really, while Robert's mother was sawing off half the table legs, I do think she should have done the same thing to the chairs, don't you? I'm in acute danger of being tipped head over heels and exposing my French knickers to All and Sundry. He's All," she explained, pointing to one of the two young men at the table; and then, pointing to the other, "and that one's Sundry. Confidentially, darling—good heavens, I'm just full of confidences and confessions this afternoon, it must be that Catholic cathedral of a face of yours that's causing it—I find these alfresco rituals of jam and cucumber most awfully boring. I suppose it's just faintly bearable on a gorgeous summer day scented with hay and honeysuckle, but in these clammy conditions with one's heels sucking in the most dreadfully suggestive way into this slanting pasture, under a cloud cover like a shroud—I stole them, you know."

"Hah?"

"These shoes, darling. From Harrods, last week. I know it's simply awful, but I just couldn't help myself. I was with Robert, and I saw them on a rack in this absolutely gorgeous display, and I thought to myself, I've just got to have them, but I didn't have nearly enough of the wherewithal, and neither did Robert, and just as Freud says, I was seized by this absolutely uncontrollable impulse. It just couldn't be denied, you know, so I took them while Robert kept watch for me."

I looked at Robert. He gazed back indifferently.

"Your lady friend tells me you work in a hospital," he said. Sounds almost as bad as my job. I tout for a nightclub."

"Oh?"

"The Catacombs," he said, throwing cucumber sandwiches at a pair of wood pigeons. "I'm paid to stand around for six hours or so. The idea is it gives the place 'class,' you see."

"What lady friend is that?" Bubba asked. Khooshie had

described her as having a great deal of warmth. This was certainly true in a physical sense. In the cool air of the side garden I could feel a quite extraordinary amount of heat radiating from her.

"What?" Robert replied flatly.

"You said his lady friend."

"Yes. Sigridur."

"Oh, you mean the bleached whale." She turned to me. "No, but who is she, anyway, darling? With a scale like that, one expects her to burst into some dreadful Wagnerian aria at any moment."

"Stop it," said one of the young men. Then a couple of seconds later: "Stop it!"

"What?"

"You pinched me."

"I did not."

"You did so. Ooh, you fibber!"

While All and Sundry were busy nipping each other like quarrelsome crabs, I saw Mrs. Lewis watching from two tables away, her brow like a summer storm.

"Drop in some time," Robert said indifferently. "Bring Sigridur with you, if you like."

"Only if she pays."

"Bad as that, eh? Well, I wouldn't let that stop you. You'd have plenty of company. At the Catacombs, the women have always got their hands under the table. At first I thought they were giving their officers a thrill, until I realized they were passing across fivers to pay for the ersatz champagne."

Then, looking me over with a defiant jauntiness that six years ago would have been quite foreign to his lonely, stilted nature, he said, "Talking about money, any luck so far? Has our Aryan brother offered you your weight in platinum yet?"

"No."

"I'm surprised you're not with him now, giving him your deserving look."

"I don't think they want Westerners at their table."

"How are the mighty fallen. By the way, I don't suppose you remember that motorcar you left with us—the old Rolls?"

"Uh, faintly. Why?"

"I'm afraid I've rather demolished it, old man." He laughed at the memory. "Few months ago, in London."

"Oh. That's too bad."

"Got fined twenty quid for that one," he added peevishly. "Oh, and that French painting of yours. The one Kath liked so much. I gave it away. It reminded me of her too much."

"I see. And my samovar. Gave that away, too, did you?"

"That Russian tea thing? Good Lord, no. What do you think I am? That belonged to you. No, it's still around, somewhere. I think I saw it in the attic a few months ago."

The garden party was almost over before I could get near the Maharajah again. Just as I managed to get within toadying distance, his secretary reminded him that it was time to leave.

"But I have not had a chance to talk," the Maharajah protested, causing my heart to jump as he turned in my direction, "to dear son. Where is he, where is dear son?" he asked plaintively, as if we were all conspiring to separate him from the young prince.

Then: "Oh, my goodness, there he is over there, playing with those flighty girls," squealed His Highness, which earned him a pained look from the vicar, whose flighty girls they were. The Maharajah did not appear to have eaten anything that afternoon except one or two cups of tea without milk or sugar. Perhaps he was too full up from all that toffee. Beige saliva was dribbling from the corner of his mouth down onto his jutting chin.

"Oh, goodness, is he not the Casanova?" he cried, dabbing his chin fastidiously with his purple sleeve.

Discreetly summoned by the secretary, Khooshie reluctantly came over. "You are away to the races then, Father?" said he, looking relieved.

"The races? Oh, no, dear son, I am away to my boat, not to the races."

"Never mind, never mind. It is just an expression, Father," Khooshie said, so impatiently that the old man's face collapsed more than ever.

Several guests glared indignantly at the boy for causing his father distress. He didn't appear to notice. "Did you have a good talk with Bartholomew?" he asked indifferently.

"Which one is that, dear son?" the Maharajah asked timidly. "I have met so many odds and sods this afternoon, you see."

"For God's sake, this chap here, Father. He's the reason you came along this afternoon."

"Of course, of course," His Highness squealed. "The one who fished you out of the beverage."

"Really, Father," Khooshie grated; and flushed in the region of his beige cheekbones as he became aware that the vicar's pretty daughters were giggling at him and his father. And he thought he had been hitting it off with them so well, too.

"If you must use slang," Khooshie shouted suddenly, "you should at least use it correctly. The word is drink, not beverage! 'He is fishing me from the drink,' is the correct expression."

"I understand completely," the Maharajah said humbly and fell to studying his son, perhaps trying to understand why the boy, who was quite affectionate when the two of them were alone, grew so impatient whenever there were other people around.

Then, sensing that the Westerners around him did not approve of his humility—as a representative of Indian royalty he ought to be more autocratic and dignified—he looked around for a way to assert himself. Seeing his diminutive chauffeur nearby, gobbling jelly from a bowl held barely an inch from his face, the Maharajah ran over and hit the little fellow with his fly whisk. Then he glanced around, to see how we were taking it.

"And this time, do not abandon the steering wheel in order to peer under the instrument-panel thing whenever you think I am putting my foot on the wrong pedal," the Maharajah shouted; and whacked the chauffeur again, to show us that an Indian could be just as authoritarian as any European.

Next, without a second's emotional readjustment, he aimed his orange smile straight at me. "Give me your arm, Mr. Bandy," he said in his screechy voice and, upon receiving it, leaned on me as heavily as his dehydrated form would allow and started toward his car.

The chauffeur, quite unfazed by the incident, quickly polished off the rest of his jelly, then scuttled ahead of us.

"Perhaps you are wondering, Mr. Bandy," the Maharajah said, "why I did not search for you like mad after I heard what you had done for dear son."

"No, no."

"Yes, I am sure you are wondering. It is only that I was expecting *you* to get in touch with me, you see. That is what usually happens," he said with a resigned twitch of the lips. "When I am in debt to somebody it is never long before I am reminded of the fact. So I was most surprised, you see, when the weeks passed and there was not a word from you, not a single word."

"Ah," I said, perhaps a trifle noncommittally. I had decided not to tell him that I had failed to approach him only because I had not realized that he was indebted to me.

"I couldn't understand it, you see, because people are always cultivating me, and I know it is not for the pleasure of my company," he said, gesturing at himself with feminine grace. The gesture suggested that he was drawing an invisible veil over his frying pan of a face. "So when you didn't appear, in spite of all the fuss and botheration in the newspapers, what a surprise that was, Mr. Bandy, what a surprise!"

Reaching the car, he gently disengaged his arm and climbed into the front passenger seat, from which vantage point he thanked Mr. and Mrs. Lewis profusely for their hospitality.

Then, suddenly behaving as if we had all disappeared into thin air, he turned away and ordered his driver to proceed; which the chauffeur did, swishing over the gravel driveway until the car was in the correct position to reverse straight into the rare tree fern from the Solomon Islands that Mr. Lewis had been cultivating for the past twelve months.

"Hard luck," somebody murmured to me as the open Ford disappeared round a bend in the driveway, "but there you are. I knew all the time that the stories about his generosity were greatly exaggerated."

* * *

Two weeks later, however, the Maharajah summoned me to an address in a side street off Belgrave Square, which turned out to be Irwell Court, one of the city's most elegant blocks of flats. The lobby contained several thousand tons of gray marble, and an elevator surrounded with elaborate ironwork.

According to the doorman, who was an ex-serviceman with numerous long-service and good-conduct ribbons on his uniform, it was actually Khooshie who was renting the flat upstairs. The Maharajah was merely staying with him for a few days while his yacht was having a barnacle scraped off it.

"His young nibs is out shopping with Miss Carruthers at the moment," the doorman confided, referring to Khooshie, who had been occupying this realm ever since his arrival in England several months previously. "But the old nibs is in, if you want to go up. First floor, turn right at the top and don't pay no attention if they tell you there's nobody home. They always say that."

The skinny, wrinkled retainer who opened the door did at first announce that there was nobody at home, but resignedly admitted me when I refused to go away. He led me through two or three large rooms to a thirty-foot lounge containing an Adam fireplace. Opposite the fireplace was a glorious, semicircular window with a view of a church spire. The rest of the light came from a chandelier that, crystallizing in the blue-and-gold ceiling, must have required its own power station.

Khooshie obviously had a handsome allowance. The room was richly furnished. Several landscapes in elaborate frames hung from the walls. You could tell they were important paintings because most of them were too grimy to allow the subject matter to be distinguished.

The Maharajah appeared almost immediately, smiling shyly. After arranging me comfortably in an armchair, he asked without further preamble whether I had heard the stories about his extraordinary generosity.

"I do seem to remember hearing an anecdote or two about it," I whined.

"Tee-hee," he said. "I spread the stories myself."

"Lovely."

"It helps in one's negotiations, you see, to have people think they are to be handsomely rewarded," he said gleefully, tapping my knee with his Woolworth whisk. "They are more ready to compromise their principles, you see."

I wondered why he bothered to carry that fly whisk of his. I'd noticed at the garden party that though more than one fly had buzzed around his head, he had made no attempt to swat them; similarly, he was taking no action today, though two or three tempting bluebottles were droning around the room. Perhaps it was a purely ceremonial instrument, the Indian equivalent of the imperial orb and scepter?

The wizened little man with the caved-in face was regarding me quite seriously, now. "Are *you* ready to compromise your principles, Mr. Bandy?" he asked slyly.

"I would in a moment, Your Highness, if I had any."

"I am sure that is not so," he said politely. Then, after regarding me in silence for a moment: "You are not in a terribly patriotic mood then, Mr. Bandy?"

"Not terribly."

"Ah. And why is that, Mr. Bandy?"

"Oh, I don't know."

"You are thinking the same way as Robert Lewis, I heard. He is saying that the people who started the war and conducted it cannot expect any more respect or loyalty from his generation. Is that it, Mr. Bandy?"

"I don't know. Maybe."

He regarded his fly whisk carefully for a few moments in silence, as if counting the tiny holes in it; then sighed. "It is such a problem," he muttered. "While most debts are easy enough to repay if you have the money or the influence, the trouble is, Mr. Bandy, that you have done something for me that I can never pay for, you see."

I nodded, admiring his cheek. It appeared that he was refusing to discharge an obligation because he had decided that it was too great a debt. It occurred to me to try that on my tailor, some time.

"So I will not insult you by offering you money, Mr. Bandy."

"Go ahead, sir, I wouldn't be the least insulted."

"No, no," he tittered. "I wouldn't hear of it. There is a contempt, you see, in the giving of a reward."

"It's a contempt I could easily put up with, Your Highness."

"No, no. Instead, I am ready to offer you a job, Mr. Bandy."

"Oh, good."

"In India."

"Oh, hell."

"There is a very good salary, Mr. Bandy. Though of course it is much less than you deserve."

"Naturally."

"Fifty thousand a year. I have considered it very carefully, you see, and that is what I have decided. It will go a very long way in India, you know."

"I suppose so."

"For example, I pay my clerks only two hundred rupees a year to start with—and many of them have wives and children. So you see, you are not exactly starting at the bottom," he said, tittering again.

Fifty thousand, eh? I happened to know the value of the rupee, because after meeting the Maharajah, Sigridur had looked up the rate of exchange in a financial newspaper. A rupee was worth one shilling and four pence. Thus fifty thousand was . . . gosh—well over three thousand quid. Three thousand, three hundred and thirty-three pounds, to be exact. That was six times what I had made as a member of Parliament.

However, I was nothing if not a negotiator of uncommon subtlety. So, with a crooked smile: "We're talking about fifty thousand *pounds*, of course," I said, preparing to look somewhat insulted when he replied that he had been talking about nothing of the sort. But it would signal to him that I considered fifty thousand rupees a low offer, and thus perhaps encourage him to raise it another notch or two.

"Yes," said the Maharajah.

After all, he was an Oriental and would be accustomed to bargaining. I mean, if I accepted his first offer he would certainly think less of me. Hence that ridiculous response of mine, which was further designed to inform him that when it came to money I tended to think big. So if he wanted my services he would be well advised to think in rather more ambitious terms.

Except that his answer had rather muddied my subtle ruminations.

"Pardon?" I asked.

"I am saying yes."

"Yes what?"

"You were asking if I was offering you fifty thousand pounds a year."

"Yes?"

"Exactly."

"Exactly what?"

"I *am* offering you fifty thousand pounds sterling a year," he said.

"Oh."

"If you are willing to take on the responsibility."

"Yes, I . . . I'm quite willing to be responsible for fifty thousand pounds. . . ."

"I am talking about the job, Mr. Bandy. But you are not asking yet what the job is."

"Oh, aren't I? Oh, no. Uh . . . what is the job?"

Whereupon he told me; and it sank in almost straightaway, that he was proposing to appoint me deputy commander of his independent state's new air force.

PART II

Outside Supreme Headquarters

Once before, when good fortune embraced me, I had swanked around London so excessively as to turn the stomach of even the most indulgent among my friends. In 1918, unexpectedly raised from captain to lieutenant colonel, I had visited everybody I knew, many of them of such slight acquaintance that after I had shown off my pips and crowns there was nothing left to talk about. I traveled to outlying messes on the flimsiest excuses for the satisfaction of having my inferiors spring to their feet when I appeared. I found excuses to enter one particular mess three times in a row, until the pipsqueaks foiled me by remaining on their feet, loudly discussing tactics and strategy, or at least I assumed that was what they were talking about, as the word "offensive" featured so prominently in their discourse. I even visited wounded comrades in hospital. Naturally I didn't expect *them* to jump to attention, especially as most of them were too incapacitated even to reach for the emergency button. But that was all right, I just wanted to demonstrate that I had succeeded in spite of all their prognostications to the effect that my only connection with the ladder of success would be to hold it steady for others. One wounded chap on whom I paid a call was Lester Pearson, or Mike Pearson, as they called him in the Royal Flying Corps; but he was so bitter about the conduct of the war, and even about the fact that it was taking place at all, that I failed to impress him in the least with my pips, crowns and red tabs. As it turned out I had another fine opportunity to win young Pearson's respect and admiration five years later when I became a member of Parliament. He was then a lecturer in modern history at the University of Toronto. Unfortunately, just as I appeared in Burwash Hall to savor Lester's stupefaction at the news that I actually represented even a tiny fraction of the Canadian people, my former professor of anatomy stalked in and proceeded to tick me off for having given up a career in medicine for one in politics. The sight of tall, glorious me trying to defend myself from a small, hairy anatomist had not exactly convinced Lester that I had greatly improved since the days when I attempted to bayonet him during some gentlemanly army training exercises in the Don Valley.

Now once again, in securing such a post, I was in a position to impress the world with my worthiness. Deputy commander of an entire air force, no less. I wanted everybody to know about it. Unfortunately, secrecy had been strongly enjoined upon me. For commercial, political and various other reasons, said the Maharajah, there was to be no publicity. Even my title must be kept confidential.

"Can't I even have cards engraved, saying B.W. Bandy, Deputy Commander, Royal Jhamjarh Air Force?" I pleaded.

"Oh, dear no, nothing like that, Mr. Bandy."

It was somewhat frustrating, until it occurred to me that there was hardly anybody left to impress anyway. Most of my friends were dead or scattered. And when I mooched along to the hospital to tell them that I was quitting, I couldn't bring myself to blow my own trumpet. I had lost my lip. While it had been fun to preen in front of my fellow officers, there was little satisfaction to be gained in posturing in front of a group of underprivileged porters or fagged-out charge nurses. Similarly I departed from the boarding house for rather more spacious accommodation on Ponsonby Terrace as modestly as possible, not because I was modest but because the attitude of the boarders toward my good fortune might have been one of deference. I could put up with almost any form of contumely; but deference—no, not that.

Naturally I informed the Lewises that I now amounted to a row of beans, but as it was they who had done the gardening, the occasion was somewhat lacking in dramatic effect.

"You are looking quite repulsively puffed up," thundered Mrs. Lewis. "Nevertheless, that is certainly to be preferred to your former hangdog look—or perhaps one should say your hanghorse look. A diet of humble pie may be good for a curate—or Lady Penruddock—but it does not suit you in the least, Bartholomew. Pray do not allow yourself to be downtrodden again."

"I shall do my best, dear Mrs. Lewis."

"Oh, you shall have to do a lot better than that," she said severely.

Perhaps another reason for failing to brag was that I was still not entirely convinced that it was all true and that the offer was genuine. I kept expecting to discover that I had been the victim of some elaborate confidence trick, even though Mr. Lewis had vouched for the authenticity of the Maharajah. Which is why I continued to check up pretty thoroughly on the wizened little ruler, to make sure his credit was good and that he was not a lunatic or a rebel of some sort. I even traveled down to the Isle of Wight one day, to make sure that he really did own a yacht. While reading up on his native country, I had discovered that the independent state of Jhamjarh lay in central India, two hundred miles from the nearest ocean. So what on earth was he doing with a steam yacht? True, its ownership was clearly established in Lloyd's register, but I still felt the need to see for myself. Which was why I had myself ferried across to Yarmouth, where the vessel was said to be berthed. It was there, all right, a long, narrow, white-hulled beauty, all teak, brass and laminated glass, with the Jhamjarh flag at the masthead: a pair of crossed hatchets on a green ground. Good Lord, he had even named the vessel after his son. It was painted on the white stern: *Khooshie, Bristol.*

Even so, it was only when I saw the balance of the funds that had been placed originally at Khooshie's disposal that I finally came to believe in the authenticity of the enterprise. Despite the boy's profligate and usually irrelevant expenditures, there was still nearly five million pounds left in the special account in the bank. *Five million.* My God, the Maharajah really meant business.

It also placed my salary in proper perspective. Until I saw how much the Maharajah was prepared to spend on his schemes, I had considered mine to be an unbelievably extravagant salary. Afterwards—I wondered how soon I could apply for a raise.

There was only one person that I was looking forward to impressing, and that, of course, was Sigridur. I was hoping to put her into a state of shock from which she would never recover. After the way she had been treating me all these months, that was the very least I could do for her in return.

It was all planned. First I intended to invite her to a slap-up dinner at the Café Royal. In fact I had the entire evening planned, right down to the dialogue. I would be direct, sincere and modest as a banana. I would refrain from braggadocio. My revelations would be terrifically casual. First I would inform her that I was now rich, and when, inevitably, she expressed scorn, I would take out my wallet and gaze at her coyly from behind a fan of fivers. Naturally, she would then accuse me of carrying out some spectacular robbery. Whereupon I would show her a receipt, proving that the sum of £12,500 had been credited to me by Deacon's Bank, Birchin Lane.

Next I would inform her in quiet, reserved tones that I was now senior adviser to the Maharajah of Jhamjarh. And the moment she uttered a pshaw, I would whip out the impressive-looking letter addressed To Whom It May Concern, affirming that Mr. Bartholomew W. Bandy, fomerly of Ottawa, Canada, was an official representative in Europe of His Highness the Maharajah of Jhamjarh, and that said Bandy had authority to negotiate contracts, leases or other agreements and make purchases on behalf of the State of Jhamjarh up to a limit of £1,000 without additional authorization, or beyond that limit if suitably authorized. For once, Sigridur would make no response other than to turn pale and regard me with reverence and respect. And at that point I would bring out the narrow velvet box containing a terrifically expensive lady's wristwatch studded with diamonds and toss it across the slap-up dinner table with the peerless nonchalance of a peer to whom the expenditure of sixty-two pounds, ten shillings and sixpence was a mere bagatelle. "Here, this is for you," I would say with the utmost fiscal suavity. Then, while she was still goggling, slavering and showering me with kisses and apologies for ever having doubted me, then and only then would I light the dynamite. After explaining that the watch was a recompense for her financial aid over the past few weeks, I would then inform her that it was also a good-bye gift.

"Good-bye? I don't understand," she would falter; whereupon I would explain that her behavior at the garden party had been the last straw; that I could put up with her insults without bursting too many blood vessels, but that when she made the Maharajah look like a feeble-minded old idiot, that was it. I had decided there and then that I was through with her.

"I see. Now that you are well off, you don't need me anymore," she would respond, "and I am to be cast aside like a handful of cod guts."

"Not at all, Sigga," I would say warmly, patting her hand. "I've been wanting to be rid of you for ages, long before I became rich."

"Why are you doing this to me?"

"Why? Don't you see, Sigga? It's because you're so awful."

"How?"

"How? You've done nothing but bully me, correct me and interrupt me ever since—"

"But I was looking after you."

"Sigga, I've been looking after myself for thirty-one years—"

"Thirty-two. You are now thirty-two years old."

"For thirty-two years, and for most—"

"Your flies are undone. Here, I'll see to it."

"Let go of my manhood this minute!" . . . at which point it occurred to me that the dialogue was not going entirely my way. Even in my imagination she was getting the better of me. Next I'd be visualizing her as she moistened a corner of her napkin and leaned over to wipe my mouth.

So I decided that there was only one way to deal with Sigga, and that was to treat her firmly, fairly but uncompromisingly, so that she would be in no doubt as to where we stood. It was quite obvious from the foregoing conversation—which admittedly hadn't actually taken place, but was almost certain to do so if I was foolish enough to face up to her—that she would never understand how much I resented her unless I made it actively plain. Accordingly, instead of presenting the wristwatch to her in person, I mailed it to her at the hospital residence and, the moment my unfurnished flat on Ponsonby Terrace was ready for occupancy, I marched firmly, fairly but uncompromisingly out of the boarding house, leaving no forwarding address.

There was one other reason why I didn't feel like explaining it all to Sigridur face-to-face. I feared that all her doubts and disbeliefs might be greatly reinforced if I was ever compelled to admit that, while it was true that I was to be deputy commander of the RJAF, that air force did not yet exist.

That was the real reason the Maharajah was employing me. He needed someone to create such an air force from scratch.

After that first interview in Irwell Court, several other meetings followed, mainly to enable us to agree formally on terms. These included an advance that loaded my bank account with the largest single sum I had received since that flirtation with the films back in '22. Mentally converted into dollars, the sum came to more than $60,000. And that was to be only a *quarter* of my annual salary. After months of poverty it seemed so immense a sum that at night I sweated, sleepless, every time I thought about it; while at the same time trying *not* to think about the reason why the Maharajah so urgently desired an air force.

Despite an attempt at dispassion, the urgency was there right from our first meeting in Khooshie's apartment. (Khooshie himself took no part in any of our discussions.) I wasn't aware of the urgency at first, because I myself was so benumbed with surprise. I was even slower at grasping the idea of a private air force in a subcontinent that I had always thought of as being owned, lock, stock and barrel, by the British.

"Surely the British government looks after all you natives," I said. "You know, imperial defense, and all that."

After he had finished twitching, the Maharajah explained slowly and patiently that his was an independent state, not under the direct control of the government of India. A sixty-year-old treaty with Britain allowed him to maintain an armed force for self-defense, and self-defense was what he was now concerned with.

"Shouldn't you first consider establishing an army?" I asked, numbly clutching a glass of fizzy orange, which was all that he was offering in the way of liquid refreshment.

"I already have an army."

"Oh, do you?"

"So now I am wanting an air force," he said, spreading his hands as if it were all as simple as ordering a dozen assorted doughnuts.

"What size of air force?" I asked.

"Oh, medium, please."

"I mean, how many squadrons do you see?"

"I do not see any. You have not started yet."

"No, I mean—" I began, but then let it drop. Finding out precisely what he wished to accomplish with his air force, which would thus establish its size, was not nearly at the top of my list of queries. In fact several hundred others had priority, especially the cost. Was he really prepared for the enormous expense involved in equipping, training and transporting even a single squadron of aircraft?

"It seems to me that it is you who are boggling about all the money," he said, raising his bare feet in the air. He was wearing a white dhoti on this occasion, with apparently little on underneath, in spite of the English summer. "Don't worry, Mr. Bandy. What is important is results. They assure me, you see, that you were a very good organizer in the war." He was now tapping his feet together. "Well, that is all I am wanting, most especially the speed and the energy you are noted for, because it is all a matter of top priority, you see."

As he went on to discuss other matters, I stared at him curiously. There was a businesslike tone to his voice quite different from his usual fumbling delivery. Gone too was any suggestion that naiveté was to be the order of the day. Judging by some of his remarks he had been checking up on me as assiduously as I had been checking up on him, in his case with remarkable thoroughness considering that he had learned my name only three weeks previously.

"You are perhaps wondering why I am offering you such a very big salary when I am aware of what you are earning at present?" he said at one point. "You are thinking to yourself, 'This wonderful Indian fellow could have offered me very much less, and I would have accepted it in half a mo'. But you see, Mr. Bandy, it is a very big job indeed, that perhaps only a man like you can do. You were once a general, but you do not have the, shall we say, the attitude of such officers. I am also paying you so very highly because I have to be quite sure of your loyalty in the face of danger and, no doubt, of a lot of pressure, and I am realistic enough to know that loyalty must be paid for."

"Danger?" I asked uneasily.

"Did I say danger? I meant safety," he said quickly.

I looked suspiciously at his sunken garden of a face, but it expressed nothing but age. He looked so spent that it caused a shock every time one remembered that he was only fifty-two years old.

"I don't know what conclusions you've arrived at about me, Your Highness," I said, praying that the guff I was spouting would not cause him to withdraw his offer, "but I must make it clear that however I feel about governments, and the System, and so forth, I could never fight my own people."

"Why not?"

"Well, I might get hurt."

"Anyway, it is not my intention, Mr. Bandy, to fight the British in India, if that is what you mean."

"Are you sure?"

"Oh, yes, I am sure, thank you. Though in my opinion it would do them a world of good to have a few bombs dropped on them. A terribly stuck-up lot, the British in India, you know."

"Are they?"

"Oh, yes. Are you sure you would not like to machine-gun a few of them, Mr. Bandy?"

"Well, maybe after I've got to know them better, Your Highness."

The Maharajah tittered for a moment, then, serious again, started to unfasten me with the buttonhooks of his eyes. "If only I could confide. . . ." he began; but then he stopped himself by putting a hand over his queer, orange mouth.

"Go on, you can tell me," I wheedled, as if he had been about to confess to some abominable vice or other; but he merely plucked at his dhoti in a preoccupied way.

We remained silent for a good two minutes, each of us occupied with his own thoughts. I don't know about his, but mine were tumbling like circus acrobats. Money. A tremendous challenge. The chance to fly again. Command. Travel. Money. Adventure. Fifty thousand pounds a year.

I jumped up, startling the shrunken little man out of his brown study, and strode to the high, semicircular window. The sun was just setting. The walls of the lounge were glowing red hot. The only sound came from the traffic struggling around Belgrave Square, and from a bluebottle that was butting its head against the glass. I looked round automatically for the Maharajah's fly swatter, but he was not carrying it today.

"Actually, I'm still having trouble understanding the situation, Your Highness," I said at length, watching the bluebottle. It was now lying on the sill, holding its head and complaining. "I mean, forming a private air force. . . ."

"It is not private," he said patiently. "It is public, for my independent state in India."

"But, presumably, to be a real air force, it will have to be armed with guns and bombs and things."

"Of course."

"And what's the government of India going to say about that?"

"My dear Mr. Bandy, they have no objections to my army, so why should they worry about my air force?"

"Still, it all seems very odd to me. . . ."

"What do you think of Khooshie?" the Maharajah asked quickly.

"What?"

"Khooshie. What do you think of him, Mr. Bandy?"

Wrongly assuming that this was a conversational parenthesis that was irrelevant to the original subject, I said, "Oh. Well, I imagine he inspires quite a bit of affection."

"Do you think so? Do you really think so?" he cried, delighted. "Then I am not alone in thinking he is a ripping sort of fellow? And he likes you very much, Mr. Bandy. He says you are like an Indian."

"Thanks very much."

Tears formed in the Maharajah's glowing brown eyes. "When I think how very nearly he was lost to me . . . and what you did . . . I am quite speechless, quite speechless. . . ." He snatched up a handful of dhoti and dabbed at his eyes. And I think it was from that moment that I began to love that queer, vulnerable, emotional, giggly old coot.

"But you know, Mr. Bandy," he went on when he had recovered, "it is very hard for me to rein him in, because he is so like me when I was that age, sewing his wild porridge. It would be wonderful if he could be left alone to enjoy himself. But there is no time, you see. And also I see now that I was asking too much from a boy of eighteen."

"Asking what, sir?" I asked, strolling back from the window.

"Well, you see, Khooshie was supposed to have been organizing the new air force."

"Khooshie?"

"That is why he came to England. To start my air force and learn to fly."

"Khooshie was to organize things?"

"He has done very well, very well indeed," the Maharajah said defensively. "He has already designed an air force uniform."

"A uniform. In only five months, too."

"And he has visited many airplane manufacturers, and so forth. Also he has leased some very nice offices in London."

"Ah."

"I know what you are thinking, Mr. Bandy."

"I'm not thinking, sir. My mind's a blank."

"No, no. You are thinking that Khooshie, a wonderful boy as he is, has not accomplished terribly much in five months. And I am afraid you are right, Mr. Bandy. But of course it is not his fault. The various manufacturers and people he is talking to simply will not take him seriously, even though he has the money to buy anything he wants."

"I can see there might be a slight problem there," I said, visualizing the reactions of grizzled veterans to the approaches of a willowy princeling who looked sixteen years old and who had no experience to speak of, even of flying.

An awful thought suddenly occurred to me. "By the way," I said casually, but sitting down, just in case. "You said that I would be *deputy* commander of the air force."

"That is so, yes, yes."

"Who would the commander be, then?"

"Ah," the Maharajah said, his voice muffled, possibly because he had half buried his face in his whitish clothing. "That is a very good question, Mr. Bandy," he said, looking as if he hoped not to answer it.

"That would be you, wouldn't it, sir?" I asked, perhaps a shade pleadingly. "As titular head of your armed forces? Yes?"

"That is true," he said eagerly. "I would be basically responsible, of course."

"And official commander of the air force. Splendid, sir, splendid," I said, hoping that my firm tones would revamp the potential hierarchy . . . just in case the hierarchy needed revamping. But the Maharajah looked so guilty and defensive that my heart sank into my socks; where it indubitably belonged; for after a few more minutes of prevarication, he finally confirmed one of my many fears: that the chap in charge of the new air force was to be his son.

"Though actually," he added, brightening, as if it were a mitigating circumstance, "he wants his title to be just a little more imposing than that of commander. He wants to be called Air Chief Marshal Khooshie. Will that be all right with you, Mr. Bandy, do you think?" he asked, placing his thin brown hands together as if praying for a tolerant response.

Another three meetings followed that particular get-together before the Maharajah departed on the long voyage back to

India. The final meeting took place at Khooshie's Supreme Headquarters.

That was what he called the offices he had leased in the east-central area of the city, off Cannon Street. In fact he had already placed an order for a brass plate to be inscribed to that effect.

The offices occupied the ground floor of an otherwise empty building on Laurence Pountney Hill, which was not a hill at all, but one of those charming London gardens tucked away behind the begrimed facades of the city. Initially the headquarters comprised a reception area, a large general office and, at the rear of the building, one handsomely proportioned chamber that served as Khooshie's private office. However, we were soon to lease the second floor of the building as well, and ultimately the third floor.

Khooshie's bolt hole was a high-ceilinged space, and it had a lovely Persian carpet on the wall. The window provided a pleasant view of the irregularly shaped square.

Even given the Jhamjarh budget, it was expensively furnished. As well as the carpet, there was an eighteenth-century mahogany table that served as Khooshie's desk, the legs carved into the shapes of court sycophants. It had a marble top on which stood a sterling-silver telephone and a pen-and-ink stand in silver and jade. His office chair was also a product of Elizabethan craftsmanship, a stout affair of carved oak, the back inlaid with an arabesque design and surmounted by all sorts of fancy cresting.

It was remarkably tidy, too. There wasn't a single piece of paper on the entire desk, not a single catalogue, reference work, brochure, contract or even a dunning invoice. On a side table stood a stack of stationery, unused. There was nothing in the desk drawers either, not least because there were no desk drawers.

I caught the Maharajah's eye. He looked away moodily.

"Well, you sure haven't been idle the last few months," I said. "You've furnished the office very nicely." I gestured through the doorway toward the long, general office, which was crammed with brand-new office equipment.

"Thank you," Khooshie said, taking his seat at his desk and proudly placing his delicate hands palm down on its antique surface. "There are a few paintings as well, but they have not yet been hung. The janitor says they are too heavy."

Meanwhile the Maharajah, after another despairing look around Khooshie's HQ, seemed to shrink into himself. His head drooped and he stared at the floor, totally motionless except for the twitch of a muscle in his sunken face.

I could guess how he was feeling. He was realizing that his son had accomplished even less than he had feared. Perhaps the Maharajah had hoped to discover this morning that some progress had been made, some action taken that Khooshie had forgotten to mention; but after shuffling through these expensive chambers and seeing the empty filing cabinets and the new typewriters nicely protected by their dustcovers of dust and failing to spot a single employee—unless you counted the janitor, who had been eating his lunch with his feet on the front reception desk—His Highness could have no further illusions. Khooshie had issued not one contract, purchased not one item of essential equipment, booked not one cubic foot of space in a ship. His only concrete accomplishment—or rather brass accomplishment—was to order a plate etched with the words "Supreme Headquarters Royal Jhamjarh Air Force," with the intention of placing it at the street entrance. And even that work was undone when the Maharajah pointed out as tactfully as possible that, given the nature of the enterprise, he would prefer to avoid publicity rather than attract it.

(The brass plate that finally went up at the front entrance read, "The Prakash Purchasing Commission." Prakash was the family surname.)

By now, Khooshie had sensed that his father was registering something less than his usual approbation. Immediately the boy went into a sulk. "Now what's wrong, Pater?" he asked rudely, driving his fists into the pockets of his flannel bags.

"It is nothing, dear son."

"You do not like the offices? They can always be changed, you know."

"Oh, no, they are wonderful, Khooshie, just wonderful."

"Then why are you emanating waves of distress, Father?"

When the old chap could not bring himself to reply, I thought I had better help him out as tactfully as possible. So I interjected gently, "I think that what is bothering your father, Khooshie, is that you don't seem to have done a scrap of work round here."

"I pay other people to work," he replied, looking surprised.

"Yes, but what other people? Where are they?"

"Obviously they are late for work," he explained, with a restrained smile, showing how tolerant he could be in the face of such feeble mentalities.

"Oh, then you have taken on a few employees, have you?"

"Me? Certainly not. That is up to the office manager."

"But at least you have an office manager?"

"Who knows? I do not concern myself with petty details," Khooshie said, fussing about inside his trouser pockets.

"Well," he burst out angrily a moment later, glaring at his hunched parent, "do you think it can all be done in just a few days?"

"But it is *months*, dear son," the Maharajah faltered, his eyes imploring the boy not to be too angry with him if he now ventured a mild criticism. "And you remember I told you many times, many months ago, dear son, how very important it all was."

"Well, I was busy," Khooshie mumbled defiantly.

"Yes, yes, of course," his father said miserably, looking at Khooshie's beautiful carpet, perhaps wondering why it was on the wall rather than on the floor. "I am well aware that it takes time to do these things. But as you know, it is already August, and I had hoped, dear son, that we would have much accomplished long before next April."

"Why, what happens in April?" I asked quickly, hoping to catch him away from the home base of his guarded replies.

"It is the time of the southwest monsoon, when there is very heavy rain, you see, and flooding."

"Oh, I see," I said, not realizing for months that he was being evasive—the rainy season in Jhamjarh did not begin until about June.

So it was not that that caused me to start to my feet. "But good Lord, sir," I cried, "I hope you don't expect to have a complete air force delivered before April."

"Of course. It is essential."

"But that's impossible, Your Highness. Stap me, I assumed we were talking about some quite distant date, like, well, next leap year. We can't possibly manage it by April."

"See," Khooshie cried triumphantly. "Even he cannot manage it."

"Sir, it would mean we'd have to have everything organized here by next January—hundreds of men, hundreds of tons of equipment, thousands of cubic feet of aircraft—"

"Oh, I am sure you can do it, Mr. Bandy."

"I mean, in effect, you're only giving me a few weeks."

The Maharajah looked at me with his glowing eyes and said softly, "If we cannot have our new air force in place at Djelybad very soon, and certainly before the monsoon season, then I am afraid, Mr. Bandy, that all our efforts will be entirely wasted."

"You mean . . . ?"

"Of course. You might as well give up the whole idea right this very minute and hand back all that lovely money I have already paid you, you see."

"I'm sure we can manage it by next April, Your Highness," I said.

Two days later, he sailed for India, after formally extracting a promise from me that I would deliver the agreed five squadrons of aircraft, together with a full complement of pilots, support and administrative staff and all necessary stores and equipment, to his central Indian state by April first.

All Fools' Day. For it was a promise almost impossible to fulfill.

I mean, it was ridiculous. I was expected to find hundreds of professionals and skilled tradesmen who would be willing to commit themselves to a foreign adventure whose purpose had not even been defined. I mean, it gave me less than six months—and three of those would be needed just for the passage to Bombay. It was absurd.

On the other hand, fifty thousand was not absurd, no sirree bob. So, assuming that the Maharajah needed the assurance strictly for the record without regard to its feasibility, I promised lightly enough; until he added that if I failed to deliver, then his life, and what was much more important, the life of his son, might be forfeit; and the lives of a good many others.

"Forfeit?" I repeated, wearing a smile designed to force him to modify this exaggeration. He did, but the modification was even worse. "It is perhaps already too late," he said softly, so softly that I had to form myself into a question mark to hear him. "But I must try, Mr. Bandy. I must try, for Khooshie's sake."

Me and the Gang

I had familiarized myself to some extent with the aviation scene while seeking employment, so I was able to pass the word around fairly efficiently that I was looking for personnel with flying or ground-staff experience. A few discreet advertisements also went into the aviation journals. Within hours, enquiries began to trickle into the office. Among the first to apply in person was Sylvius Hibbert.

"Hibbert. By heck. Good old Hib. I'll be darned. Are you available? Say no more—you're hired," I cried, drawing him delightedly into the general office and clearing a space near my desk at the far end. "Say, this calls for a drink and a celebration. It's not too early for a drink is it?" I looked at the clock on the wall. "No, it's okay—it's after 9:00 A.M."

Hibbert was a pilot whose flying career had been cut short in 1916 after a crash. He had subsequently become my adjutant at the Dolphin squadron and had proved to be an excellent administrator, particularly adept at securing scarce whiskey and champagne.

"Sit down, sit down, Hib," I went on, perching on my desk and looking him over to see if he had deteriorated as badly as the rest of us; but he appeared to be in a reasonable state of repair, apart from his advanced baldness. Otherwise his mild face with its intelligent blue eyes, snub nose and small, firm mouth was unaltered either by life's laurels or thorns.

"You've developed quite a fallow pate, Hibbert," I remarked, looking wonderingly over his shiny summit.

A slow smile spread over his face as if, after many years abroad in the land, he had finally come home. "You're not exactly trichomic yourself, Bart," he responded, looking up at my own topknot, where the shoreline was threatening to join up with a bald island farther back.

The reply reminded me of one of Hibbert's most marked characteristics, his fondness for expensive words with Greek and Latin forebears. That was what had first earned me Hibbert's undying respect. Not my flying skill, or my lightning wit, or even my beauty, but the fact that I had understood one of his posh words. In conversing with his new CO, he had used the word "mnemonic," but, knowing that military men were often simple, untutored souls, he had immediately defined the word. I had responded testily that I was perfectly familiar with the word, thank you, from which point on he assumed that I was his glossological equal, and began positively to bombard me with foreign roots, not realizing that mnemonic happened to be one of the only three expensive words I knew. Then, to top it off, he found out that I owned a painting by his favorite artist, Matisse, whereupon his respect and admiration for my taste as well as my erudition (one of the other big words I was familiar with) knew no bounds.

If people receive an unfavorable first impression of you, that unpromising start can very rarely be overcome—as I had discovered many times in my career. This was a converse example. Hibbert had been searching for intellectual friendship ever since joining the military. Not surprisingly, he had rarely encountered it. An intellectual was more likely to be found in a road gang than in the Flying Corps. Hibbert was convinced that he had finally encountered a mental and esthetic equal, and from then on I could do no wrong in his eyes . . . though admittedly he was having trouble suppressing persistent doubts by the time I left the squadron.

"Well, this is just great," I exclaimed, hurrying to the filing cabinet. "Let me see, now, what's the Scotch filed under, S for Scotch, or W for . . . ? Ah, here it is. Well, now, tell me everything about yourself, Hib. What are you up to now, for instance?"

"It's a pretty dull story compared with your life, sir," he said in that familiar self-deprecating way of his.

"Good Lord, Hib, you mustn't address me as sir," I said happily, filling up my own tumbler. "A bow or curtsy will be quite sufficient, you know. Bottoms away." I swallowed half the contents of the glass. "How d'you mean, compared with my life?" I asked.

"I've followed your career with a great deal of interest. From the steppes of Russia to the steps of Parliament, as it were."

"Ah, well, I can explain that, Hib," I said defensively.

"What I can't understand is why, with all your achievements, you aren't a household name."

"What name would that be?"

"I mean, you did so much for this country. And what did you get?"

"A CBE?"

"And this latest exploit—crossing the Atlantic single-handed—that was a superb achievement. But—"

"Yes, well, you have to see my side of it, Hib," I said, avoiding his shiny gaze. He had still not entirely overcome a tendency to hero worship. I wondered if I could put him and Sigridur together, to average their assessments. "Anyway, tell me all about yourself, Hib. What are you doing now?"

There wasn't much to tell. After the war he had gone back to university with the intention of taking up teaching but, finding teaching jobs scarce, he had ended up working for a wine merchant. He was still vinously employed, as he put it.

"I told you it was pretty dull," he said, as I suppressed a yawn.

As he talked, I watched carefully to see how he took his whiskey. If he hurled it at his uvula too eagerly, I would have to backtrack on that first hearty invitation. Quite a number of former acquaintances seemed to have become alcoholics. Anxiety, depression and other symptoms of a sustained trauma were the lot of perhaps most of the men who had fought on the Western Front. Only alcohol seemed to afford some protection. Freudian treatment certainly had no effect. The terrifying dreams of the shell-shocked, for instance, could hardly be interpreted in terms of sexual symbolism.

I felt really lucky that I myself had come through the war unscathed, with only occasional periods when I couldn't decide whether to kill myself or have another cup of tea. In common with the others, I had lost all belief in God, church and state, in the inherent goodness of man, in outwardly imposed discipline, in authority, even in virtue itself; but these were minor penalties compared with the furies and terrors that beset so many former fighting men. Would those poor souls ever recover from the shock of war and the discovery that their leaders had marched them over a quicksand? Even Hibbert, serene as a bowling green, would confess in time that he was sometimes afflicted with daylight brainstorms in which he saw himself eviscerating bishops, shredding newspaper proprietors into crimson spaghetti and obliterating square miles of government buildings, complete with howling occupants.

"Drink up," I exhorted, quickly polishing off my own drink. This was to get it out of the way, so as to obtain a clear view of Hibbert's problem, if he had one. I watched very closely, to see if he followed the classic pattern of the confirmed drinker: the first, fast, desperate snatch and gulp, followed by a quickly poured second drink, which, however, would be sipped with studied indifference, as if the imbiber were trying to prove that he could take it or leave it. Accordingly, as I hurriedly poured another for myself, I was really pleased when Hibbert not only declined a second drink but seemed to be having difficulty in coping with the first, a half-tumbler of malt whisky from the Isle of Islay. (I could afford the very best, nowadays.)

"So," he said after a pause. "What's it all about, sir? The aviation community's buzzing with rumors that you're recruiting for the Canadian Air Force. Is that it?"

"Not quite. . . . You're still in touch with the aviation community, are you, Hib? That could be a help. I need at least eighty pilots."

"Eighty!"

"But all I've signed up so far is two."

"Eighty pilots!"

"And a good many hundred ground staff."

"Good heavens."

A moment later I learned to my delight that he had even kept up with a few of the survivors of our Dolphin squadron. One of them, John Derby, had only recently left the air force and might still be available. In fact, Hibbert had tried to organize an annual reunion; but after a couple of years it had fizzled out. "We found that we were spending most of the time talking about you," he said with a pale smile. "Your exploits, eccentricities and such."

"Eccentricities?" I frowned.

"Flying with that matted fox fur of yours, persecuting your superior officers, things like that—jumping on top of prize peacocks."

"That was an accident."

"We laughed for hours about things like that," Hibbert said, shaking his head negatively as I wiggled the bottle at him before pouring another for myself. "But anecdotes about you didn't seem quite enough of a justification for an expensive reunion, so. . . ."

For more than an hour we gossiped about people we knew, until the inevitable silence fell.

"Well," I said, sliding my starboard buttock off the desk and sitting rather more officially in my chair. "I'd like to offer you a senior position on the staff, Hib. We'll sort out your precise duties later, if that's all right. The pay is exceptionally good, by the way."

When I told him how much, he started. "Just as I thought," he said. "It *is* an illegal enterprise."

"No, it isn't."

"What, then?"

I clicked the whiskey glass ruminatively against my teeth for a moment. Then: "The rumors are fairly close, Hib. Except that I'm recruiting for an Indian air force."

He drew back his head like a startled tortoise.

"I'll tell you all about it, Hib, but it's to be treated as highly confidential, okay?" I said, and proceeded to summarize the several discussions I'd had with the Maharajah, leaving out only his final words.

When I finished, Hibbert continued to stare intently for several seconds as if I were still speaking. Then he arose and paced up and down the long office, repeatedly smoothing his balding head with a pale, artistic hand. That was another familiar mannerism. He always did that when he was agitated.

Finally he halted in front of one of the new Remington typewriters. He ran a forefinger through the dust that coated it, then started to turn the platen thoughtfully. The clicking sounded loud in the long, unpopulated office.

"Somehow," he said slowly, "I can't see the government being too pleased at the idea of an Indian ruler forming his own air force."

"Why not? He already has an army," I said, pleased to have, at last, someone with whom I could discuss the situation, but disturbed to hear him expressing the same doubts that were assailing me.

"Yes, but an air force? The very last word in military sophistication?" He paused, to allow for comment. There was none. "And though you say you're only planning on five squadrons, good Lord, Bart, the way India Command has been transfusing some of their strength to the trouble spots in Iraq, that's probably more than the RAF has out there."

"He assures me we'll never be asked to fight the British, you know."

"I doubt if that would reassure the government. I mean, why does he want it?"

"Ambition? To create a modern state? Gratify his ego? Make him feel puissant or contemporary? An excuse for a fancy air display? At the moment we can only speculate, Hib, and I'm not one to waste my energies waving useless ifs and buts and maybes about. He swears it's not for use against us, and that's good enough for me."

Finally Hibbert said that he would think about it and let me know; that if it was anyone but me in charge he would not have considered the proposition for a moment but would have turned it down out of hand; which was what he was still likely to do.

To my relief, he returned on the following day to accept, after reassuring me that he was doing it strictly for the money. "My attitude is purely mercenary," he said earnestly. "There's not one iota of idealism or ideology involved. I just want to reassure you that my motive is one of pure greed, that's all."

"Of course. Loyalty to the rupee is all we ask."

He then volunteered to do what he could to spread the word among his aviation contacts. The result was an increased flow of applicants of all kinds, from flight observers to military policemen.

Though some were unemployed, a surprising number had secure jobs. I asked one former armorer why he was willing to give up a steady job in a Midlands engineering shop for the discomfort and uncertainty of a life in far-off India.

"I dunno," he said.

"You're ready to face the heat, the smell, the flies, the hostility and the peculiar culture out there, just for much higher pay?" I asked.

"Well, yeh."

"And you're prepared to give up your mother and the local pub . . . Sunday papers in bed, . . . holidays in Llandudno or the Isle of Man . . . going round the garages picking out that new motorbike for yourself . . . rousting about with the lads at weekends or flirting with the mill girls . . . eating toffee apples down at the market . . . playing football on the waste ground? You're prepared to give all that up?" I said admiringly; but received no reply. This was because he wasn't there. He had departed in a hurry, having apparently come to the conclusion that he would be better off where he was.

Luckily, John Derby was not so easily discouraged. Contacted by Hibbert, he turned up at the office one Saturday, and we had a delighted reunion.

"Good to see you, John," I said, "even if you do look more dissipated than ever."

"And you still look like a Roman ruin and as impertinent as ever toward your betters," he replied in that humorously sour way of his. After which we shook hands and smiled happily, reminded of the only good to have come out of the war, the comradeship.

Derby's history over the past six years was a familiar enough story. As with so many combatants, he had been psychically damaged by his war experiences. He still did not feel that he had regained a normal perspective on life. "I even went to live in your country, in 1919," he said. "That just shows how disoriented I was."

"You mean in Canada? Why didn't you look me up?"

"I wasn't in the mood for company."

"Well, I wasn't there, anyway. I was in jail."

He had lived almost as a hermit on Vancouver Island for eighteen months, he said, trying to overcome feelings of rage and depression. He had returned to England in 1921, and rejoined the RAF; but the prospects were so poor—"I wasn't due to be promoted to flight lieutenant until 1927"—that he had resigned his commission just a few weeks previously and gone to work for Handley Page, flying passengers in C400s. But the pay was so poor, five pounds a week, that he had been about to give up aviation altogether.

"Do you still have good contacts in the air force?" I asked.

"I suppose so. I even did a stint at the Air Ministry, just down the road."

"That might come in useful."

"What's this Maharajah of yours going to do with his air force?" Derby asked.

"Same as with his private army, I suppose: hold a march-past and fly past every few months."

"I gather you don't know for certain?"

"I have his assurance that we'll never be asked to fight our own chaps, and with the money he's paying, that's all I care about," I said.

"Well, if that assurance is good enough for you, it's good enough for me, I suppose," Derby said.

Another useful member of the staff was Roland Mays. It was Hibbert who recommended him for the job of paymaster. He said that it would not be easy to find an accountant with military experience who would be willing to leave the country for an indefinite period, however much we were offering; but Mays, Hibbert thought, might jump at the chance, for he was anxious to leave the country even sooner than we had planned. He wished to escape from his wife.

When I heard this, I naturally pictured a timid, henpecked type with eyes as jumpy as fleas. He turned out to be one of those supremely polished and confident English gentlemen, forty-six years old and of a distinguished appearance, right down to the artful touch of gray at the temples. He owned the kind of well-fed, contented and self-confident face that would surely bring waiters scurrying to his side from all corners of the restaurant. The tie of a famous public school hung from his neck, and precisely the right amount of white handkerchief peeked from the top pocket of his perfect suit.

Being a careful custodian of his own dignity, he had been at pains to explain his personal circumstances to his friend Hibbert, so as to avoid exposing himself to embarrassment when he met the boss. He had no wish to put himself at a moral disadvantage, not least because the boss was an unknown quantity. All Mays knew about the fellow were the facts, which, of course, told him nothing. The boss was not a public-school man, that was certain. He wasn't even English. I mean, gad, he might even be another uncouth colonial, like Lord Beaverbrook.

"Bartholomew Bandy," Mays was reported to have murmured. "Got an alliterative name, I notice. That's not in very good taste for a start."

So he conveyed the somewhat embarrassing personal details to Hibbert, who was then expected to pass them on to me. It didn't do Mays a bit of good. Practically the first thing I said to him at the interview was, "So—I hear you're on the lam from your wife."

Though not a twitch disturbed his perfectly manicured countenance, no doubt all his fears about the couthness of the boss were instantly realized.

However, as Hibbert had given me the rundown, I didn't nose too closely into the reason why Mays was prepared to give up a vice-presidency in a firm of chartered accountants for the rigors of military life in a not particularly salubrious sector of the globe. It appeared that he had made the mistake of marrying late, after he had grown used to his bachelor freedom, and had compounded the error by marrying for money without looking carefully enough at the cash box. Worse still, his wife was the daughter of the man who had founded the firm of chartered accountants. Mays's wife, I understood, was attractive enough, but she had a marked distaste for the side of marriage that "centered in the bedroom" as she put it—though Mays had offered to do it in any room of her choice, or even in the orangery on warm days. Consequently, a decent interval after the marriage—ten months—Mays established a mistress in a Bayswater flat. His wife found out and ejected him from their imitation Tudor abode, while his father-in-law proceeded to make it difficult for him to remain in the firm. But then the wife, believing that she had little chance of bagging other marital game if she lost him, attempted to get him back. The more he resisted, the more determined she became to hang onto him. Twice already she had tracked him down, and her persistence was starting to unnerve him. It was bad enough being driven out of his London flat, then out of his mistress's flat, he told Hibbert, but he had been forced to give up his club as well, after his wife created a scene in the lobby. So India was beginning to look like a safe haven.

Actually, Mays had provided me through Hibbert with so much information about himself, that there was practically nothing for us to talk about after the first few minutes of the interview. So we talked about me, instead.

"That's very interesting," he said, his plumpish jaw quivering with the effort to suppress a sequence of yawns when I'd finished telling him about my early struggles. Nevertheless, his light blue eyes were alert enough as he asked various subtle questions in an attempt, I think, to get a handle on me and fit me into the right pigeonhole.

It wasn't easy. He was having difficulty in reconciling my Savile Row suiting with the Gothic entity that it enclosed. For instance, he had been trying quite hard to find out if I belonged to a decent club. You could tell a lot about a chap by his choice of club. He set great store by a decent club.

"Mine's the Junior Carlton—at least until my wife finds out," he said. "Yours is the Grosvenor I think somebody said?"

For a moment I was tempted to tell him that it was the Whippet and Greyhound Fanciers' Club, but then reminded myself that I was now a pillar of the community and such frivolities were no longer seemly.

"I'm hoping to be proposed for the United Services," I said. "Anyway, Mr.—"

"Really?" he said skeptically. "Isn't that just for senior officers?"

"I was a senior officer. Now, Mr. Mays—"

"Yes, of course you were. I do apologize, Mr. Bandy," he said with a charming smile. "All the same, I should have thought you'd apply to a political club," he went on, sounding as if he didn't think I'd get into one of those either. "You were a member of Parliament in Ottawa, weren't you?"

I wondered how it was that a perfect stranger could find out so much about me in a few hours, while Sigridur had been unable to manage it in months.

"For a while, yes," I said. "Now, Mr. Mays, I—"

"And before that you were a film actor, I believe."

"Look here, Mays, who's interviewing whom here?"

"Of course. Carry on," he said with silky equanimity. But before I could do so: "As a matter of fact, sir, your name cropped up in the club just the other day."

"Oh, yes? Anyway, Mr. Mays, I don't—"

"The present Chief of Air Staff, I believe he is."

"Concerning the position of paymaster, I . . . what?"

He raised a polished hand and covered his mouth at this double take. I had the impression that he was thoroughly enjoying the interview. I was sure of it when he looked up again to reveal a sparkle of well-bred amusement in his powder-blue eyes. "The Chief of Air Staff heard your name being mentioned in my corner of the lounge, and it produced quite a marked reaction. The old boy does not appear to approve of you, Mr. Bandy."

"The CAS is a member of your club?"

"Yes. I shouldn't call the old boy an old boy, of course; he's only five years my senior."

"I hope you didn't tell him what we were up to, Mr. Mays."

"How could I, Mr. Bandy?" he said with a smooth smile. "You haven't told me yet."

In the silence that followed we stared at each other unblinkingly. Though he was the sort of person whose company I could enjoy—the frictionless, imperturbable, not entirely lacking in humor sort—I wasn't too happy that he was clubby with the CAS, who was quite likely to make things difficult for us if he ever found out what we were up to.

"You're a bit old for this job, Mr. Mays," I said tentatively.

That startled him for a moment. But then he looked more interested than ever, as if I were only a mildly amusing spectacle, but nonetheless original enough. "I'm in excellent shape, you know," he replied, complacently smoothing his waistcoat over his flat stomach.

"It's likely to be a grueling service."

"You won't get anyone else of my age with my experience, you know."

"I don't *want* anyone with your experience."

"It won't be easy finding another adventurous accountant, old boy—that's practically a contradiction in terms. So if I were you, sir, I'd grab me while you have the chance."

We stared at each other for several seconds; and ended up laughing.

"I quite like the idea of being a member of an independent air force," he added.

My face folded up again. "Oh, hell," I said. "You know about that, too?"

"You don't think I'd apply for a job like this without a spot of investigation, do you?"

"I guess not."

"The very fact that you're trying to keep it a secret is bound to stimulate even more curiosity than it already warrants."

"I suppose so."

He paused, carefully caught my eye and said quietly, "Whether you take me on or not, Mr. Bandy, I'm a seasoned club man, you know—discretion itself."

He was telling me that whatever the CAS learned about us, it would not be from him. I decided then and there that I liked Roland Mays and was prepared to trust him, despite his past record: he had been assistant paymaster general of the British Army.

After two weeks of interviews during which Hibbert, Derby and I signed up more than twenty pilots and dozens of ground staff, I was getting over my surprise at how easy it was proving to be. I had expected much difficulty in attracting the right kind of pilot, the kind with experience and a spirit of adventure. In fact the majority who applied *were* unsuitable, lacking either one quality or the other, or both. But that still left many excellent applicants, including a few Canadians and Americans. Among the English applicants were a couple of boyhood pals who seemed more like refugees from the music hall than responsible officers. Even their nicknames sounded like a variety turn. Their real names were Fletcher and Carberry, but they had been known since childhood as Fetch and Carry.

They were inseparable. They even came into the interview together, arm in arm, a pair of fresh-faced youths three years out of Fallow Grammar School, the first flyers I had met who had not served in the Great War. Nevertheless, they had nearly two hundred hours each in their log books. Some wartime pilots didn't have that many.

Backed by their families, who had forked out for two war-surplus Avro 504s, they had been joyriding passengers up and down the country for the past three summers. The foul weather this year had finally defeated them. They had been looking for alternative flying work since the beginning of July.

"What else have you flown, apart from the 504?"

"Just the DH4, sir," Carry said, then jerked his thumb at Fetch. "And he's flown the Crumpler."

"The name is Rumpler, old bean."

"It was Crumpler after you'd finished with it."

"Look who's talking—the chap who dunked that town councillor johnny in a sewage farm."

"He didn't seem to mind."

"Probably didn't notice any difference from his usual habitat."

"No, it was because he'd already fouled himself during the takeoff."

"No wonder, the way you fly."

"I fly with élan."

"Elan, your French instructor, is he?"

"Gentlemen, gentlemen," I said heavily. "Is this the way you usually carry on?"

"Yes, sir, he always carries on that way. It's disgusting, I think."

"That's true, sir, it's disgusting the way he thinks."

"Yes, well," I said firmly, "you're not in the lower fourth now, Fetch."

"I'm Carry, sir, He's Fetch."

"This bickering is all very childish, you know."

"Yes, sir."

"Very well, then." I cleared my throat, rearranged some paper on my desk, then asked them why they wanted to join my team; and promptly learned that it was because I was organizing it. It was I who had first roused their interest in flying.

"Me? How?"

"You remember when you delivered that speech at Fallow, sir?"

"Vividly."

"Well, we were in the audience. We were only fourteen at the time."

"I was fifteen."

"You were only a month older than me."

"And through sheer talent I'm still your senior, so shut up when I tell you to."

"All right, I will."

"But you haven't."

"Yes, I have."

"No, because you've just spoken, therefore you haven't shut up."

"Because you haven't told me to, yet."

"Yes, I have."

"No, you haven't. You said I was to shut up *when* you told me to—isn't that right, sir?"

They looked at me expectantly. I shook my head in disgust. "Look here," I said. "We have no time for this sort of nonsense in our organization. We have another three applicants to see before noon, so—"

"There's only two, now," Derby said. "Cook isn't coming."

"Yes, he is," I said.

"No, he isn't," Derby said.

"I've definitely got the catering officer down for eleven-thirty."

"Oh, yes, *he's* coming."

"There you are, then."

"It's Cook who isn't coming."

"You've just said he was."

"No, I didn't."

"You said the catering officer was coming."

"That's, right."

"Well, that's what I said—Cook's coming."

"No, he's canceled."

"He's canceled but he's coming?"

"Wait," Derby said. "I'm beginning to suspect that a slight misunderstanding may have arisen. Who are you talking about, sir?"

"Yes."

"Yes, what?"

"Surely you mean yes, Hoo."

"Who?"

"That's right."

"What's right?"

"Hoo."

"Who what?"

"Hoo's his last name."

"Who's last name?"

"Right."

"Oh, you mean Mr. Wright's last name? Now I understand! It was another misunderstanding! You're talking about somebody called Wright, aren't you?"

"Who?"

"Wright."

"No, I was talking about One Lung Hoo, the Chinese catering officer."

"Ah, now I understand," Derby said blandly, glancing at Fetch and Carry, who were looking a trifle bewildered.

When they had left and Hibbert had come over to find out what we were laughing about, John said, "By the way, I've been meaning to ask. When am I going to meet the boss?"

"Here I am, how d'you do?" I said, still feeling silly.

"No, not you—the real boss. This Indian prince of yours."

That sobered me up all right. I caught Hibbert's eye. Both of us looked away.

"I've only met him once myself," Hibbert murmured, moving private correspondence around my desk until I slapped his hand away.

"Really?"

"He rarely comes into the office until after lunch," I explained.

"But I've been here for days, and I've never seen him," Derby said, staring at us suspiciously.

Inevitably the day arrived when Khooshie actually came to work. He sauntered in unexpectedly one morning while I was holding a meeting with Hibbert, Derby and "Mays the Clubman" as I had taken to calling Roland, to his decreasing amusement.

The first disturbing sight was that Khooshie was wearing mustard plus-fours. The second was that he was clutching a roll of drawings.

"Ah, Bandy," he said in the upper-class drawl he had picked up from his fashionable young friends, "I want you to look at these designs that I am specially commissioning from that artist fellow. The one that Bubba introduced me to. What is his name again, the one in the beret with the very big bow tie? Anyway, here is the one I like myself. It is our pilot badge. What is your opinion?"

"Ah, Khooshie," I cried. "I'll be with you in a moment. These gentlemen are just leaving."

"What d'you mean, just leaving? We work here," Derby said; so I was forced to introduce Khooshie.

"So this is the new design for our pilots' wings, is it?" I cried, unrolling the drawing. However, I calmed down pretty quickly once I saw it.

"An owl?" I asked.

"Yes."

"It's an owl."

"It is most artistically drawn, is it not?"

"Yes, but an owl? Sitting on a park bench?"

"It is a branch."

"But Khooshie—are you sure that's appropriate? For pilots' wings?"

"It is true that I asked for an eagle with wings outspread in flight, or perhaps a falcon. But Bubba's friend the artist has convinced me that outspread wings is the most appalling cliché."

"Yes, but—"

"By the way, you have not yet told these gentlemen who I am," Khooshie reminded me, smiling a shade reprovingly.

"Ah, yes," I said. "Well, this is Prince Khooshie."

"I mean, who I am in our new air force."

"Ah. Well, Khooshie is our. . . . He's also involved in this enterprise of ours, you see," I said in a forthright way; and rolling up his design for the new RJAF pilots' wings, I attempted to guide the lad into his office at the back of the building.

"Please, you are holding my arm as if in a vise," he squealed. "I am wanting to talk to my men, if you don't mind."

"Course, Khooshie, course. But won't you be late for lunch?"

"I am waiting for my new uniform to be delivered," the boy said irritably; but the mention of the uniform replaced the sulky expression with one of glowing delight. "Oh, Bartholomew, it is just beautiful. Wait until you see it!"

The expression changed again, to one of concern. "But perhaps there is something else you can advise me on, Bartholomew. I cannot decide whether to have six or seven gold rings on my sleeve. I have been working my fingers to the bones, Bartholomew, deciding on the various ranks, and according to this cogitation, I, as commander, should have seven rings. But you see, the seventh ring reaches the elbow, so that I cannot quite bend the arm, you see."

"I see. Yes, yes. That *is* a problem. But now—"

"Commander?" Derby asked.

There was a shrill silence. "Ah," I said, after half a mo. "Perhaps I should explain that as the Maharajah's official representative in Europe, Prince Khooshie naturally has to have *some* say in the, the general running of the, the. . . ."

"I am to be supreme commander-in-chief of the air force," Khooshie said proudly.

Derby looked at me. I moved slightly, farther out of reach. "Though of course the actual title has not been definitely decided on," I said quickly.

"That is true. I have not decided. Perhaps Air Chief Marshal would be better, do you think?"

"Prince Khooshie is . . . how old?" Derby asked.

"Eighteen."

"And how many hours has he?"

Khooshie went over to the calculating machine, and worked it out. "A hundred and fifty-seven thousand, six hundred and eighty hours," he said.

"I meant, how many hours *flying* time."

"Twenty."

"And he is to command the air force."

"In a sense, John, that is true. That is, he will command in his capacity as, how shall I put it. . . ."

As it turned out, there was no need to put it. Khooshie's uniform arrived from the tailor at that very moment.

His handsome, beige face aglow, Khooshie rapidly unwrapped the deluxe parcel and removed the tunic. This he hung on the coat rack from a hanger. Then, unfolding the trousers, he held them below the tunic so that we could admire the ensemble.

And we certainly were impressed. No one moved a muscle for at least ten minutes.

The suit was pure white. It had royal blue epaulettes six inches long, with gold stripes. It had multicolored enamel badges on both the left and right breast pockets. One portrayed the god Siva; the other was the emblem of the new air force, depicting a falcon clawing at a decayed carcass. Gold badges were pinned to the lapels, and temporary pilots' wings had been pinned to the left breast, underlined by a row of ribbons. And as Khooshie had said, there were seven gold rings on each sleeve.

"The tailor has assured me that these medal ribbons here are all color coordinated," Khooshie said. "And as for what is to be worn under the tunic, I am suggesting a green shirt with a red tie, though possibly that might not go too well with the rest of the uniform. What do you think, Bartholomew? I am insisting that the overall effect must be tasteful, of course," he finished, looking at each of us in turn with his spiky-eyelashed eyes.

"I . . . yes," Mays said.

"Definitely," Derby said almost inaudibly.

"M'oh," I said, intending to say, "M'oh yes," but finding my throat too dry to croak more than the initial vowel, which produced a brief lowing sound.

Later, of course, when Khooshie had gone, I had to assure the chaps that they would never, ever have to wear a uniform even remotely similar to the one that had just blinded them.

"I mean, my God, Bart," Derby said faintly. "A South American dictator would think twice. . . ."

"Yes, don't worry, we'll change it."

"And the badges."

"Yes, them too."

"Specially the gold one featuring the ice-cream cornets."

"Those are the Himalayan mountains, not ice-cream cones—"

"I mean, even for a musical comedy there are limits—"

"Yes, yes."

"And what's this about air chief marshal? Good God, he's hardly old enough to be an aircraft apprentice."

" 'S okay, John, I'll soon talk him into accepting a more appropriate title . . . I hope."

And so forth. But it was another reminder that Khooshie would have to be kept busy on various false errands for the next few months.

Signing Some Contract or Other

The formation of a small air force from scratch soon involved Hibbert, Mays, Derby and myself in prodigiously long hours of talk, travel and plain office drudgery. There seemed to be a thousand wrinkles a day to be ironed out, uncountable conferences to attend, trips to be made, negotiations to be conducted and obdurate Indian princes to be cajoled. To handle the ever-increasing weight of work, we were having to take on more and more temporary staff: receptionists, assistant-typists and various other assistants, messengers, managers, agents and clerks. Our ground-floor offices were soon jammed, and we had to rent space on the floor above and, a month later, on the floor above that as well, until we ended up leasing the entire building on Laurence Pountney Hill.

In addition to the crush of staff, we were trying to cope with hordes of visitors a day—salesmen, shipping clerks, manufacturers and representatives of the various companies we were dealing with—while at the same time attempting to interview dozens of applicants skilled in the fifty different trades that were needed to run just one squadron. We were also having to see to their present and future financial, transport, health and social needs, and their work requirements.

As if all that weren't enough, we were frantically busy making the shipping arrangements for an extraordinarily complicated range of new and used equipment, from ten-ounce tensiometers to two-ton Huck starters. Even Hibbert and Roland Mays could hardly keep it all straight in their minds and notebooks, while I could have used twice as many business hours in the day. I loved every minute of it.

This in spite of some quite worrying problems in obtaining the aircraft types that we had decided on. I must confess that I hadn't anticipated any problem there, for literally tens of thousands of new fighter and bomber aircraft, assembled or nearly so, had been left over after the war ended. Large numbers of these machines had been put on the market. They had gone principally to scrap merchants, who were supposed to dispose of the aircraft only after they had been transformed into scrap. But many of the merchants merely slashed an easily mended fuselage, or took a sledge hammer to an engine and, by an amazing coincidence, always managed to strike only the easily replaceable number plate. In this way, otherwise unharmed engines went for £15, and brand-new airframes for £50. I had snatched up several such bargains myself after the war.

The British government got rid of many additional aircraft by presenting them to Commonwealth countries, or through sales to other governments. Even so, despite this profligate distribution, there should have been thousands of aircraft left over. Yet after weeks of traveling as far north as Dumfries and as far west as Bristol, the most we could scrounge together were two Vimy bombers, half a dozen used Camels, three DH4s and a decrepit Harry Tate. This mixture, fixed up, flown to a base near Tilbury and lined up at the edge of the field preparatory to crating for overseas shipment made, I thought, a very unimpressive showing. I had been visualizing impeccable lines of sparkling new fighters and the very latest bomber/reconnaissance machines.

There were a large number of surplus aircraft around. They were owned by the RAF and stored throughout the country in hangars, yards, lots, depots, stations and aircraft parks. But as we were still trying to keep our activities secret, we stayed well clear of that source of supply, for the time being, anyway. Even at this early stage, we had a sneaking suspicion that the government might not take kindly to the idea of our buying RAF aircraft so that we could establish a rival air force in their most prized overseas possession.

The only course left to us was to turn to the manufacturers and get them to build the equipment from scratch, a pretty frustrating alternative considering the enormous number of aircraft sitting idle in the country. But even here we hit a snag. As far as bombers were concerned, the only type that could be delivered on time and in the required numbers was the DH9, which was still being manufactured for overseas customers. The only trouble was that I wasn't too keen on the DH9, as I had fallen out of one at fifteen thousand feet. But there was no alternative; so, with no great satisfaction, I finally placed an order with de Havilland for thirty of the type, complete with spares; and these were actually delivered before the blade of the guillotine fell.

As for fighter aircraft, I had been hoping to acquire the latest Vickers design, but it turned out that the only machine that could be delivered in sufficient quantities by our deadline was the Snipe. However, that did not dismay us. Though six years old, the Sopwith Snipe was still probably the best production fighter with an exceptionally strong airframe.

On my previous visit to the Sopwith company's successor, the Hawker company, I was a job applicant. This time I turned up as a customer. Naturally I exploited the situation to the utmost, arriving in one of Khooshie's chauffeur-driven limousines and accompanied by my paymaster general, Roland Mays, and an aristocratic aide, Freddy Montglass. Twenty-six-year-old Freddy was more than six and a half feet tall, but tended to hunch and stoop, as if fearful that his height might be construed as pretentiousness. Despite a substantial entry in Burke's Peerage, he was almost pathologically humble. "I'll quite understand if you can't use me," he'd said at the initial interview. "I've dashed little to offer, I suppose, except I know a few people in society. But of course that's not what you're looking for, is it?"

"Well, not really. But—"

"Of course, on the very slight chance that you did consider taking me on, I might just possibly be useful in running errands for you, getting you a good table at the Savoy and things like that. . . . But of course a girl typist could probably do that for you just as well."

"Not at all."

"And though I don't expect much in the way of salary, I expect a girl would cost even less."

Even when I told him that I would try him out as my personal assistant, he tried to dissuade me. "Are you sure you really need me, sir?" he asked earnestly. "I mean, when you get right down to it, I don't know anything. I went to Oxford, you see."

Finally I said, "Look here, Montglass, if it makes you feel any better, I'm only taking you on for snobbish reasons. I quite fancy the idea of having a viscount for a personal assistant."

"Oh, I see. It's not because of any merit on my part?"

"None at all."

"Ah, well, that's different. In that case I accept . . . unless of course," he added anxiously, "you've changed your mind in the last forty-five seconds . . . ?"

Naturally the three of us were accorded the red-carpet treatment at Hawker from the entire board of directors. Among them was the Fred Sigrist who had turned me down so regretfully just a few months previously, and the great T.O.M. Sopwith himself. It was all wonderfully satisfying, this reception, not least because Sopwith had followed my wartime career and was aware that much of my success had been accomplished in his aircraft designs. But best of all was the reaction in the boardroom when they heard that I was prepared to place an order for sixty aircraft and spares. They needed to call on every ounce of British self-control to save themselves from the shame of exhibiting profound satisfaction. It was the largest order they had received since the good old wartime days.

"Mm, I think we can fit you into our production schedule," Mr. Sopwith said, "with a bit of juggling." But then he betrayed his excitement by responding to some feeble jest with a cacophonous and totally uncharacteristic guffaw. Pure nerves and elation.

Quickly recovering, he turned to Fred Sigrist and said in an undertone that was meant to be overheard, "Though we may have to open up E Shed along Elm Grove, eh, Fred?"

"With such a rush job," Sigrist told us cautiously, "I'm afraid it'll increase the cost of the aircraft a little."

"Speed is essential, regardless of cost," I said, ignoring Mays across the table, as he winced at me pointedly. Sigrist, however, closed his eyes ecstatically. He was busily multiplying £7,000 by sixty . . . and then adding in the spares . . . and waterproof casing. . . .

He had good reason to be happy. Three technical and financial conferences later we handed over the first of two payments of about a quarter of a million pounds each. During the elaborate lunch that followed, practically the entire work force looked into the company dining room to admire us as we stuffed food into our faces, while the directors quietly worshiped us with their eyes as they slavered into their fresh fruit cups and attempted to suppress their curiosity as to why we needed thirty bombers and sixty fighters and racks of bombs and tons of guns. They were afraid to find out, in case it queered the pitch. And in that their attitude was identical to ours. We didn't want to know either.

Police, Investigating

After a couple of attempts were made on Khooshie's life, I began to suspect that somebody was out to kill the lad. For a moment I even wondered if I were the somebody.

Having so recently been impoverished, I was more than normally concerned with economy, which made Khooshie's spendthrift ways all the harder to bear. It wouldn't have been so bad if the money he was flinging about was contributing even indirectly to the organization, but he was spending it in feasting and frivolity; on nightclubs, jaunts and expeditions, on excessive tips and gratuities, on wagers, women and motorcars. A great deal of money also went on equipment that might be nice to own but had precious little to do with building an air force. He was purchasing every electrical item that took his fancy, including not one but several of the latest battery-operated wireless sets, console gramophones, moving-picture machines, electric hand warmers and toys. He was particularly thrilled with one toy, a machine like an eggbeater that emitted colored sparks when the handle was turned. He would sit in the dark for hours, turning the handle and expressing delight over the electrical bouquet.

There were plenty of presents for his English friends, too: cases of champagne and loans of cash for the males and, for his lady friends, hiking outfits, taffeta frocks, tennis rackets, presentation sets of silverware and the settling of bills that seemed to be run up whenever he was in the vicinity. And then he had the nerve to complain when I asked him to sign a check for £1,100 worth of surplus RAF bench equipment.

"That is a terrible lot of money to pay," he said. "Do you realize that such a sum would keep the average Indian family fed and clothed for sixty years?"

In the next breath he would complain that we were buying too much secondhand material. He felt this was undignified, and that we should buy only the best.

"If we bought only the best, Khooshie, in this particular case you would be signing not an eleven-hundred-pound check but one for three thousand."

"That's all right. Father has plenty of money," he said; and to prove it, went out and bought a walking stick and a house in Buckinghamshire, explaining patiently that, "Good Lord, Bartholomew, one has to have *somewhere* to take one's friends at the weekends."

Understandably he was reveling in his new freedom from family restraint and in the sophisticated freedoms of Europe. We just wished that he had not fallen in with the particular bunch that were led by the socialite Bubba Carruthers, the girl he had met at the Lewises' garden party. Some of her crowd were shameless. The police had been called to their last escapade when citizens reported some quite unacceptable behavior in a public park. Khooshie had escaped arrest only because he was the only one not intoxicated with liquor. His Hindu culture forbade it. He was thus able to make good his escape, half-dressed, into the rhododendrons, while the rest of the pack, except for Bubba, who never seemed to get caught, were heavily fined the next day in magistrate's court.

Days later we learned that they had prevailed upon Khooshie to pay the fines. These chums of his included a few young officers who could not afford to take menial jobs for social reasons but who were unqualified for any other kind of work; but for the most part, Bubba's crowd were younger men and women who had not contributed to the war, but who had absorbed—or were imitating—the cynical disgust of those who had.

What particularly annoyed us about his excesses was that his association with the flappers, artists, poets, unemployed officers and samples of privileged youth interfered with our work.

When he treated a dozen of his friends to a jaunt to Paris one fall day, we decided on a showdown. On the Friday of his disappearance, he had been urgently needed to append his signature to a particularly important contract. Five days elapsed before his return. This aroused on our part not only exasperation but anxiety. He was, after all, in my care. But when I expressed my concern he replied testily that I was not his father, and when I remonstrated over the way he was keeping so many freeloaders in luxury, he was furious. "Money, money, money, that is all you think about," he stormed. "Every time I come into the office I have to sign another fifty checks for thousands and thousands, but the moment I spend a few quid on my friends, you have a face like a gallon of vinegar."

However, there was one useful result from his social excesses. They distracted him from flying. I had delegated one of our most reliable pilots, Philip Brashman, to take over Khooshie's training, but after only two attendances for ground-school instruction, Khooshie quit, saying that map and compass reading, Morse, theory of flight, engines, rigging and navigation were just too boring for words, and anyway he didn't see why he should learn all about struts and carburetors and things. Surely it was up to the ground staff to deal with details like that. As for learning the Morse code he just knew he would never grasp it, not in a million years, so why waste time on it?

Yet even with flight instruction, he sometimes failed to turn up, if a flying lesson clashed with, say, the races at Epsom Salts, or wherever it was that he and his buddies kept losing so much money.

Finally Brashman, a former colleague of mine at the Gosport School of Special Flying, announced that he was washing him out. "The lad has not only no aptitude for flying," he reported, "he doesn't appear to have any reflexes. He's dangerous, Bart. He has more than forty hours in his log book, and I still don't dare let him solo."

"But he already has soloed."

"Well, all I can say," Brashman said in his calm, measured voice, "is that the instructor who allowed him to do that should have been tied to a bomb rack and released over the Brooklands sewage farm."

That was yet another worrisome problem. Khooshie had given practically everybody the impression that he was a veteran pilot who lacked wings only because the new badge with the condor design hadn't yet come from the emblem manufacturers. (We had finally persuaded him that a condor with outspread wings would decorate the breast of an intrepid birdman rather more appropriately than an owl huddled on a twig.) If it became known that he could not pass the Royal Aero Club tests, he would be made to look foolish—and Khooshie was excessively sensitive to the attitudes of us Westerners. I was unwilling to tell him that he was being washed out, as I needed him in a good mood so he would go on signing checks. I tried to wheedle Brashman into doing the dirty work, but he pointed out that the boy would come to me anyway for confirmation, so I might as well save a detour. "A tactful wash-out will be better coming from you," Brashman said.

So I told the boy, next time he came into the office. "I'm afraid you're a really rotten pilot, Khooshie," I told him sympathetically. "But don't feel bad about it. Some people have flying ability, others have none. You just happen to have reached a standard no better than that of a trainee with two hours' dual instruction, and you'll never get any better. It's not just my opinion, Khooshie. Everybody agrees that you're an absolute dud."

Just as I feared, Khooshie took it badly; unlike everybody else in the office who had overheard our conversation. The moment Khooshie stormed off: "That's telling him, Bandy," Mays cried, his dignified face crumbling with the effort to dam a wave of emotion. "Tell me, have you ever thought of joining the foreign service? Gad, Hibbert, what a loss to the diplomatic corps."

Even Hibbert was laughing, the tears streaking his cheeks. I stared at them in haughty astonishment, but this only increased the hysteria, which had now spread to Derby and several others, and even to normally imperturbable Philip Brashman. I could only assume that they were cracking up from overwork. "Oh, oh," Mays gasped, clinging onto his ribs, "isn't he the most tactful man you've ever . . . ? Oh, what subtlety, what sublime . . . oh, oh."

"I do not think he was at all tactful," Khooshie said furiously, returning at that moment. "I thought he was quite rude to me." But this only increased the disgraceful howling sounds, until Khooshie shouted that he would just go to another flying school, that's all, and show us all up.

"Now see what you've done," I shouted at the others. "You've offended him." But even that failed to restore order. In fact Mays actually laughed more than ever, and finally had to cling to a filing cabinet, moaning in pain, to prevent himself from falling. I could only conclude that overwork had temporarily deranged the lot of them.

Luckily, Khooshie abandoned the idea of applying to another flying school, but contented himself with sulking for several days. Finally I realized that it was the thought of losing the wings off his uniform that was bothering him rather than his performance as a pilot. "But you see, you can't wear wings without earning them," I explained. "It's just not done, Khooshie."

"I am Supreme Air Commander-in-Chief, I must have wings. It will not look right if I do not have wings on my uniform."

"Look, Prince Albert is in the RAF, the Prince of Wales's brother, and even he cannot be awarded his wings unless he qualifies for them—and he's second in line to the throne."

"You mean even an English prince must pass all the tests and examinations?" Khooshie asked, looking impressed. All the same, he continued to argue stubbornly that he could not possibly be Field Marshal of the Royal Jhamjarh Air Force—or Supreme Air Lord; he had not yet decided on his exact title—without wings on his tunic. Finally I agreed that he could be an honorary pilot and keep the wings, provided he undertook never to fly an aircraft without being accompanied by a qualified man.

No sooner was that problem settled unsatisfactorily when the second assassination attempt occurred.

The first try had been passed off, at first, as the work of a common footpad, despite the rather novel method, for London, of garrotting. On that occasion, Khooshie had stayed behind in the office to write his usual weekly letter to dad, and it was dark when he emerged onto Laurence Pountney Hill. He was saved only because he was wearing a neck brace, the consequence of a wild party the previous weekend at somebody's country estate. When the attacker crept up behind, slipped the cord round Khooshie's mackintoshed throat and tightened the noose sufficiently to ensure a quick kill, he must have been pretty surprised to hear his victim respond in quite normal, unstrangulated tones, "What the devil are you playing at? Bartholomew, is that you who is mucking about?"

Strangely enough it was the affront to his dignity rather than the flirtation with death that upset him most. When the would-be assassin slipped the wire round his neck and pulled, Khooshie was dragged backwards and, in order to maintain his balance, was forced to flail his arms in a most ungainly fashion. The boy was self-consciously proud of his natural grace, which he knew he possessed because he had been told that he possessed it by so many people, from adoring relatives back in India to the fashionable crowd who were currently fattening his ego as assiduously as they thinned his wallet. He resented the offence against his dignity far more than the fact that somebody had tried to kill him.

Though attacks on citizens in the darker London purlieus were not uncommon, the *modus operandi* was distinctly unusual. Chief Inspector Frank, who had been called in when it was learned that the victim was some sort of prince, was quite intrigued. "Our English footpads aren't usually so unsporting," he said, sweeping a forefinger under his mustache before remembering that he had shaved it off. You could tell he'd recently owned a mustache. There was a white band under his nose that made it look as if he were suffering from frostbite. "They usually employ just a lead pipe or a belaying pin or an old spanner—some decent, civilized weapon like that." He paused to examine Khooshie's neck brace closely. Actually, not all that closely. He had to hold it at arm's length to bring it into focus. "H'm, yes, you can plainly see the score marks," he murmured. "Strange . . . we have very few cases of attempts at strangulation. In the streets, that is. It's common enough in the home, of course. . . . But you say, Prince . . . uh. . . ." He paused and whispered to me, "What's his name again?"

"Prince Khooshie Avtar Prakash."

"Oh, yes. Uh, you say, Prince . . . uh, that you are unable to give a description of your attacker?"

"How could I? It was dark and he was behind me. All I know is that he had the most foul breath," Khooshie said, disgusted all over again by the olfactory recollection.

"Hm. He used piano wire, I suspect. Probably with some sort of grip or handle at each end. The wire, I should say, was a D-sharp string from a Steinway. . . ."

"You think it was just an ordinary robbery attempt?" Hibbert asked.

"Hardly ordinary, given the irregular weapon," Chief Inspector Frank said, lofting a superior eyebrow. "But otherwise, yes, I should say the motive was robbery. That ring on the prince's left forefinger," he pointed out, proud of his powers of observation, "would alone provide ample incentive.

"Anyway, we certainly can't allow important visitors to this country to be attacked with impunity," the chief inspector continued. "Rest assured, sir, that we shall do everything we can to bring your assailant to justice . . . even though, as a clue to his identity," Frank added with a hint of reproach in his voice, "halitosis is not much to go on."

Owing to the paucity of clues, the chief inspector probably never expected to visit Khooshie again; but in fact he was back within two weeks when the prince was attacked a second time, and in the same manner as before, with a loop of wire whipped over the head from behind and tightened across the throat.

The attack, which took place just after dark, occurred in almost the same spot, the courtyard outside our offices on Laurence Pountney Hill. "An interesting square, this," Chief Inspector Frank said. "These charming irregular-shaped gardens were the site of Corpus Christi College, you know, which was destroyed in the Great Fire of 1666—or was that the year of the Great Plague . . . ?"

This time, it was a gift parcel that saved Khooshie from almost certain death. He had been out shopping that Thursday morning and had returned after lunch with the result, armfuls of presents for Bubba Carruthers, well known, as the chief inspector put it, for her high jinks with policemen's helmets. Being unable to deliver them immediately, Khooshie had left the parcels at the office. As motorcars were not allowed onto the hill, the parcels had to be carried a good many yards back to the car. That evening, Kapur, the diminutive chauffeur, collected most of the parcels and disappeared into the passage leading to Cannon Street. Khooshie was to follow with the remainder. The moment he emerged from the office, the assailant struck from behind, looping a wire over Khooshie's shiny black hair and tightening it lethally across his throat. The wire created painful contusions on both sides of his neck. After treating these injuries, the doctor surmised that if the wire had been drawn tight over the throat itself, Khooshie would have been dead in only a few seconds.

What saved him was a fortuitous piece of timing. A second before the assailant struck, Khooshie parked one of the parcels under his chin—it was a silk scarf in a longish, flat box—in order to free his hand to reach into his pocket to make sure that his wallet was in place. He knew that he would need plenty of cash, as he was going out with Bubba that evening. Consequently the wire snapped over the box instead of the Adam's apple. The box was very nearly sliced in two by the murderous pressure.

The diminutive chauffeur returned before the assassin could amend his grip. Though Kapur failed to give chase, he did manage to catch a glimpse of the assailant. The assailant was dark skinned.

"Dark skinned, eh? That puts an entirely different complexion on things," Chief Inspector Frank said, looking quite relieved to learn that the person who had resorted to such a filthy foreign technique as garrotting was not English. "I think we had better look into that. Are you aware, sir, of anyone from your part of the world who might harbor a certain amount of ill will?"

"No."

"Nobody who might be bent on revenge, perhaps?"

"No."

"Maybe in retaliation for some act committed by you or a member of your family, perhaps?" the chief inspector asked hopefully.

"No," Khooshie answered, with a shrug. "Nobody could possibly want to kill me."

"Oh, I don't know," I said.

The chief inspector looked at me. "Couldn't it have something to do with our activities here?" I added, gesturing around at the office.

"Who knows?" Khooshie said, shrugging again.

"What activities?" Frank asked.

"I've told you, Chief Inspector. We're purchasing various supplies for the prince's father in India. You've seen our cover—I mean, our brass plate on the door—the Prakash Purchasing Commission?"

"Yes, I've seen that. Incidentally, what exactly *is* a prakash?"

"Eh?"

"These prakashes that you've been purchasing—what are they, exactly?"

"Eh?"

"I mean, sir, who knows—maybe somebody in India doesn't want you to purchase them."

Seeing me gazing dumbly at the copper, Derby chipped in, "Good Lord, Chief Inspector, do you mean to say you've never tried a prakash?"

"Well, I. . . ."

"You should try them. They're delicious. You just haven't lived until you've tried one, you're just not in the swim."

"Yes, of course," Frank said coloring, obviously stung by the accusation of unfashionability. "Never mind that now. Let's stick to the point. The point is that someone appears to be intent on eliminating the prince." Thoughtfully he swept a finger under his mustache, or where it used to be. "All right, let's summarize what we've learned so far. First, possibly the malefactor is a fellow Indian."

"You too are an Indian?" Khooshie asked skeptically. "What part of India are you from, Inspector?"

"Chief Inspector, actually."

"Chief Inspector? That does not sound like an Indian place to me."

"No, no, I was just putting you straight, young man — Prince. I don't come from India at all. I'm from Much Wenlock."

"But I don't understand, Inspector," Khooshie persisted. Then, hesitating: "Sorry, I do not remember your name."

"Frank."

"Yes, Inspector, be as frank as you like."

"That's my name, Frank."

"And what is your second name?"

"That *is* my second name."

"You are called Frank Frank?"

I thought I had better clear up the confusion, so I piped up, "No, it's Caesar, not Frank, Khooshie. See, it says so on his card here."

"César Franck? Oh, dear me, what a very distinguished name."

"Do you think so?" the chief inspector asked, preening doubtfully.

"Well, he was a famous composer, wasn't he?"

"Who?"

"César Franck," Hibbert put in.

"Yes?" the Chief Inspector asked, turning to Hibbert.

"I'm talking about César Franck."

"Oh, you mean grandfather!"

"César Franck was your grandfather?" Derby asked, looking really impressed. "The great composer?"

"Certainly not. Grandfather was a banker. What's this about a great composer?"

"César Franck."

"Yes, I'm listening."

"The famous symphony in D minor," Hibbert tried to explain.

"What about it?"

"It was his."

"Whose?"

"César Franck's."

"I never knew grandfather wrote music."

"No, no," I said. "Don't you remember, he was a banker."

"But he wrote music on the side?"

"On the side of what?"

"Oh, balderdash!" Frank exclaimed.

"Balderdash—that's in the north of India, isn't it?" Derby asked. "There you are, Khooshie, the inspector comes from Balderdash."

"Will you be quiet!" the chief inspector shouted, plainly still annoyed at the way Derby had exposed his ignorance about prakashes. Then, recovering somewhat: "Naturally we shall proceed with our investigations, but in the meantime there is the security of the prince to be considered. We can, of course, arrange for police protection, but—"

"It will not be necessary," Khooshie said haughtily. "I do not wish it."

"Just as well, I suppose," Chief Inspector Frank said. "We don't have the manpower for it anyway."

Khooshie seemed disturbingly undisturbed by the narrow escape from being burked. I couldn't decide if it was Indian fatalism or the result of a defective nervous system. But then Khooshie rarely behaved in a typical fashion . . . unless, of course, his behavior was typical among Indians.

After Roland Mays, Hibbert and I discussed the situation next morning, we decided that Khooshie must have a bodyguard whether he liked it or not. Indeed, it seemed an extraordinary oversight that he did not already have one. He was, after all, a prince and heir to a treasury said to be comparable to, if not to rival, that of the Aga Khan III. Yet even Khooshie's household staff, which might have provided some sort of protection, was feeble, consisting as it did of a cook who was about as fleet as an oyster, an elderly Indian who acted as a butler, and a major-domo who seemed to spend most of the time in his room sleeping.

Khooshie continued to resist the idea, fearing that the presence of a bodyguard might inspire ridicule among his sophisticated friends; until Bubba decided that he should have one. After considering the matter, she informed him in her toffee voice that it might be a jolly good idea to have some sort of protection, and moreover she knew just the one, somebody who would make a divine bodyguard.

Aware of her reputation for mischief, I was highly suspicious of this helpfulness on her part and tried to persuade the boy that the selection of a competent professional should be left to us; but he knew that if he did not accept her suggestion, Bubba would be displeased, and as Khooshie would go to any lengths to earn her approval, it was her nomination that carried the day.

"Who is this bodyguard?"

"There's nothing to worry about, sir," she replied respectfully. "It's the bouncer at the Cafard Club." And she promised to introduce Khooshie to his new bodyguard on Saturday. That was the day that Khooshie was to throw his first big party.

"After all, I wouldn't dream of putting Khooshie-whooshie into the hands of anyone who wasn't totally competent and trustworthy," Bubba bubbled. After that first encounter at the Lewises, she had taken to calling me Bar-folomew, but changed it to Barty Darling when she saw that I was not overly enchanted by her cute little lisp. Still later, when she saw that I disapproved of her influence over Khooshie, she began to address me with exaggerated respect as "sir," to emphasize that at the age of thirty-two I was now out of it, not one of the crowd. I was to be considered a has-been, or at best an authority figure, part of the System, no longer capable of joining in the fun without a hearing aid, a truss, glasses, a wig and a diet of oysters, ginseng and powdered rhinoceros horn.

Irwell Court

When I entered the lobby of Irwell Court that Saturday, the racket was gushing down the staircase like a tidal bore. Khooshie's party appeared to be well under way.

"Good Lord," I said, cocking my napper at a forty-five-degree angle. "Is that a jazz band up there?"

"It is, sir," said the maroon doorman with all the medals. "And I hope, sir, you can do something about it. We have already received numerous complaints, and it's not even midnight."

"What's that barking?"

"That's Lady Lavender's hounds, sir. I suspect they have caught the scent."

"Scent?"

"One of the prince's young friends, sir," the doorman said stiffly, "insisted on going up there with her pet fox."

It was true that the neighbors didn't look too happy. When I reached the apartment, half a dozen of the building's big league burghers were gathered in the corridor outside, mouthing complaints that could be safely assumed to be furious, though they were going unheard over the racket from within. One of them, a duke with wild hair and a dressing gown, was beating at the door with impotent fists.

"Here, let me try," I said; whereupon the duke, after looking over my impeccable formal wear and my cloak with the crimson silk lining, made way for me gratefully. So I opened the door, went in and closed the door after me.

Not that the door opened all that easily. As I thrust it open, the woodwork caused a young woman to go shooting across the polished parquet. She must have been lying on her back with her feet against the door. She did not appear to resent the parquetry glissando.

"Sorry."

"That's all right. I'm used to being pushed around."

"Isn't anyone answering the door tonight?"

"I didn't hear it say anything, darling."

None of Khooshie's household staff appeared to be on duty at the front door. I shook my head at this lax security, turned and locked the door, with the result that four hundred and sixty-seven guests subsequently failed to gain admittance and had to return home for Horlicks instead of champagne.

As there was no space left in the entrance-hall closet, I made my way to the nearest bedroom, which appeared to belong to the majordomo, and there dumped my cloak and topper. I assumed that it was the majordomo's room because the majordomo was in it. He was sound asleep under layer upon layer of silk, cotton, satin, wool, fur and gabardine. I tiptoed my way back into the passageway and headed toward the nearest liquor supply.

So many people had turned up for the party that it was difficult to make much progress. It took me ten minutes even to find the jazz band. It was playing in the lounge in front of the semicircular window. A girl with a tiara perched at a rakish angle on her head was dancing dreamily atop a table by herself, holding her skirts at garter height. Through a bedroom doorway I recognized some of Bubba's friends. They were quarreling. The conflict seemed to be principally between two young men with long necks.

In the blue reception room, somebody had dropped a dollop of food onto the royal blue carpet. Remembering some of the pork pies I had eaten in Paddington station, I stared at the mashed paté or trifle or whatever it had been. It was being trampled deep into the fibers by battalions of shiny shoes, pumps, boots and slippers.

Searching with increasing thirst for something to drink—I had been working late and my filing cabinet had run out of booze—I came across a concentration of glasses and thought there must surely be a few bottles nearby. Dozens of glasses were ranged on the mantelpiece, some half full, some empty, and all lipsticked, smeared, cracked, upended or overturned. When a pimply youth in white tie and tails barged alongside, I started to ask if he knew where the bar was, but he was busy chasing a girl with a soda syphon. She was screeching; rather unnecessarily, I thought, as the syphon was empty.

I caught sight of Khooshie. He was dancing with Bubba. I tried to attract his attention, but his eyes were closed ecstatically, his cheek against her fuzzy hair. He looked as if he were about to be lovesick down her back. Her eyes, however, were wide open and alert. She saw me, wiggled her fingers and wrinkled her little nose in that cute way of hers. She made no attempt to wake Khooshie.

A middle-aged man outfitted in mothballs said, "I really don't know why that girl invited us. The one dancing with the darkie. She hasn't spoken a word to our group all night."

"What group is that?"

"The Catford, Putney and Herne Hill Bicycle Club."

"Oh, yes?"

"She invited all the membership, but only six of us could come. She told us to bring our bikes."

Ten minutes later I came across the buffet. The tables were ranged along the wall near the passage to the kitchen.

It was a comestible shambles. Salmon mixed with chocolate cake. Sandwiches floating in the punch.

Nearby, leaning against a joint of roast beef, was a young man whose eyes were panning drunkenly back and forth. There was a bottle of whisky sticking out of his pocket. Assuming that he had filched it from the bar, I reclaimed it on Khooshie's behalf and gently pickpocketed it.

The bottle was still sealed. I opened it and, after glancing around to make sure that Emily Post wasn't at the party, swigged from the neck; then, knowing that one swallow did not make a summer, I swigged again.

After that, I recorked the bottle and took it for a walk.

"Bartholomew," Khooshie cried. "You have arrived. Where have you been? It is late. Mr. Hibbert has also arrived."

"Where is he?"

"He has left. I think it was too noisy for him. This is a very successful party, don't you think? But perhaps it is too noisy for you, too, Bartholomew?"

"Pardon me?"

"Is it too noisy?"

"What?"

"Noisy? Too noisy?"

"Oh, no, it's just right."

"If so, I can dismiss the band and order everybody to be silent, just for you, Bartholomew. I owe you everything. Did you know, Bubba, he saved my life?"

"Yes, sweetie, you told me."

"He was ready to give up his life for me."

"No, I wasn't."

Yet another lovely girl—every woman there was lovely, except for one redhead in a sequined gown, and that was a man, anyway—came up and slipped an arm through Bubba's. Her chest was so determinedly suppressed as to be almost concave. "So this is your very own rajah," she said to Bubba. "My, just look at those gorgeous eyelashes."

"I know, darling. And they give the most thrill-making butterfly kiss," Bubba sang back, plucking a half-smoked cigarette from her ebony holder and dropping it into her half-filled champagne glass.

"But darling, do tell: what's it like, going around with a man who's prettier than you?"

"It's a new experience for me, I must admit," Bubba said. "But I expect you're quite used to it, aren't you?"

The new girl smiled, her lips not unduly influencing her eyes. "Talking about butterflies," she said, "how's Michael Arlen these days?"

"Darling," Bubba said quickly to Khooshie, handing him her glass, "be a dear and get me another, would you?"

That was a part of the conversation I understood, and why

she was so eager to get Khooshie out of the way. Striving to live up to the public's view of her as a postwar girl rebelling against society, Bubba had indulged ostentatiously in quite a few affairs. She even told me that she had slept with Michael Arlen, whose *The Green Hat* had just been published, to noisy acclaim.

"How was he as a lover?"

"Imaginative enough, but infirm of purpose," she replied, after making sure that Khooshie was not in jealousy range.

Tonight Bubba was wearing a gown that exposed her smooth shoulders. At the Lewises' garden party, I had noticed that she radiated an uncommon degree of heat. I noticed it again now when she intercepted me in the passageway to Khooshie's bathroom.

"You don't approve of me much, do you, sir?" she said, twirling a new champagne glass between her fingers. The fingernails were painted blue. "I suppose you think I'm leading Khooshie astray." She moved closer, and the heat increased. The waves of warmth emanating from her were quite amazing, as if she had just emerged from the oven. "Well, of course I am leading him astray, aren't I? And high time, too, surely. He was the most frightfully naive boy when we first started going out—you don't have a gasper on you, do you, sir?" She wiggled her foot-long cigarette holder. "And after all, a girl has to live. Ever since I chucked over one of daddy's young men—my God, you've never experienced true boredom until you've met Roger the solicitor—he's been refusing to pay my allowance—daddy, I mean, not Roger. I mean, you've no idea what it's like to be absolutely desperate for money. Khooshie is an absolute godsend, he can't refuse me anything, he's such a darling, and I really am quite fond of him, you know."

"He's crazy about you."

"I know, isn't it a bore? But there you are, there's no accounting for tastes, is there, sir?" she said, and issued that loud, debutante laugh that made me feel like blowing a poisoned dart at her through a rolled-up finishing-school prospectus. "I mean, it's not my fault if he's fallen head over proverbial heels, is it? It becomes a bit of a strain sometimes, he goes into the most dreadful huff if I'm not behaving all the time like the vicar's daughter. Mind you, I've known some pretty untrammeled vicar's daughters. . . ."

As she moved still closer, the heat from her smooth round shoulders increased still further. "Personally," she said, gazing up at me with a calculating look, "while I absolutely adore him when he's being as restrained with the sick-making homilies as he is free with the exchequer, I prefer men who are rather more mature."

"Oh, darn, that lets me out. Nobody's ever called me mature," I said uneasily. She had a habit of standing so close that one couldn't help wondering if one had cleaned out one's nostrils recently.

"Oh, I don't know. You have a face that's done a lot of living."

"I guess that's a polite way of saying it looks ravaged," I said, moving away laterally, like a sliding cupboard door. She can't have realized that our pelvises were so close that they had almost bonded.

"Hello, John. Didn't know you were here."

"I'm not."

"Have a swig."

"You trying to get drunk tonight, Bart?"

"Well, John, I'm not trying not to."

"I'm getting squiffy on the racket alone. I sense an atmosphere of crisis, don't you? The doorman's complained again."

"Doesn't seem to have made much difference."

"I don't think you're supposed to give parties like this in Irwell Court. Even stirring your teacup too loudly will usually bring a frown."

"The residents are gathering outside. Do you think they'll attack?"

"My God, that's a thought," Derby said. "Wave after wave of dowager duchesses."

There was a howling noise from the lobby, and we wondered if the attack had already started. But it was just another clot of idlers, pretty girls and willowy wisps of chaps with haw-haw voices, who had just come from the show at the Garrick: *Tiger-Cats*, with Robert Loraine and Edith Evans.

"I knew Robert Loraine when he was a squadron commander in France," I said to one of the crowd.

"Yes," he said. "I suppose you're both old enough to have served in the war."

John Derby returned with a friend in tow. This was a shy young man wearing Harold Lloyd spectacles. His name was Kenneth Francis. Derby introduced him as the RAF's top wireless expert.

"Are you interested in coming to India?" I asked, but he hurriedly explained that he was quite content where he was.

"He couldn't believe all the things he's heard about you," John said. "He just wanted to meet you and see if you really were such a paragon of vice."

"Really, Derby," Kenneth said; and to me: "But I was interested, sir. You sounded like one of those remarkable North Americans who have done everything. Like the description of the author on the dust jacket of a book. You know—before taking up writing he'd been a lumberjack, burlesque performer, farm hand—"

"Oil rigger, kindergarten teacher," Derby contributed. "Sewage worker, neurosurgeon, felt-hat-pouncing operator, coprophiliac—"

"Coprophiliac? What's that?"

"Don't ask, sir. Knowing Derby, it's bound to be disgusting."

We paused for a moment to watch a couple of girls nearby. They were holding crayons and were busy writing on the boiled shirtfront of a guest who was either unconscious or apathetic. They were playing noughts and crosses.

Kenneth Francis was busy telling us about his work on wireless communication between aircraft when we were interrupted by a loud, hoarse voice. "Talking through the old titfer as usual, eh, Flying Officer Francis?" it said.

The newcomer was a beefy, red-faced man with a voice so hoarse that he had to summon considerable respiratory pressure to force out the syllables.

Kenneth began to stammer nervously. The other cut him short. "Well, come on, man, introduce us," he said quite genially.

Kenneth did so, with no great pleasure. The beefy one proved to be a Group Captain Kempt. "George Kempt, actually," he said, acknowledging Derby's presence only with a curt nod before turning back to me. "Of the Air Ministry. So you're this fellow General Bandy, are you?"

"No."

"What? But I thought—"

"I don't use the rank."

"Ah. Yes, well, that's understandable enough, isn't it, old man? It was only a very temporary appointment anyway, I gather. In some back-of-beyond place like Russia, eh? Mostly you were a, what? lieutenant colonel, weren't you? That's below the rank of group captain, you know."

"M'oh, yes."

"Just thought I'd get it straight, eh? So many people think that a group captain is, well, like a mere captain. It's pretty annoying. Personally I don't see why they had to change over from the old army titles. I'd have been a full colonel."

"You still are a fool colonel," Derby said; but fortunately Kempt was busy staring at the bottle in my hand through bulging, bloodshot eyes.

"I say," he said, licking his lips, "is that your whiskey, or can anyone join in? You have a bottle with no glass, and I have a glass with no bottle. Perhaps we should get together, eh?" he said, and laughed heartily.

"Here, I'll get you a glass," he went on, and managed to find one in less than a minute. It was clean, too. "You *are* the one who's organizing an air force for some wog, aren't you?" he went on, looking me up and down doubtfully.

"Yes. The Indian over there," I said. "He's your host."

"Yes. Not much of one, though, is he—if he invites the likes of Flying Officer Francis here," he said, and laughed again, and drove an elbow into Kenneth's ribs. Kenneth waited for Kempt to look away again before he winced.

"At least Ken got an invitation—Captain," Derby said evenly. "Did you?"

"As impertinent as ever, eh, Derby?" Kempt said calmly enough as he drained his glass. "Yes, I got an invitation, if it's any of your business." He turned his back on Derby, and gripped my arm and drew me into a stream of traffic. The movement of the crowd did the rest, separating us from Derby and his friend.

"I hear," Kempt said in his painfully hoarse voice, "you're paying a pretty decent *dastur*, as we used to say in India. Paying a lot even to the lowest ack emma, what?"

"Yes."

"I don't suppose you have room for the top man in the supply and services department of the Air Ministry, do you?"

"Why, do you know where I could find him?"

"Talking about myself, old man. I could use a spot more of the old wherewithal, you know, the way prices are going up every dashed week."

Playing for time, I asked him about his job and listened intently, or as intently as was possible over the yelping of some animal—a fox, perhaps, or one of Bubba's friends—as Kempt bragged about the trials and tribulations of being director of materiel in the Air Council. The sum total of what he had to say was that there was never enough money to replace the RAF's worn-out equipment. They were so short of money that some appalling penny-pinching had to be resorted to. "My lady secretary, for instance," he hoarsed, "has to make do with a prewar Blickensderfer, for God's sake."

"Your aircraft are getting pretty old too, aren't they?"

"Aircraft?" Kempt repeated vaguely, as if he had never thought of aircraft as being part of the air force economy. "Yes, I suppose. . . . Though the chief bullyboy himself usually clutches that side of things to his own bosom."

"Pardon?"

"Talking about the Chief of Air Staff, old man."

"Oh, yes."

"He mostly deals with aircraft, even though the sale and purchase of aircraft is supposed to be within my purview."

"Ah, yes."

"Well, he can have it, if he wants all the extra work. Our chief seems to think," Kempt sneered, his beefy face glistening, "that everything else ought to be subordinate to his precious squadrons."

"You don't mean to tell me that he thinks airplanes and pilots are more important than anything else?"

"Exactly. Well, I can tell you, he wouldn't get far without the clothing depots and the soup tureens and all the rest of it—blanco and brass polish and everything—that we have to order."

"I gather you don't get on too well with the Chief of Air Staff," I slipped in with a kowtowing smile.

"And our trophy cabinets," Kempt added, flushing with remembered humiliation.

"Trophy cabinets?"

"Beetle-browed bastard."

"Pardon?"

"You wouldn't believe the way he spoke to me. As if I were a bloody erk, or something," Kempt said, his hoarse words forced out even harder under the pressure of his indignation. And he went on to describe the gross interference his department had been forced to put up with from the office of the CAS.

I asked what had happened and listened with more difficulty than ever, for Kempt's anger was interfering with his coherence, as he described how he had ordered four thousand pounds' worth of trophy cabinetry for the officer's mess at Hendon and one or two other aerodromes. The CAS had learned about it and had practically gone into convulsions over the expenditure. He had spoken very rudely indeed to Group Captain Kempt. "Practically accused me of being a crook, by God—just because the cabinet manufacturer was my brother-in-law. I tell you, Bandy, if I hadn't had two mouths to feed I'd have resigned my commission there and then, the way he talked to me."

Apparently in upbraiding the group captain, the CAS had pointed out that he had been forced to restrict personal flying by squadron COs only a few weeks previously. And here was Kempt, giving thousands of pounds' worth of nonessential business to a damned commode manufacturer.

The CAS had even had the nerve to suggest that Kempt's relationship to the furniture manufacturer had had something to do with the order.

"As if that would have made any difference," I snorted as scornfully as possible, to encourage the group captain.

"Exactly," Kempt said. A speck of spit spat from his lips. "Did he think I'd actually accept a commission or anything like that from my own brother-in-law?"

"Course you wouldn't."

"The most my brother-in-law's ever done for me is make me a small loan, that's all. And I can assure you I've never had the slightest intention of not paying it back. Eventually."

I was genuinely angry at the way Kempt had been treated by the Chief of Air Staff, and I said so.

"You really feel that way, old man?" Kempt asked gratefully.

"I do indeed. I haven't felt so angry for years as I do now at the way he's treated you," I said. What I failed to add was that my annoyance resulted from the fact that the CAS's attitude toward Kempt lowered the tone of his hostility to me and placed me on Kempt's level. I felt really upset at the idea of sharing the Chief's hostility with someone like Kempt.

"Damned good of you to say so, old man," Kempt said, squeezing my arm. "Anyway, if there is anything doing for a man of my position and experience you'll let me know, eh? Perhaps something in the London end of things. I'm not too keen on India, actually—though of course I'd go if it was worth my while. But it drives you to drink, you know, India," he said, filling his glass and then mine as close to the brim as he dared, considering the danger of being buffeted by the crowd. "No point in earning heaps of the old folding stuff if you have to give up a liver or two, is there? It's the heat out there. I know, I did the five-year tour. As for the Indians, they're worse than the heat. They . . . ."

His voice trailed off as he became aware that somebody was lying on the carpet nearby. It was one of the young men who had been quarreling in the bedroom several hours ago. He was holding a blood-dappled hanky to his beezer.

"One of Bubba's pansies," Kempt said, and gave the boy a kick.

By the time I got away from Kempt with vague promises of future consideration, I had made myself a friend for life. John Derby was disgusted with me. "God, you must have changed, to get on with a bloat like that," he said, and would hardly speak to me for the rest of the night.

As the hours staggered by, I started to get the feeling that someone was watching me. But every time I looked around, he or she was looking elsewhere.

I in my turn was watching Khooshie, with some concern. He was kissing one of Bubba's hands. She was lying down, stretched out on a sofa, exhibiting her silver-stockinged knees. Khooshie was kissing one of her hands over and over, passionately. Unknown to him, the other hand, dangling over the back of the sofa, was being kissed by somebody else, a fellow called Rabbit-Hutch, or some such double-barreled name. He was sucking her fingers one by one.

It was when I turned away from the sofa that I discovered the watcher. I found myself meeting the eye of an ox-shouldered fellow who yet managed to look quite elegant in his white tie and tails. He started toward me.

My first impression was that his dark, fleshy face with its accouterment of jowls was geniality itself. The impression was not contradicted by the square black mustache that had been applied to his face. It looked rather comical. As additional backup, a gleam of humor glinted from his small brown eyes. The skin of his face was rough and dark.

"Mr. Bandy?" he enquired.

"Mr. Stanley, I presume?"

"Eh? No, my card," he said, passing over said card, which had expensively engraved lettering; but the letters spelled out nothing except his name and the address of a flat in W1.

"At last. It's an honor to meet you, Mr. Bandy," he said, far too heartily for that time of night, and wearing as frank and open an expression as his big, deadpan face and its hairy locus would permit. "My name, as you see, is Skelton." And he leaned away with a triumphant look, as if he had successfully explained Kierkegaard.

"Yes, so it says here: Rupert Skelton, Loathsome Mews, W1."

"That's Lothian Mews, Mr. Bandy."

"Oh, is it? You've been watching me all night, haven't you? I expect you've fallen in love with me. But it's no good, Rupert, I'm spoken for."

He looked startled for a moment, then laughed heartily. "No, nothing like that," he said, still chortling. "But I see we can talk frankly, and that's good, Mr. Bandy. There's nothing I like better than to get it all straight without shilly-shallying or evasions, eh?"

"So who are you?"

He leaned forward again, looking really serious. "I'll tell you," he said. "I assure you, I don't beat about the bush, Mr. Bandy. I always prefer to come right out with it, and put my cards on the table, and proceed as straight as a die. Is that the correct phrase, as straight as a die? The thing is, I'm not sure because I grew up in an underprivileged household, Mr. Bandy. In our family we could never afford any clichés, or platitudes, or even a few well-worn phrases like that. From morning till night, not one well-worn phrase ever passed our lips. We couldn't even afford common says or old saws. There was never a single aphorism in the larder.

"It wasn't in aid of sound linguipotence either, you know. It was simply poverty and neglect. The result was that I grew up knowing almost nothing of those expressions that are so commonly to be found on the breath of even the least sophisticated. Consequently it came as a blinding revelation whenever I heard a hackneyed phrase, even in Hackney. This sublime discovery particularly applied to proverbs. You cannot imagine the thrill that ran through my very being the first time I heard somebody say 'Every cloud has a silver lining.' The sheer observation of it! Especially as it was so true, as everybody can see in certain conditions when the sun vanishes behind a narrow cloud. I was quite overwhelmed, Bandy. 'Look before you leap.' 'He who hesitates is lost.' Marvelous! Why had I never expressed such great truths myself, when they were so obvious? Obvious, of course, only because nobody, I thought, until now had had the genius to formulate them. But then most great discoveries are basically simple, aren't they? The idea of using a long pole to lever a heavy object is so obvious that it is difficult to imagine not how it was first thought of, but how man failed to think of it for so long. 'Getting down to brass tacks.' 'As dead as mutton.' Every cliché, every saw, almost every simile and metaphor even, were new to me, and arresting in their vitality, their immediacy and, above all, their appositeness.

"And yet how obvious! You know how you come across a passage in a book, some thought or idea that electrifies you with its insight, yet instantly strikes you as being profoundly true because it confirms what you already knew without ever having reached the point of formulating it. It's only now, in weak moments, that I occasionally experience a stab of suspicion—absurd, eh?—that such phrases are a public convenience for relieving one of coherent thought. But, 'What is home without a mother?' Oh, Bandy, how I wept the first time I saw that on a sampler. The perspicacity, the insight, the sheer—from my point of view—originality of it. Even today, I have to be careful not to make a fool of myself by expressing excited appreciation over some worn adage or frayed maxim, for fear that the other party will suspect me of satire. I must be even more careful not to bring home phrases picked up in the gutter and offer them as genuine currency, in case I'm suspected of passing counterfeit maxims so debased as to render them useless as a means of exchange . . . . Mr. Bandy? Mr. Bandy?"

"Oh, sorry. Must have dozed off. Just having forty winks. Not as young as I used to be."

"Of course. Anyway, now you know who I am."

"Er, yes."

"And now you know that—"

We were interrupted by a hullabaloo from the entrance hall. While I was still trying to work out whether Skelton had told me who he was or not, Khooshie came stitching through the mob and seized my arm. "It is my bodyguard," he said breathlessly. "Come."

"Who? Oh, yes, the Cafard Club bouncer."

"I want you two to meet. Come, come."

"He's reasonably presentable, is he, Khooshie? I mean—"

"Oh, yes, very presentable."

"Stop pushing," somebody said.

"What do you mean, stop pushing? I want to get through.

Besides, this is my party, I shall push whoever I wish. Bubba has arranged everything, Bartholomew, so there is nothing to worry about."

I wasn't so sure of that, and I was less sure than ever when I met Khooshie's new bodyguard, though there was no doubt that our latest employee was large enough for to the job, being about six feet tall, and thus towering over Khooshie, and positively protrusive with avoirdupois. The unusual thing was that Khooshie's new guardian was female and black.

"Muriel, this is Mr. Bandy," Bubba was saying, expressionless as yogurt. "Mr. Bandy, may I present Miss Muriel Tombola?"

"Hell," I said, "lo."

A giant smile split Muriel's features, revealing several hundred teeth, one of which was crooked. "Hello yourself, chief," she said, her voice clearly audible over the music—a particularly raucous version of "Alexander's Ragtime Band." "I am pleased to meet you." She turned to Bubba. "He is the big cheese?" she asked, and upon receiving an affirmative, she seized my hand and shook it (and the rest of me), saying, "Well, here I am, chief. I have sacked myself, and I am now ready for anything."

" Oh, good."

"I will guard Prince Khooshie his body as if it was my own," she said; not a particularly reassuring pledge as she did not appear to have looked after her own body all that well. It must have weighed enough to prevent a takeoff in any known airplane. She had arms like thighs . . . which made me wonder what her thighs must be like.

"I will be happy to take care of your body too, chief," she added, looking me up and down with a gloriously uninhibited smile. "I am well qualified. I have been to Oxford University. You have heard of it? The one in Bompala?"

"Well I never."

"The rector was a good friend of mine. The rector his name is Dr. Mgoolie. I have a diploma from there. It is a diploma in . . . what is the name again?"

"Sociology," Bubba said.

"That is it. Sociology. I have not brought my diploma, though, as it is goat skin, and smells badly. And besides, there is nowhere to keep it on my person. Do you like my dress, chief? This shade of orange is very popular in Bompala this season."

"And the, the pearls go very nicely with it too, Miss Tombola."

"Thank you," she said, smiling at me coyly as she ran a hand over the lower part of her abdomen.

I recoiled slightly, buffeting Khooshie, who was looking pleased with his choice of bodyguard—because Bubba was pleased.

"I got these pearls at the Cooperative System," Muriel continued. "The object of this system is to provide members with inexpensive merchandise at a reasonable price. I am a member. I always shop there," she said, speaking with as much pride as another might have mentioned the name of Paquin of Dover Street.

"You look very nice, Miss Tombola," I said; adding in a high, pleasant sort of voice, "Oh, Khooshie, could I see you a moment?"

As I turned away I caught Bubba's eye. Her face was pink with suppressed emotion.

I soon learned that at first Khooshie had objected to Bubba's choice as strenuously as I now did. He felt that such eccentric employment might detract from his dignity. But Bubba had convinced him that it would be unfashionable of him to reject Muriel merely because she was a woman. "Or are you against her because she is black?" Bubba asked. "Of course I am not prejudiced," he replied. "I was just thinking that she might consider the job—er—beneath her." But Bubba had quickly worn him down by the usual, simple means of lowering the temperature of her apparent emotional regard for him; whereupon, in a panic, Khooshie agreed to take on Miss Tombola for a trial period.

"She is quite spectacular, is she not?" he murmured, staring in fascination at Muriel as she proffered her references—demonstrating her prowess as a bouncer by throwing one of Bubba's friends into the Adam fireplace.

I argued, pointing out that apart from anything else, it would attract attention to the Prakash Purchasing Commission, "And you know that's not what your father wants."

"It can't be helped, Bartholomew," he said, not looking completely happy about it now. "But Bubba will despise me if I change my mind now, Bartholomew. I love her. She is so wonderful, so gentle, so. . . ."

"You're talking about Muriel?"

"No, no, Bubba. She is so wonderful. I am wanting all the time to save her, to protect her from the cold and wet and people, and painful things, even from some of her friends. Oh, I am not blind, Bartholomew."

"No?"

"I can see that they are not all jolly decent chaps, and I know most of them are looking down on me because I am an Indian, but Bubba is different, it is quite obvious she loves me and would do anything for me, short of sharing my bed. That is not something she would ever do."

"No."

"Though I yearn for her, Bartholomew, I very much yearn for her."

"Mm, that's too bad," I said.

At five in the morning when I found myself proposing marriage to a girl with ice-cold hands I decided that it was time to leave. I felt sufficiently fortified by now to handle a brief sojourn in my empty flat before starting work again at nine. The decision firmed when I noticed that the girl with cold hands and I had been dancing cheek to cheek in the middle of the floor accompanied only by the sound of distant altercation. The jazz band had packed up and left some time previously.

Skelton appeared as if by magic. "Why hello, Skelton," I cried. "What an amazing coincidence, seeing you here."

"I've been waiting for an opportunity to finish our conversation."

"Oh, wasn't it finished?"

"Though in the meantime I quite enjoyed watching you—with admiration, I might add. It's your face."

"Of course it's my face," I said truculently. "Whose face did you think it was?"

"If you always talk like this," said my dancing partner, "I don't think I'll marry you."

"What about my face, anyway?" I asked, consumed with indifference.

"Oh, just that whether you're furious, frustrated, amused or whatever, your face never seems to change expression. It's quite uncanny."

"I expect," my fiancée said, "that it's been buried in the Arctic for eons and has only recently been unearthed."

Meanwhile, the noise from the direction of the front hall seemed to be getting louder. "What's all the commotion?" I enquired.

"Trouble of some sort. I believe somebody's called the bobbies."

"Oh, lawks," my betrothed said, and disappeared into the madding crowd, never to be seen again.

"It might be a good time to leave, actually," Skelton said, taking my arm, either to steady me or to lead me somewhere.

"Somebody's called the cops?"

"That's right."

"I'll get my coat."

"I have it right here, Mr. Bandy. The cloak, right?"

"Hope you didn't disturb the majordomo. He was asleep under all those coats and things."

"Actually he was dead. He couldn't get out from under. He suffocated."

"Oh, lawks."

"That's what the commotion's all about. They've sent for Chief Inspector Frank of the Yard."

"Christ, let's get out of here."

"This way, through the kitchen."

"Poor old majordomo. I knew him when he was only a corporal, you know."

As we shoved through the mob I said rather more soberly, "You've obviously reconnoitered the joint pretty well, Mr. Skelton. By the way, I still don't know who you are."

"Surely I explained earlier on?"

"Did you? Tell me again."

"Very well, Mr. Bandy," he said. "I'll be frank."

"Oh, no, you won't. One Frank is quite enough."

There was the sound of breaking glass. Bubba, giggling, escorted by Rabbit-Hutch, scuttled ahead of us through the kitchen exit. A few feet away a member of the Catford, Putney and Herne Hill Bicycle Club was being sick into the kitchen sink.

"Bandy?" Skelton said in a queer voice.

"Yes?"

"That wasn't a fox I saw just now, was it?"

"Indeed it was."

"Good God."

Skelton was peering along the corridor outside. I peered too, lurching. A small pack of fox hounds were racing toward us, barking.

Skelton hauled me inside again and slammed the door and put his back to it, looking almost disconcerted.

The argument at the far side of the apartment was growing either louder or closer. The hounds continued to bay outside the kitchen door.

"Trapped like rats in a trap," I said conversationally.

"Oh, well," Skelton said resignedly, "I suppose I'll just have to show my hand."

"What hand?"

"I suppose," he went on, lighting a cigarette with exaggerated gestures, as if playing to the gallery in an exceptionally large theater, "that your jolly old Maharajah wants this air force of his to lord it over all the other rajahs. Is that what you gather, Mr. Bandy?"

He extinguished the match with a flourish. Graceful tendrils of sulfurous smoke hung in the air.

Without waiting for a reply—which wasn't forthcoming anyway—he continued, "All the same, he must know perfectly well that our jolly old government is hardly likely to do handsprings through sheer joy at the prospect of an armed force out there that's not just on their doorstep but practically in their drawing room.

"In fact," he added, puffing on his cigarette in an amateurish way as if he had only just learned to smoke, "it would be understandable, wouldn't it, if the government did something about it before that happened?"

"Like what?" I enquired, rather more attentively than heretofore.

"Oh, making things just a teeny bit more difficult for everybody involved."

"Are you with the government, Mr. Skelton?"

"Lud, I hope you don't suspect me of being an envoy, or anything as melodramatic as that," he said with a plump smile that urged me to embarrass myself by confirming such an absurd, childish or bizarre supposition. "You'll be using the words 'secret service,' next. Good Lord, that would be positively *outré*, whatever that means, the idea of a secret agent approaching a respected citizen in the middle of the night to warn him," he said, his voice changing and his small eyes steadying, "that the government would look very unfavorably indeed on any attempt to upset the balance of power on an extremely sensitive subcontinent."

There was a moment of silence, soon broken by the baying of hounds, breaking glass, shouts, screams and a Victrola.

"I see," I said at length. "But suppose a secret agent did approach such a respected citizen, what do you think the citizen should do about it, Mr. Skelton?"

"Don't ask me, old man," Skelton exclaimed, looking astonished. But he crushed out his cigarette with decisive force. "I mean, who am I to tell a free citizen what to do? I only know that if I were him—or is it he?—I would think very carefully before continuing to earn the displeasure of a democratic government. There are all kinds of ways of making things difficult for a chap, you know," he finished, with only a faint smile.

Somebody buffeted me as he ran past, shouting. I grabbed for support at a standard lamp. A dizzy pattern of light flitted briefly over the ceiling.

After what seemed like a long time Skelton asked lightly, "So? What do you think, Mr. Bandy?"

I thought about it, still hanging on, rather nervously, to the floor lamp. "I don't know," I said finally. "You see, a bird in the hand is worth two in the bush."

It took Skelton a few seconds to exclaim admiringly over this phrase. "A bird in the hand is worth. . . . I must remember that," he said, his eyes shining. And he continued to look fairly admiring as he added, "You know, I have the impression that you're cocking a snook. They thought that might be your response, Bandy, but they thought they'd give you a chance before they said. . . . What *do* they say, anyway, in the films, when they want something to happen?"

"Uh . . . 'Action'?"

"That's it," Skelton exclaimed, looking pleased as anything. "That's the word."

Then he reached for and shook my hand. "Thank you, Bandy. And it was a pleasure meeting you at last. I really mean that," he said, and, wishing me a sincere good night, he opened the door and hastened along the corridor from which all the other hounds had departed.

I found out what he meant only three days later when I was summoned to the Canbury Park Road works of Hawker, and was there informed by a dejected Fred Sigrist that they would not be able to fill our order.

Something had come up. It concerned future orders from the Air Ministry. These might be jeopardized if the work on the sixty Snipes was carried out. He was sure I would understand that they could not risk their future in aviation for the sake of a mere sixty aircraft. So they would just have to go on making pots and pans and hope that the ministry would give them enough work in the future in order to prevent a second and final liquidation of a Sopwith enterprise.

I looked at Tom Sopwith, who was also at the meeting. "This was from the Chief of Air Staff, I suppose?"

"I'm afraid we're not at liberty to say any more," Sigrist began.

"Oh yes, we are," Sopwith said quietly. "Yes, naturally the word came from the government via the CAS."

"I see. Our concrete order worth up to half a million is to be canceled, just in case you get an order from the ministry some time in the vague future?"

"That's the situation," Sopwith said. "I suppose you understand what it's all about, Mr. Bandy. I'm sure I don't." He flushed and raised his voice. "Except that when the British government starts to blackmail British industry—"

"Tom," Sigrist said.

"When they start to blackmail industry," Sopwith repeated forcefully, "I think it's about time we stopped thinking of ourselves as the world's greatest power and started behaving properly, as a banana republic should."

Wearing an Ill-fitting Smile

It was just prior to that warning from Rupert Skelton that the brilliant designer and test pilot, Geoffrey de Havilland, had shown me his latest fighter-reconnaissance aircraft, the DH42. The prototype had been flying successfully for more than a year, though the machine that Mr. de Havilland invited me to try out was a more advanced version, with a metal fuselage.

I accepted his invitation to test-fly the DH42 with alacrity, took off from the field at Edgware and was never seen again; or at least not until teatime.

When I finally returned to the company sheds, stunting like mad, de Havilland had difficulty in suppressing his annoyance over the thoroughness with which I had tested an experimental machine. Luckily we had recently made the final payment on the order for thirty DH9s. This made me his most valued customer, so he couldn't afford to fulminate.

"I didn't actually mean you to drain the tank and strain the machine to the limit, Mr. Bandy," he said with a smile like a set of worm gears. "I just expected you to do a quick circuit and bump, you know."

However, he quickly regained his aplomb when I praised the DH42 to the skies and asked how soon he could deliver sixty.

"Beg your pardon?"

"If you can complete half that number by next January, I'm prepared to place an order as soon as you like."

"Sixty."

"I was going to go for single seaters—the Snipe, to be exact—but this machine is so superior that, assuming we can agree on price, I'm prepared to abandon the order for the Snipes."

"*Sixty*? You did say *sixty*?"

"Yes. Five dozen assorted DH42s, please."

"Come into the office, Mr. Bandy. No, please, take the best chair, the one with the cushion. Would you care for a cigar . . . tea . . . champagne . . . my sister?

"Actually," he went on, as soon as he'd calmed down, "the DH42 is a government contract, but I see no difficulty there. It's their practice to order just one, or two, or, very occasionally, three examples of a new design, in order to keep development going until they have the money to reequip the service. It's hard on us, of course, but we go along with it because if they don't order a new type in quantity this year, maybe next year they will. Incidentally, sir, you've made a wise decision. Our machine is technically up-to-date with a superb engine, not one of your old-fashioned rotaries, as in the Snipe. So if you're willing to sign a letter of intent, Mr. Bandy, I could approach the ministry right away for their approval. There's no need to worry about a favorable response either. They've never stood in the way before. After all, we're the ones who count, eh, we're the ones who build the aeroplanes, aren't we, ha, ha, ha."

So we had gone ahead on this basis, and everybody was pleased, especially our pilots, who were thrilled at the prospect of taking part in fly-pasts, circuses, exhibitions, reviews, tattoos—or whatever the Maharajah wanted us for—in the very latest fighter aircraft, while our administrators were happy because the machines were to come from a company noted for the excellence of its products.

Until Mr. de Havilland came to us a few days later to inform us that the authorities had vetoed the deal. De Havilland were not to be allowed to exploit their own work.

"They were quite happy about the sale to another customer at first," de Havilland said. "In fact, one official told me that if a production run could bring the price down a few hundred, they might consider placing an order themselves.

"The Third Air Lord himself said there was no reason we couldn't go ahead with it. And then yesterday the head of the Air Ministry telephoned to say there'd been a change of policy. The DH42 project was to be considered strictly government, and the special tools and jigs were not to be used on anybody else's behalf."

There was a vicious pause. "You don't look terribly surprised," he said.

"No."

His good breeding prevented him from asking what it was all about. He went away thoroughly angry at the government, but furious with us for failing to let him know that we were enemies of the state.

As for our feelings, we weren't surprised, because by then it had become clear that neither de Havilland, nor Hawker, nor any other aircraft manufacturer would now sell us so much as a spark plug. The word had been passed around in that delicately ruthless way of theirs—over lunch in private clubs and at carefully arranged accidental encounters—that any firm that supplied us with airframes or engines might just possibly find government contracts a little harder to obtain in the future.

We couldn't really blame the manufacturers. They were clinging on to an economic precipice as it was; it would be folly to antagonize the rescue team.

"So what are we going to do now?" Derby asked at our next Monday afternoon conference.

The crisis was such that even Khooshie was present—complete with his new bodyguard. She was lurking just outside the frosted glass door of the conference room on the top floor. We could hear her sighing impatiently every now and then.

"About the only thing we can do now," Roland Mays said, "is to move the entire operation out of the country."

There was a shocked silence. The long paneled room shuddered as heavy lorries and buses rumbled past in nearby Cannon Street.

"With the government determined to stymie us, I don't see what else we can do," he added.

We all thought about it with a pang. Several pangs, in fact.

"Dash it all, I've just renewed the lease on my flat for six months," Freddy said. "Can't we stay in London and simply buy the rest of the aeroplanes abroad?"

"The French would certainly be delighted to receive the order," Hibbert said, "not least because it would give them the opportunity to poke Perfidious Albion in the eye."

Everybody nodded gloomily. France and Britain were practically at war with each other these days over France's merciless treatment of Germany, the French occupation of the Ruhr and various other areas of conflict.

"Unless we started from scratch again, it would be impossibly complicated, Freddy," Hibbert added. "Just the revised paperwork alone would be an awful headache. New licenses, bills, port certificates, not to mention having to adjust all the financial arrangements."

"I agree," Mays put in. "Besides, the government would certainly find alternative ways to blow the bridges."

"So it looks as if our arrival in India will be delayed quite a bit," somebody said.

"No," Khooshie said.

It was the first word he had uttered at the meeting. We all squinted toward the head of the table. While the rest of us were in clothes rendered stale and wrinkled by yet another hectic day's activities and emergencies, he had shown up in a freshly laundered white shirt, yet another new jacket and a Fair Isle pullover. His black hair, brushed straight back without a parting, shone like a helmet.

We waited patiently for him to expand this negative into a telling phrase.

"I have heard from father," he said in a subdued voice. "He has reached home at Djelybad. He says it is more important than ever that we get there soon.

"He says that everything will be ready," Khooshie continued, meeting nobody's eye. "They have laid out the airfield at last. He is employing engineers of the Societé Anonyme Industriel Bessoneau. They have started work on the hangars and other buildings. Father is trying very, very hard to be in a rush. It is up to us to be in a rush, too." He looked toward the window. "He says he has written to you about this, Bartholomew."

"Yes. He wants us to get there even earlier than planned."

There was a brief silence, broken only by a loud sighing noise from without—Muriel Tombola, growing lonely or impatient. As we now knew, she hated having to hang about for longer than a few minutes.

"I just don't see how we can meet even the *original* deadline," Mays said. And then proceeded to ask the question that we didn't really want answered, in case it was unfavorable and forced us to give up our splendid salaries. "Why is it so urgent anyway, Khooshie?"

"I cannot say."

We sat there wondering whether he meant that he was not prepared to say, or that he didn't know the answer.

Now that the question had finally broken cover, everybody was suddenly keen to run it down. "I mean, you're not actually going to use your air force *as* an air force, are you?" Mays prompted. "You know, bombing people, and so forth?"

"It's just for air displays and things," Hibbert added, nodding his head as if in the hope that this would set up a sympathetic oscillation in Khooshie's noodle.

Khooshie merely fiddled with one of the gold rings on his fingers.

Observing the uncertainty of the response, Derby said casually, "I heard from a pal of mine at Adastral House that India Command had been thinned out quite a bit recently. They've had to send most of their planes and pilots to handle that trouble in Iraq." He tapped an unlit cigarette on the tabletop, making an effort to smooth out his usual wary, cynical expression. "This sudden urgency of yours wouldn't have anything to do with the urgency of theirs, would it?"

Outside the frosted glass, Muriel Tombola began to whistle loudly and quite tunefully.

"I know," Derby continued carefully, inspecting the cigarette for flaws, "that few of us have any love for the authorities. But not even we would be willing to confront the RAF in India, even if we outnumbered them. Some of them we know personally."

"Your father fully understands that, doesn't he?" Mays asked.

When Khooshie's beige face remained expressionless, I put in, "M'oh yes, we're all agreed on that. The Maharajah recognized that from the start."

Yet Khooshie continued stubbornly silent. We peered at him in frustration. Initially tolerant of his oat-sowing operation, irritation over the boy's randy frolics was now drifting over the company. It might not have been so bad if he had simply gone out and enjoyed himself. After all, he was only eighteen, freed from domestic restrictions—assuming he'd ever had any—for the first time in his life. But every now and again he would put in an appearance for as much as half a day, making difficulties about signing checks, complaining about people using his big, ground-floor office as an interview room or pestering us for our opinions about his fancy designs, the latest being his aircraft symbols, the Jhamjarh equivalent of the German cross and the British and French roundels. Khooshie's design showed two crossed forearms ending in hands that wielded bloodstained hatchets. I had pointed out that the purpose of such insignia was to render aircraft identifiable, not to make an editorial statement. In the case of his artistic composition, it would be difficult to make it out from a distance of more than five feet. At which Khooshie lost his temper and shouted that I was always throwing buckets over his ideas. Look at the way I had squashed his beautiful uniform and insisted on a plain, blue-gray tunic. And I had offended his artist friends by turning down their lovely cubist-style badges and Bubba's air force cap with the feather. "I mean, hang it, Bartholomew, what could be more symbolic of flying than feathers?" he had shouted in defence of her creation.

Today in the conference room his face was suddenly that of a stranger. It was hard with determination. We were quite impressed and assumed that this resolve had something to do with the letter he had received from his father that morning.

"This is as good a time as any to clear things up," Mays persisted. "We must know once and for all, Khooshie. Is your air force for any aggressive intent?"

"No, it isn't," Khooshie said quietly, and apparently with complete sincerity.

There was a noticeable lessening of tension as Mays added, "It's strictly a defensive weapon, then, just as your army has been for so many years?"

"Of course."

That was the reply that Mays had been looking for. He said quickly, "Good. So it can't be all that important that we reach India on time. A few weeks can't make that much difference."

The boy stared fixedly at the center of the long table, his lips compressed.

I had my pipe going by then. After a judicious suck or two, I raised my eyebrows at the lad.

"I am sorry, Bartholomew," he muttered, digging a thumbnail into the edge of the conference table, "but we have had an agreement right from the beginning, and we are insisting that you stick to it." He hesitated; then, as if on parade, he straightened his shoulders and raised his handsome head to attention. "If you don't think you can manage it, father says we are to give up the whole idea, and that is all there is to it."

"Abandon the whole project? Close this office, everything?"

"Yes."

A heavy silence descended. Hibbert opened the top pocket of his shirt and peered into it. Freddy examined his nails and adjusted a cuticle or two. Philip Brashman, who was to be—was to have been?—one of our squadron commanders, stuck out a boot, examined it with a frown then leaned over to flick at a speck of dust that had had the effrontery to mar its brilliant finish.

And Muriel Tombola stuck her face into the room and called out, "Hey. Hey, Khoosh—how much longer you going to be, Khoosh?"

Whereupon Khoosh jumped up and said, "Oh, my goodness, yes, I am forgetting about the tea dancing. Yes, righty-ho, Muriel, I shall be ready in two ticks of a lamb's tail."

After Khooshie had left, silence descended again with a heavy thud. Mays joined in the fiddling contest by jingling the coins in his pocket, his well-cared-for phiz drooping. Derby bit his pencil, then examined the teeth marks to see if they were evenly spaced. Hibbert drew a figure on a notepad, 428,776,242½, then divided it by 7 and Freddy looked at everybody else's expression for guidance as to how he should compose his own.

"Well, decision time," Mays said at length.

"What decision?" Derby muttered sullenly, knowing perfectly well what decision.

"Do we go on or not?"

Hibbert was the first to answer. "I think what you really mean," he said quietly, "is, do we believe him or not?"

"If one buys a shotgun," Freddy said suddenly, "surely one intends to use it."

We all twisted in our seats and stared at him.

"I mean . . . don't you think so?" he faltered, blushing.

"Nobody forks out millions merely for ceremony," Derby said.

"Something is going on that we don't know about."

"Right. Khooshie has obviously been enjoined to silence."

"There's a great deal of unrest in India just now. Anti-British feeling. Resistance to our God-given right to order the world's affairs—"

"Apart from a few intransigent areas like America and Russia."

"I mean, look at this India Congress thing. Look at Gandhi. If the Maharajah Prakash put a well-trained army and air force at their disposal. . . ."

This time the silence was ominous.

"The Royal Family does," I said suddenly, out of the corner of my pipe.

They all looked at me. "What?" Brashman asked.

"The Royal Family does."

They all sat there with glassy eyes, trying to work out what I was talking about.

Brashman was the first to give up. "Does what?" he asked.

"Fork out millions for ceremony."

"Oh, yes. Well, they're the Royal Family, after all."

"And the Maharajah's had an army for years and never used it."

"That's true," Mays said, nodding his head judiciously, though he had not the slightest idea whether it was true or not. But I was the boss, and he preferred to agree with me whenever possible.

They all watched keenly as I relit my pipe and sucked noisily to get it going. After a moment Derby squeamishly averted his eyes from my cheeks, which were sucking in and out in what he plainly considered a revolting fashion, while Brashman, getting tired of waiting for this performance to end, went for a walk to Trafalgar Square and back.

"Personally," I said, puffing with utmost sincerity, "I am determined to believe the Maharajah's assurance that he has no aggressive intent toward the British in India."

"Quite," Mays said, in a tone designed to suggest that he agreed, disagreed, felt noncommittal or all three.

"It may be appallingly naive of me, but there you are," I said, puffing.

"Yes, there you are."

"And," I added, examining the stem of my pipe for leaks, "my conviction has nothing to do with the fact that my salary would cease the moment I was no longer convinced."

"No, course not."

"Course it hasn't."

"That has absolutely nothing to do with it."

"I would never let an income of well into five figures influence my moral or patriotic judgment."

"Certainly not. Neither would we."

"So, gentlemen, I say we go on."

"Right."

"Quite."

"Jolly good."

"Agreed."

"Actually," Freddy said, "old Lord Liver bought a Purdy shotgun and never once used it."

"There. You see?" I said triumphantly.

"He popped off just afterwards, you see."

"Anyway," I said, after glaring at Freddy for a moment, "the point is, not *do* we go on, but *how*. But there, too, I am utterly confident that some way will be found to get round this disgraceful, immoral government obstructionism."

"Hear, hear," Mays said.

But days later we were still no closer to acquiring the operational and spare aircraft that were to have made up our two fighter squadrons. In a sudden attack of gloom, Hibbert confided, "I just don't see how we can solve the problem without divine intervention. If not a *deus ex machina*, then at least a few pulleys."

"Sometimes I don't understand a word you say," snapped Brashman. Hib's intellectualisms were starting to get on his nerves.

"Anyway, we already have divine intervention," Derby said. "We have Bandy."

He looked annoyed when nobody chortled as they usually did at his sallies.

After a moment Freddy said in his timid tones, "You wouldn't think old MacDonald and his socialist chums would care all that much about imperial India." He was referring to the Prime Minister, Ramsay MacDonald, who had formed the country's first Labor government at the beginning of the year.

"Them?" Mays said. Freddy's naiveties usually made him smile in a kindly way, but this time he felt that a snort was in order. "My dear fellow, it's the permanent types in the Home Office, Foreign Office, Colonial Office, India Office and War Office who've got together with the Air Ministry over this. I don't suppose MacDonald knows a thing about it."

I looked up. "Oh?" I contributed.

"Oh, what?"

"Tell me more. Why wouldn't he know about it?"

"Well, for one thing, he's his own foreign secretary, and he seems to be spending most of his time in Geneva these days, involved in the League of Nations and other scandals."

While the others talked back and forth, I thought about it.

"Has Hawker sacked any men recently?" I asked suddenly.

They all raised their eyes to heaven, or held their heads in their hands. He was off again, with his peculiar asides.

"Don't know."

"Give Mr. Sigrist a ring and find out, Freddy."

Ten minutes later he was back with the answer. "They sacked two men a couple of months ago for whittling on a wooden airframe, that's all," he reported. "But it had nothing to do with our canceled order."

"What've you got in mind, Chief?"

"Does anyone know the Prime Minister?" I asked.

They all held their heads again.

"Nobody knows him personally? Nobody got any contacts in his office?

"Then I think," I said, "I'll have to call in a six-year-old IOU."

Four days later I was at 10 Downing Street, waiting to see the Prime Minister.

I had had dealings with one other occupant of this grimy row house off Whitehall six years previously. The occupant then was Lloyd George, and readers of these memoirs will know that he was indebted to me; that, back in 1918, the Welsh Wizard had spellbound me into helping him get rid of the commander-in-chief in France, Field Marshal Douglas Haig. The PM had armed me with certain damaging facts about Haig's conduct of military affairs, and I was to fire them at the press and public during a speech at Fallow Grammar School in Chester. But the timing had not been too good. The speech was delivered on March 20, and on the next day the Germans made their massive attack on the Western Front, which threatened to win them the war. At such a critical juncture, Lloyd George simply could not proceed with his plan to dismiss the c-in-c.

This, of course, had left me horribly exposed as solitary gaff-blower, to be vilified in the press as a jumped-up Air Ministry colonel whose behavior was close to treason. I had, as the famous military correspondent of *The Morning Post* put it, stabbed my own commander-in-chief in the back while he had his back to the wall. Which, of course, was the occasion when the Chief of Air Staff, a good friend of Haig's, had slung me out of the Air Ministry and, with the characteristic vindictiveness that he invariably exhibited when dealing with yours truly, placed me in the forefront of that same German attack.

Lloyd George assured me that he would not forget the little service that I was rendering him, and when I went to see him now at the House of Commons I found that, by some miracle, he really hadn't forgotten. Even so, he looked pretty relieved when he realized that it was someone else who would have to supply the favor, not him. All I was asking of the fiery Welshman was his help in obtaining an appointment for me with Ramsay MacDonald.

"Is that all you want, bach?" he said, and there and then set the wheels in motion to carry me to an appointment just far enough ahead to enable the government watchdogs to check up on me and make sure that I was not an assassin, a paid-up member of the Conservative Party or a canvasser for some worthy charity.

I was kept waiting in an anteroom for only a few minutes before being ushered into the cabinet room. There I found the Right Honorable seated alone at the long table, gloomily surveying a hillock of despatch boxes that had greeted him on his triumphant return from Geneva.

Without a word he gestured for me to sit opposite him at the cabinet table while he finished snatching his way through a report. "Och," he said finally, "ah'd like tae tossue the wanchancy lhield who skelloched the speerings of thus bogle-wark."

I opened my mouth to express an enthusiastically sycophantic agreement; then slowly closed it again. "Eh?" I enquired.

"Makkin' me greet and grane with thus routh o' doited collogue—the hirpling bitcallant."

"Really?"

"An' the noo I hae tae throle a jaloused deray."

"Is that right?"

He slung the report aside and looked at me squarely for the first time. "So," he grunted. "Cothrom na Feinne, ye warrand whilk mair a scowp or a flitt of siller?"

"Ha?" I said, in the Icelandic fashion.

"Or is it a birling glisk that has caused you tae glunch in the clamjamfry?"

"Uh. . . ."

"Weel, oot with it, mon."

"Oot with what?"

"With your routh, drookit cantrips and brawly loanings."

"I haven't come for a loan. I—"

"Loanings means bypaths. Do you no' understand plain Sco'ish?"

"Certainly. I spent my honeymoon in Scotland."

Mr. MacDonald stared at me fixedly. However, he soon turned away and massaged his eyes. I was quite pleased. Plainly, I was a sight for sore eyes.

"All the same, I suppose I'd better talk to you in your own language—whatever it is," he muttered. With an effort he stared at me again. "So you had your honeymoon in Scotland, did you? You married the poor wee Lewis lassie, I believe?"

I stared. "You know the Lewises, sir?"

"I do. William Lewis was the only human being I ever encountered in the Foreign Office."

I had been looking forward to the appointment with Ramsay MacDonald with some apprehension, for he was, after all, a socialist. I regarded socialism with slightly more respect and admiration than I accorded pederasty. Still, MacDonald probably wasn't a *real* socialist, as, so far at least, he had made no attempt to redistribute my wealth. In no time at all I found myself chatting to him almost as if we were old friends.

I mean, perhaps it wasn't his fault—something nasty in his childhood, perhaps—that had made him a believer in the overthrow of the profit motive, self-interest, fortune hunting, feathering one's nest and everything else that was good in man. Forsooth, he seemed quite a decent old fellow.

On his part he seemed quite impressed that the great David Lloyd George had spoken up for me. Somehow he gained the impression that his Liberal predecessor sympathized with my problem. Of course, I may inadvertently have given MacDonald this impression when I dwelt at length on my long-standing relationship with the fiery Welshman and on our common efforts to rid the country of that slaughterhouse superintendent Field Marshal Haig.

"Lloyd George is concerned, is he, at this attempt to scuttle your contract with this aircraft manufacturer?" MacDonald asked.

I sneaked around the question in my usual forthright way. "It's not just an attempt, sir," I said. "They've succeeded."

"Who is they, exactly?"

"I gather it was originally the civil servants of the Colonial and India Office, Prime Minister."

"Oh, them."

"But now it seems to be mostly the Chief of Air Staff."

"Aye. I got on to him the moment I heard from David," the Prime Minister said, "to get his side of it."

Oh, damn, I thought. That's torn it.

"But at the mention of your name he became so incoherent I found it difficult to understand what his objections were. Mind you, even normally, he tends to be a man of few words," MacDonald said, adding, "and even those few are often delivered as if he were dictating a telegram."

"That's not my experience of him," I said ruefully, sticking my hands deep into my pockets and stretching my legs under the cabinet table. "He says what he thinks of me all too fluently."

"Anyway, I did gather he felt that letting this Maharajah chappie have his own air force was not a very good thing at all for the security of the Indian subcontinent."

"Yes, sir," I said, pasting a confidential expression onto my face as if he and I were already on the same side against the duffers. "He's simply not aware that the Maharajah has had a private army of from two to three divisions for half a century without ever using it in any way counter to British interests in India."

"Is that so?"

"Yes, sir. He's had a standing army for more than fifty years," I said, with an emphasis justified by the fact that I was telling the precise truth for once. "He has never caused the Indian government a moment of concern, as far as I can determine. In fact there's a firm treaty between us and the State of Jhamjarh. We also have a political agent in the capital, to keep an eye on things."

"Aye, laddie; but they say an air force is a different kettle of fish altogether; that it would gravely upset the balance of power out there."

"A mere five squadrons, sir?" I asked with a light laugh. "A few antiquated aircraft, none less than six years old, some of them ten? Yet," I added darkly, "they represent much-needed work for a good many working-class families, Prime Minister."

"Sticking in the political knife, are you, Bandy?"

"Yes, sir."

MacDonald stared for a moment, then laughed briefly through his nose before looking stern again. "A few aircraft canny be all that much of a loss to this Hawker Aircraft Company."

"Sixty aircraft, sir? It's the most substantial order they've received since the end of the war."

"You know, Bandy," the PM said softly but warningly, "I can check every claim you're making."

"Please do, Prime Minister," quoth I, looking tremendously honest. "In fact, I don't believe any aircraft company has had such a huge order as that since the war."

"A huge order is it? That's funny. A moment ago I had the impression that in numbers your air force was a mere bagatelle."

"Ah. Ah, yes," I floundered. "But though sixty aircraft is not really a significant force, it *is* a significant order for a company that's desperately short of work.

"Dammit," I cried, "they've been forced to make pots and pans to keep going, when they should be building a future for the country in aviation. The industry ought to be encouraged instead of, of treated in this fashion. But of course, they're no longer needed for a war, are they?"

"Now, now, Bandy. I'm not a mother's meeting."

"Sorry, sir," I said, cursing myself for speaking out like that. I believe now, though, that this outburst impressed him more than any of the facts and figures I threw at him that afternoon. Except among the most desiccated intellectuals, emotion is the most telling argument of all.

Though, mind you, I suspect that he equated my abrupt indignation with the plight of the workers rather than the manufacturers; possibly because, only seconds later, I was combining the outburst with the information that the Hawker Aircraft Company was already sacking men.

"Oh?"

"Yes, sir. We checked with them about it only the other day, and they confirmed it," I said.

"And that may not be the end of the calamity," I continued. "While we're whittling away the country's future in aircraft manufacturing, the cancellation of our contract may lead to much more extensive sackings." I didn't tell him that the sackings would be at the Prakash Purchasing Commission.

"Aye," MacDonald grunted, staring at me unblinkingly. "Not content with sticking in the dirk, now you're giving it a wee twist, eh?"

"Sir?"

"I can see now how you managed to win a by-election against all odds."

"You know about that?"

"Don't worry, I've found out quite a lot about you in the last two or three days."

"You haven't found out too much, I hope," I said.

I had replied with genuine anxiety, but he must have thought I was joking, for he chuckled. "And I must say I'm not unimpressed—despite what people say about you."

"Ah."

He sat back, tapping a pen on the edge of the great cabinet table, and stared at me ruminatively. "Talking about aircraft," he said at length, "what do you think of the situation in Iraq?"

"Ah, yes, the situation in Iraq," I said, and paused, apparently giving it my most serious consideration. And in fact I was. I was trying desperately to work out what the situation in Iraq could be, and why on earth he had suddenly brought it up.

The trouble was that these days I had no time for reading newspapers. I mean, great Scott, I hadn't even realized that a Socialist government had been in power for nearly a year until quite recently; so I was hardly likely to know what was happening in Iraq. In fact I didn't even know where Iraq was. I had hardly even heard of Iraq. Nobody had taught me about Iraq in school.

He had said, "Talking about aircraft. . . ." So obviously Iraq had something to do with airplanes. And I seemed to remember seeing the word Iraq on a newsagent's placard. But that was as far as I could get.

So for once I was forced to forgo bluster and tell the truth. "I don't know a thing about it," I said.

Oddly enough, he looked pleased rather than disillusioned at this reply. It was a while before I realized why. He thought that as an intelligent and concerned citizen, I knew quite a lot about it, but not in the detail required of a person involved in governmental affairs. Hence my modest rejoinder.

But even more oddly, he did not follow up this sudden change of topic, but instead proceeded to ask me questions about myself. Presumably he was filling in the gaps left in the report on me compiled by his security services.

Then he returned to it without warning. "How," he asked abruptly, "would you like to go to Iraq for me, Bandy?"

"Eh?"

"You heard, laddie."

"Go to Iraq?"

"Yes."

"Me?"

"You."

"Go to Iraq?"

As he was beginning to show signs of impatience, I added hurriedly, "Uh, no thank you, Prime Minister."

"I cannot for obvious reasons trust these newspaper reporters who seem to be the only outside observers on the spot. I am badly in need of an unbiased account of what is really going on out there," he said, pinning me to the chair with his unblinking gaze.

"So would you be able to get there and back inside two or three weeks?"

"No, sir. Because I'm not going."

"It seems to me you're just the man for the job, Bandy. You are not one of us, and nobody could say that you were sympathetic to the old school tie, or the capitalist system as symbolized by the newspaper lords, the bankers or people like the Chief of Air Staff."

"What's he got to do with it? The CAS."

"I don't need to tell you that, young man. The bombing campaign was his idea."

So they were bombing somebody out in Iraq, were they? And the CAS was involved in some way or other. Now we were getting somewhere.

Except that I had no intention of getting anywhere.

"Anyway, the point is, nobody could accuse you of being partial to either side," MacDonald added.

"I simply can't afford the time, Prime Minister," I said, and to prove how poor a choice I would be, I hunched my shoulders like Uriah Heep and adopted a craven whine.

I might just as well have recited the *Lay of the Last Minstrel* for all the note he took of my posture. "While at the same time," he went on, "you are an experienced military man and aviator, with enough political experience to ensure that you won't drop too many goolies when you make your report to me before the House adjourns this year."

"It's very flattering that you should want me, Prime Minister," I whined, "but I fear I must decline. You see, we're at a critical juncture in the affairs of the Prakash Purchasing Commission."

"They might possibly," the PM said carefully, studying his pen, "become somewhat less critical in the immediate future."

I opened my mouth, then clopped it shut again. Then opened it again. "Ah," I said.

"Good lad. I knew there was a spark of intelligence and self-interest in there somewhere."

"You will see that our contract with Hawker is honored, if . . . ?"

"Let's not be too bald about it, Bandy."

"I don't see why not. I am bald, or increasingly so." I took a deep breath. "How long would it take, this trip?" I asked, hoping that he might provide a clue as to where Iraq was by telling me how far it was.

But, "That would depend on you," replied the unhelpful old swine.

"And you want me to report on the situation there, that's all?"

"To report just as you saw it—fearing and favoring neither side. You're good at that, aren't you, Bandy?"

"Yes," I said glumly. "Both sides usually end up hating me."

"Splendid. How soon can you leave?"

I still had my hands in my pockets and my feet under the cabinet table; so far under, in fact, that I was in danger of sliding off the chair and disappearing from sight—a fate that I should have welcomed at that moment.

Instead, I straightened up and said carefully, "How soon might the Chief of Air Staff be ordered to cease his interference with the proper functioning of British industry and with the livelihood of its workers?"

"Aye, you were in politics all right," MacDonald said, looking not all that pleased about it. He tilted his head while he thought. "Well, let's say, as soon as I receive word that you've reached Iraq—how would that do? It's not," he added smoothly, "that I don't trust you, Bandy, but it will take a few days anyway before I can prepare the proper request to the Air Ministry—"

"The proper order, Prime Minister?"

"All right, order. An order to the Air Ministry to the effect that, having carefully assessed the situation—" He stopped and regarded me coolly. "And I have carefully assessed it, laddie. I'm not a fool, you know. It seems to me that you could be taking a very considerable risk by maintaining your faith in the good intentions of this Maharajah. Situations in India can get very tricky, you know, and I'm no' sure but what I don't smell a rat.

"However," he concluded, "the smell isn't quite powerful enough to overcome the seductive scent of expediency. I desperately need an objective report on the situation out there, as much to quieten my own backbenchers as anyone. So I'll pass the word to the Air Ministry chief and make sure he obeys."

"And you'll pass the word to Hawker that they may proceed with the contract without fearing the future?"

Suddenly he looked much less avuncular. "Dinna try to drive any more bargains, Bandy. You're no' in that strong a position.

"So," he said after a chilly pause. "You'll go, then?"

"Delighted, Prime Minister," I said morosely.

"You will, of course, pay your own way out there, and all other expenses," he said, placing his big, rawboned hands on the cabinet table to indicate that the interview was nearly at an end. "It would be best if you receive no recompense from us. We wouldny wish to risk anyone accusing us of paying you for your opinions, eh, Bandy?" he said, resuming his hearty manner. In fact he even winked. "Actually that's the main reason I've chosen you for the job," he said. "So it'll no' cost me a single bawbee."

Seven days later I was in Egypt, anxiously awaiting the arrival of an aircraft that would enable me to continue across the desert to where Iraq was said to be located, in the biblical land between the Tigris and the Euphrates.

That's Me in the Middle East

Gad, it was good to bask in the heat again.

The voyage along the Mediterranean had not been particularly warm. In fact the late-September breeze had been cool enough to keep me in the American Bar since we had passed Malta. I hadn't realized how hot it had become until I stepped on deck as the *Messageries Maritimes* ship braked to a halt off Alexandria with a screech of sirens. The wind stilled, and the sun blazed as if being refueled by a trillion demented stokers.

After an expectant pause the ship shuddered, belched, then got under way again and limped toward the harbor mouth. I padded across the deck to the rail. I had the deck almost to myself. Most of the passengers were too busy panicking over their luggage and how much to tip the cabin attendants. I had only one piece of hand luggage and, having accumulated some experience in these matters, had tipped my attendant even before we left Marseilles.

As the sun furnaced down, I closed my eyes and, lizardlike, tilted my creased visage to capture a vitamin or two. In England, the sun had only broken through the clouds a couple of times in five months.

By the time I opened my eyes again, the Alexandria lighthouse was drifting past and hiding behind the ship's funnels. Now the inner harbor came fully into view. I gazed around, greedy for my first view of fabled Egypt, hoping to see some exotic, bare-bellied frail lolling in a gilded barge; or at least a row of filthy-postcard sellers. But there was hardly any sign of life at all. Nothing seemed to be moving anywhere. Even the dockyard cranes were frozen in mid-gesture.

Ah. A couple of natives, at last. A mahogany speedboat grumbled past over the glassy surface of the harbor. I peered down into it, eagerly. It contained two red-faced Englishmen in pith helmets.

There wasn't even a pyramid in view. Nothing but the steamy flatness of the Nile delta, half-eaten by the teeth of skulls, or sun-bleached buildings. The row of ships along yon pier were all from London or Rotterdam.

Still, this was only Alexandria's dockyard. Presumably there was a bit of mysterious East beyond the dockyard gates. There was certainly a mysterious odor in the air. It was like nothing ever sniffed before, compounded, it seemed to me, of sandalwood, sewage, raw tobacco, hot sand, Greek *eau de Cologne*, perspiration and Bovril.

M. Bourguignon joined me at the rail. A businessman, he was on his way to Pondicherry, the French colony in India. He was the only Frenchman who had deigned to converse with me during the voyage from Marseilles—perhaps because he wasn't French at all, but Belgian.

"Just look at those people down there," he said, pointing.

I looked over the side of the ship. "What, those?" I asked. "Those aren't people. Those are rags—bales of rags, presumably imported for making paper, because the Egyptians have run out of papyrus, you see."

Then a couple of the bales stirred, to confirm that they were, indeed, people.

An hour passed before those few of us who were landing at Alexandria were allowed to straggle ashore; then another hour in a hot, dusty shed waiting for customs clearance. Finally, in my case, a wait of two hours for the train to Cairo; the journey taking us through a flat, white-hot plain dotted with villages made of cow pats. The inhabitants, drifting along streets that looked like bacteria-harboring fissures in the walls of hot, steamy kitchens, were so thin that crocodiles would surely use them only as toothpicks and stalk instead the emaciated ibis for a relatively meaty meal.

Occasionally from the carriage window I glimpsed a naked child or two playing in the dust. One of them seemed to have rickets. That was a condition familiar enough in England, but there the children had iron leg braces to enable them to get about. The boy here was mobile only because he was dragging himself along the ground, seeking the cooler shadows.

In Egypt I came to the conclusion in ignorant haste that between the poor and the rich there was no comfortable middle class as in western countries. The houses seemed to be either mud pies or palaces. That was my conclusion. A fat lot I knew. Cairo in 1924 was a city of colonies, Western, Copt and Levantine, each with its own flourishing middle class of merchants, engineers, financiers and even artists. They set brilliant tables at which strangers like me would never sit, or even know about. The British caroused in their circumspect way while keeping the treasury from going bankrupt and building the roads and irrigation works; the French ran the museums and formed string quartets; the Copts, the truest Egyptians, manned many of the top positions in the government; the Jews ran the banks; the Greeks employed the fellahin at wages of sixpence a day to build their marble palaces; and the Syrians made the pastry, or lived off their Palestine estates. The Turks, who had only recently lost Egypt, were still here in large, affluent numbers. They were the aristocrats among the Moslems, though they did not consider themselves Egyptian and made no great attempt to learn Arabic. But all tourists like me ever saw was conscienceless wealth and grievous poverty. Child labor still obtained, despite the labor laws, with children as young as six working in the raw-cotton workshops for eighteen hours a day.

The sanitation didn't seem much more progressive than the working conditions. When I reached Cairo at six-thirty on the day of my arrival and stepped out of the railway station, I saw a mule lying dead in the middle of the concourse. Judging by its expansion it had been there in the stifling heat for about two days. It quite took me back to the bad old days in the trenches on the Western Front.

Evading a mob of importunate porters and unctuous urchins, I hopped aboard a gharry and directed the driver to the Semiramus

Hotel—where I received yet another forceful impression. As we reached the hotel, a fellow with a grin like the San Andreas Fault appeared and offered me a spot of entertainment. He had with him a goat and a monkey, and for a few piasters he would encourage the latter to mount the former. Indeed, the monkey almost did so freely, when, misunderstanding a signal from its master, it erected and scuttled toward the goat. I understood later that, for a few additional piasters, the animals would do it balanced on skittles.

By ten o'clock that night I had partaken of an excellent dinner in the splendid dining room of the hotel and was sprawled contentedly in my room or, to be exact, outside the room on the tiny balcony. Even that late at night, the heat had diminished only slightly. Which was okay with me. I think this was the first time I had been consistently warm since abandoning my overheated office on Parliament Hill so many eons ago.

I was determined to make the most of it. I had even switched off the ceiling fan in the bedroom so as not to reduce the temperature below ninety degrees until it was time for bed.

Gad, this was the life, I thought, sighing with pleasure as I gazed through the balcony grillwork at a night sky the color of pearls, and at Cairo's half-Turkish, half-Edwardian silhouette of minarets and bank buildings, and listened to some chap who was either being tortured by the traffic police or calling the faithful to prayer. On a small table at my elbow stood a tray and a bottle, one of several bottles of French brandy purchased on board ship. (I had heard that some people in these parts rather frowned on booze and discouraged its use.) I even had a bulbous glass to drink out of. What more could one ask of life?

Actually, plenty more. As prearranged, the Semiramus Hotel was to be our *poste restante*, and I had been hoping that a message would be waiting for me when I arrived. But my pigeonhole was vacant. I was annoyed. Still, it would give me a few hours to purchase some tropical gear. And the delay would also enable me to orient myself to the Orient before my transport arrived to carry me over the desert to Baghdad.

* * *

By now, I had learned a bit more about Iraq and about why Ramsay MacDonald was so anxious for a reasonably objective report on the situation in that corner of the world: so that he could answer, with a semblance of conviction, the critics in his own party and in the newspapers, or mollify them with a change of policy.

It seemed that Iraq was a brand-new country, born of Britain's almost accidental acquisition of Turkish territory in the Great War. In 1914, when Turkey came into the war on the wrong side, a British force had landed at Basra to safeguard imperial interests in the Persian Gulf against the Turks. As the British were in the vicinity, they thought they might as well wander inland into Iraq, or Mesopotamia as it was then, to see if there was anything worth pinching. Liking what they saw, they decided to secure their backs by proclaiming that they had come to free the Arabs from the Turkish Empire. They then proceeded to conquer all the Turkish territory in sight throughout the Middle East. The part of it that was formerly Mesopotamia would be renamed Iraq, and everybody in it would live happily ever after.

The leaders of the numerous tribes in that region had other ideas; or rather, their ideas of living happily ever after were to gather as much loot, carry off as many women and spill as much blood as possible. Besides, they were miffed at having a non-profit government imposed on them instead of a decently corrupt Turkish regime. Accordingly, a few of the sheiks raised various revolts and had been doing so ever since.

This apparently was where our friend the CAS came in. After the war, these local rebellions had been holding down a sizable force of British troops at enormous expense. When Winston Churchill, who was then Minister of War and Air, consulted him, the CAS asserted in his usual forthright way that there was no need for the government to spend millions on maintaining forts, levies and regular troops all over the desert. He could handle the warring sheiks from just one base and with five squadrons of aircraft in conjunction with a few fast armored cars. He could control the sheiks at a fraction of the cost and with infinitely greater efficiency.

(This was one of the things that made it so difficult for me to antagonize the CAS as enthusiastically as I had antagonized so many others in authority. This proposition of his was fine, original thinking. It had never occurred even to professional military pundits that control of vast territories might be accomplished solely through air power, an idea that had major implications for an empire that owned a quarter of the entire world's real estate. Such bright ideas kept reminding me to my annoyance that the CAS was by no means the usual brass hat with the imagination of a cod. The man was almost worthy of respect. Worse, his originality produced this terrible suspicion that for once it was I rather than my antagonist who might be wrong.)

Fortunately, Mr. Churchill also proved to have a spot of imagination. He decided to try out the Chief's concept of controlling a country without actually occupying it. And the air force policy of responding to uprisings by trouncing disaffected villages began.

At first it was jolly successful. Since the establishment of the British mandate, several uprisings had been quelled by bombs, bullets and righteous indignation. Lately, though, the revolts had become more serious. Consequently so had the response—the bombing; and then the response to the response—noisy protests from the pacifists back home and from those sections of the community that would use any battering ram to get at Ramsay MacDonald's socialist fortress. By September of this year, some reports by newspaper correspondents of heavy casualties among the revolting Arabs had created storms of protest from the back benches and some vicious slanders in the press about a noncombatant premier—MacDonald was a pacifist during the war—who apparently had no moral objections to the wholesale slaughter of foreigners: men, women and children.

That was where I came in. Mr. MacDonald felt that the accounts of the correspondents were so biased and bloodily sensational and so at variance with the RAF's own account of what was going on that he needed an impartial eye. The fool thought I had one.

Still, it was possible that I might remain objective. It all depended on what was in it for me, whether my advantage lay in gaining the approval of the PM, or in sucking up to the CAS in the hope that he would ameliorate his hostility and leave me in peace to my warlike activities.

As soon as I sped back from 10 Downing Street to Laurence Pountney Hill that day, I had rushed into the office with cries of, "Quick, where's Iraq, and can I get there and back before it's time for my cocoa?"

I lost ten minutes right there. It took that long for the astonishment to die down and for Hibbert to draw on a look of determination. He proceeded to insist that I would have to travel by train and by ship. With luck, that might get me to Egypt in only six or seven days. Then from Cairo—

"You can forget that right away, Hib," I said. "I have to get there and back by the weekend. I have an appointment with my manicurist on Saturday."

This was just what Hibbert had feared, that I would plan on flying all the way. He argued vehemently that an aerial journey was much too risky. He could not permit it under any circumstances. Even a minor injury from a crash en route—an almost inevitable crash, given the distances involved—might disable me long enough to ruin our entire enterprise.

"Nonsense," I said. "Just this year I flew across the Atlantic practically via the Arctic Circle. By comparison, flying to the Middle East should be as easy as pie."

"The more I hear about that improvisate circumnavigation, the more I believe it was a miracle you survived," Hibbert said, his face stiff with stubbornness and prolixity, "given the state of navigation even in these parts, let alone anywhere near the magnetic pole. Anyway, we simply cannot allow you to fly all the way, just when things look so promising."

"You see, Bart," Derby said in a kindly fashion, "it's not so much your skin we're worried about; it's our jobs."

"Especially when you can probably get there by ship almost as expeditiously," Hibbert said.

It took another half hour of argument and some desperate slashings through shipping timetables before we reached a compromise. Our only available long-distance aircraft, a converted

Handley Page C400, could not be readied for the trip for another five days at the earliest. So I would go on ahead, by flying to Marseilles—Philip Brashman would pilot me in a DH9—and take the first available eastbound ship. There was a French vessel leaving for Alexandria in about thirty-six hours. If I caught it I could be in Egypt in a week.

Meanwhile, the Handley Page, flown by two of our experienced C400 pilots, would follow on as soon as possible. If the transport had not caught up with me by the time I reached Cairo, I was to wait at the Semiramus Hotel until it did. I was advised by somebody who knew the area well that I should definitely not attempt to travel onward from Cairo by land. Apparently the nomads did really disturbing things to your gonads if they caught you in the desert, and although there was not much call on mine lately, still, you never knew, they might just possibly come in useful, one of these days.

After two days in Cairo, haunting the lobbies, dining rooms and reception desk of the hotel, my euphoria had faded to nothing and come out the other side as irritation and frustration. Not only had the Handley Page failed to arrive, I hadn't even received a cable telling me which part of the world it *had* reached. I'd despatched several cables myself, asking for information—any information—the football scores, even. Nothing. I had even tried telephoning, but after two hours I had gotten no farther than Portugal. At least I think that the incomprehensible babble heard at the far end of the line was Portuguese.

Attempting to see something of Cairo while waiting for news was almost as frustrating. One could hardly swing an elbow without jarring it against Egyptian touts of various sorts and small, hungry boys, literally hundreds of them, who swathed me the moment I emerged from the affluent portals of the hotel, all offering to act as my guides to the tomb of Ramsay II, or trips to Pyramus, Thisbe, Chops or the temple of Fred Karno, or to sell me themselves or their sisters. At first, aware of how rich I was compared with them, I ventured forth so laden with coins that I feared my new cream-colored tropical suit would never recover from the pregnancy, and I would toss handfuls of piasters toward their convulsive paws. But there were just too many of them, and besides, the largesse was causing near riots that were drawing me to the attention of the police. Like the mysterious Turk in the room next to mine in the hotel, I was most anxious to remain as inconspicuous as possible.

The Turk, a massive fellow in a maroon fez, had twice reacted to the presence of British army officers in the lobby of the hotel, which was what had first drawn my attention to him; that and his pained expression when the desk clerk had addressed him too loudly as Mr. Kekevi.

Anyway, I was forced in the end to stop handing out any money at all to the mendicants. Instead I learned to shove heartlessly through the throng until they gave up or were unable to follow me through the narrower streets.

Once free of the importunate unfortunates, though, I was able to tour without being unduly pestered. In the process I was surprised at how colorless Egypt was and, indeed, all of the Middle East that I saw. In reading the *Thousand and One Nights*—properly expurgated, of course—I had come to think of the Middle East as a positive riot of color. The reality was like a sepia photo. Though I guess it was hardly surprising, considering the power of that sun, burning in the cloudless, washed-out sky. Still, the bazaars were colorful enough, with their amazing stalls of embroidered clothing, glittering brassware and vivid foodstuffs, strange fruits and vegetables shaped like outsized teeth, homunculi, candles or other shapes obscene enough to excite the attention of a Havelock Ellis.

The way the surrounding desert trespassed on the city was almost as fascinating. Right where the buildings of Cairo ended, the desert began, a desert perpetually doing its best to infiltrate and form sand dunes in fountains and bald patches on grass verges. When storms formed the sand into a blanket and drew it over the city, it smothered even the ferocious sun.

I knew all about the desert because I spent two or three hours in it one afternoon. I joined a tour to the pyramids, along with other guests from the Semiramus, including a pair of American girls of about twelve or thirteen and their mother; and, to my surprise, Mr. Kekevi. He had not struck me as being the tourist type.

As a ride on a camel was included in the price of the tour, I took advantage of it, yawing and pitching over the foot-burning sand and causing the American girls to stare first at my face, then at that of the camel, then back at mine, and break into fits of giggles.

Shortly after the camel had genuflected me back to earth, Mr. Kekevi approached with the absurd excuse that he needed a light for his cigar. From them on, he never left my side, but trudged faithfully alongside, talking on and on about himself, but actually conveying very little information, and asking me very few questions but somehow receiving a great deal of information.

By the time the party was heading back to the hotel in the bus, I was beginning to feel quite pestered by what I thought was his inconsequential small talk until, halfway to the Semiramus, he asked, "By the way, you are interested in politics, Mr. Bandy?"

"M'hm. Why?"

"I have come into possession of certain information that might be of interest, perhaps?"

"M'hm? Why should it interest me?" I asked drowsily.

"You are concerned with important matters, I think, judging by telegrams you are sending and receiving?"

I turned to stare at him—not an easy task, as he was seated next to me, and his bulk was jamming me into the corner.

"I think you are interested in Iraq. Yes?"

"What makes you think that?"

"If only you consult me, Mr. Bandy, I could tell you all about trains to Suez, and from El Kantara to Palestine, and how to get from there to Baghdad. I can help in all ways. You are an important man, with much money at your disposal, and government facilities, airplanes, so on and so forth."

"Look here, Mr. Kekevi—"

"Please, no indignation," he said with a plump smile, as if declining flowers. "I know who I am talking to. You are agent of the British government, close associate of your Prime Minister, so on and so forth, and you have important work in Iraq. Well, it is about Iraq that I have the information."

I started to blurt indignantly, but then subsided, not least because I was half-tranquilized by his perfume. "Military information?" I asked.

He nodded.

"About the bombing?" I asked eagerly.

"Bombink?"

"From airplanes. You know, bombing?"

"Ah, yes. Bombink."

"It is? It's about the bombing campaign?"

"Please?"

I subsided again. It was not about the bombing.

Lethargically flicking away the flies, I tried to concentrate on Mr. Kekevi rather than on thoughts of cool running water in a shower stall. Kekevi's perfume was not the least of the distractions. Over the next few hours I was to become thoroughly familiar with Harem No. 5, which was what he was doused in, I believe. Even so, it could not quite overcome one or two body odors that were emanating from him, nor the smell of his cigar.

He was lighting another cigar now, looking me over through eyes narrowed by cunning or smoke. Lowering his voice so that it was hard to hear over the racket of the ancient autobus, he said, "What I have is details of great interest for you English—about trouble that is to happen in a few weeks in Iraq.

"There now," he finished triumphantly, waving his cigar dangerously close to my new suit. "I do not think I am giving away too much if I say that."

It occurred to me, as I sat there in that noisy bus, feeling as if the sweat and sand were combining all over my skin to form muffins, pies and tarts, that his information, if genuine, might just possibly be worth purchasing, even if it had nothing to do with the bombing. After all, it wasn't my money. His information might just possibly come in useful—perhaps earn me points with the RAF if the information was something their intelligence people didn't already know.

"What form is the information in?" I asked.

I had to rephrase the question several times before Kekevi understood. Though he spoke English fluently enough, his comprehension of the language was somewhat shaky. "Ah," he exclaimed finally. Then: "I do not think I am giving too much away if I say it is few pages, five pages, details from. . . ." He hesitated, glanced around fearfully, then took a deep breath. "From commanding general of Forty-first Salahaddin Division," he finished, looking around again; though the other bus passengers were much too wrapped up in their own sweat and grit even to glance in our direction.

"Details of what?"

"Ah," was all he said in reply.

As the bus pulled into the driveway of the hotel, I told the scented Turk—I had now identified another of his odors, that of McVities and Price biscuits; the man was a positive symphony of smells—that the price would have to be reasonable and I would have to see a sample page before so much as a piaster changed hands.

The negotiations that took place in Kekevi's room that afternoon and evening are largely irrelevant, especially as they were abortive. Naturally I wasn't parting with five hundred pounds without getting at least one of the pages translated, while Kekevi kept insisting that there was no time for this, as he was leaving the hotel in a day or two.

"Can't help that," I said. "I'm not handing over three hundred pounds—"

"Four hundred fifty."

"—pounds to someone I know nothing about, in exchange for a few sheets of cheap paper written in a language I don't understand."

"You English are so unreasonable, so on and so forth," he moaned, removing his fez for the first time that day to mop his brow. The maroon fez had left a maroon line on his puffy forehead. "Look, if you will pay by tomorrow night, I will ask only four hundred English pounds."

"Why tomorrow night?"

"I have told you," he said exasperatedly. "The agents of

Atatürk. They will kill me if they find me. I am living because I never stay in one place for more than three days. I am already too long here."

"Oh, sure," I said, though he did sort of behave as if in fear of his life from Atatürk, whoever that was.

Really, if Kekevi was a con man, I must say he was not very good at it. The few details of his background that he had volunteered sounded so improbable that it was hard to see how he could have had any faith in them as inventions. He claimed to have been a distant cousin of the almighty Sultan of Turkey, and through no fault of his own—he said—he had been forced to flee when the Sultan was deposed. And, instead of coming out with a plausible reason why he had been forced to leave the country, he had acted evasive and sullen; from which one derived the impression that he must have done something pretty bad to force him to leave Constantinople and skulk around the Middle East in fear for his life . . . unless, of course, the evasive and sullen mime was part of the confidence trickery.

Anyway, we parted without coming to an agreement, I proceeding to the American Bar in the hotel and he, evidently irritated and dismayed at his failure to conclude the business there and then, to whatever nefarious activities he indulged in of an evening.

By the time I had tossed down three drinks I had reached the conclusion that he was definitely a confidence trickster and that I would be an utter fool to believe that the copy of the military orders he was offering was of the slightest interest to anybody except some future writer on the history of the Salahaddin Division—assuming that such a unit even existed.

I mean, did the scented Turk expect me to part with a small fortune in exchange for a piece of writing that he had probably knocked off whilst sitting on the toilet in some Egyptian train—except that you couldn't sit on the toilet in an Egyptian train as they didn't have toilets, all they had was a hole in the floor and a couple of metal plates on which to place your feet—I mean, did Kekevi take me for a simpleton? I congratulated myself for refusing to give way to the impulse to purchase the five pages. I had my pride, after all—I couldn't possibly allow myself to be taken in by a confidence man, even though I could easily afford Kekevi's final price, £350.

So why did I feel dissatisfied? Was it because I had resisted an impulse of the sort that I usually gave way to, often to my advantage? Resisting the impulse, was it a sign that I was growing staid and cautious with age?

I had an urge to return to Kekevi's room and pay him the £350. I half rose to my feet to do so. But then I resisted that impulse as well. So now I felt worse than ever.

It was all very well for me to take risks and surrender to impulses and things when I was the one who was paying. But it was the Maharajah who would be forking out. Did I have the right to throw his money around on a hunch? Certainly I did. Why not? That was what he was paying for, my experience, skill and judgment. God help him, then, I thought gloomily, when his representative couldn't even find a safe route to Baghdad, let alone make up his mind to gamble £350 of somebody else's money.

And so went my thoughts, round and round, as I sat at one of the tables in the bar, huddled over my fourth Scotch; until finally, with an effort, I mentally elbowed Kekevi aside and concentrated on my own business. And I was quite relieved when it took me a mere half hour to decide that if there was no word from Hibbert by ten the next morning, I would press on to Ali Baba-land regardless . . . somehow.

The decision taken, I sprawled back in the chair and scowled around to see if there was anyone worth talking to . . . so to speak. I was suddenly feeling randy, in the mood for debauchery. For months I had been too poor or too busy to think about such matters, but with all this inactivity, first on the ship, and now in the electrifying atmosphere of an exotic city, I was building up quite a head of steam, sexwise. I was rather hoping to espy a loose woman or two. But the bar was almost empty. A group of four were talking quietly at a table in the far corner, a couple of British administrators and their wives.

Kekevi had mentioned that he might join me in the bar later that evening. I would almost have welcomed his presence by then, to distract me from libidinous thoughts . . . for as I sat there, sighing and sipping, I was seriously considering the idea of going out to rent somebody's sister. After all, it was still only ten o'clock.

Thinking sinkingly of honey-colored hips brought me back to Sigridur. Since we had parted, I'd had very little time to think about her, but surprisingly whenever I had, I did. As time passed and her faults faded, I found myself dwelling on her more and more fondly. Sometimes I even felt some compassion. It seemed to me that there was a resistance there to letting herself be loved. She made it hard for people to feel affection for her when she bullied them so mercilessly. Even harmless old fellows like the Maharajah. She was a sergeant major trapped inside the body of a northern goddess.

At that point I became aware that somebody was watching me. Naturally I assumed that it was the scented Turk again, and I turned toward the entrance, the direction from which the scrutiny was coming. But the person standing in the doorway was a tall, thin fellow of about thirty-five, dressed in a blazer that fitted him as perfectly as it might have fitted a harp seal.

Catching my eye, he moved toward the table hesitantly, almost shyly. "It's Bandy, isn't it?" he asked; then, before I could answer: "My word, yes, of course it is, nobody else could—" But then he stopped in confusion, obviously too polite to complete what had apparently started out as a joshing insult.

His face looked familiar, as indeed it should. When I agreed that I was Bandy, he smiled delightedly, exposing an upper set of teeth that looked false but were real, and a lower row that looked real but were false. What with this orthodontal riddle and that large Victorian mustache draped over his cheeks he looked remarkably like a scarred walrus. And that reminded me.

"Greaves!"

"Absolutely, old man, absolutely," he cried, humbly grateful that I still remembered him.

He put a hand on my shoulder in an affectionate way; but then, perhaps fearing that the gesture might be considered presumptuous, he quickly withdrew it. "As I live and breathe—Bandy, the great parachutist."

Yes, it was Greaves, all right—down on his luck, judging by his blazer.

"Sacred blue, this is absolutely splendid," he went on delightedly. "Imagine meeting you here of all places after all these years. I've often thought about you, and you're still my favorite anecdote.

"But listen, what are you drinking—Bart, isn't it? I remember you asking me to call you Bart," he added anxiously, glancing quickly over my impeccably starched front with its pearl, and the dinner jacket that had been packed in such a hurry. It was as if Greaves feared that I was now too important a personage for him to presume on our past friendship.

He himself had apparently fallen on hard times. His blazer had obviously been snatched off the rack and purchased without his making sure that it fitted. It didn't. In fact there was something disheveled about his whole appearance that even the heat could not explain. The collar of his white shirt was worn, as well as being mushy with sweat. And he needed a shave.

Of course, he had not been the best-dressed man on the Western Front even when he was commanding officer of a DH9 squadron, but he had never looked quite as damp and seedy as this.

"Of course," I cried enthusiastically, to show that even though I was now far superior to him, there was nothing toffee-nosed and snobbish about me. "And yours is Cyril, isn't it? What'll you have, Greaves?"

"No, no, this is on me, my old," he insisted, and ordered a couple of whiskies. When the waiter presented the bill, I had to pretend not to notice when Greaves poked carefully and with an air of anxiety at a handful of silver piaster coins and copper milliemes, to see if he had the right change. Plainly it was important to him that he not break a bank note. If he had a bank note, that is.

As I had nothing to do that evening except check with reception every so often to see if there were any messages, I deigned to remain in the bar with Greaves, reminiscing about old times, including the memorable occasion when we first met. This was when I flew into his aerodrome for a parachute demonstration one bright July afternoon in 1918. I remembered it particularly well because it was I who had to do the demonstrating.

What happened was that for weeks I had been harassing the authorities, particularly my brigade commander, Soames, about parachutes. Having learned from Soames's wife that parachutes were at a much more advanced stage of development than I had thought and could now be considered quite reliable, I kept badgering the brigadier about the need for parachutes in the air force, pointing out on every conceivable occasion—and some that were inconceivable—that a great many lives could be saved if pilots and observers were supplied with the new Guardian Angel parachute. But the idea was novel, and the brass hats believed that if airmen were given parachutes they might be tempted to use them. It never seemed to occur to people like Soames and that swine the CAS, who had also been against parachutes (good Lord, could I possibly still be feeling hostility to the CAS over that long-dead issue?) that quite often, jumping out of an aircraft was the only way to survive. The best friend I ever had, Richard Milestone, could have done with a parachute. He went down from fifteen thousand feet, burning all the way.

Anyway, Brigadier Soames paid me back for my harassment quite neatly by challenging me to test the Guardian Angel myself under simulated combat conditions. No doubt he hoped that I would be killed. In fact, I very nearly was when, on my third jump, the parachute snagged on the tail of the DH9.

Cyril Greaves was the pilot of the DH9 and, when I finally emerged from the quarry whose soft though stinking waters saved my life, he was so overcome with emotion over our narrow escape—for he had been in as great a danger as I—that he embraced me and held me in his arms for at least a minute, though a large number of signalmen, French civilians and staff officers were present. I had felt terribly embarrassed.

But then he had obviously taken a liking to me, even before

the near disaster, while we were waiting for the demonstration to get under way. We had stood at the bar for hours, talking shop, exchanging the latest jokes from Bertangles, slandering our superiors and generally gossiping garrulously and guffawing and, as we got steadily more blotto, exchanging confidences that we would regret when we were sober.

As was happening again, in Cairo, six years later; with one change, that I was doing most of the talking, this time, while he listened, apparently with unreserved admiration and enjoyment.

"What gets me, my old," he said after I had explained how I had come to be based in England, "is that you don't seem to realize what a magnificent achievement that was, flying solo over the top of the world. But then I always did say you were the epitome of the unknown soldier, reverenced but obscure."

"Obscure? I like that."

"In the sense of deserving to be enduringly famous but, through no fault of your own, never quite managing it," Greaves said, looking at me anxiously in case I was as insulted as I looked.

While I was wondering how much longer it would take him to ask for a loan—for it was obvious that he was leading up to it; why else would he be dishing out these dollops of adulation?—he asked what I had been doing lately. "I mean, what are you doing in Cairo, if you don't mind my asking, Bart? Taking over the government, perhaps?"

"They're not ready for me."

"Nobody's ready for you, Bart," Greaves said, his tone growing vague as his eyes strayed to the broad, wrinkled back of Mr. Kekevi. The scented Turk had just entered the bar and was now settling himself on two end bar stools. He had seen me, but after a hard look at Greaves had given no further sign of recognition.

"Do you know him?" I asked, lowering my voice.

"Kekevi? Yes, I do, matter of fact."

"So who is he?"

"Oh, you know . . . there's quite a few people like that floating round the Middle East. Even a few English officers have gone to seed," Greaves said, suddenly morose. "Human wreckage of the war and all that."

Obviously in an oblique way he was talking about himself, offering an explanation for his own seediness and trying to excuse it. Wreckage of the war, indeed. Why didn't he pull himself together like a man and make an effort to be industrious, morally upright and sober—like me?

"He was a cousin of the deposed Sultan of Turkey I believe, but had to flee when the nationalists took over. You know—Mustafa Kemal."

"Tell me more about Mr. Kekevi."

"I believe he's been trying to sell the British authorities here the details of some Turkish involvement in Iraq or something."

"Yes, he approached me," I began.

"But of course nobody would be simpleton enough to consider buying it."

"No. No, course not."

"I suppose he still has a few contacts with people in Turkey who aren't overly enthralled by the new regime, but I can't see he'd have anything useful on the nationalist army, not after all this time."

"No, I guess not."

"Not that we have anything to worry about. The RAF have the situation well under control."

"I guess so," I mumbled, feeling rather annoyed at Greaves for confirming my decision not to buy the material from Kekevi.

By now it was almost midnight. Even so, I was still remarkably sober, and if there was a tendency to giggle and for my face to collapse now and then, that was because of the debilitating heat, not because between us we had consumed nearly two bottles of Scotch. In fact, to show how sober I was, I had enough presence of mind to avoid the truth when Greaves again asked what I was doing in Cairo. Why was I bringing corn to Egypt? as he put it. I suspected that if I told him about the Royal Jhamjarh Air Force, he would want to join up, and I was not at all sure he was the right man for the job. I mean, look at the way he drank, for one thing. And then there was his appearance. As commanding officer at Frévent, he'd had an amusing if somewhat unfinished appearance. The large Victorian mustache that drooped heavily down his sunken cheeks had done nothing to improve the symmetry of his face. But at least his faculties had been intact, compared with the mental deterioration he was now manifesting through his wild laughter and the sycophantic admiration that he had been lavishing on me all evening. In those days he had a splendid reputation as a leader, much loved by his men. He had behaved in a thoroughly competent and professional manner. Now look at him—like a bag of groceries. His skin was pallid, even though he had apparently been living in the Middle East for some months. His eyes were bloodshot and staring, his cheeks ill-nourished, his hair receding. Sweat trickled down his neck in sordid streams. His chin was pocked with stubble.

He had left the air force in 1919, he said. The poor devil had obviously gone completely to the dogs since then. By the time we left the bar at one in the morning I thoroughly intended tucking a few Egyptian pounds into his pocket when he wasn't looking. I would have done so, too, except that I wasn't looking either, and by mistake tucked the money into the pocket of the bellboy who had helped me to my feet. . . .

My third day in Cairo was the worst of the lot. I started it with a hangover and ended it with a failure to discover any means of reaching Baghdad except by camel train.

Then in the evening I received not just one cable but two. I read them standing in the middle of the hotel lobby, getting in the way of the other guests, officers in desert uniform, red-faced administrators, smart-looking Egyptian businessmen in fezzes with tassles, stern English women in unfashionably long skirts. FORCELANDED FRANCE STOP read the first cablegram, which was from the senior pilot of the Handley Page. LONDON INFORMED STOP ETA CAIRO NOW EARLY OCTOBER STOP GATES.

October? *October*? October was still days away. And it was a bleeding fortnight since my rushed departure. And they had still only reached *France*?

Steaming, I tore at the other message. It was from Hibbert. It read: GOOD NEWS STOP AIR MINISTRY BARRICADES DOWN STOP CONTRACT REACTIVATED.

Which cooled my vile temper only slightly.

Then, to round off a sweating, frustrating day, I went and bought the five pages of rubbish off Kekevi after all.

I mean, it was a patently absurd and totally illogical thing to do, to fork out a small fortune for five sheets of practically toilet-paper quality. To make the impulse more ridiculous, it was not until I had been back in London for several days that I had the army orders translated, and found that they referred to an infiltration by the Turkish regular army onto Iraqi territory in support of some Iraqi sheik or other, to take place at the beginning of December—an operation that did not, in fact, take place on that date. I wondered if I was going mad in the heat. At the time the five pages of Turkish squiggles and Arabic and Roman numerals didn't even *look* official. There wasn't even an emblem or symbol or coat of arms or anything on the pages; it was just a hasty scribble in pencil, with numbered lists and signs within brackets, and subparagraphs and numerous colons: military people love colons. The only sensible explanation I could offer to account for this absurd expenditure was that I was reacting against Cyril Greaves. My reasoning may have gone something like this: Greaves had always had a high opinion of me, and not only had it failed to diminish with age, maturity and experience, but it had actually increased, until now his belief and faith in me was impregnable to everything except irrefutable proof that I had been certified insane by a panel of thirty doctors. It therefore followed that Greaves's judgment was exceedingly faulty. He had judged Kekevi's reliability to be doubtful. Therefore it might well be worth my while taking Kekevi seriously.

Even so, I despised myself for being so impulsive; so I was not exactly in the best of tempers when I met Cyril Greaves again in the bar that night. "Well, well, if it isn't you again," I said shortly.

"But we arranged to meet here, Bart," he said, his face falling.

"Did we?"

"Incidentally, my old, do I remember rightly or not? When we were leaving last night, did you grab hold of a bellboy and stuff money into his pocket?"

"Certainly not."

"He thought you wanted to take him up to your room for the night."

"Good God."

Greaves was trying to stifle a laugh, though he was pretending that he was merely straightening his mustache. "The rest of the staff were quite surprised," he added, "because the bellboy you seemed to be fancying was the oldest and ugliest bellboy of the lot."

"If you don't mind, Greaves, I'd rather not talk about such things."

"Yes, of course," he said quickly, straightening his face.

After a while, when the silence started to become oppressive: "I say, Bart," he said timidly, "is there anything wrong?"

"No."

"Not got a touch of Gyppo stomach, have you? A lot of people get it when they first arrive."

"No," I snapped; then in an outburst: "I'm only likely to be stuck here in this oven of a country for the next several months, that's all," I shouted, viciously dabbing my neck with a bunched-up handkerchief. "God, this bloody heat."

"How do you mean, my old?"

"Oh, nothing. Don't pay any attention to me, Greaves. Cyril. Somebody was supposed to be sending aerial transport for me, that's all, and they've been delayed for several days. I've just heard."

"Oh, I see." Greaves combed at his mustache thoughtfully with his fingers. Actually he ought to have used them to excavate his eyes. There were grains of sand in the corners of them.

Today had been hotter than ever. On top of that, a storm had blown up out of a clear blue sky, heaping sand against the white walls of Cairo almost as deep as the February snows of the Ottawa Valley. When I got back to the hotel I found that I had left my suitcase open, and it was half-filled with grit. Every garment had turned into smartly designed sandpaper. Every time my teeth met they crunched sand.

"Where did you want to go, Bart?" Greaves asked.

I hesitated, but could see no harm in telling him, so I said sulkily, "Baghdad."

"Oh," Greaves said, looking relieved. "I thought it might have been the other direction."

"What difference does that make?"

"Well, I couldn't really have justified a trip westbound."

Hardly listening, I ordered another two whiskies, though Greaves had barely had time to drink his first.

"Just so long as it's nothing to do with parachutes this time," he said with a smile.

"What?" I asked rudely.

Seeing that I was still not in a terribly good mood, he rearranged his expression and said respectfully, "I mean, I could get you to Baghdad easily enough, you see."

"You? How?"

"You know. Through the air force."

"You know somebody in the air force?"

"Yes. Me."

"You?"

"Of course. Didn't you know? I'm terribly sorry," he said, as if it were his fault that I was so dense. "I thought you knew."

"But you said you'd left the air force."

"Yes, in 1919. But I'm afraid I wasn't any good at anything else, so they were good enough to take me on again.

"Of course," he added, "I couldn't get back my old rank. You know how it is. I was lucky to sign on again as a flight lieutenant."

"Let me get this straight. You could get me on an RAF flight to Baghdad? But how would you get me past your CO?"

"I know we're not supposed to take civilians, but they would certainly make an exception for you, Bart."

"What makes you so sure the authorities would allow it?"

"Well, I'm one of them, you see. I'm Chief Staff Officer to the AOC, Middle East."

"What?"

"I'm terribly sorry, my little cabbage—didn't I mention that at all? I'm a group captain now, I'm afraid. In fact it's even worse than that. I'm just waiting for my promotion to air commodore to come through."

It began to occur to me that my flight across the Atlantic by the northern route was something of an achievement when I saw the extremes the RAF had to go to simply to get from Egypt to Iraq. The distance, about a thousand miles, was nothing compared with the distance I had flown with little help except from drawing instruments, a compass and a theodolite. Yet the air force was forced to establish emergency posts every few miles across the desert, not just as insurance against engine failure, but to keep their aircraft heading in the right direction. They claimed that even by 1924 aerial navigation wasn't up to the problems of flying across featureless terrain. My goodness, I'm glad nobody had told me before I left Labrador.

But perhaps the desert was even more tricky than the ocean, what with the heat, atmospheric conditions, the danger of falling into the hands of the nomadic Bedouin and, perhaps worst of all, the clever mirages that could sneak up on a fellow and convince him that he was upside down or about to crash into a volcanic escarpment.

The air force had solved the problem by abandoning the navigational hardware altogether and relying on the eyeball. Two years previously, their surveyors and work teams had drawn a straight line right across the desert for eight hundred miles, the first formal track that the desert had ever known. Where the terrain was soft or sandy, the track was a furrow easily seen from almost any altitude. Where the ground rose into the lava fields, the route was marked with a continuous line of white paint. The track ran all the way from Amman in Transjordan to Baghdad, deviating from the straight and narrow only when a wall of rock forced it off course down some convenient gorge or gully.

Because of the ferocious conditions of the desert, emergency landing points had also been established about every fifty or sixty miles along the route, each with its stock of fuel and spares. Though valuable, the emergency supplies were unguarded. At first, the Bedouin had poked curiously around the dumps, but having no use for spark plugs or gasoline, had long since lost interest.

"Fascinating," I said, peering down at the track from a thousand feet. Already halfway to Baghdad, we were just flying over a convoy of supply trucks, shepherded by a couple of armored cars. Somebody waved from one of the trucks. Our aircraft, a great fat Vernon, waggled its wings.

I had been on board since ten to seven that morning; for Greaves had been as good as his word. Barely seven hours after our conversation in the bar, we were airborne, bound for the Baghdad area.

Greaves had intended to return to Iraq that morning anyway, after attending a conference in Cairo with the air officer commanding, so it had been easy enough for him to fit me into a spare seat in one of the big transports of Forty-five Squadron, which flew regularly between Egypt and Iraq—or Mespot, as Greaves insisted on calling it.

Before taking off from the RAF base at Aboukir, I had studied the route carefully, just in case I ever had to fly it myself. You never knew. The first part of the journey had looked like an easy spot of navigation, given the cloudless skies. We had simply turned northeast and flown to the Nile delta, then along the Mediterranean coast to Jaffa in Palestine, then inland to Amman, in the newly created kingdom of Transjordan. It was only from there that the furrows and the white lines had become necessary.

After Amman, the terrain at first had been quite rocky and the color of tawny lions; but as we droned along the white line, the ground flattened into desert, fuzzy and shimmering. I could see why they needed a continuous mark if they were to fly solely by visual reference. Had the line been intermittent, it would have been easy to miss the next section, even if it were only a few hundred yards farther on. The scene was totally featureless. Worse, the land and sky were indistinguishable from each other. When I peered ahead through the big, oblong windows of the Vernon, I thought at first that we had made a hundred-and-eighty-degree turn without my noticing and were heading back to the Mediterranean. I could quite plainly make out an ocean five miles ahead. But it was just more desert.

As the blinding light was giving me a headache, I turned away from the window and squinted around. We were sharing the spacious cabin of the Vernon—the military name for the Vimy Commercial that I might have been flying across this same terrain had it not been for the CAS—with a party of airmen and a corporal. At first they had behaved self-consciously at traveling with a senior officer. Greaves was in his khaki uniform today, with blue rings halfway to his elbows. Soon, though, the young lads had settled down, and most of them were now dozing, their faces, sallowed by the sun, polished with sweat. Even at a thousand feet it was hot as sausages in the cavernous fuselage.

"In Basra, I've known it reach a hundred and thirty degrees," Greaves said. "But it's not too bad at this time of year."

He had not yet asked why I needed to get to Baghdad, and I had not so far volunteered the information. I wanted him to confide in me in an objective spirit. If he suspected that my report might damage his beloved RAF, he might be tempted to color in the picture.

I had already asked him a few carefully casual questions about the bombing campaign in Iraq, and had received what sounded like frank answers, to the effect that the air force was particularly careful to avoid inflicting any casualties at all. Having served in the RAF myself, I was aware that its bomb aimers had never been all that concerned about civilians. So I found this hard to believe, and said so. Being too polite to argue, he just shrugged.

By the time we reached the HQ airfield at Hinaidi in Iraq, though, I thought I had better come clean, so as soon as we had collected a beer at the officers' mess and retired to a corner of the lounge, I told him what it was all about, that I was spying on the RAF on behalf of a bloody politician, and a socialist one at that.

As I had waited a humiliatingly long time before trusting him with the truth, his opinion of me should have gone down quite a few notches. I was really hoping it would. It was a terrible strain being looked upon as a great man and a hero. In fact, for a few moments he looked quite cross because he felt that I had encouraged him to speak frankly without warning him that everything he said might be taken down and used in evidence. Then he learned that my opponent was his chief, the head of the air force. Most officers and men in the peacetime RAF loved the fierce, intolerant incorruptible air marshal. Had Greaves been quite normal he would have been bound to assume, out of loyalty and affection, that it was the CAS who must surely be right, and that I was the villain of the piece.

But old Greaves turned out to be one of the exceptions. He had met the CAS only once, when he visited the DH9 squadron in France, but Greaves's opinion of the Chief was based on an objective assessment very similar to mine: that the CAS had been responsible for the slaughter of thousands of pilots and observers in the name of an insensitive, brutal and bankrupt air policy.

"So you have my full support," Greaves said, adding with a wry smile, "so long as you don't tell anyone you have it. I do have my career to think of, you know."

"Of course, Cyril."

"However, in all fairness, I should point out that the Chief has been very civilized in his approach to the Iraq problem."

"Oh?"

"As long ago as 1921, he gave us strict, written orders that no rebel village was ever to be bombed without our dropping leaflets twenty-four hours ahead of time, warning them that an attack was coming, so that they could get out. I can let you have a copy of that order, if you wish," Greaves said. "I've made the same offer to quite a few newspaper fellows, but the fact is, Bart, not one of them has ever used it, far as I'm aware. I suppose their exaggerations make much better reading than the poor old dull facts. But seeing as it's you, I'll go even further. If it was up to me I would send you out on the next punitive raid, so you could see for yourself. Obviously I can't do that, but short of that I'm willing to give you complete freedom of action to investigate. You can go anywhere you like, and you can interview anyone you wish, British or Iraqi, without interference from us. Because I know just what you'll learn: that if, acting on behalf of King Feisal of Iraq, we are faced with a revolt by the tribesmen, we do our damnedest to make them think twice about fomenting trouble again by ruining their houses and knocking off as many of their goats as we can in one raid. But as for actually killing them, that's something we very rarely do, and only then usually by accident.

"A lot of the current fuss was caused not by us but by a civvy out here who ordered us to make an example of one particular village. We bombed hell out of it and machine-gunned the villagers when they ran into the river.

"But we were the ones who protested, my old," Greaves said, "and in fact Fox, the High Commissioner at the time, sacked the civilian administrator for issuing that order. And *that*'s the true situation out here, not these hysterical distortions they seem to be feeding the public back in Blighty."

A Trifle Tipsy

I arrived back at Croydon on the morning of October eighth, having completed some very fast though quite extensive travel around the Kingdom of Iraq, and I reached our London office shortly before 1:00 P.M. on that ill-starred day.

By then I had confirmed to my own satisfaction that what Greaves had told me was accurate, and I was all ready to carry out my side of the bargain and reward the PM with an interim report showing that his critics were talking through their hats.

As it turned out, the report was never to be written. Instead I went out to the pub.

I had returned to Laurence Pountney Hill to find a strangely underpopulated office. On being informed that the senior staff were celebrating in our favorite pub, I veered thence gladly.

As I emerged from the smoke that choked the lounge of the Boar's Head, an ironic cheer went up from the assembled officers, and within seconds I was being plied with drinks, queries, insults, gossip and information.

"How did you manage to get back from Iraq so soon?" Mays asked.

"I don't suppose he went any farther than Malta."

"Assuming he even got that far."

"Probably did all the work from his hotel room with his notepad on one knee and a dusky Malteser on the other."

"Just like a reporter."

"No, but how did you get on, Bart?" Hibbert asked.

"Look, what's all this about? I get back to the office at one in the afternoon to find you've all repaired to our favorite tavern for some sort of celebration."

"And having repaired thence, are now in a state of disrepair," said Freddy Montglass, and giggled.

"What's the occasion?"

A moment later I was celebrating too, when I learned that, just that day, Hawker had officially and ceremoniously handed over the first of the Snipes.

Just as Hibbert had advised me in his cable, Ramsay MacDonald had carried out his side of the bargain. He had ordered the Chief of Air Staff to cease all interference with our perfectly legal business arrangements; and the order had been promptly if furiously obeyed.

"Hawker have been working flat out ever since," Hibbert reported. "We should have the whole order ready for shipment by the end of January."

"We've won," somebody cried. "Nothing can stop us now."

Derby said gravely, "You know, I'll never ask any more of life than this: an exotic destination, a few personal servants to attend to my every whim, a nubile maiden or two for the asking, a glorious hot climate, about a thousand quid a month and a chance to fly again. I know my demands are modest, but there you are, I'm nothing if not restrained."

"It's almost too good to be true," somebody else said.

"And we owe it all to Bart," Mays said, his smooth, gentleman's face expressing profound satisfaction. "We didn't have a chance to congratulate you, Bart, on your successful negotiations with the PM before you flung yourself into the blue, but let us do so now. I never thought for a second that you would manage it. You must surely be the first person ever to defeat or outmaneuver the Chief of Air Staff. I don't think that in his entire life he ever failed to have it all his own way, until you came along." He stood up and raised his glass. "And so, a toast to pure genius—that great Canadian novelty, Bartholomew W. Bandy, Deputy Supreme Being of the Royal Jhamjarh Air Force."

There was a roar, a forest of bent elbows and Freddy Montglass had to be restrained from flinging his heavy beer glass into the fireplace.

Even Derby, who seemed to think that I tended to turn into the most awful swankpot whenever I brought off any sort of coup, congratulated me on the ministerial intervention. "I don't know how you managed it, mind you," he said. "I expect it's because old MacDonald's been so harried lately by both sides of the House, and didn't know whether he was coming or going."

"You don't have much faith in the brilliant logic and penetrating persuasiveness of my submissions, or the breadth of my experience in dealing with heads of state, do you?"

Derby thought carefully for a moment, then said, "No."

Even the people at the next table laughed. We had been talking so boisterously that they couldn't help overhearing some of the conversation.

"Anyhow," I cried, lifting a fresh glass of beer, "a toast, to my friend Ramsay."

"Listen to him, toasting the socialists. Bandy, the arch-reactionary."

"I am never arch," I said severely. "A trifle roguish at times, perhaps, but. . . . No, but credit where credit is due, you know—Ramsay has done us proud. A Tory or Liberal wouldn't even have let me into Number Ten, let alone given me a hearing, let alone acted on what I had to say, let alone—have I let enough things alone, yet?"

"Yes," came a chorus.

"But I must confess that even I am just a tad surprised at how susceptible to reason these socialists can be," I said. "Mind you, it's quite true that Ramsay was looking pretty distracted."

"Yes, but how did he look *before* you started on him?" Derby asked, to another crash of laughter.

"Anyway, how did you get on in Iraq?" Mays asked, and I spent the next twenty minutes telling them that Ramsay would be amply repaid for his intervention.

"Jolly good," Mays said, patting me on the shoulder and smiling owlishly. He was only on his fourth pint, and it had gone straight to his tongue.

"Know what?" Hibbert asked suddenly.

"What?"

"Know what?"

"What?"

"Brilliant conversationalists, aren't they?" Derby said.

"What is it you want to tell me, Freddy?" I enquired.

"I'm not Freddy," Hibbert said indignantly. "I'm—hic."

"You're a hick?"

"No, no, I was telling you my—hic—name."

"I never knew you had a hickname. What is it, Hibsy-wibsy, Owly wowly, Specky-four-eyes?"

"You're just being silly," Hibbert said, gazing distantly out the pub window at the pedestrians as they threaded through the parping, palsied taxis. For once the streets out there were dry. Now that winter was approaching, the weather was improving daily. The October air was almost as warm as the beer.

Inside the pub, caught unawares by the warm spell, the proprietor had banked a fierce fire in the grate. The coal fumes and those from all the cigarettes were making my eyes water. In self-defence I reached for my pipe and started to nudge tobacco into it.

"Well, I guess we should get back to work," I said with an air of finality.

An hour later Mays was talking about his barber, who had had a backyard fence and three garden gnomes knocked down by a runaway lorry. "But he didn't turn a hair," Mays said.

"Fat lot of use he is," Derby said. "A barber who doesn't turn a hair." And he and I dissolved into snorts and giggles.

"I say, Bart," Freddy whispered, blushing. "That woman over there is rolling her eyes at me."

"Well, roll them back," I said, "you've already got two." And once again Derby and I snorted and wheezed with merriment.

"Well," I said a while later, "I guess we'd better get back to work." And I ordered another round of drinks for everybody except Hibbert. I didn't order a drink for Hibbert because he had left, weaving industriously and muttering something about his mother.

"Yes, I suppose we'd better get back to work," Mays said. He was looking a bit put out at the way Derby and I were behaving in such a childish, pally way. Mays had a jealous element in his character. Moreover, as second in command, he felt that only he should be on intimate terms with the boss.

"John, I think you've got that training report to finish," he said smoothly.

"Finished, old boy. It's on your desk," Derby said with a smile that caused Mays's smooth surface to become distinctly choppy. A fair amount of roughness had begun to mar the surface of the relationship between Mays and Derby. Derby was the sort of flyer who felt that anyone who wasn't a pilot, and a fighter pilot at that, simply didn't count. Mays considered himself to be one of nature's elite, and everybody else was there only to take orders; so naturally they didn't get on terribly well. Mays stood in the middle of the pub lounge wondering whether to make an issue of what he knew to be a fib: Derby had not nearly finished the training report.

Deciding that this was not the right occasion, he produced one of his charming smiles, smoothed the gray hair at his temples and said, "Well, I suppose I'll be off, then, much as I should prefer to remain in your fatuously incoherent company." And so saying, he departed, jimmying his way through a sudden rush of business. Now that it was about to close, the pub was suddenly filled with toffs and tarts and other latecomers. The noise banged furiously on our eardrums. My eyes were drooling with the smoke.

John gave me a nudge and nodded toward Freddy. Seated opposite us, Freddy was sunk in gloom. He had been desperate to cultivate the sexy-looking bloom who had been ogling him, but he had not had the nerve. Now she had left with another man.

He sat there, miserable as virtue, refusing to look at anybody, hating himself.

"Last call, gentlemen."

"Good Lord, is it that time?"

"Better get back to work, I suppose. You coming, Freddy?"

"Suppose so. No point in staying here, now."

"Especially as they're closing."

We pushed off through the crush, buffeted by last-minute beer-bearing patrons. I was gluey with perspiration in the odorous heat. It was like being back in Iraq.

" 'Ere, watch it, 'oo you shoving?" shouted one fellow.

The moment I stepped outside, I received a violent blow to the head. It was obviously lethal. I felt very sad at the thought of dying. First Khooshie, now me. It wasn't fair.

"I've been attacked, Derby. Is my head bleeding?"

"Not that I can see, old bean."

"You can't see anything, you're drunk."

"That's true."

"I'm dying, John. You'll have to take over," I said; but I soon realized that it was merely the cool air that had delivered the blow.

"One thing about drinking," I said. "It sure shaves the expense of lunch."

"You should worry, with your income."

"That's true. I keep forgetting I'm a plutocrat now," I said, wishing that the buildings on the opposite side of the street wouldn't hurtle past so fast, like an express train made of granite, brick and limestone.

"Gad, it's quite a relief, you know, getting the problem sorted out, John. I can tell you now, I was getting a bit worried at the thought of me opposing the might of the British Empire, an empire covering a quarter of the entire world surface, an' administered by positive battalions of dukes and lords, viceroys, governors, governors general, general governors, residents, agents of various sorts and high commissioners, not to mention low commissioners—every one of whom," I said with a catch in my voice, suddenly overcome with self-pity, "was just about to put a black mark against my name."

"You're right," John said, adopting a peculiar whining drawl that almost made Freddy smile, "you against four hundred million citizens on seven continents. The odds would have been a trifle daunting."

I lurched. Freddy reached over to steady me with an unexpectedly strong arm, considering his weedy height. He propped us both against the wall of the pub. "You two wait here, I'll call a cab," he said, sounding hideously depressed.

"Poor old Freddy."

"Listen, Bart."

"What?"

"Listen."

"I am listening. I can't hear a thing."

"Mean to say you can't hear the motorcars bleating, the traffic policemen whistling, the hooters hooting, the babies howling, the trains steaming, the barges sirening? Good Lord, he must be going deaf as well as alcoholic."

"Whatjamean, alcoholic?"

"Oh, nothing."

"Alcoholic? I'm not alcoholic."

"Where the hell's Freddy? He's been gone for thirty seconds. Poor old Freddy. He's a mass of complexes and stuff, isn't he?" Derby said quickly. "He'd keep old Freud busy for years."

"I'm not alcoholic," I repeated. "Just because I have a few drinks now and again."

"You mean again and again."

I thought about it in churlish silence all the way back to the office. "Well, I'm not," I said, lurching against a desk in the general office.

A couple of temporary clerks looked up, then averted their eyes squeamishly. Hibbert came up and said, "We were just about to send out a search party."

"Ha?"

"They want you along at the Air Ministry as soon as possible."

"Now?"

"It's the Chief himself."

"Sent for me? Oh, crumbs."

"Oooh, *now* you're going to get it," Mays said.

Hoping to make as good an impression as possible on everybody at the Air Ministry, I borrowed one of Khooshie's limousines, complete with snooty chauffeur, and bowled down the Strand in a state—in state, that is. The gesture was quite wasted. The only one to notice me was the chap outside the front entrance who was sweeping horse buns into an outsized tray and dumping them into a steaming cart.

They were attentive enough in the lobby, though—"Oh, yes, sir, we've been warned about you"—and I was escorted immediately to the sixth floor in an unreliable elevator and deposited in an anteroom that contained two chairs and a large porcelain jardiniere.

The next thing I knew I was waking up with a start, realizing with hectic embarrassment that I had nearly fallen sideways into the jardiniere.

I focused, yawning hugely, on my watch, then looked again, sharply. It was nearly four-thirty.

The bastard. He had summoned me peremptorily, then kept me waiting for well over half an hour.

Damn the CAS. I hated him. No, I didn't. That was one of my problems. In facing up to the air marshal I was already partially disarmed. The CAS was the only bigwig who had ever impressed me as being as great a man as everybody said he was. Which was why his vindictive intervention at the Imperial Airways interview had been so surprising. He had never struck me as being a mean sort of person. He had a lot of genuine sympathy for the men under his command, and his reputation as a leader was in most respects well deserved. Only his wartime determination to force the RAF into an aggressive role regardless of the cost diminished him. He had insisted that the air force be unrelentingly aggressive purely for its own sake or, as he put it, in order to obtain "moral superiority" over the enemy. John Derby had talked to a few German pilots after the war and said that no German ever confessed to feeling the least inferior, morally or in any other way. But there you are. In his attitudes, the CAS had been typical of practically the entire military leadership. . . .

Once again I seemed to have regressed from a certain admiration for the man to something resembling hatred. So I thought I had better pull myself together. I wasn't likely to defend myself effectively if I merely sat in his office glowering. So I turned my mind to something rather more constructive; that is, I fell to speculating about whether the CAS would defer to me now that I was an important if pesky civvy, who had the ear of the Prime Minister himself, or whether he would greet me in the usual way, with a snarl.

At least the long wait enabled me to sober up somewhat, before his service secretary finally wheeled me into the inner sanctum. Once there, I was really pleased to see that the Chief had risen; like the gentleman he was, he had climbed to his feet regardless of his feelings toward me. I was really gratified—until I realized that his posture was a compromise. He had not considered it fitting that he should remain seated, but on the other hand he just couldn't bring himself to rise respectfully when I entered. So he had jumped up and hurried to the window and was now standing there with his back to me.

Still, all was not lost, manners-wise, for after the secretary, a decent enough air force officer by the name of Marson, had spoken my name and withdrawn, the CAS safeguarded himself from accusations of boorish behavior by acknowledging my presence with quite a friendly sounding grunt, delivered with just the right touch of preoccupation. His abstraction suggested that, important as I might be, the report that he was absorbed in was even more so. To prove it, he would glance through the window every now and then with a worried frown, as if the destiny of the nation hung in the balance.

As the seconds marched past his reviewing stand at the window, I took the opportunity to familiarize myself again with his spacious office. It had a comfortable visitor's chair—into which I had not yet been invited to sink—and a handsome desk, a fine piece of furniture with a green leather top on which a green glass lamp burned brightly in the late-afternoon gloom.

Also on top of the desk were several freshly typed pages on Air Ministry stationery, two book ends with but one book between them—*King's Regulations*, naturally. The CAS was not much of a reader.

He was not much of a host, either. A minute later he was still standing at the far end of the room, reading the report by the gray light from the Strand. So while I was waiting for him to acknowledge my presence properly, I looked around for something to do. There was a pile of new memo pads on a side table. As there were plenty of them and I could always use a memo pad, I took one. There was also a box of India rubbers, but I didn't take any of them, as I already had an India rubber.

Next I read a very nicely typed letter on ministry letterhead. It was to Winston Churchill, and it was quite interesting. It was all about Singapore. Apparently the Royal Navy was intent on turning Singapore into the Gibraltar of the Far East. The CAS was vehemently opposing the navy. He had no objection to the idea of turning Singapore into a major base with a floating dockyard and extensive storage and repair facilities. What he objected to was the way the admirals were going about it, as if the airplane had never been invented . . . or, for that matter, as if the army had never been invented either, for the base was to be defended by fixed fifteen-inch guns pointing *out to sea*—as if that were the only direction from which an enemy was ever likely to approach.

I got so involved in the letter that unconsciously I directed my haunches toward the chair behind the desk, and I very nearly sat down in order to read in greater comfort. What dissuaded me was the realization that the Chief had finally turned and was now glaring at me with a ferocity that quite took me back to the good old days when we all had a purpose in life, a goal to be scored, an idealism to be consummated. His frightful stare really brought back nostalgic memories.

He had obviously whirled round with the intention of getting down to business without delay; of unfurling his tongue and giving me a good lashing with it. He was universally feared for his damnatory vigor, and usually expressed it the very second that the conversational essentials—one could not say niceties—had been cleared away like so many dirty dishes. But upon turning and observing the reason for my own preoccupied silence, he was, as I say, quite diverted, and the best he could manage at the moment was to stride forward and snatch the letter from my hand and slap it back on the desk. He then stood there, quivering eloquently.

"My God," he said at length. "You haven't changed, have you?"

"Why, thank you, Air Marshal."

"That was not a compliment, damn you," he shouted.

"Didn't really mean to read it, Air Marshal," I said in a placatory, not to say obsequious fashion, and checking up on his sleeve to make sure he was in fact an air marshal. The broad and narrow stripes indicated that this was so. "It's typical of the navy, isn't it?" I went on with a nudging expression. "They're so practical-minded they have to see their ships sunk before recognizing the possibility that they might be. I mean, look at General Mitchell of the American Army Air Service. He keeps urging the other two services to recognize that air power has rather changed things in war, but will they listen? Will they, eh?" Realizing with a certain amount of unease that I was still somewhat tipsy, I attempted to slam on the verbal brakes; but they failed to hold. "Why," I careened, "there's even talk of air-martialing him for being so uncouth in his attempts to drag the army and navy out of the nineteenth century. Did I say 'air-martialing' him just then? I meant, of course, court-martialing him. Anyway, here you are, sir, saying the same things about our admiralty. I don't know," I went on admiringly, "is there no end to your genius? Great military thinker, Father of the Royal Air Force, architect of our aerial victory, major theorist on air power—and much too generous-minded a fellow, eh? to hold a grudge against a young and naive Flying Corps officer at Gosport, just because he trod on your heels once or twice whilst lobbying on behalf of our pilots on the Western Front—"

"You were pestering me about distributing egg timers among the squadrons!"

"Well, you must admit I was right, sir," I said, with barely a hint of reproach in my voice. "I mean, now that we have the war in proper perspective, we can see that there was, indeed, a desperate need for egg timers among our front-line squadrons; for as I emphasized in the mess that time, Air Marshal, as I pointed out repeatedly while I was following you up and down the length of the bar at Gosport, we desperately needed egg timers in order to obviate guesswork—"

"Yes, I remember that too," he shouted, quite puce with ire. "Obviate! Using the damn word repeatedly, in and out of context, whether appropriate or not—"

"Well, you see, I'd only just learned the word, sir. Anyway, I'm sure you were as concerned about morale in the service as I was, and I can assure you that morale went down every time we sliced off the top of an egg—or in some cases, when we tapped the top of the egg with a spoon, depending on one's personal preference—then picked off the pieces of shattered shell casing with our fingers . . . or in the case of one pilot named Dougal—No, never mind him, let's stick to the point, shall we? And the point is, sir, that when our Dawn Patrol eggs were hard-boiled, it made it very difficult to dip our soldiers in the yolk, you see."

"Soldiers?" the air marshal enquired, beginning to look quite disoriented.

"You know, lengths of toast, sliced into narrow strips and dipped into the—I particularly like mine done that way, don't you, with just a few grains of salt on the tip of each soldier, and—"

"What the devil kind of squadron did you belong to?" the CAS asked, very loudly. "Sprinkling salt on our soldiers and dipping them in—whatever it was you were babbling about dipping them in. And they were prepared to put up with that sort of treatment? By God, I'd've ordered an enquiry if I'd known that was the sort of thing going on in your squadron—"

"No, no, you know, soldiers—lengths of toast. . . . Anyway, as I said, the Dawn Patrol egg was always so hard-boiled, you couldn't enjoy them that way, a direct result of the cooks not being issued with enough egg timers, you see."

He seemed to get a grip on himself just then. "Mr. Bandy," he said, almost calmly.

"And all I was trying to tell you, sir, at Gosport, was that we pilots liked our eggs done to a T, but the cooks never seemed to get them right, the eggs being—"

"Mr. Bandy."

"—being either underdone and slimy, or overdone and of the consistency of Blackpool rock—"

"Mr. Bandy!"

"Wot?"

With a face like a granite outcropping, his thick, black eyebrows quivering, he took a deep breath and his place behind the green-topped desk.

"Sit down, and let's get on with it," he grated, gesturing at a chair. "I haven't much time."

"Oh, dear, I am sorry. Incurable, is it?"

"What?"

"And, good Lord, you're only—what?—sixty-one years old."

"Fifty-one, damn you!"

"So young. But there you are, these disgusting diseases can strike even the youngest of us."

"I haven't got a disgusting disease!"

"Heart trouble, then? I suppose so, judging—"

"I haven't got heart trouble either!" he bellowed, gasping for breath.

"Well, you certainly have dyspnea, with that shortness of breath. I know because I studied medicine at one time, or in fact more than one time. Still, it might be better to get a second opinion. After all, I could be wrong."

"You're always wrong, by God—it's practically a law of nature!"

"Sir," I said with some dignity—though not a great deal—"are you trying to say you don't have much confidence in me?"

With one more attempt at restraint, though still panting a bit, he said, "That's putting it so mildly as to make even the word 'understatement' an understatement. I don't even have the faintest stirrings of confidence in you—for reasons that have quite recently been enormously buttocksed—*buttressed*"—the air marshal's face whitened with fury over the slip. "When you were at the Air Ministry during the war, I very soon realized," he gasped, "that whatever position you adopted must *ipso facto* be wrong, and therefore it was perfectly safe for me to adopt the contrary position!"

"Ah, yes," I said archly, "but did the contrary position always prove to be the right one?"

"Invariably!"

"Oh."

"In fact I seriously considered having it written into *King's Regulations* that any course of action opposed by you must by that very fact be the correct course, and is to be adopted forthwith—and vice versa!"

"Yes, I know," I said with a companionable laugh that had to be suppressed hurriedly when it turned into a hiccup. "My boss at the time, the Secretary of State for Air, his ideas were always a trifle impractical—"

"I'm talking about your ideas, your schemes, your proposals and lobbyings, damn you," he screamed, "not those of your half-witted master!"

"You're quite right, sir, his don't bear talking about," I said with a really nice smile, to show that, regardless of our differences, deep down the CAS and I thought alike, basically.

His great black eyebrows merged forthwith into one hairy growth. He seemed to be trying to force his teeth apart, judging by the way his quadrate muscle was straining.

However, after yet another Herculean effort, he relaxed; sufficiently, anyway, to overcome the lockjaw. "Do you know, Bandy," he said unsteadily, "I deeply regret that I stopped you from joining Imperial Airways—"

"I know. I thought it was a bit mean of you, sir. Still, no need to apologize."

"Oh, God," he whispered to himself; then, trying to maintain the restraint: "I was not apologi—"

"I realize that you were just trying to get your own back after I'd made an ass of you—so to speak—in hospital."

"Silence!"

"So it's okay, Air Marsh, I forgive you."

"Will you be quiet! I was trying to say I regret it because, if I hadn't interfered, you might not have become involved in this Indian business."

"By George, that's right," I said wonderingly. "So you were doing me a favor, really."

There he went, gritting his teeth again. I didn't think his dentist would be too pleased about that, assuming he had one.

"Let's get to the point," he said, after still another fresh start. "I have called you in because we are disturbed at the speed with which this, this enterprise of yours is being organized. We understand that a great deal of equipment, including bombing machines, has already been despatched. And now we learn that your order for fighters is proceeding at an alarming pace as well." He paused, treating me to a glare famous for its ability to penetrate armor plating of almost any caliber. "Now, I cannot disregard a direct order from the Prime Minister," he said. "It appears that the most I can do is appeal to your. . . ." he swallowed. "Your better judgement.

"Dammit, man," he continued, slamming a fist onto the desk. "You must see that it's an intolerable situation, a rival air force in India! It would be an ever-present temptation for this rajah fellow to defy the imperial authority."

"He swore it would never be turned against the British."

"And you're naive enough to believe that?"

"There's no way our pilots would ever fight your pilots."

"There are other ways of challenging us or opposing our authority that could make things impossible for the government of India, don't you see? Suppose he declared his support for this Indian Congress, which is agitating for Home Rule? His military capability would put real power behind their political ambitions. He could swing the balance of power to the nationalists without a shot being fired and make our position there untenable. Good God, why couldn't the Prime Minister see that? But all he could talk about was his responsibility to industry, and the workers, and. . . . I think he's so utterly confused by all the things that have been going wrong for his socialist party since he took over that he just can't think straight anymore—especially with you facing him, by God."

The argument continued for a remarkably long time considering that the CAS was used to disposing of his inferiors in a matter of seconds. And I couldn't help admitting to myself that there was an uncomfortable weight of truth in his contentions. He was saying what I and many of the others had been trying not to think about, because we wanted the job, the money and the opportunity to fly. In my case, the situation was crucial. Twice previously I had earned substantial sums only to squander the money on wine, women, song and experimental aircraft. I had a dread feeling that this was my last chance to succeed and make life tolerable for myself.

So, if my life depended on being stubborn, blind and obtuse, so be it. I was determined not to listen to reason; or rather, I convinced myself that a reasonable attitude was one that no longer perceived virtue in placing the national interest ahead of my own. After all, look where national interest had led the world: to the Great War, a chaos in Europe of anger, frustration and inflation and, in the rest of the world, a cynicism about the honor of governments that boded ill for the future of ordered society.

So, stubbornly, blindly and obtusely, I argued, while he pointed out with increasing agitation that if I persisted in arming an independent state, I would be doing great harm to the cause of democracy and the national interest of India as well as that of the empire.

Until finally: "You mean," I said, "that whenever you lot decide what the national interest is, it automatically becomes unpatriotic to oppose it?"

He seared me one more time with that stare of his, before nodding slowly. "No," he said at length. "I told them it would be useless to appeal to your better nature. You're as Bolshie as you ever were, aren't you, Bandy?

"Well, it appears we can't stop you," he added; but was stopped himself when there was a hurried knock at the door and his service secretary hurried in without waiting for permission to do so. He crossed to his boss, leaned over and whispered urgently in his ear.

The CAS listened, jerked back his head to stare at the secretary and leaned over to listen again. Then he jumped up and strode out of the room, gesturing for his secretary to follow.

I arose too, or, to be exact, half rose, looking as if I were trying to do my business on his carpet, and gazed after them, wondering whether I had been dismissed or not. But he had closed the door, which seemed to suggest that I was not expected to leave immediately. So, slowly and uncertainly, I sat down again.

Five minutes trotted by before the air marshal reappeared. When I saw his face, I started.

He was smiling.

"I have news for you, Bandy," he said without preliminary. "I have been informed that the MacDonald government has just been defeated in the Commons."

An expectant silence fell. The CAS continued to smile happily, tapping his foot as if suppressing the urge to break into a tarantella.

"What does it mean, exactly?" I said rather stupidly.

"It means what I said, man. Your socialist friends are out. The government lost a vote this afternoon, and it means it will have to resign immediately."

While I was thinking about it, he continued, "It alters the situation a bit, what? I don't think we need pay much attention to Mr. MacDonald's wishes any further in this regard, until the next government is formed."

"It can't be true," I faltered. "The Liberals had promised to keep them in power."

"I don't know anything about that," the CAS said, still smiling happily within the parentheses of his facial creases. "Read all about it if you wish. It's already in the evening papers."

"You can hear the newsboys from here," Marson, the secretary, said, inviting me to listen by cocking his own head toward the window.

"I don't know whether MacDonald will win the general election or not," the Chief went on, taking in two lungfuls of ministry air. "I suppose he will. They say so. But until then, I'm reverting to our former position, Bandy. No manufacturer of British aircraft will be carrying out any more work for you, if they know what's good for them. And I will not allow the Snipes that have already been completed to be handed over to you."

I protested of course, but I knew I was beaten. Though theoretically the Prime Minister's orders were still valid and would remain so throughout the general election, I knew from personal experience that in practice the CAS and others in his position, including the permanent secretaries who ran Whitehall's departments of state, would certainly stall any orders that might not be to the liking of the opposition. You never knew. Though it was thought to be unlikely, the opposition might form the next government. You certainly didn't want to upset people who might be your new masters.

In this case the opposition was the Conservative Party, which believed fervently in the empire, and which was therefore highly unlikely to countenance the establishment of an independent air force in India. So, even had he been sympathetic to our cause, the CAS would have been strongly advised to lie fallow, administratively speaking, until after the general election.

This, of course, did not hinder me from arguing with increasing desperation; until finally the Chief wearied of his bit part as a gleeful herald of bad news and ended the conversation by thundering, "Until MacDonald is once again in a position to force me to do it, that's the way it's going to be. As long as I am able, Bandy, I will make quite sure that you don't acquire one more aeroplane for this treasonous air force of yours. And now kindly leave my office."

He even shot me in the back as I was leaving. "And another thing," he shouted after me down the corridor. "I'll even do my best to stop you exporting the aircraft you already have. So there!"

As soon as I reached the street I grabbed the nearest evening newspaper and read the lead story with such evident wrath that pedestrians walked around me as carefully as if I were an open manhole, and a policeman started and half drew his truncheon.

Blast MacDonald. Blast the damn fool. He had been defeated on an entirely feeble Liberal motion. It was one calling for a committee of enquiry, not even a major issue. The commission was to enquire into the government's handling of the Campbell case. John Ross Campbell, acting editor of a rag named *The Workers' Weekly*, had published an article inciting the armed forces to mutiny. He had been charged and remanded.

But when he appeared in court a few weeks later, the charges were withdrawn.

This had caused an uproar in the press and Parliament. After my own experience of political life, I had been doing my best to avert my eyes from the squalid gavotte of Parliament. But even I could not help but be aware of the scandal, which roused suspicions that there were quite a few communist sympathizers in the socialist government. Yet the Liberals had tabled quite a mild motion on the affair, and it was confidently expected that the Prime Minister could accept it without incurring much of a political penalty. He could easily have obscured the issue once the committee was formed. After all, obscuring the issue was what parliamentary committees were for. But for some reason—perhaps he was afraid that even a small ray of light might emerge from the committee room—MacDonald had decided to defy his erstwhile allies, and today when the Liberals had voted in favor, the Conservatives had gleefully marched after them into the lobby and defeated the government.

For the next few days there was considerable gloom and despondency on Laurence Pountney Hill, especially when it became evident that this time the word had gone out not merely to the aircraft manufacturers but to practically everybody in the country involved in aviation, even the surplus arms dealers. The Chief of Air Staff was being very thorough indeed in his efforts to block the formation of the RJAF.

Nevertheless, I exhorted everybody in sight to carry on regardless. We would solve the problem somehow, I said. And such was my optimism, and so frequent were my assertions that old Ramsay would never have to move his cheap furniture out of 10 Downing Street, that I even convinced myself. And there was ample justification for my cheerleading. As I told a crowded meeting of air crew, maintenance and administrative personnel on the top-floor conference room in late October, all the surveys indicated that the socialists would regain power. They were expected to poll as many as three million votes more than in the previous general election, which would give them an overall majority.

Gosh, this was fun. Addressing the jam-packed supporters was just like the good old days on the hustings. "And it's not just me making these assertions," I cried, remembering to make the appropriate politicians' gestures—pointing at heaven, but crooking a compromising finger slightly so that it also pointed at the horizon, just in case some of my listeners were unbelievers (I also remembered to raise an uncompromising fist three inches above the lectern, the gesture suggesting that I was tamping lumps of starch with a mortar and pestle)— "the fact is that I am quoting from informed sources. It is generally agreed that Ramsay MacDonald has more than made up for the occasional fumble on the home front through his accomplishments in foreign affairs. He is almost single-handedly responsible for the splendid achievement, for instance," I harangued, "of the Geneva Protocol."

"What's that, sir?" Fetch asked.

"Yes, what's that?" asked Carry.

"The Geneva Protocol? Why, it's . . . it was signed in Geneva, that's what it was."

"Yes, but what actually *is* the Geneva Protocol, sir?"

"Yes, sir, what is it?"

"It is a splendid achievement, Fetch, let's leave it at that."

"That's not Fetch, sir, that's Carry. I'm Fetch."

"Well, whoever you are, shut up. Where was I? Yes, the point is that these socialist swine are bound to get in again, and this is a very good thing, you see. For as you know, I have the ear of the Prime Minister, and—"

"Where is it?" Carry asked.

"Where is what?"

"His ear. Do you carry it around with you, sir, or do you keep it in your desk?"

"I expect he has it in his pocket, so he can take it out every now and then and have a word in it."

"Carry. Leave the room this minute."

"That's not Carry, sir, that's Fetch. I'm Carry."

"In that case, both of you leave the room. This is a democratic meeting—I don't want to hear another word from either of you. Uh . . . would you summarize what I've said so far, Hib?"

"You were confirming that the Labor Party was certain to get in again, sir."

"Exactly. And when they do," I said, placing a hand inside my natty gent's suiting and over my redoubtable ticker in a really convincing and authoritative pose, "I can assure you that I shall have a word in the PM's . . . I shall have a word with him and see that something is done about this unwarranted interference on the part of this Air Ministry lackey, don't you worry."

As polling day drew nigh, it became increasingly evident, even to other political experts, that the socialists would win the general election quite handily. *The Times*, for instance, said that if any party suffered it would be the Liberals, who had offended many a middle-of-the-road voter through their support for Labor. And this, in fact, proved to be an accurate forecast. The Liberal Party was decimated on polling day.

And so, despite the air marshal's mean behavior, the situation looked really promising—until the famous Zinoviev Letter appeared in the *Daily Mail* shortly before polling day, which was Wednesday, October 29.

Mays and Hibbert brought the great black headlines to me on the previous Saturday morning while I was engaged on a vital administrative task—attempting to pick the lock of my filing cabinet. I had lost the key.

Then I read the letter: "Oh, my God," I said.

"Yes, that's really torn it," Hibbert said.

The letter, dated at Moscow, September 15, 1924, purported to have come from Grigorii Evseevich Zinoviev, a member of the Soviet government. It was addressed to the Central Committee of the British Communist Party.

"This will scupper the socialists all right," Mays said.

Indeed it would; for the letter, in the typically turgid prose that communists love, was an exhortation aimed at the British proletariat, encouraging them to indulge in subversive activities.

"It's already causing something like panic in the city," Mays said, "and it's only been out a few hours."

Panic would prove to be almost an understatement. The uproar was riotous, with the Conservative Party seizing on the letter with whoops of joy disguised as moral outrage, while the newspapers were to scream so loudly about Soviet subversion and to predict so frighteningly that there might easily be a British October Revolution if the socialists were returned to power that, from the moment the letter appeared, Ramsay MacDonald never stood a chance.

Naturally, in self-defence, the Labor Party attempted to refute the letter by casting doubts on its authenticity, but their counterbarrage went almost unheard. There simply wasn't time to establish whether the letter was authentic or not.

Personally I should have said that the letter sounded thoroughly genuine, and after all, I should know. I had written it.

For the infamous "Red Letter" in the general election of 1924 was the "student exercise" that I had composed for that swine Ian in the boarding house in Norfolk Gardens some months previously. And it certainly did the trick. It was directly responsible for Ramsay MacDonald's defeat at the polls four days later.

Khooshie Snaps

Misfortune has a tendency to overdo it, and so it was in our case. It continued to kick us after we were down. In mid-November, while we were still searching desperately for replacements for the Snipe, Rupert Skelton reappeared. He turned up at the office with an evening newspaper that contained the worst news yet, news that would make it impossible for us to carry on.

He did not immediately show me the item, however, but first issued a statement, as if addressing a roomful of journalists whom he hoped to convert to his point of view before he imposed total censorship on them.

"I am sure that, like us, you are genuinely interested in the welfare of India," he began, inserting his black bulk between the arms of the visitor's chair in my office and gazing at me as earnestly as a vicar. "I'm sure you believe that its best interests will not be served by the irresponsible arming of one of its petty princelings. It's nothing to do with me, of course, but I have heard that India Office deeply regrets its previous inaction in allowing this Maharajah to build up his army to the point at which it threatens the security of our garrisons in central India. And on top of that, you must surely be able to comprehend the consternation felt by the government at the prospect of an independent air force as well. It could create an intolerable situation."

Having completed this statement, he suddenly relaxed and, with a manicured forefinger, scratched vigorously at the little black mustache in the middle of his big, fat face. "There," he said, looking as if he might even be smiling under the adipose tissue, "I was told to say that. So there you are, that's done with. Now we can settle down and tell a few dirty jokes."

"I don't see that you needed to recapitulate," I muttered as I completed my toilet. I was molding a tiny lavatory out of plasticine. "Your side is winning all along the line."

"Good heavens, it's not my side, Johnny. I'm just a messenger boy."

"You're a member of the Foreign Office's Intelligence Department," I said meanly, "at their headquarters on Parliament Street. Your room number is 405. Your assistant's name is Arbuthnot."

Skelton sat motionless for several seconds before heaving about as he searched for his cigarette case. He finally located it in his hip pocket. It was so cheap-looking, at a time when a handsome cigarette case was a mark of sophistication, as to seem ostentatious. Moreover, it was deformed. Presumably this had been caused by the weight of his hip. After all, it was hardly likely to have been deliberately maintained in a bent condition, as he appeared to be quite anxious to get it open. He was digging his big yellow thumbnail into the appropriate slot so determinedly that I expected his nail to snap at any moment.

Finally he managed it, and lit a cigarette, using an ordinary gunmetal lighter, with a show of relief.

"Where did you get that stuff, Johnny?" he asked at length, evenly enough.

"It's amazing how much you can find out when you have plenty of money at your disposal."

He thought about it for a moment. "Yes, I suppose so," he murmured vaguely, tapping his knee with the folded newspaper.

After a moment he continued more briskly, "That's all nonsense, of course, but we won't waste time arguing about it."

"Why are you here, Skelton? We've been thoroughly shot up by the Air Ministry, isn't that enough?"

"Some people thought it might be enough, but I wasn't so sure you'd give up that easily. I thought I'd better make quite sure."

"Inflict the *coup de grâce*, you mean, with that speech about the empire?"

"Oh, that was mainly to redress the set, so to speak, before I came sauntering on stage through the French windows, holding the evening newspaper and saying, 'I say, Bartholomew, old chum, have you seen the *Evening News*?' "

He handed over the newspaper. "Page two, at the bottom," he said. "Just wanted to show you that our concern was not entirely unjustified."

The item had an explosive force out of all proportion to its length. It was quite brief: a despatch from New Delhi, dated the previous day, stating that the State of Jhamjarh had expelled the British political agent, and that its ruler, the Maharajah Sundar Avtar Prakash, had declared, according to the agent, that it was his intention to abrogate unilaterally his country's sixty-year-old treaty with Great Britain.

I read the few lines again, more slowly this time, before saying blindly, "I see."

Puffing away at his cigarette, which, in harmony with his cigarette case, was bent, Skelton said gently, "You believe now that he's up to something, Johnny?"

"Do you call everyone Johnny?"

"Well, I don't think I would address the Foreign Secretary as Johnny."

"I've thought all along he was up to something," I said bitterly. "I just didn't think it was anything to do with the government of India. Not directly, anyway."

"And now what do you think?"

I rummaged around for something nasty to say and finally settled on, "By the way, Skelton, you could do with some new recruits in your assassination bureau. They're not too competent, are they?"

"Assassination bureau?"

"Don't tell me you know nothing about Prince Khooshie's being attacked a couple of times?" I asked, watching him closely to see if he fell to his knees and confessed. And in fact his carefully tutored facial muscles slackened sufficiently to make him look quite startled for a moment.

"Yes, I'd heard about it. But my dear Bandy, they may be in the cloak-and-dagger business over on Parliament Street, but they don't exactly wear them and wield them, you know."

"No, I don't know. I'm not sure of anything anymore," I said, rising and pacing over the early Indian handwoven pile carpet that I had pinched from Khooshie's office. (Well, it had seemed absurd, having a beautiful old carpet like that on the wall instead of on the floor where one could wipe one's feet, spill coffee and trudge up and down, as one was doing now.)

Skelton stared at me curiously, making a face as he dragged at his cigarette. I had noticed that habit before. Whenever he inhaled, his face so far forgot itself as to allow an expression of discomfort to trespass, as if inhaling was a painful activity.

There. He was doing it again: wincing as he dragged.

"You don't seriously believe that the people you're talking about would have anything to do with physical attacks, do you? I've always understood that the secret service fights clean."

"Yes, so they'd have us believe," I snapped, dragging out my pipe, blowing down it, then putting it away again. Abandoning the carpet, I marched back to the window and glared down into Laurence Pountney Hill. A nurse in gray cotton and white celluloid was wheeling a bicycle along the path between the beds of dank rhododendrons and withered heather.

"What's the significance of his giving the political agent the heave-ho?" I asked at length, turning back to my desk.

"Well, I suppose it means that there's some activity in them thar hills that the Maharajah doesn't want us to see."

"Christ."

Wincing over his cigarette, Skelton watched appreciatively as I sat there, raging internally at the Maharajah. Oh, the skinny little bastard. How could he have picked now of all times to challenge the might of the empire—just when I was about to collect the next installment of my salary?

* * *

If the Zinoviev Letter was a knock-out blow, the Maharajah's action in expelling the King's representative was the demise and the funeral combined. However much we all needed the job, we couldn't continue now.

I utterly failed to understand the Maharajah's reasoning. How could he possibly believe that we would proceed with the enterprise after he had shown his hand by using it to slap the imperial authority on the kisser?

And now, misfortune, not content with a knock-out blow and a funeral, inflicted an indignity on the remains. There was another attempt on Khooshie's life. And this time it succeeded.

Saying nothing to the others, I left the office early that evening and somehow ended up in a pub. I was surprised to find myself still there, supperless, at closing time. I was beginning to suspect that I was drinking just a shade too enthusiastically these days. I would have to watch that. I had heard that overimbibing could be disastrous in India's hot climate. . . . But then I remembered that I wasn't going to India, now. So it was all right, I could have another drinkypoo.

Even before Skelton's visit, I had decided to inform the prince this evening that I could see no way to establish the fighter squadrons in India by the agreed date. I had done everything I could to find another source of supply. I had even sent Philip Brashman to Amsterdam to investigate the possibility of ordering a former enemy aircraft, the Fokker DVII. He had returned raving about Anthony Fokker's latest fighter, the DXIII, which could do 170 miles an hour; but neither it nor the VII would be available for at least a year. To our fury and chagrin, we learned that we had been just too late to acquire as many Fokkers as we wished. Two hundred of the Great War fighters had been available up to the previous month, but somebody had just bought the lot. Fokker had refused to divulge the identity of the purchaser.

Now I would have to inform Khooshie that we were not merely fighterless but air-forceless as well. And if he protested, by God I would rage at him. How, I would ask, how could his father have chosen this moment to further inflame British suspicions? Quite apart from the consequences for the RJAF, didn't he realize the danger that the British might take action against him, just as they had done with that other independent state in India a few years ago, Khaliwar? They had marched into Khaliwar and deposed its rajah, Omar Khayyam, or Sherif U. Scaliwag, or whatever the British Museum reading room had said his name was. Sharif-ul-Khalil, that was it. How could his father have been so bloody *stupid*?

My rage was soon cooled by the downpour that hit London that fateful night, and I was feeling pretty miserable by eleven o'clock when the cab let me off at the inconspicuous entrance to Irwell Court in Belgravia. Remarkably, Khooshie was still living there, despite all the efforts to get rid of him after that housewarming party of his. His expulsion had been demanded by about half the inhabitants of the building under their spokesman, the Bishop of Penge. However, after a heated interview, Khooshie had finally cooled the managerial forehead with the cold compress of his check book.

It had not been difficult to sway the management, despite the additional embarrassment of the death of the majordomo, who had been crushed to death by topcoats. They were not eager to lose a prince, even an Indian one, especially as, dazzled by the family boodle, they were already overcharging him. They finally agreed to let him stay provided he agreed to an increase in the rent, and the payment of an exorbitant sum to cover the damage to the suite and to the corridor where Lady Lavender's hounds had finally cornered the fox and torn it to pieces.

"We'd have been quite sorry to see the lad go," the doorman admitted. "He thinks nothing of dispensing pound notes as gratuities, you know."

"Is that right?"

"On the other hand, the Bishop could leave any time, far as we're concerned. All *he* hands out is threepenny bits."

That evening there was only one servant on duty in Khooshie's apartment, the ancient Indian retainer named Imdad. Even he was in bed when I called, unless it was his custom to answer the door in his nightshirt. That garment was short enough to reveal a pair of thighs like banister spindles. He knew little English, and though I'd had a couple of Hindi lessons from Khooshie, the only word I recognized was "Khooshie." As he pronounced the word, he gestured toward his master's bedroom, then promptly went back to his own bed.

With only one inadequate servant about, it occurred to me that Khooshie's household seemed to be encouraging the assassination plot. Any determined assassin could have broken in here with ease. There was no sign even of the bodyguard.

When I walked through into the private suite, I found that Khooshie was busy in the bathroom. I also discovered that Miss Tombola was on duty after all. She was watching Khooshie take a shower. She was standing only four feet away from the stall, studying his every move.

"What's wrong?" I asked.

"There is nothing wrong, my man," Muriel said. "I am guarding him."

"Oh," I said, retreating from the clouds of scented steam. "Do you usually guard him this closely?"

"Only when he is taking a shower, my man."

"I see."

"He likes me to guard him most careful of all, you see, when he is taking a shower."

I caught Khooshie's eye. He looked away quickly.

"If you don't mind, I am not the least wanting to listen to your silly conversation," he said angrily and snatched at the shower curtain and swished it shut.

Naturally I assumed that he was taking a shower before retiring. It was, after all, twenty minutes past eleven. But when he reappeared in the lounge, he was attired in flawless formal wear. Almost flawless, that is—the boiled shirt front was bowing slightly.

"Your dickey is bent," I pointed out. But for some reason he looked more insulted than ever.

"Are you really going out?" I asked. "It's important we talk, Khooshie."

"I have signed enough checks for one day," he said huffily. He crossed to the big, semicircular window and peered out to see if his car and chauffeur had arrived.

"It's quite urgent, Khooshie."

"It is always urgent," he snapped.

"Haven't you heard the news from India?"

"What news?"

"Your father has expelled the political agent."

"Good."

"Good?"

"I did not like him," Khooshie said, his fine, dark eyes flashing. "He was condescending."

"But don't you see, it's as good as challenging Britain to a duel."

"So?"

"Khooshie, over and over again we have made it plain that no way can we take your part in any conflict with the British."

"There is no conflict," he said, and he continued to argue even when I told him what the evening newspaper had reported, that his father was about to denounce the treaty with Britain.

"Who says so?" the boy asked offensively.

"The political agent, in a press conference. He—"

"Well, he is a liar," Khooshie said contemptuously, and continued to argue along those lines until, losing patience, he stamped his foot and shouted, "I have no time. I am going to a midnight do with Bubba, as soon as she comes for me in my motorcar."

His temper dissipated as fast as it had gathered. "She has had the Rolls-Royce now for nearly a month," he said, biting his nails—a brand-new habit. "She makes Kapur sit in the back while she drives. He is not happy."

"Khooshie, it really is important that we discuss—" I began.

Seeing that I was reviving the old argument, he decided to fly into another rage. He jumped to his feet. "I have been thinking. My father is paying you a lot of money, but you are not doing anything. It is a fine thing, isn't it, when we are paying you all that money and you are not doing anything except gallivanting off to Egypt and other nice, warm places whenever you are feeling like it?"

That sobered me up quite a bit. "Perhaps," I said stiffly, "I might have done better if you had told me what was really going on."

"Nothing is going on, that is what I am complaining about," he shouted, wrenching at his choler. "Oh, yes, I can see you looking superior as anything. You think a mere Indian has no right to criticize. You treat us Indians as if we were children to be indulged or thrashed when we are naughty, you British, but the moment one of us is talking back you very soon put us in our place.

"Except I do not have a place to be put in," he added, unhappily. "At home I am to be borrowed from, or flattered, because my father is rich as Jesus, and I am not looked on as a real person. In India I am looked up to. Here I am looked down on. Oh, yes, you are polite enough, all so very nice and considerate, but I can feel. Bubba is the only one—it is as obvious as anything—" He stopped, choking.

"Khooshie—"

He snatched his shoulder away, showing that he had absorbed enough Anglo-Saxon stoicism to wish to conceal the tears of unhappiness and mortification in his eyes.

I stared at him helplessly, wits dulled by bucketsful of beer. Before I could summon a bromide, Muriel heaved into the room from the direction of her bedroom.

"Hey, Khoosh," she bellowed, "what's all the hullabaloo, my man?" She wagged a forefinger like a shillelagh. "If you are not careful, we will be kicked out again. I don't want to be kicked out; I like it here. It is a lovely place. So you stop that at once, you hear?"

"Yes, of course," Khooshie said quickly, and began to eat his bootlaces. Until I realized that they weren't bootlaces but lengths of licorice. He was fond of licorice.

After upbraiding Khooshie a little more, Muriel turned and beamed, as if calling on me to admire how well she could handle the boy. Storming at him, she seemed to be saying, was part of her job as bodyguard.

At the moment she was certainly the most lavishly dressed bodyguard I'd ever come across. She was attired in two acres of white satin covered with approximately four million beads. One of the sleeves of the gown had split at the seam where her massive black arm emerged.

She was also wearing a hat. It looked like the buffet table at the Café Royal. Tucked under her arm was a handbag like a decayed otter.

"It is time for the party?" she asked.

"But why are you not in bed?" Khooshie asked, swallowing nervously. "I said you are to go to bed."

"You are going out, Khoosh. I am coming too. Boy, am I looking forward to the party or am I not?"

"You're not. I am going alone to the party."

"I am going with you. I am your bodyguard."

"I am not wanting you tonight."

"All the same I am coming. I am being paid to guard your body as well as admire it."

"No, you are not coming," he said, raising his voice. "You disgrace me."

"When do I disgrace you?"

"All the time."

"What all the time?"

"Like, like when we went into the cathedral of St. Paul and you said in your most terribly loud voice, 'What are all these people doing here? Why are they not all working?' "

"Well, it was not a Sunday. It was a Wednesday."

"You do not understand these things," Khooshie said loftily. "It was probably early closing day. That is probably why they were all in there, worshiping like mad."

There was a rapping from the front entrance. When Khooshie and Muriel continued to glare defiantly at each other, and nobody else made a move, I crossed the lounge, living room, sitting room, drawing room, etc., and answered it myself.

It was Kapur, the diminutive chauffeur. When I returned to the lounge to inform Khooshie that his car had arrived, he and Muriel had already patched up their quarrel. Only two minutes had elapsed, but they were chatting quite amicably. Muriel, busily sweeping a fox fur around the Doric column of her neck, was saying that she was looking forward to the hunt, she surely was.

"Can we give you a lift, Bartholomew?" Khooshie asked, looking at me anxiously to see if I was still offended. Just to show that he himself was prepared to forgive and forget, he allowed me to hold his top hat and white silk scarf for him while he debated whether to wear an overcoat.

"Oh, my, you look lovely," Muriel said, winking at me behind his back.

"Thank you," he said gratefully, and with a view to returning the compliment, looked her over. Given her bulk, this took quite a while. Finally and perhaps a little lamely he told her that she looked very nice.

Giggling with excitement, she linked herself to him by a wobbly black arm, and together they led the way into the passageway outside and along to the ancient open-cage elevator. Muriel was talking animatedly and with little squeals of laughter. They were discussing the treasure hunt through the London docks that Bubba had organized. Khooshie had been persuaded to put up the prize, an eighteenth-century French fan that had cost a sum equal to the annual wage of a slush-jollier.

As the elevator reached the poorly lit marble lobby, we saw several persons gathered at the front entrance. They had just returned and were waiting for friends to disgorge themselves from other cars or taxis. Hearing the chortles and giggles, they turned, and their faces turned into lemons when they saw who it was.

Khooshie fell silent, abashed, when he saw that the Bishop of Penge was among them. It was plain that, despite Khooshie's hefty contribution to the church's leper colony, the bishop still regarded Khooshie with some reserve. The resident next to him, a cabinet minister's wife, looked even less welcoming.

Through the open doorway of the building came the loud slap of water on the sidewalks and cobbles. It was raining, the elements making up for several dry days. Through the beveled glass doorway, we could see a flustered young man in a dinner jacket scuttling up and down outside in the gleaming dark, trying to cope with a vehicular chaos. Half a dozen private cars and cabs were all trying to crowd under the canopy of Irwell Court. There wasn't room for them all, and the competition was leading to some ill-tempered complaints.

Even as we watched through the glass, the rain turned into a drenching downpour. I was glad I had accepted Khooshie's offer of a lift, and when the little chauffeur, Kapur, appeared in the doorway with an umbrella, I got ready by turning up the collar of my jacket. At which moment a man wearing spectacles and a black beard moved out of the shadows and lunged at Khooshie.

Muriel screamed and lashed out. She caught me in the mouth with her huge fist. As I staggered, I saw that the attacker had a knife with a broad, six- or seven-inch blade. It burned as it reflected yellow light. He was near a yellow lamp in an ornate bracket near the doorway. He raised the knife high over an astonished Khooshie.

For a fraction of a second the man hesitated, as if unwilling to desecrate the gleaming shirtfront that guarded Khooshie's breast. How else to explain his change of direction of thrust? The assassin did that, altering the angle so that the knife would strike home just beside the boiled shirtfront. The knife did indeed strike laterally, embedding itself in the side of Khooshie's chest, the blade driving in the direction of the heart.

It must have slipped between the ribs, for the blade sank right to the hilt before the assassin withdrew it. With a shout he hurled himself between the cabinet minister's wife and the bishop's wife, sending them reeling back with puffs of outrage. The cabinet minister's wife tripped and fell on top of me just as I was scrambling up.

I was somewhat scrambled mentally, what with a heavy evening of drink and cogitation, a blow from Miss Tombola, and the abrupt descent of two hundred pounds of cabinet minister's wife on top of me. Meanwhile the assassin made his escape—driving everybody back with his flailing knife, before smashing his way through the crowd at the entrance and disappearing into the wet, shiny night.

Screams, harsh as grinding metal, shrilled off the marble walls.

A howling Muriel was now lashing out at the bishop with her beaded purse as if it were all his fault. Only Khooshie remained silent. With both hands to his chest he had staggered back against the grillwork of the elevator. The entire contraption, from fifth floor to cellar, clacked and shuddered under the impact. Somebody kept shouting "Police! Police!"

By the time I reached him, his legs had given way, and he was sliding slowly to the floor, his face as gray as the marble walls.

The doorman, back from a quiet drag in the cellar, came running up the stairs. He stopped dead and stared, open-mouthed, at the frenzied scene. Some idiot was still screaming. Two of his wealthiest tenants were on the floor, one silent as death, the other rocking and moaning as she soothed a soiled silken kneecap. "Look at that, my best silk stockings."

The doorman's expression changed from shock to dread. Someone in a business suit was busily disrobing. That was me, using my jacket as a pillow for the dying prince, whom no flights of angels would sing to his rest. The only descant came from that idiot wife of the high court judge, with her continuous screaming.

"He's been stabbed! He's been murdered! Get the police, for God's sake! Has anyone gone for the—?"

"Ambulance. He should have a doctor. Hospital. Doctor. Hospital. St. Pancreas is good. My sister was in there. They—"

"Should give him air. You're supposed to give them air."

"That Indian. You know the one. God, he looks—"

"Awful. He's not dead, is he? I've never seen anyone dead. What's he saying?"

"Bartholomew."

"It's all right, Khooshie. Don't fret, it'll be okay."

"I'll fret if I want to. Gopala, he was my personal servant. He was very good at fretwork. He showed me how."

"Don't talk. The ambulance will be here soon. Has anyone sent for the . . . ? Good. Yes. Any time now, Khooshie."

"There's a Harley Street man living here, they've sent for him. Of course, he's a dermatologist, but I don't suppose—"

"He stinks of beer," the bishop's wife hissed at the bishop.

"Hush, dear, he's dying."

"Not him, the other."

"He had a beautiful inlaid box containing five saws," Khooshie said dreamily. "Delicate as silk, and he made a bit of extra money for himself cutting screens and selling them in the bazaar through his relation . . . I have forgotten the name. . . ."

"Khooshie, could you move your hands, so I can see the, the minor wound? I'm sure it's just a minor. . . ." But his fists over the dreadful wound were as rigid as if he had already died and rigor mortis had set in.

"What was his name, what was his name?"

"Gopala, you said."

"No, I mean the name of Gopala's relation. He sat always between two toddies. It was the best place in the bazaar and there were always many arguments about who should be there, but Gopala's relation was always there."

I couldn't get him to remove his fist from the side of his chest, and I couldn't bring myself to use force. Khooshie's face was gray with shock. He just wouldn't move his hand from under his shirtfront at the side.

The others fell silent at last, or relatively so. They were whispering instead of bawling. They pressed around. There was a flash of purple. It was the Bishop of Penge, his face struggling for pathos.

"I was only away for a minute," the doorman was saying, looking almost as desperate as Khooshie. "A couple of minutes at the very most. But they'll say it was my fault he was done in, I just know it. And a prince, too, and it'll be in all the papers."

"Stop whining, man, and do something."

Khooshie clutched at me with the blood-drained fingers of his free hand. "Bartholomew? Are you there?"

"Shhh, don't talk."

"Am I dying?"

"Yes," the bishop's wife said firmly. Then, when everybody looked at her: "Well, he ought to know, oughn't he? It's always best to know."

"Bartholomew, you must tell my father that he must go on, in spite of it. He will want to give up, he will not . . . he is only doing it for me, and I have let him down. I have not learned to fly and to take my place." A tear welled in each of his spiky eyelashed eyes, the eyes that made girls and matrons come all over queer, as if those eyes were physically pressing on erogenous zones. "He wants an air force only so that our independent state will survive. We would like a navy, too, but there is no sea that is available. . . ."

"You shouldn't be talking this way, Khooshie."

"I am not saying anything disgusting am I, Bartholomew? I have not got to that part yet." The bishop's wife leaned closer. "You see, we have many enemies, Bartholomew. For instance there is Khaliwar. They have always been envious of our riches and our fertile soil and our trees. And then there is—"

He coughed. What looked like gore trickled from his mouth. In the hall's inadequate lighting it looked black. The bishop's wife moved away again.

Khooshie's voice was fainter when he continued. "My family, you see, have ruled Jhamjarh for centuries, but I am the last of the Prakashes, and now that I am dead, it is possible that father might lose confidence in the survival of our family. He will give up, and then we shall be overwhelmed. . . ."

His dark, prominent eyes dulled, then slid upward. Somebody whimpered. The doorman removed his cap. But it was only because Khooshie's attention had been attracted by a movement from the bishop. The bishop had been glancing surreptitiously at his watch.

"Next, there is the matter of the apparent attempts on my life," Khooshie continued. "Alas, more than apparent, in this case. I have been thinking about it, and I have come to the conclusion that somebody has been trying to kill me four times."

"*Four* times?"

"The first time I think it was my flying instructor."

"What? Philip Brashman?"

"No, not your man. The other. The first."

"Your first instructor? Bernard Hive, you mean?"

"Yes. But it doesn't matter now, as they have finally succeeded," the boy said, so sadly that somebody sobbed.

After a while, however, people began to fidget, especially when Khooshie started to go into details as to the disposition of his property. He was particularly anxious, he said, that I should have one of his radiograms because, though I had quite often been a thorough pest, on the whole I had treated him quite decently.

"Then there is Bubba," Khooshie continued. "I know you think she is being so friendly because I am rich, but I assure you, Bartholomew, even if I was as poor as anything, and in rags, and diseased up to the eyebrows, and prematurely aged, she would still love me. I love her so much, Bartholomew. So, as I have not made out a will, I want you to see that she gets something. Say, a million pounds? Though of course that might be difficult as you are not permitted to sign checks for more than a thousand—"

"Look here, Khooshie," I said. "Isn't this dying speech of yours taking rather a long time? Some of us want to get to bed, you know. And I haven't had my dinner yet."

"You haven't had dinner?" Lady Cowper said. "But it's midnight."

"Well, I usually eat late."

"Personally I don't know where you're going to find a decent restaurant open at this hour."

"How can you be so heartless?" the bishop hissed.

"What, just because I haven't had dinner?"

"Talking that way in front of the boy."

"Yes, well, I'll hurry it up," Khooshie said, just as the dermatologist arrived in his dressing gown, his face full of grave wrinkles. Within seconds he was kneeling by the body and prying Khooshie's hand away from his heart, to reveal, as I had already realized, that the assassin's knife, though it had driven right to the hilt into the side of Khooshie's chest, had left no wound whatsoever.

Muriel in Belgravia

I stayed overnight in Khooshie's apartment and next morning chatted to him for a few minutes while he lay in bed, polishing off a large breakfast. The alarms and excursions of the previous evening had evidently not diminished his appetite.

"It is quite plain," said he, emitting a deprecatory English-style laugh to show that he was not to be considered credulous, "that I am under some sort of divine protection."

"I wouldn't exactly call Muriel divine."

"I am referring to the Miracle," he said, smacking away my hand as I reached over for a slice of toast. "I mean, dash it all, Bartholomew, did you or did you not observe the assassin's blade plunging deep into my breast?"

"I did."

"And I assure you, I felt it. I felt the steel driving deep into my heart. I felt the blood under my hand, forcing itself between my fingers in a sanguine ooze, its curling crimson fingers retaining that distinctly animal smell—"

"*Please*. I'm eating my breakfast."

"It is *my* breakfast that you are eating," Khooshie said crossly. He was annoyed because I was not regarding him with the awe and reverence due to one so markedly favored by his favorite deity, Siva. The rest of the staff were showing a much finer sense of proportion. The new majordomo who had supervised the delivery of the breakfast tray had actually trembled in Khooshie's presence, while the underling he was supervising had withdrawn backward with bows galore; so many that his oily black hair had come undone and started to trail on the floor . . . unless of course he was mopping the floor in this fashion in accordance with some Eastern-style obeisance.

Khooshie was thrilled by the tokens of respect. Why even Muriel, seated in her usual position near the entrance to the bedroom, was according him silent homage. For the last half-hour she had been staring at him whenever he wasn't looking, staring with such wide-eyed intensity that the whites of her eyes seemed to banish every shadow from the bedroom.

She was also unusually subdued this morning. Even Khooshie had begun to notice it and to glance at her curiously; but whenever he glanced in her direction, she would hang her head until he had looked away again.

I supposed that she was feeling low because on the occasion of her first real emergency she had not done spectacularly well. Perhaps she was wondering what they would say down at the bouncers and bodyguards' hiring hall when they heard that she had fainted.

"After all, you saw what happened," Khooshie persisted.

"Yes."

"So you cannot deny that I was assassinated," he said, watching me carefully in case I snatched again at the fodder. "And yet the grievous wound that was inflicted was completely healed by the time the doctor arrived. If that is not a miracle, Bartholomew, then there is no meaning in life."

"Yes, it was amazing."

"You must write to my father describing what has happened, Bartholomew. You must write in exquisite detail. He is greatly interested in omens and marvels, you see. He has experienced many strange happenings himself. Once when he was out at night, strolling near the Chokka Hills with his adviser, Mr. Hafeez, a blue fox came right up to father and bowed. When father asked what it meant, Mr. Hafeez said it meant that father's worst enemy would die in a few weeks. Accordingly, father watched his relations very carefully and, sure enough, one of them died within the specified time. It was somebody whom father suspected of diverting much of the betel-leaf crop into his own warehouse."

"Gee whiz."

"The victim was Mr. Hafeez himself. He died of rabies after the blue fox bit him, you see."

"I see."

"Things like that happened many times to father, though of course, being a king that is only to be expected. But this is the first time I personally have been touched by a divinity. Unfortunately, father is suffering from disillusionment just at the moment, and if I write and tell him, he will take it with a pinch of snuff, and not believe one word of it. So you must tell him, please, in great detail. It will very much hearten him, I am sure."

Khooshie clapped his hands, and smirked when a servant arrived within seconds. With a lordly sweep of a slender wrist he ordered the removal of the breakfast tray.

"By the way, Prince," I said, "did you really mean what you said last night about your first instructor?"

"Who?"

"Your flying instructor. Bernard Hive?"

"I don't remember everything I said. I was delirious with pain, you see."

"You indicated that he might have been trying to get rid of you."

"Oh, that," he said, shrugging somewhat irritably. He would much rather have gone on discussing the miracle. "Who knows? Perhaps I was in a suspicious frame of mind. It just occurred to me, that's all, because when I was doing my solo and the engine conked out, I just happened to look at the fuel tube thing, and it was empty. But I had only been flying for a few minutes."

"For God's sake, why did you never tell me this before?"

Khooshie shrugged again and brushed crumbs off the sheets.

I had been intending to follow another line of enquiry that morning, but now I decided to postpone it until the evening.

"Khooshie," I said, "may I borrow one of your motorcars?"

"Of course, my dear chap, no need to ask," Khooshie said,

brightening. He liked doing things for me, provided it did not involve him in any effort. "You may even have a chauffeur to go with it. Take the one with the white hair. In fact, you can keep him. I do not want him back. I do not admire him, even though he was the chauffeur of Lord Hynd-Waters for twenty years until the Daimler conked out. Every time I go out in the car, this chauffeur looks inside as if to make sure that I have not disgraced myself on the upholstery."

Thinking about the chauffeur caused Khooshie's delicately handsome features to turn awry. His bulging brown eyes glowed fiercely within their palisade of eyelashes. "I tell you, Bartholomew," he said indignantly, "if it were not so absurd, I would suspect him of the most awful snobbery. He is always comparing me with his former employer, this lord of his. But I ask you, who is more important, a twopenny knight whose family were probably court sycophants only a few hundred years ago, or I, who am not only a prince but one who is under the most particular protection of the god Siva? I ask you."

The blaze dampened with the usual suddenness. Now he sounded quite lordly and condescending. "By the by, Bandy," he said, lying back on the silken pillows, "we have given some thought to your concerns and have decided that there is nothing for you to worry about. I suppose it must be disturbing to those who do not understand these things to hear that father apparently intends to sever connections with the Raj." He leaned over and actually patted my hand. "But do not worry, my dear chap. This threat to abrogate the treaty is merely a diplomatic feint. You underestimate father, you know, if you assume that he has no skill or subtlety in these affairs." And he flapped his hand dismissively and informed me that I was now at liberty to leave the presence.

As he lay there, he looked so wise and mature that, had there been a custard pie handy, I should cheerfully have applied it to his face. Fuming, I made for the exit.

"I suppose you need the car for more of your urgent business?" he asked, so wearily but indulgently that I mentally substituted a grenade for the custard pie.

"No." I gritted my teeth. "It's such a nice November day, I thought I'd take a trip to the seaside." But he wasn't even listening. He responded with a wave that could only be described as utterly dismissive of the world's trivial vicissitudes. A semidivinity obviously had higher things to think about.

When Khooshie first suggested that his flying instructor might have been out to eliminate him, I had dismissed it as the babblings of a shock victim. But after thinking about it, I wasn't so sure. I was beginning to recollect a few details about that instructor, his character and his behavior. The more I thought about Bernard Hive, the more certain I became that a spot of investigation might not go amiss.

I still couldn't believe that an instructor would deliberately send a student aloft alone knowing him to be hopelessly incompetent. Yet the fact was that Hive *had* allowed Khooshie to solo when he must have known that the boy was a positive menace as a pilot. Moreover, he had pointed Khooshie out to sea — a most unnatural heading for even an advanced student — where his chance of survival, if he came down, was almost nil. And what about that almost empty fuel tank? Could Hive have drained the tank, relying on Khooshie's carelessness and unobservant nature to ensure that he *did* come down in the sea?

Murder by airplane. I had never heard of that before. But what was in it for Bernard Hive? And what did it all have to do with India?

However, it was Hive I should be questioning, not myself. Which was why I was borrowing a car and chauffeur that morning, to take me to Southend aerodrome.

First, however, I tracked down one of the lads who had been with Hive in the pub when I walked in so very long ago . . . or was it only a few months? It took an annoyingly long time to do so, but I finally located him at a nearby horse-riding establishment. Whereupon a pound note passed in one direction and some useful information in the other, to the effect that Bernard Hive had owned only one training aircraft, so that when it went into the sea it should have been a financial disaster for him. Even when it was still flying, Hive was usually pretty hard up. But soon after the loss of his only visible possession, Hive was suddenly flush with oodles of pelf.

"Mind you, he's spent it all now," the stable lad said, " 'cause the landlord down at the pub is starting to remind him again about settling up, like. No, he ain't in the flying business no more, he's just waiting for the right job to come along. You know how it is with officers. Can't be just any ordinary job, you know, like the rest of us common herd. Where'll you find him? In the pub, of course."

As it was opening time by then, I had the chauffeur drive me straight there. The chauffeur, incidentally, was indeed proving to be a stuck-up fellow, though my main objection to him was that he had such a fine head of hair, even if it was white.

Hive was in residence. He was sitting alone at one of the benches sulkily nursing two inches of ale when I joined him and handed him a fresh pint. This time it was my turn to expose a wallet packed with currency.

"Haven't I seen you before somewhere?"

"In this pub, a few months ago."

"Oh, yes." He looked wonderingly out the window at Khooshie's Lancia Lambda. He had seen me drive up in that long, low beauty.

"Yes, you were asking about a job. You seem to have found one, all right," he said, smiling ingratiatingly. "Haven't got one for me, have you?"

"Well, the answers to a few questions might be worth a few quid."

"What questions?"

"Like, who paid you to ensure that the Indian prince, Khooshie, did not return from his solo."

Bernard Hive was not overly self-controlled. He started so violently about half of his beer slopped over the scarred wooden bench and cascaded onto his starboard kneecap.

By the time I arrived back in London it was too late to pursue the other line of enquiry, which was far more important than the confrontation with that miserable ex-officer, Bernard Hive. So I directed the chauffeur to Irwell Court.

When we arrived and I told him to wait, he said stiffly, "I have been on duty since seven this morning, sir. It is now nearly 11:00 P.M."

"Oh, this is nothing," I said as I climbed out. "You'll be working quite late from now on."

Well. He had no right to flaunt all that hair.

Inside I found Khooshie camped outside Muriel's locked bedroom door. He was busily pleading through her keyhole.

"Muriel," he was saying in a voice already growing hoarse, "why are you not being reasonable?"

"Go away."

"Open the door, Muriel, so we can talk in a civilized manner."

"So now you are saying I am not civilized."

"I am not saying that at all. I am saying—"

"But of course to you white folks I am just an ignorant black person from Zambuk."

"I keep telling you, Muriel, I am not a white folks, I am a very high-caste Indian fellow."

"You look down on us just as much as them."

"But Muriel, how can I look down on you when you are so huge and I am only—"

"You only want me so that I can stand there and admire your bare bum," she said tearfully through the woodwork.

Khooshie glanced at me, then away again quickly.

"It is all your fault," Muriel was saying.

"I am sorry, Muriel."

"I am not coming out until you apologize."

"I have said I am sorry."

"And another thing, you don't treat me like a lady, just because I am black."

"I do. I—"

"Then why do you always walk in front? Have you never heard of the expression 'ladies first'?"

"But Muriel, you are not a lady, you are a bodyguard."

"It is always me who has to open the door for you and hang about all the time, waiting for you to finish your meetings. You are ashamed of me, that is what is the trouble."

"I am not ashamed of you. I—"

"You are. You never ask me to have dinner with you and your fancy friends. I have to wait in the kitchen and starve."

"You had dinner with us at the Café Royal only last week."

"Only because Bubba said I could. She said I must sit at the table so I could impress the *maître d'hôtel* no end with the headdress of my tribe, the one with the shrunken heads."

"And you certainly did impress him," Khooshie said. "He fainted."

"There you are, you see? You are making me feel bad again."

"How?"

"You are reminding me that I fainted last night instead of coming to your aid. Well, it is not my fault that you have such a big jujube."

"Such a big what?" I asked.

"Who is that voice?"

"It's only Bartholomew. Look here, Muriel," Khooshie said angrily, "I cannot continue to hold a conversation through all this wood. It is not seemly." And he rattled the doorknob.

This instantly changed Muriel's tone from resentment to fear. "No," she screamed. "You must not come in. It is your jujube."

"What rank superstition," Khooshie snorted and rattled the doorknob again, producing another scream.

Intrigued by his discovery that rattling a doorknob produced a nerve-jangling shriek, Khooshie rattled it yet again to produce a similar reaction. A mean smile played over his delicately proportioned features. It looked as if a certain resentment had been building up over Muriel's refractory behavior, and he was seizing the opportunity to get his own back, while at the same time researching a brand-new area of the conditioned reflex.

Eventually Muriel grew tired of screaming. When she finally emerged, she condescended to return to Khooshie's employ on condition that certain changes be made in the arrangements, which included a raise of a pound a week, sponsorship of members of her family in Zambuk to enable them to come to England, a dress allowance and saxophone lessons. Khooshie balked only at providing her with a maid, not because he objected to her choice of maid, her sixteen-year-old niece, but because the niece would be expected to act as bodyguard whenever Muriel was busy with her memoirs, and Khooshie feared that Bubba might be jealous if she saw him being accompanied by a nubile young woman.

Some time after seven the following evening, I directed the chauffeur to my old lodgings in Norfolk Gardens.

As I clambered out of the magnificent, ivory-colored Lancia Lambda, I glimpsed Mrs. Wignall's sharp nose twitching in the gap in her net window curtains.

"Working in a garage now, are you?" were her first words upon meeting me in the flaking hallway.

"Certainly not. I've just gone up in the world, that's all."

"Gone up? You're a lift attendant?"

"No, I am not an elevator operator," I translated. "Does this natty gent's suiting look as if it belonged to an elevator operator?"

"You had that suit before you left."

"Uh . . . yes, so I did. All right, but what about that beautiful car out there? Doesn't that tell you something?"

"Why, is it yours?"

"Well, no, not exactly. But—"

"There you are, then," she said with a snotty nod. "And if you want your old room, you can't have it."

"I don't want it," I said, feeling really peevish over her abject failure to recognize a man who had made good when she saw one.

"What are you here for, then?"

"For one thing, I came to see if there were any letters for me."

"Why would there be any letters? You don't live here."

"I thought there might have been a letter from home."

"I don't know why you think there'd be letters here for you. Are you in the habit of going up to people's houses and asking if they have any letters for you?"

"Darn it, woman, I didn't leave a forwarding address, so I thought—"

"There isn't."

"What?"

"There aren't any letters for you. Why don't you try the house next door? Maybe they'd be able to spare you some letters."

By then I was hoping that some other boarder would appear, one who would be rather more impressed by my air of affluence and authority; and as luck would have it, Mr. Ribble returned from his travels at that moment. As he entered the front door, he was listing heavily under the weight of his steel sample case.

"Oh, aye," he said, his coarse face red and sweating in the humid November evening. "Pinched anyone's bath night, lately?" And he carried on up the stairs as if he didn't really expect a reply.

I gazed unblinkingly out the front door. Ribble had not properly secured it, so that it had groaned open again. Through the doorway I could see the leaves of the plane trees drifting disconsolately to earth. Perhaps they had been hoping to hang on until next spring.

At least it was raining leaves rather than rain. That seemed typical of England. Now that winter was almost upon us, the weather had greatly improved. At the present rate we would be sunbathing by Christmas.

I made to close the door. "Aren't you going to say good-bye?" Mrs. Wignall asked.

"I was just going to close the door, that's all."

"Leave it open for a few minutes," she ordered. "It'll help to air the hall."

"Yes, it does need airing. A tornado might help."

"Anything else?"

"What?"

"I was enquiring if there was anything else you wanted."

"No. Well . . . . I just dropped in to see how everybody was. They're all really good friends of mine, you see. I'll never forget them. So, how's Miss . . . the little old lady who lives next to the bathtub? And Mrs. . . . the lady on the top floor? And the two music students, er Ian and, er . . . ."

"Ian and Betty? They are no longer with us. They had to go. They were playing ducks and drakes with their bath nights."

"Surely playing with rubber ducks and things in their baths was no reason to get rid of them, Mrs. Wignall. I myself—"

"They were abusing their ablutionary privileges," she said sharply, but failing for once to stare me in the eye.

"Abusing their . . . ?" I began. Then: "By any chance—they weren't sharing their bath nights, were they? So they could enjoy two baths a week?"

"Enjoy is the right word," she said tartly. "It was the sound of their enjoyment that first alerted us—the boarders, that is—to the fact that something untoward was going on. For the sake of my guests I was forced to ask them to leave."

"Well, I never," I said. I was now my turn to look away, suspecting that it was I who had first put the idea into the heads of Ian and Betty.

As if unwilling to lose the conversational offensive, Mrs. Wignall asked sharply, "And what d'you mean, music students? They weren't students."

"Yes they were. At the Royal Academy of Music."

Plainly pleased to be able to correct me, she said, "She was. He was a journalist."

"What?"

"If you don't believe me, buy the *Daily Mail*. You can see his name in it any time."

"I see," I said, through my teeth.

"While you're here, there's one thing I'd like to ask you, Mr. Bandy," Mrs. Wignall said, two dabs of color staining her sulfuric face. "About Mr. Drane."

"Who . . . ?"

"Him, of course." She gestured along the corridor to the first door on the left. "What I want to know is, did he ever say things about me when you were here?"

"Say things?"

"Slanderous things."

"I don't remember."

"People have been looking at me queerly for a long time now, and I'm sure it has something to do with him. Are you sure you don't know anything about it?"

"No. Sorry," I said, avoiding her eyes more than ever.

I was spared any further grilling by the shrilling of the telephone from the front room. After staring at me fixedly for a couple of seconds, she turned on her heel, hurried into her room and closed the door with a force that was not quite a slam; while I on my part walked thoughtfully deeper into the gloom and knocked at Mr. Drane's shadowed door.

There was a faint scuffling sound from within, but half a minute later he had still not answered. Remembering that something like this had happened the first time I met him, I waited patiently enough, if somewhat uneasily, meanwhile reviewing what I had learned from Bernard Hive. Which did not take long, as I had learned almost nothing.

It was too much to expect that even a bribe of several pounds sterling would elicit a confession of guilt from Hive. For all he knew, I might have turned him in to the police; though he had been quick enough to point out with a shakily triumphant nod of the head that there was no proof of any of my filthy accusations. That he had deliberately despatched Khooshie seaward in an airplane that was not meant to return—it was utter nonsense. Worse, it was slanderous. He had a good mind to call the police himself.

"Look, all I want to know," I said patiently, turning my hand palm up on the table to show how frank and open I was being, "is whether you had a personal motive for killing Khooshie? There, now, that's not an unreasonable thing to ask, is it?" Realizing that my knuckles were resting in a puddle of ale, I removed my hand and shook it over his trousers.

"Clear off," he responded.

"I have the resources, you know, to find out if there was anything between you and Khooshie other than as instructor and student."

"Well, you won't find anything, because there isn't," he said triumphantly.

"Ah, thank you, Bernard. That's one thing I wanted to know. Here's your five pounds."

"I don't want it," he said, staring at the ridiculously large white bank note. "Clear off, I said."

"So therefore somebody else paid you to eliminate him from the human race."

He sat there and sneered.

"Unless, of course, you can explain how you were suddenly so flush with money after you lost your only aircraft."

The sneer slipped a bit. "It was insured," he muttered, his eyes flickering. "That's where the five thousand came from."

"I wouldn't stick to that story, Bernard. Too easily disproved. Besides, you forget, I'm in the flying business myself, and I know that insurance companies won't insure private aircraft."

"Says you."

"Even if they did, they sure wouldn't insure an Avro 504 for that amount when you could buy an almost new one for less than a fifth of that."

"Bollocks."

"Listen, Hive. If you don't talk to me, you'll be talking to a certain Chief Inspector Frank of Scotland Yard, and he'll have you whimpering in no time at all," I said, hoping I looked suitably threatening.

Apparently not. "No, you listen, old man," he sneered. "There's no way you can possibly prove anything except that I came into some money. So bollocks to you, old man, bollocks to you."

After issuing a few threats, I tried bribery again, but his reluctance to confess to an attempted murder even without witnesses proved to be even stronger than his need for a spot of the ready. Still, the confrontation had been useful. I had come away convinced that he had had no personal reason to dunk Khooshie into the North Sea, and therefore that somebody must have put him up to it. Five thousand pounds was a handsome compensation for the loss of an Avro 504 and the almost negligible risks involved.

By now, whole minutes had elapsed with no answer to my imperious knocking in the corridor of the boarding house. I rapped again, adding to the percussion with some impatient foot-tapping, while listening to the faint sound of Mrs. Wignall's voice on the telephone in her room. Then I glanced idly out through the front door.

And received a terrible fright. Striding across the lamplit street of the square was an all-too-familiar figure in a tweed suit and light-colored blouse. She was struggling with a parcel. As she reached the steps, a snatch of light from Mrs. Wignall's front window caused her topknot to gleam bright gold.

Instinctively I looked around for somewhere to hide. Closed doors everywhere. I was trapped.

So be it. I turned to face her, shoulders back. Contemptuously I waved away a blindfold. I was too mature for that sort of thing, now. Thirty-two years old, after all. I was past all that—evading awkward confrontations by skittering into concealment. In the past I had responded to crises in that cowardly manner far too frequently. But I had finally learned that it did not pay to evade one's responsibilities or postpone an unpleasant confrontation by skulking. It rarely solved the problem, and the burning humiliation when one was ultimately discovered was invariably worse than the encounter it was designed to avoid. So I turned to face her squarely as she started up the steps to the open front door.

Amazingly, she had not yet espied me. As well as her handbag, she was carrying an awkward parcel. Laundry. She was having trouble with it. The brown paper was shiny and kept slipping from under her arm. She had not yet looked ahead into the house. The corridor was not particularly well lit anyway. And as she reached the top step, the parcel again started to slide from her grasp, so that she had to grab for it, which distracted her still further.

It would have been genuinely impudent of me to have snubbed the fates when they were thus offering me another spin of the wheel of fortune. So I turned and reached the stairway in one bound. Possibly more than one bound, as it was a good ten feet away, but I was in no mood for exactitude. Another bound carried me to the top of the stairs, and there I hid, concealed by spindles and shadows. And I watched with thumping pulse, expecting her to . . . I don't know what. It hadn't yet occurred to me to wonder what she was doing in the boarding house, or whom she was visiting. So I don't know what I expected her to do.

What she actually did was to start upstairs after me, clutching her parcel, and whispering to herself in Icelandic.

I backed deeper into the gloom, instinctively turning toward my old room. By the time I remembered that the corridor on that side of the house led nowhere but to a grimy window that overlooked the back garden, it was too late to turn back. Trapped again. I could hear her approaching, feet dragging tiredly over the floorboards. It was nearly eight o'clock. She had probably spent twelve hours in the sunless basement of the hospital.

Obviously there was only one course of action for me to take. Praying that my old room was not occupied by some nerve-shredded spinster who would scream like an unoiled mangle and land me in jug on a charge of rape, murder or selling encyclopedias, I opened the door, raked the interior with a lightning glance and slipped in, excuses already buttering my lips. "Health inspector—any cockroaches?" I was ready to say, or, "Paddington Station—all change," whichever seemed more appropriate in the circumstances.

My luck still held. The room was unoccupied. Apart from a pair of lace curtains at the window—they were already turning grimy at the hem in the smoky London air—the room looked just as I had left it. No—there were a few odds and ends on the dresser that weren't mine, dimly visible, courtesy of the street lighting that came sneaking along the brick wall outside and reflected itself in through the window.

Merde. My luck wasn't holding, after all. I could hear Sigga's footsteps in the uncarpeted corridor outside. I could even make out the crackle of her brown-paper parcel. And the sounds were coming closer.

I stared unbelievingly at the door. Surely she wasn't visiting the very room that I had chosen as my sanctuary?

She was. The doorknob was starting to turn, clumsily. It was only then that it occurred to me that she actually lived here.

One, two, three paces round the end of the bed. I snatched at the mahogany wardrobe. For a frantic second I failed to locate the familiar little knob. My nails scrabbled at the crack. The door to the room was opening. I could hear her breathing and muttering as she wrestled with the parcel. My fingers encountered the knob. Foot over the high sill at the bottom. Lucky I was a horseman, and instinctively put the offside foot in first, otherwise I should have been stuck in there facing the wall with my back to the room, horribly exposed. So I slipped inside, a split second before Sigridur switched on the ceiling light and entered.

And that is how I came to be in the mahogany wardrobe.

Oh, this was appalling. Sooner or later she was bound to open the wardrobe door and see me standing there with my chin resting on a steel clothes rail and my stunned expression directly above it. It could confirm her very worst suspicions about me, assuming I had not already sunk so low in her esteem as to make further depreciation nonsensical. So I resolved, with all the strength of will for which I was renowned, to step out of the wardrobe immediately and face the music, even if it was by Schönberg. Seeing me emerge couldn't possibly be more of a shock to her than if I remained and she opened the wardrobe to reach for, say, the cotton vest that had been slung over the clothes rail three inches from my left eye. So that is what I decided, to give myself up. However, first I would wait to ascertain whether she intended to remain in her room. It would be silly to step out of somebody's wardrobe just as they were leaving. Mind you, that wasn't very likely. She had looked so tired I didn't think she would be going out on the town. Nevertheless. Or maybe she'd go to bed soon, and I could tippytoe out as soon as she fell asleep.

I was fooling myself. She was bound to open the wardrobe sooner or later. Apart from the chest of drawers opposite—I could see it easily through the slightly ajar wardrobe door; it had brushes, combs, aspirin and photographs of her family arranged on it—there was nowhere else for her to put her clothes.

Wait. Was it possible that she might open the wardrobe and still not see me? It would be quite like her to sling her clothes into the cupboard without looking. Take the cotton vest suspended from the rail more or less in front of my eyes. It, for instance, had been tossed in here carelessly. I myself was in the habit of treating clothes with respect, putting them away carefully in drawers or upon hangers and folding my trousers very carefully, and so forth; but not everyone was as respectful as me. Sigga certainly wasn't, she was downright indifferent as regards both clothes treatment and clothes sense. Look at that green tweed suit she was wearing. It was totally unsuitable. It made her look bulky. After all, she was already a hefty piece of work, with a set of bones borrowed from *Homo erectus* before being refined for use in *Neanderthal man*. Further, the bones were padded out with a good solid diet of cod, cream, lamb and so forth. She certainly didn't need to augment all that with a layer of hairy Hibernian mutton material.

Of course, it was possible that I was reading too much into the vest dangling there before my very eyes, but nobody could say I was not an optimist, always ready to see the positive side of things. But, oh God, this time the situation was utterly hopeless. She had now been sitting there for at least half an hour. She was certain to revive at any moment and start bustling about, putting things away in drawers and wardrobes. It was surprising that she hadn't already revived. The moment she entered she had plonked herself on the side of the bed with her back to me and the wardrobe. After ten minutes or so she had picked up the laundry bill and had studied it carefully, not finding it much to her liking, judging by her back. Damn it, I would step out of the wardrobe right now and get it over with. If she opened the door without warning there was a distinct risk that a scream would pierce the night's dull air. Sigga might scream, as well. Probably just before bringing up her knee to end forever the prospect of Bandy progeny.

(Many people believed that that would be a good thing. I knew this because they had told me. "The thought of another Bandy loose in the world is just too ghastly to contemplate," they had said. Actually I had a child, but it had been taken over by the mother's billionaire parents.)

Twenty minutes later, Sigga was still sitting on the side of the bed with her back turned, and I was on the rack. For the past many minutes I had been attempting to ease the pain by pointing my knees in opposite directions and sinking into an obscene squatting position, but I couldn't get my chin past the clothes rail. Already I had very nearly alerted her to my presence. When I started to bend, one of my knees had pressed against the side panel of the wardrobe and made it creak. My heart nearly downed tools. I don't know how she failed to hear the squawk of the wood, unless the rest of the house was being particularly unruly that evening. I remembered that during many a sleepless night in this place, the house had creaked, thudded and grinded quite noisily sometimes, as well as settling and rotting. Perhaps the creak had coincided with one of those sounds.

Unless she was locked in that brown study of hers and couldn't get out. She had long since finished reading her laundry bill, but had not stirred from the side of the bed. There was something dispirited about the set of her back that quite disturbed me, despite a certain preoccupation with my own discomfort. Her broad back tapering neatly to the waist—you could identify the waist, now that she had removed the jacket of her green tweed suit to reveal an old-fashioned ivory blouse with frills and things at the wrist and collar—looked really depressed. I felt quite concerned. Now she was examining her big, chemical-stained hands, and sighing. This wasn't like her at all. She should have been bustling about, getting ready for a night on the tiles. Her silence and the resignation of her posture as she sat hunched on the side of the bed were not only uncharacteristic, they were annoying. Go on, get out there and enjoy yourself, you dope.

She continued to sit there for hour after hour, or so it seemed, with slumped shoulders and golden head bowed, as if deliberately to cause me discomfort, emotional as well as physical. If I wasn't careful I might soon start to feel compassion. This was a woman who had been made for wide fiords, hot springs and cool breezes over volcanic plains, but who was now confined in a dispiriting room in a bath-rationed boarding house in a distant grimy city, without relatives or even the dubious companionship of the fellow who she claimed had inspired her to come here in the first place. I had a feeling that she had still not made any friends. Despite her beauty and basically unselfish nature, she did not make friends easily. Men tended to be scared off by her powerful personality and tactless behavior, and women because she tended to overwhelm them physically. Not that it bothered Sigga. In the presence of small, dainty or slender females, large-scaled Sigga should have felt awkward and clumsy, but her manner, swagger and bossiness suggested that there was nothing unusual about her, there was no reason for her to feel self-conscious. She made other women feel decadent, as if she was the female of the future, an Erica the Red, while they still had a long way to go to emulate the brawling vitality of a Jane Austen. As far as I knew, the only woman who had ever taken a liking to Sigga was Mrs. Lewis. But there you are, Mrs. Lewis had an impregnably powerful personality herself, and so did not begrudge it in others.

Finally, finally, Sigga made a move. She stirred, uttered a deep sigh and with an effort arose—and, turning toward the door, passed out of my line of sight. My heart bumped. She was about to leave the room. Of course. To go to the bathroom before an early retirement. I waited, holding my breath in order to hear the door opening and closing.

She reappeared a few seconds later, holding a towel and toilet bag. Splendid. She would be out of the room in a few seconds.

Now that escape was certain, even the agony of cramp diminished somewhat, and I had time to wonder why she had come to live in this house when the residence behind the hospital had been perfectly adequate and a good deal more private. I had seen her room once, and it had suited her perfectly: lofty, spartan, white washed, so hygienic as to be almost sterile. Why on earth would she have given that up for this seedy space with its splendid view of a gritty brick wall? She was undressing.

Oh, my God, she wasn't. She was. She was going to disrobe before going to the bathroom. She was unbuttoning her blouse.

Worse, she was standing directly in my line of vision, courtesy of the gap in the not-quite-closed wardrobe door. She was even looking in my direction, almost right into my eye, which was practically glued to the gap, not because I was eager to inspect her underwear, but because I did not dare risk removing it—the eye, that is, not the underwear—in case she caught the movement. I was afraid even to blink in case my eyelashes acted as semaphores.

A large brassiere hove into view, complete with creamy slopes that proved that her exquisite complexion did not end at the upper thorax. Now she was shrugging out of the ivory blouse and tossing it carelessly over the back of the room's sole chair. That's fine, I thought, that's enough. It's not your bath night, Thursday—I assumed that she had also taken over my bath night—so all that's necessary is for you to stand at the sink in your skirt and bra and have a good wash, right? Just sling on the old dressing gown, okay? and nip along to the bog, okay? The toilet was bound to be available at this time of night—now she was unfastening her skirt.

The striptease continued. "Put it on, put it on," I whimpered, and for a moment I thought she actually was going to leave the skirt in place, for now she was reaching behind to unfasten her bra; and in fact she did unfasten it, and one of the straps slipped down over her shoulder. However, she left the appliance in place for the time being, while she got busy again on her skirt. She held it in place for a few seconds, then abruptly tossed it aside onto the bed, and stood there, exposing the most complex arrangment of belts, clips, fasteners, silks, cottons and elastics that quite reminded me of the clever linkage geometry of the Gander amphibian.

My eye started to water in the draft through the gap in the wardrobe door. I blinked frantically to clear my vision before remembering that disaster could follow if she caught even the slightest twitch from in here. Now, still facing me, she was putting one foot on the bed in order to disconnect a suspender. The leg was encased in black silk from wiggly toe—she had slipped off her shoe—to silvery thigh. The leg seemed to be as long as most women were high. It was a superb leg. I only wished that I had been in the right frame of mind to admire it.

At which point it became evident that I was in the right frame of mind, a condition that I tried hard to deny, as there was no room in the wardrobe for us both. That Sigga was rolling her stockings only halfway down her limbs and was now removing her brassiere entirely did not help in the least. Oh, Lord. Oh, Lordy. Oh, lawks. What orbs, that went so well with my scepter. And to make matters better, I mean worse, she was stretching her arms above her head so that those delectable convexities flattened into mounds mere enough to make one thoroughly appreciate the beauty, rhythm and grace that the sculptor divined in the divine female form. Now her arms were spread sideways as if she were preparing to take wing, or send the signal Engage the Enemy at Close Quarters.

Next, sighing as she stretched, she put her hands behind her neck and arched her back. I'm not sure but I think I whimpered aloud, and the side panel that had groaned under the pressure of my knee groaned again, not under the pressure of my knee.

As she stretched, her belly button rose like an inconstant moon from the horizon of her elastic. Belly button? A veritable excavation, a discovered lost Atlantis, a refuge for weary hunters, a speleological find, a hymn to Hymen, Sun, stand thou still upon Gibeon; and thou, Moon, in the valley of Ajalon; the valley clearly visible now, as the soft white pants too were cast aside, but not before she had turned her back to expose another two treasures from the imperial regalia, the skilful copy of the bosom by the Great Artist Himself; which waggled briefly before disappearing round the corner of her pelvis as she turned and sat on the bed again, this time in profile, with one long leg outstretched almost to the foot of the bed. She picked up her laundry and began to search through it for a clean towel. I noticed that she had sat on the bed in much the same way as she usually got to her feet, in a muscular, no-nonsense way, as if nobody had ever told her that it was unladylike to plonk yourself like a load of coal down the chute, or to stand up as if unsticking yourself from a puddle of molasses. Sometimes she even emitted a grunt. Sometimes she even sat with her knees apart. That was all right when she was wearing her old-fashioned skirts, but what if she ever brought herself up to date with a short skirt? Yet I loved many of her gaucheries, perhaps because there was innate grace there, a looseness and freedom in her overall motion, the grace of a wild animal arching after game.

It was at that moment that I experienced the pain not only of cramp but of overwhelming emotion. It was her sigh, involuntary, I think, that triggered it, so suppressed but so deep, so lonely a sigh. I suddenly found myself awash with a strange sort of heat. It flushed the face and fired the stomach as if I had swilled some corrosive but somehow inoffensive chemical: the same chemical dissolving my intestine to produce the sort of feeling as at the commencement of a stall or spin. Why . . . I loved her. I loved Sigga.

Was that why I had thought about her more and more often as the weeks passed? It was true. I loved her and had never realized it until now, now that I had been forced to look at her through eyes cleared of the glaucoma of irritation and prejudice; to look at the true Sigga, behind the stifling screen of her ghastly motherliness, to see, in a way, into her soul as she sat naked there, attired only in that sigh. And I longed to spring out of the wardrobe and take her in my arms and give her a little protection in return for her concern for me. . . . Yes, that was true, too. She had been deeply concerned about me. But why had she bothered, when she was convinced that I was a wash-out? She genuinely cared for me? It was hardly likely, but what other explanation was there? She had cared enough to . . . Lord, yes, to occupy my room in this boarding house, simply because it had been my room? And because that was the bed I had slept in? Because she loved me, too? Good Lord, how could I have been so dense? Until now it had never even occurred to me that that might have been the reason she had come to England.

I decided that when she finally nipped along to the bathroom, I would emerge and wait for her to return, and then hug and kiss her and tell her I loved her, and yes, yes, tell her that I loved her enough to marry her when I got back from India.

How overjoyed she would be! First to see me again, then to hear that I had finally come to my senses. How wonderful it would be to be married. To have a home to come back to of an evening, with a wife and a wireless set and everything. And I was busily imagining such a domestic scene, with Sigga togged out in a lightning series of costumes from pinafores to ball gowns, and, for an unguarded moment, attired solely in those black stockings of hers—when the cupboard door opened and Sigga said, "Pass me my dressing gown, would you, Bandy?"

A few seconds later she was wrapped in her old-fashioned dressing gown with the velvet cord and calmly folding and refolding her towel. And wearing an expression that did not quite match the welcoming version that I had created only a minute or so previously. In fact, she was busy expressing the hope that the cramps I was suffering from might develop into rheumatism, sciatica, lumbago and arthritis, separately or in combination, as it would serve me right.

"What a miserable coward you are," she said.

"Not at all," I said, trying to straighten up.

"Yes, you are. Hiding in there, spying on me. Do you think I cared a fig whether you came back or not? You did not need to hide, I was not going to hit you. You think I care because you went away without a word? You are nothing to me. In fact, you are nothing at all," she said, far too loudly for that time of night. Flinging down the towel she started for the door. She turned almost immediately. "What am I doing?" she said. "This is my room. It is for you to get out. Go on, get out! Go on!"

"Shhh."

"Don't you shush me! And how glad I am that you are suffering. That is why I didn't let on that I knew you were in there. So that you would suffer."

"I see," I said, attempting to respond in a dignified way, which wasn't easy considering that I was bent over as if one shoulder was lashed to the opposite hip. "And you undressed on purpose, too?"

"Certainly," she said haughtily. "I wanted you to see what you had missed."

"Sigga, listen: I realize now—I love you."

"Oh, really? That is why you scuttled up the stairs like a rat as soon as you saw me?"

"I've only just realized it."

"It is a matter of complete indifference to me."

"I've only just understood that you love me too."

"I? Love you? I am laughing like anything. I haven't the slightest interest in you. Love you? Ha! You worm, you fake, you—rotter!"

Someone thumped on the far wall.

"Sigga," I whispered imploringly.

"So just go," she said loudly; and when I failed to move, "Go on, get out, get out," she said, so loudly and fiercely, and on a rising note that suggested that a loss of self-control was imminent, that I thought it best to obey, muttering as I hobbled out that I would come and see her again as soon as I could. "Don't bother. If I never see you again, I will be very happy," she shouted, but with a catch in her voice that might have been a sob, before she slammed the door and inspired another muffled thumping on a common wall.

Though it was now rather later, I returned, in a much less concentrated frame of mind, to Mr. Drane's room on the ground floor, and knocked; softly this time, in case Mrs. Wignall came out and gave me hell as well.

This time, Drane answered promptly, sticking his bizarre, streamlined face out of the woodwork and looking up and down the passageway before admitting me to his lair.

"Was it by any chance you who was knocking last time?" he asked in an unsteady voice.

"Yes," I said, trying to wrench my thoughts away from Sigga and back to the business in hand.

Before sitting, I looked around carefully in case he had spent the intervening time preparing a few other surprises for me, like last time with the pickled eye, the wriggly worm and the dangling spider.

"I thought it was—" he began.

"You thought it was who?"

"Nobody."

A card table had been drawn up in front of his favorite armchair by the greasy stove, with the remains of his supper on the green baize surface: bread, cheese, pickles, jam and a nice cup of tea. It looked as if he had eaten very little of the meal. The cheese looked powdery, the jam had a dead fly in it, the bread was curling and the cup of tea, almost untouched, had a cold, discolored look.

Drane must have been sitting there for hours, having lost both his appetite and the energy to clear the table.

He did so now, albeit wearily, collecting the tea things onto a tray, and putting them aside in an alcove that served as his kitchenette. He folded the card table, leaned it against a wall and then stood still, facing in no particular direction and looking at no particular object.

I stared at him. Some time during the evening he had removed his jacket, and the extreme narrowness of his shoulders was further emphasized by his dishabille. Apart from socks and shoes, he was wearing a pair of trousers that were too wide for his gangleshanks, and suspenders—or braces he would call them—over a striped shirt. The shirt was collarless, exposing an Adam's apple that seemed like a miniature replica of his head, shaped like a wedge.

Until a couple of nights ago I had forgotten how strange a face that was. I couldn't help thinking that its shape would give him a great advantage in some aquatic pursuit, like championship swimming. With that sharp, jutting nose and those cheeks sloping so sharply backward, his face resembled the bow of a ship.

"So, how are things with you, Mr. Drane?" I asked as, bonelessly, he sat opposite me in his armchair.

"Oh, fine."

"How's everybody in the boarding house?"

"Fine. They've curved Mrs. Wignall's gonorrhea. Now there's only her D.T.s to worry about."

"She's getting suspicious of you, you know that?"

"Yes. I really ought to stop. It's hard, though."

"Tell me, when I lived here, did you ever say anything about me?"

"Only that you kept whips in your cupboard."

"Surely there was more than that?"

"No."

"I got off that lightly?"

"Well . . . I did tell Miss Delisle that you had been caught interfering with a sheep. But I did say," Drane added hurriedly, "that you had been acquitted."

After a moment I said coldly, "It must have been a shock to you to see me there the other night."

"Yes. I was wondering when you'd come."

"People think Khooshie has mystical powers, now. You know, like a fakir."

"I didn't see you until you started after me."

"Somebody got in the way."

"I saw you'd recognized me. I don't see how, though, when I was wearing a beard and mustache."

"You have a rather distinctive face, Mr. Drane. Not even a beard like a bear's pubis could disguise that."

When he failed to answer, I continued, "Among the many things I don't get is why you did what you did with what you did it with."

"You mean the trick dagger, with the blade retracting into the hilt? Our deluxe model, five and sixpence. . . . We haven't sold many of them lately. I don't think mothers like seeing their kids plunging knives into each other, or into dear old Nanny's behind. It gives them such a turn, they say. . . . What're you going to do about it?"

"If you tell me what it's about, maybe nothing."

"Maybe? That ain't good enough, Mr. Bandy."

"It's all you're getting, Mr. Drane. The police are taking it seriously, you know."

"I know, I know. I can read."

"They're particularly concerned, of course, because that building is filled with influential people."

"I know."

"Not to mention your target. You can't stick knives, real or otherwise, into princes and not expect a serious investigation."

"Yes, yes, you don't have to keep on about it. Jeez, you're driving me mad with that whine. God, my head."

"Perhaps most of all—"

"Oh, Jeez."

"It's the kind of joke that makes the gendarmes feel very mean, Mr. Drane."

"Except," Drane began.

"Except what?"

"It wasn't a joke," he said.

Me, in the Dark

I arose and went for a stroll around the room—first making sure that no unpleasant surprises from Drane's novelty shop awaited me, such as bakelite turds or clockwork tarantulas.

Next I admired the artistic pattern of fluff, dust and fat on the wall above his hot plate, though I was careful not to touch it, or indeed anything else in his greasy abode. I doubt if the various surfaces had been wiped since the Treaty of Versailles.

And finally, needing a drink, I raised one of my polished, handmade shoes from Wootton's and edged open the sideboard door, hoping to catch sight of an incriminating liquor supply; but failed to do so.

"Stabbing somebody with a retracting knife wasn't a joke, you say?" I asked.

"No, but it was the only way."

"To give him a heart attack?"

"I had to swear I'd do it, so I did it."

"I see," I murmured, seeing nothing whatsoever.

"And that's all I'm telling you. I don't owe you an explanation."

I considered his answer for a moment, then nodded and completed my perambulation by turning to the door. "Fine," I said. "If that's how you want it."

"Where you going?"

"Hm? Police, of course."

"See if I care."

I opened the door. "Here, wait," he said; so I waited in the doorway. "Look, shut the door, for Godsake."

Still trying not to think of Sigga but to concentrate on one thing at a time, I closed the door and, in order to look reassuringly detached from the penny dreadful of his confession, took out my pipe and pouch and filled the bowl with rich expensive tobacco; which would also serve to camouflage the odor of his clothes, victuals, breath, etc.

"Maybe we can talk. Would you like a drink?"

"Now you're talking," I exclaimed, as he opened the crude cupboard under the hot plate and brought out a bottle of Irish whiskey and two tumblers. The glasses were so smeared they would have kept a fingerprint expert busy for days.

"Supposing I told you. What about the bobbies?"

I gulped gratefully. "I can't promise not to tell them until I hear what you have to say," I replied.

He stared into his glass for what seemed like minutes before he said abruptly, "I'm ready to tell anyone about it. I've been pretty scared, I don't mind telling you. Like I said, it was no joke. I was supposed to kill him."

"Supposed to?"

"What happened was, I was in the Unicorn, see, the one I always go to on Sat'days after the game. A pub. I go every Sat'day on my motorbike. Westham. And over a few pints I was telling them all about how I was living with my girlfriend, Harriet Delisle, and that's how the misunderstanding come, see."

"Wait a minute. Your girlfriend Harriet Delisle? You mean the little old lady living here?"

"Yes, I was telling them about how she—"

"You claimed you were living with her?"

"Well, I am, aren't I? We both live in the house here."

"That's true. . . ."

"Course, I give them the impression she was a bit younger, like, and richer, but. . . . Anyhow, to cut a Manx tale short, one thing led to another, and somehow they got the impression that I was planning on murdering me beautiful girlfriend Harriet, and they got this queer idea that it wasn't the first time I done something like that."

"I get it. You were up to your old tricks. Inventing stories about people."

"Yes. Jeez, I should stop it."

"Yes, you ought. Anyway, go on. You were suggesting to everybody in the pub that you were no stranger to murder."

"Yeh." Drane gulped down the rest of his drink and poured another with shaky fingers. He also filled mine again, but only after I had wiggled the glass at him. "I only meant it as a joke. I've never done in nobody in my life."

"Your jokes are lethal enough," I said censoriously.

"Well, I never killed nobody. But this fellow in the pub took me serious, see."

"What fellow?"

"He never told me his name, but I found out later. It was Shafqat."

"Shafqat? An Indian, by any chance?"

"He looked like it, anyway."

"Go on."

"Well, he was really taken in, see. I thought it was funny at first. Until he offered me a couple of thousand quid to do somebody in. Your pal, the prince."

"Well, well. . . ."

"I couldn't believe it. It was only the second time we'd met, too. He said he'd already paid out thousands, but the other chap had buggered things up. Is that right?"

"There were other attempts, yes."

"Anyway, I'd never have the chance at so much money in my life. I just couldn't say no. I tried, but I just couldn't pass up something like that. Two thousand quid, I mean.

"Then he asked how I was going to do it, and just for something to say I said—a knife.

"And he was still taking me serious. I couldn't believe it. And then last time we met he asks me to swear that I'd do in the prince inside a week. I didn't know your mate was a prince then, of course, until I read the papers yesterday. I nearly come unstuck when I saw that. Gord, a foreign prince, I said. What have I got meself into?

"Anyhow, he kept on about it and . . . and that was when I had the idea, see. So after that I was, I could promise him faithful, like, that I'd, you know, plunge the knife in him right up to the hilt. I convinced him I'd do it."

"You'd had the idea of using a trick dagger from your joke shop."

He nodded, lifted the whiskey glass to his lips and swallowed noisily. "Anyway," he went on, "he give me a quarter of the money right then—a hundred fivers. I'd never even seen a fiver before, let alone a hundred of the buggers. All brand-new, too," Drane said, sounding awed, as if reliving a spiritual experience.

"If you'd no real intention of doing the killing," I said, "how did you expect to get away with it as far as this fellow Shafqat was concerned?"

" 'Cause I thought I'd kept it from him about where I lived, and I didn't think nobody knew me name in that pub," he said, staring at nothing. "But he found out. And there he was, waiting outside this house for me one night with his push-bike."

"A bike?" I asked. "He goes around on a push-bike?"

"Yeh. Anyway, he just smiled, and pedaled off. Letting me know he knew where to find me in case I tried to be a clever dick."

"But you were a clever dick—with your toy dagger."

He stared at me with haunted eyes. "That's right, mate. Fact, I can't understand why he hasn't come after me yet." He shuddered and gulped. "I been waiting. When you knocked on me door earlier on, I thought it was him."

I very nearly remarked that if he lived long enough it would teach him not to tell lies in future, but he was quivery enough without somebody pouring moral bromides into his ear, so I got up and started for the door, muttering to myself, "I wonder how I could find him. . . ."

"Would you get him off me back if I said?"

I whirled. "You know where he is?"

"He wasn't the only one to do a bit of following. I followed him, first night I met him."

"Where to?"

"Wasn't easy, neither, with him on a push-bike and me on a Norton. You know how noisy them things are."

"So where does he live?"

"Only if you promise to help, mate."

"How?"

"You tell him that I know who he is, too, and where he lives, and if anyfink happens to me, the coppers get to know about it, see."

"All right."

"Promise?" He grabbed my lapel. "You swear you'll tell him that?"

"You'd trust me if I promised?"

"Course," he said, letting go and beginning to relax at last under the influence of the Hibernian distillation. "Toffs like you always keeps their word."

In spite of the contempt in his tone I must admit that I was quite tickled. It was the first time anyone had ever described me as a toff.

"All right, I promise. Where can I find him?"

"Actually I didn't get the exact address."

"Oh, fine."

"Well, I told you. With me on a Norton I didn't dare get too close to see which house he went into, exactly. He'd've heard me. But I knew which street, and round about where he disappeared, see."

It was so late when I left the boarding house and climbed into the back of Khooshie's ivory Lancia that I was tempted to call it a day and return home for a spot of whiskey and silence; especially as the chauffeur was obviously anxious to get home himself. He kept directing long-suffering glances at me in the rear-view mirror.

In fact I was just about to say, "Home, James"—his name really was James—when he made the mistake of saying, "Where to now, sir?" in distinctly disrespectful tones.

So I said, "Golder's Green, please."

"Golder's Green. I see. Any particular *part* of Golder's Green, or shall I just circle it for a few hours?"

"It's somewhere near the Crematorium."

"A very appropriate destination, sir, if I may say so," James said, and attempted to dislocate my neck by accelerating as fast as his foot could manage it.

The street into which Shafqat had disappeared was dismayingly long. The gas lamps on each side of the street seemed bent on proving that parallel lines did meet at infinity. As if to emphasize the difficulty of the task of finding one individual, the houses were determinedly alike: identical semidetached brick residences bathed in fuzzy yellow gaslight. There were no pedestrians abroad and capable of giving me directions to the nearest Asian. The street was populated by one cat. A black cat. It crossed my path.

I told James to proceed slowly along the street in the hope that at least one citizen might be returning this late at night to Bide-A-Wee, Mon Repos, Blarney Castle, Rose Lea or Cushy Billet; and finally one such citizen appeared. She was a jolly-looking hausfrau, who was either on her way to the electric chair, judging by the electrodes under her hair net, or was bringing home a few bottles from the pub, judging by the clinking sounds from her carrier bag.

"Par'n me," I called from the rear window. "Would you happen to know the address of a Mr. Shafqat?"

"Eh?"

"Mr. Shafqat."

"No."

"Well, do you know of any Indian who lives on this street?"

Deciding that she was not about to be set upon and interfered with, she came a little closer. "No," said she. "But there's a Mr. Shaftoe just the other side of the bridge. Would it be him?"

"Shaftoe?"

"He's got silver buckles on his knee."

"Uh. . . ."

"No, I don't know any Mr. Whatsisname," she said, taking pity on the slow-witted plute in the fancy motor; and walked on.

We had traveled no more than twenty yards when I saw the corner store, bathed in sickly lamplight. It stood at the next intersection and its two shop windows were crowded with Indian furniture and artifacts; moreover there was an undeniably Indian name spelled out in faded letters above the doorway.

As the jolly lady drew level, I wound down the window again and said, "I thought you said you didn't know of an Indian around here," and pointed at the shop on the corner of her street.

"Eh? Oh, him. Is his name Shafqat? Fancy that."

"He's new to the district?"

"No, he's been there twenty years."

"And you didn't know he was Indian?"

"Well, I just never thought of him being Indian. He's just like everyone else round here, see. He's Indian, is he? Yes, I suppose he is, with them beady black eyes. Well, I never. If you want to buy anything off him, you're a bit late though, Brigadier. He closes at five."

"Brigadier?"

"You mean you're not? Oh. I thought you must either be a brigadier or someone from the gasworks."

"Very droll, madam. Does he live here, this Indian?"

"Yes. Upstairs."

The entrance to Shafqat's private quarters above the shop was a scarred, narrow doorway just round the corner. Mr. Shafqat took quite a time answering the door, but I continued to beat at it until I heard him flatfooting down a long, uncarpeted stairway.

When he finally arrived he inserted a black eye into the space between the jamb and the battered door.

"Mr. Shafqat?"

"We don't want none."

"None what?"

"Cor blimey, it's a bit late to be out 'awking, init?"

"I've come about Khooshie."

"You won't get none of that here, mate. You want that big detached house on Burton Road, the one with the red lamp in the turret."

"I was referring to the Maharajah's son."

"Eh?"

"The young man you're trying to kill."

The door started to slam. I stuck my foot in the gap. The door hit the toecap and bounced back. Most of Mr. Shafqat appeared, holding his lip and glowering.

"You bleeding hit me mouf," he announced.

"Sorry about that," I said, cleverly suppressing my astonishment that such an accent could emerge from so Asian a face.

I stood there gaping for forty or fifty minutes before continuing, "I just wanted to ask you something, that's all."

" 'Ere, 'oo invited you into the 'ouse?"

"After you, Mr. Shafqat," I said, gesturing considerately at the bare stairs immediately behind him.

The stairs led steeply to a landing, off which was a kitchen that seemed to be made entirely of tin and lino. We did not linger there, however, but continued on into a living room whose walls were decorated in crimson flock. It made you feel as if you were in the middle of a beating heart; a heart in danger of thrombosis: in places it was peeling, stained or torn.

The room was crowded with furniture, but none of it was Indian. Maybe after selling Indian furniture for twenty years he was sick of all that carved wood and engraved brass.

While Mr. Shafqat continued to sniffle and dab at his face and then pointedly examine his fingers to see if there was any blood, I regarded him with slightly less apprehension than heretofore. I had been a trifle uneasy about going unarmed into the HQ of somebody who appeared to be in the assassination business, but Shafqat was smaller than I was and twenty years older, and he did not appear unduly aggressive. He was much darker skinned than Khooshie, the skin being thoroughly seamed as if it had been left out in the desert. His face was square and heavy, with a large, unshaven jaw. The jaw moved constantly, as if he was chewing some substance that was clearly capable of staining, judging by the condition of his teeth. He was wearing a pajama jacket with a collar so unwashed it actually shone, and a muffler I prefer not to describe.

"The name is Bandy, though I have the feeling you know that already," I said, ever so politely, in case he really was dangerous. "All I want to know, Mr. Shafqat, is, who put you up to it? To paying others, and also presumably yourself, to murder Prince Khooshie Avtar Prakash, I mean."

" 'Ere, you ain't pinning vat on me," he cried indignantly; but almost immediately abandoned the protest as hardly worth pursuing, and added, "Is 'e really all right? 'E wasn't 'urt at all?"

"No."

"The papers said 'e must be a faker. Eh?"

"A faker?"

"You know, one of them Injun magicians wot can climb up a rope wivout it being toied onto anyfink, that sort of fink."

"You believe what you read in the papers?"

"Course not. But 'e dint snuff it, did 'e, even though 'e 'ad a knife right through 'is 'eart. Everyone said vat's wot 'appened."

"Uh, yes, that's right. I guess he was miraculously preserved. Mind if I sit down, Mr. Shafqat?"

"Oi do moind. Shove orf," he said, chewing indignantly; but he made no further objection when I sat down anyway, on a chair made by the Cheapside Furniture Company.

"Anyway, to get the situation straight, Mr. Shafqat. If I go to the police with what I know, that you attempted to kill a very important visitor from India, you'll be up to the ears in bat guano. Right?"

He opened his mouth, then returned to his agitated chewing. "Why'd they believe 'im ravver van me?" he mumbled, clearly expecting an unfavorable reply.

"Well, who knows? Maybe a criminal court might give you the benefit of the doubt—if the police have failed to come up with any further evidence against you, and assuming you've no record and that everything about you and your business is on the up and up, nothing that might suggest that you're not exactly the Queen of the May."

He stared at the carpet—definitely not an oriental carpet—in an ill-done-to sort of way.

"On the other hand, I'm sure we could come to some arrangement that needn't involve the man on the case, Chief Inspector Frank." Shafqat started. I wondered if he knew Frank. "Because I'm sure you won't make any further attempts to kill Khooshie. Because if you did, you could easily end up hanged."

"You dunno nuffink."

"How about Bernard Hive and Archie Drane as witnesses for a start?"

" 'Oo?"

"You know all right," I said; but told him who they were anyway.

Several minutes cringed past before I judged that it was time to convince him that I would most definitely sic the coppers onto him unless he told me who was behind it.

"Nobody's be'ind it."

"You were killing him for reasons of your own?"

"Yer. I mean, no. I mean . . . 'ere, shove orf, will you?" he whined, sounding increasingly desperate as I exposed my pitifully few facts as discreetly as a stripper with an audience from the vice squad.

Then, to show that I was in no hurry to leave, I got my pipe going, and sat and puffed in silence for a while, practicing the familiar pipe smoker's fraud of looking as if I were deep in thought while my mind was actually a blank. I waited through another fifteen minutes of protests, one of which was that it was his bedtime and he needed his beauty sleep, and another to the effect that I was stinking out his room with my filthy tobacco.

Finally, perhaps because he was sharper-witted than Bernard Hive or merely more experienced, he began to accept that he would be no worse off admitting what I obviously already knew about his involvement.

"So now all we need to find out," I said, puffing sagaciously, "is who's paying you to eliminate Khooshie." And I went on to ask him what his connections were with India.

"Oi dunno nuffink about Injun affairs," he mumbled.

"But you're an Indian, aren't you?"

"Oi've never even been vere."

"Tell me another."

"It's true. Oi've lived 'ere me entoir loif," he replied indignantly. "My fahver stah'ed this business after 'e jumped ship back in eighteen bleeding somefink. And lyter on, 'e 'ad 'is woman shipped 'ere from India. That was me muvver."

"Ah," I said, nodding ponderously. "Possibly that explains your accent."

"Wot accent?"

"But tell me, Shafqat," I said in such a superior way that it set even my teeth on edge, "was your father from Khaliwar, by any chance?" Christ, I was even pronouncing it *chahnce*.

" 'Ere, 'ow'd you know vat?"

"Deduction, my dear Shafqat," I said airily, waving my pipe about. (Or was it inference? Never mind, he wouldn't know the difference.) "I noticed that the name of your shop was Khaliwar Imports. You said your father started the business. So I thought it likely that he was originally from Khaliwar."

That was what had electrified me, the moment I caught sight of the name above the door of the shop. "Khaliwar Imports."

Khaliwar was the name of the independent state on the Maharajah's northern border.

After building up an organization for several months, I believed that I had finally discovered what it was for.

And after only a token resistance, Khooshie confirmed it when I was granted an audience with him the following morning. "Khaliwar," he repeated, pursing his lips and trying to look thoughtful. "No, I have never heard of him."

"Come off it, Your Ethereal Highness. You know perfectly well I'm talking about the independent state that adjoins yours in central India."

"Oh, *that* Khaliwar."

"I couldn't find anything in the stuff I read in the British Museum about a history of conflict between your two states. But it makes sense if I assume that there is hostility. Enough hostility on the part of Khaliwar to make them want to kill you."

"Why would they wish to do that?"

"That's obvious. You were sent here to organize an air force, and they wanted to stop you."

"You are helping to organize it," Khooshie said in a detached way, as if the conversation did not greatly concern him. "So why are they not trying to kill you?"

"I guess that's either faulty intelligence on their part—they haven't realized I'm doing a bit to help—but more likely, they assume that if they eliminated you, they would automatically eliminate me. Believing that your father wouldn't carry on if he lost you."

"That is true," Khooshie said gently.

Heartened by this confirmation that I was on the right track, I continued, "So if they're so anxious to sabotage your air force, one might conclude that the people of Khaliwar are expecting it to attack them."

"No, that is not true," Khooshie said with godlike detachment.

"Then it must mean that Jhamjarh is expecting an attack from Khaliwar."

After a moment, Khooshie said simply, "Yes."

"Ah," I sighed.

"Father said that if I could not avoid it, I was to tell you. Incidentally, he said it is not true that he is to abrogate the treaty. He only said so in order to help you, thinking that it might keep the British off balance.

"But you are right, Bartholomew," he continued serenely. "Khaliwar is the real enemy. Khaliwar has been preparing to attack us for more than a year. And much as father hates violence he cannot allow his country to be overcome by bad men. And there are bad men in Khaliwar," he said, looking at me squarely for the first time, his dark, bulging eyes ashine with sincerity. "It is I who persuaded him, Bartholomew. I told him many months ago that I would be ashamed to be part of a country that would not defend itself. I said that God does not forgive those who attack first, but equally God does not forgive those who give up without a fight."

"That was very wise of you, Prince."

"I got it out of the *Boy's Own Paper*."

"Still. . . ."

"Mind you," he added, beginning to fade again, "I do not think he really believes in struggle. I think he is prepared to defend himself only for my sake, for my future."

"I see." I got up and wandered over to one of the landscapes on the wall and tried to see what it was about through the almost opaque varnish. "So it never had anything to do with the British in India," I murmured. "I wish you'd told me this in the first place, Khooshie. We'd have been able to work much better, without all the uneasy suspicions. . . ."

"Did we not swear right from the first place that we were having no hostile intentions to you British?" he replied gently. "We put a good deal of trust in you, Bartholomew. We expected you to trust us. It is surely not our fault if you are all cynical and suspicious."

"That's true," I said humbly, just as Muriel Tombola entered—defiantly upright on her stout limbs. Until Khooshie pointed at the floor and, slowly raising his head, stared at her fixedly. Whereupon she flung herself to the floor and started wailing, or to be exact, being too massive literally to fling herself down, she folded herself as fast as possible onto her richly padded knees, her canary yellow skirt stretching over her thighs like test material on a tensile strength machine; from which superincumbency she continued to howl with fear and adoration in what I took to be some Zambukian dialect, until I recognized the words "master," "slave" and "witch-doctor," as well as "jujube."

I caught Khooshie's eye. He smirked.

Skulking

While we could now steam ahead with renewed confidence, believing that the role of the Royal Jhamjarh Air Force was to defend the integrity of an independent Indian state against a dastardly neighbor, we had still not solved the fighter problem. Despite numerous enquiries at home and overseas in the search for off-the-shelf aircraft that could be delivered in the time available, and despite numerous brain-bashing sessions on Laurence Pountney Hill involving all the top people in the organization in the hope that one of them would come up with a brainwave— nothing. We even asked Fetch and Carry if they had any ideas. None. By the end of November we were getting desperate. And also more and more frustrated, knowing that there were literally hundreds of war-surplus Sopwith Snipes packed away in hangars and aircraft parks that the Air Board's Director of Materiel would have been delighted to sell but couldn't because he must long since have been informed of the ban against supplying the Prakash Purchasing Commission with so much as a pair of chocks.

The fighter-procurement situation was urgent enough. Even so, it was not my only preoccupation that muggy November. There was also the Sigridur situation. I was anxious to see her and advise her that I had been forced to acknowledge the truth that I loved her, and that therefore she could now live happily ever after. To this end, I waited outside the boarding house every night after work for seven nights— or, no, six nights. I took Sunday off. And to be strictly accurate, one of the nights was spent in hospital.

I managed to confront her on the very first day, but before I could follow her into the house she slammed the door in my face. On the second night I sneaked up to her room, but when she saw me sitting there, patting the bed, she threatened to biff me on the boko if I didn't leave forthwith. Given her quivering muscles, I didn't need a second telling. So on the third night I waited outside again, feeling like a lovelorn swain. I skulked for hours until, peering down the side passage, I saw a glow from her window and realized that she had come home early and had been there all along.

Thoroughly annoyed, for I was neglecting work that might have been done in the evening in order that her life might be made complete, I marched toward the house, determined to get through to her. I failed even to get through the front door. Mrs. Wignall intercepted me, warned me that I was trespassing and bade me be gone in no uncertain terms.

Nevertheless, I was back on the following night, poor devil that I was, for the weather chose that date to turn ugly. Until now, November had been uncommonly mild, the muggiest since the reign of Vic and Al. Tonight, the moment I reported for guard duty, the mercury fell like a moral principle in an emergency, and a Siberian wind, rerouted through the White Sea, Finland, Norway and across every available iceberg, came whirling into Norfolk Gardens and proceeded to lash the trees to a frenzy. When the wind died for a moment, it was only to give the rain a chance; this beat against the London façades hard enough to risk leaving them quite clean. Then the sickles of the wind, resharpened, returned to thresh afresh the miserable pedestrians and loiterers. In fact the weather was so frightful that I had to ask James to wind up the car window. Also, as I was feeling a mite chilly, I requested him to pass me his blanket.

"But what will I do without a blanket?"

"What d'you mean, what will you do? Do without. You're only a chauffeur."

"But you'll have two blankets then, and I won't have any."

"Tough teats."

"Well, all I can say, sir, is that Lord Hynd-Waters would never haven taken my last blanket."

"More fool he."

"A gentleman would never do such a thing."

"Oh, yeah?"

"It indicates a want of consideration for others especially reprehensible considering one's age and susceptibility to sudden chills," James said, and to illustrate the reproof, he put a gloved hand to his mouth and coughed—twice.

"Well, it's my car. I can do what I like."

"With respect, sir, it is not your car, it is the young Indian gentleman's car, and I am his chauffeur, not yours," James said, and we continued to bicker for several minutes, back and forth between the front and rear seats.

Until finally I said, "All right, take your filthy old blanket. See if I care."

It was lucky I had my new hip flask with me. Hours later, Sigga had still not appeared. Gradually I realized that she was doing exactly what I had done when she was pursuing me: returning home so late that the other could not afford to hang about any longer.

So I switched the guard duty to St. Pancreas and attempted to confront her in the basement; but a weight lifter masquerading as an assistant pathologist informed me that if I didn't stop annoying Miss Jonsdottir, he would reach down my throat and turn me inside out so that my scrotum ended up where my head was.

It now occurred to me to reverse the situation: to use the good offices of Mr. Lewis just as Sigridur had used them to corner me. So I got in touch and requested him to intercede with her on my behalf. At first he was most reluctant, employing all sorts of hypocritical excuses—it was too much trouble; he was simply not in the mood to help me achieve lasting happiness; and so on—but finally he admitted the real reason for his unwillingness to oblige his beloved son-in-law. "It's because I don't want to reunite you two," he explained gently.

"Eh? Why not?"

"She's not right for you, Bartholomew. You yourself said she was a terrible woman."

"That was before my eyes were opened by love."

"Gummed up by it, you mean. No, I just can't risk reconciling the two of you. The consequences could be appalling. It could even end up in marriage. No, my boy, to bring you two together again would be as irresponsible as introducing glycerine to sulfuric acid and nitric acid."

Despite his reservations, however, Mr. Lewis did his best to help, and even went to the extreme of voluteering to take Sigga out to dinner. It would provide the right environment, he felt, for the difficult task of persuading her that I was a worthwhile suitor. We arranged that we would meet later on in his club, where he would report on the evening's softening-up process.

Accordingly, instead of lingering as usual in the Lancia I tarried in the Conservative Club. I had to tarry a terrible long time. Because after dinner, instead of bringing her to me for an emotional reunion, he took her to the theater, and after that to the Catacombs for a couple of pick-me-ups. So I ended up on the street after all, for the club closed at eleven. It was after midnight when finally a taxi emptied a small, neat figure in top hat and tails onto the sidewalk outside the club.

Picking himself up, Mr. Lewis, as if illustrating the cliché of the drunk toff clinging to a lamppost, attached himself to the street lighting and smiled approximately in my direction.

"You were right, Batty, you were assolutely right," he hiccuped. "She's a wonderful, wonderful girl."

"Yes, yes, but what did she say?"

"She's changed, you know," he replied dreamily. "Lovely through and through and through." He laid his cheek against the lamppost and tried to dance with it. "I've fallen assolutely over heels in love with her. We're going to get married as soon as the church has banned the reds."

"Dammit, you were supposed to convince her to take up with me again."

"Not a chance, my boy," he said. "She doesn't care one tit or jottle for you. It's me she loves. Me, me, me," he sang, waving his arms, his shouts activating several light switches in the upper floors of the club.

However, after he had sobered up somewhat in my empty flat in SW1, he told me that he had some good news for me.

"Good news? That's wonderful," I cried, suffused with relief.

"She is now convinced that everything you said about yourself is true. You really were one of the great airmen of the war, you really were a member of Parliament, and so forth."

"Yes, yes, but how does she feel about me now?"

"Oh, that. Well, actually, she can't stand you."

"Eh?"

"You really shouldn't have made a fool of her, you know, Bart," Mr. Lewis said reproachfully. "Convincing her that you were a nobody, when all the time you were a great man just temporarily in distress."

The following evening found a dejected me at Irwell Court, carrying an attaché case filled with papers for Khooshie to sign. He had not been near the office for a week.

One of the extra bodyguards who had been employed to guard the prince against further assassination attempts answered the door. He informed me that Khooshie had retired for the night.

I didn't believe it, at first. It was only nine o'clock. I assumed that if the boy was actually in bed it was only because he had not yet risen. But when I walked into the bedroom, all the indications suggested that he was, indeed, there for the night.

Muriel and Bubba Carruthers were with him. Not in bed, of course—Khooshie had decided to renounce that sort of thing. The girls were seated in two of the straight-backed chairs that lined the far wall. The chairs had been put there to make more space for the big party of a few weeks ago, and had not been replaced.

They were not the only ones patiently waiting for an audience in the bedchamber. There was also a friend of Bubba's, a young man who needed money. And Group Captain Kempt, in a spacious civilian suit.

Sitting there against the far wall, they looked like poor relatives in a Russian play.

Muriel and Bubba barely glanced at me before resuming the watch over Khooshie, as he lay there in bed, pale and serene.

Kempt was seated at the far end of the row. I sidled up to him. "What's up?" I whispered.

"Search me, old man," he whispered back. "They showed me in here, and that's all I know."

"He is eating nothing for two whole days," Muriel whispered, glancing at me for only a split second before returning her enormous black eyes to the pallid figure in the bed.

When she added that her master was attempting to purify himself, I caught Bubba's eyes. I expected her to look amused or intolerant. Instead she seemed almost as concerned as Muriel.

Emerging from a trance, Khooshie smiled at me and held out his left hand, projecting it above the pink sheets so persistently that I was forced to take it. "I am fasting, yes," he murmured. "It's nothing. Don't worry, Bartholomew."

"Fasting? Why?"

"It occurred to me on Tuesday that it was right. It is to assert the hegemony of my spirit over my unruly organism, you see. I have so little authority otherwise, but at least I can command my own body."

I tried to josh him out of it, and Bubba came forward to help; but he just smiled and reassured us that it would be only a minor fast, just a few days, to let his substance know who was boss.

However, he was prepared to append his signature to everything that needed signing. He did so with so little fuss that I felt quite uneasy. I was used to irritable expirations of forced breath as his pen scratched painfully through document after document, squeals of protest over the number of checks being submitted for his signature and quarrels over the wording of the letters that he was being asked to sign.

For the umpteenth time I considered telling him that it had been a trick dagger, that there had been no miracle and that he was not all that divine. I felt it was time somebody dragged him off his ethereal eyrie. It wasn't good for him to live in a fool's paradise while the rest of us had to make do with the terrestrial reality. He must be restored to "normalcy," as President Harding of the U.S.A. had put it recently.

On the other hand, the illusion that he was under divine protection seemed to have restored his pride in himself. I hadn't realized until now how inferior he had been feeling.

I wondered if he felt that the others, Mays, Hibbert, Derby and Brashman, had been riding roughshod over his self-respect. I, of course, had always treated him with the utmost tact and respect, but I wasn't sure that the others were endowed with quite so much tolerance and restraint. I decided, as once again I resisted the temptation to disillusion the poor bugger, to have a word with the chaps about it.

Anyway, it was probably too late, now. The truth might come as a severe shock. No, better leave things the way they were.

"All the same, he *is* different," Bubba said half an hour later in the adjoining sitting room. "It's ever since that ridiculous attack on him."

I had mooched through to the sitting room for a few undistracted minutes while I sorted out the paperwork that Khooshie had signed. Bubba had followed me in.

"But I mean, why should that change things so much?" she went on indistinctly. She was standing in front of a mirror—or looking glass, as people like her would call it—repairing her lips. The paintwork had been smudged when she tried to kiss Khooshie and he had moved his face so that the lipstick ended up on his jaw. "I mean, the attacker missed, so what's all the brouhaha about, I should like to know?"

"Mm."

"You're not listening, are you?"

"Mm."

"You're not even listening to me saying you're not listening to me." She leaned closer to the glass to reoutline the rosebud shape that had been superimposed over her real lips. "But of course it doesn't matter to you, does it, that a girl's life is utterly shattered."

"Why is it shattered?"

"I've only been telling you for the last ten minutes. It's the whole situation. Khooshie and everything. I mean, practically overnight he's stopped being crazy about me. I mean, it doesn't do much for a girl's morale, you know, so suddenly being no longer regarded as an object of desire."

She laughed briefly. The laugh soon spent itself. "Where the hell are my gaspers?" she muttered, abandoning her face and rummaging through her purse. "I say, sir, do you have a light? And a drink? And a sympathetic expression?"

"Could do with a drink myself."

"I know. Khooshie gave all the hooch that was left over from the party to the doorman. There were about a hundred bottles. Just imagine, an absolute fortune."

As I collected the documents together and loaded them into the attaché case, she wandered over and sat on the other end of the sofa. "I mean, one moment he's telling me so, so *messily*, that he loves me—keeps telling me until I could scream, sometimes—and the next he's looking at me as if I'm his cousin from Maidenhead." She looked at me with no particular hostility. "I suppose you finally turned him against me. What have you been saying, anyway?"

"Nothing. Not a thing."

"Did you tell him about Binky?"

"I don't even know who Binky is—I'm glad to say."

"I mean, why else would he have changed practically overnight? You must have said something."

"No."

"I love him," she said loudly.

"Binky?"

"Course not. Khooshie."

"You love Khooshie?"

"Sickmaking, isn't it? It's only happened since he stopped dribbling endearments all over me. He's like a new person, and I'm in love. Before, well, to be frank, I rather despised him."

There was a layer of dust on the end table nearby. She leaned over and drew a face in it with a downturned mouth. "Well, it was the way he was flinging all that loot around. It made the chaps feel quite useless, sometimes," she said. "Trying to buy his way in.

"Now he doesn't seem to care anymore. He's treating me ever so kindly." She dotted the eyes, jabbing. "Like I'm just one of any number of people he's fond of."

I wondered what she would say if I told her she had fallen for an illusion.

Realizing that she had forgotten to smoke, she took a cigarette from the platinum case that Khooshie had given her and wiggled it at me.

"It's driving me crazy," she said as I lit the cigarette. "I mean, just when I discover I absolutely adore him, I become just another pal." She laughed. "You've no idea how utterly miserable I am."

She smoked in silence for a moment, watching as I snapped the attaché case shut. "What about you?" she asked indifferently. "Still walking out with the blonde girl?"

"She can't stand me anymore."

"Really?" She looked at me speculatively. "Robert said he kept expecting her to break into a Wagnerian aria. Personally I saw her more as a looter and pillager. You know, landing from a Viking longboat, ready to sack some Saxon village and carry off the men."

Soon I was telling her all about Sigga, defending her. Bubba was hardly listening. She was going on and on about how desperately she was in love with Khooshie.

"Surely you must have some ideas on how to restore him to his former condition of infatuation?"

"You know, she's basically a very innocent girl, in spite of her—"

"Do you think he's changed because he thought I was taking advantage—making him absolutely loopy with jealousy?"

Finally she started to pay attention. "You feel responsible for her?" she asked. "How?"

"Well, she only came to England because of me."

She dropped the remains of her cigarette into a vase of flowers. "If you believe that she moved out of her igloo and came all this way purely because of you," she said, "you're an even bigger chump than I took you for."

"You don't think I'm responsible?"

"She's a big, grown-up girl—and how. She knows what she's doing."

"Anyway, I love her."

"Do you? Well, darling," she said, reverting to that empty endearment for the first time in weeks, "if you really want her back. . . ."

"Yes?"

"Hanging about won't do it. What you should do is write."

"Write?"

"A letter. Fill it with wit, adoration and poetry, and she'll come running like a gazelle—or, in her case, a hippo."

"Do you really think a letter would do it?"

"Absolutely. If you insist on being raped and pillaged."

"By gosh, I'll do it." I got up and paced excitedly over the Indian carpet. "I'll do it. I'll write first thing tomorrow."

"I say, old man, could I have a word with you?" Kempt asked.

"Hm? Yes, I guess. . . ."

"It's you I came to see, actually. Your office was closed by the time I got there. I came along here to ask if they knew where you lived, and the next thing I knew I was being shown into that young fellow's bedroom," Kempt said, sounding bewildered.

He also looked quite tense. Derby had reported that Kempt was thought to have made one or two disastrous investments lately. I wondered if that was why he looked so anxious.

By this time I had progressed to the magnificent lounge with the semicircular window. Bubba had returned to the bedroom. On the way she had encountered the group captain and told him where I was to be found.

"God, I never knew they had apartments this size in London," he said, looking around in awe. "Funny, though—most of his servants look like policemen."

"Most of them are. Anyway, what can I do for you, Group Captain?"

"Ah. Could we sit down, old man?" he asked; and after we had done so in a couple of armchairs: "I was wondering if you'd given any further thought to employing a chap who could be an enormous asset in the supplies and services area," he said with a desperate chuckle.

My eyes, formerly flicking around apathetically, froze on his coarse red face.

"You still want a job? In spite of everything?"

"In spite of what?" He shifted uneasily. "I don't quite see what you mean, old man," he said. "Naturally I'd be delighted to be offered a job by your lot." He laughed uncertainly. "I've heard about some of the salaries you're paying."

As far as I could tell, his attitude had not altered since I had talked to him at the party. Now that was strange. Surely as a loyal air force officer, he should have been regarding me with marked disapproval. In fact, he should not even have approached me.

I suddenly felt the hairs rise on the back of my neck. Tense. Electrified.

But, careful. It might be some sly gambit by the authorities. Skelton, for example.

"So if I offered you a job—George, isn't it? If I offered you a job, George, you'd have no compunction about accepting it?"

"Of course not, my dear fellow," he said, excitement making his voice hoarser than ever. "Why shouldn't I accept it—assuming the terms are right?"

My *God*. . . . Was it possible that the Chief of Air Staff had warned practically the entire world about us—except his own ministry? That he had taken it for granted that all the departments under him had been informed? And that at least one of them had not been?

I jumped up; then tried to walk casually to the great semicircular window. I peered out interestedly, though it was dark and there was nothing to see except rooftops and a spire outlined against distant street lighting.

I said casually, though with a heart thumping like an Indian drum at a war dance, "Putting the job aside for a moment, uh, George, there's something else that might be to your advantage."

"Oh, yes? What's that, old man?"

"We're still in the market for a few aircraft, George."

"Oh, yes?"

"And I believe you have scores of Sopwith Snipes at, well, for instance, at Fifty-nine Training Depot Station, Huntingdon, Cambridgeshire."

"Do we, old man? Take your word for it," he said, but distractedly, as if I were holding things up with small talk.

"In your opinion, George—would there be any problem about our acquiring a few of those flying machines?"

"These are definitely surplus items of equipment, are they?" he asked. "Not operational, or about to become so, or anything like that?"

"No, they're definitely surplus to requirements, I understand. Being preserved—greased, waterproof-paper wrapped, and so forth."

"Well, I don't see there'd be any problem," Kempt said.

No problem? My *God*. Feeling quite giddy, I felt my way back to the armchair and pawed my way into it. "Even," I said, sounding almost as hoarse as he, "if we bought as many as, well, say—just for the sake of argument—sixty aircraft?"

"By Jove, that would be a splendid sale, what?"

"And there'd be no problem?"

The group captain went all cautious. His eyes steadied and focused sharply. Then they narrowed cunningly. Nobody was going to put anything over on *him*.

"Ah, well," he said with a crafty smile, "it would depend on how much you were prepared to pay, old man. I mean, I couldn't let a fine machine like the . . . uh . . . ."

"Sopwith Snipe."

"Yes, the Snipe, I couldn't let a machine like that go for less than. . . ." He hesitated. "Well, I'd have to look into it, but I believe the going rate for a surplus single-engined aircraft is three thousand."

"Done."

"Eh?"

"I'm prepared to pay you three thousand pounds each for sixty Snipes and complete spares."

"You are?" His eyes narrowed further. For a heart-stopping moment I thought I had ruined everything by responding so quickly.

But apparently the deal was still on. He was merely attempting to bargain. "I think the spares would have to be extra," he said carefully.

"And of course," he added, trying to look as wooden-faced as me, "there'd be a few extras, to cover administrative costs, things like that."

"I quite understand," I said. "And perhaps an extra extra? As a personal mark of appreciation from us to you, for everything you'd done for us, Group Captain?"

"Personal, old man?" he said, his voice rising to a squeak. His agitation was such that he had to clear his throat twice.

"Yes. Say one and a half percent?"

"In cash? I mean—that's usual, isn't it?"

"Of course," I agreed heartily. "Yes, in cash."

Kempt turned quite pale and started to breathe so rapidly that I felt quite alarmed for his ticker.

He was doing his arithmetic homework. I could see his lips moving and his eyes sliding over an imaginary blackboard. Sixty aircraft at £3,000 each. That was—£180,000. One and a half percent of that would be. . . . But he was too agitated to work it out.

"The commission would be two thousand seven hundred pounds, George," I murmured. "In fivers, or however you wanted it."

He gulped, and was about to say something. But then: "Five percent," he said, panting at a quite alarming rate and looking absolutely terrified.

Deep in Thought Again

Next morning when I rushed along to Laurence Pountney Hill and told the others, we actually danced around the ground-floor desks with glee, whooping like savages. Finally we were about to acquire sixty unused Sopwith Snipes that were said to be in excellent condition, together with armament, bomb racks, items of special ground equipment and as many tons of spares, including brand-new Bentley engines, as we wished to purchase from the Huntingdon depot.

Kempt and I had finally agreed on a commission of 3 percent. I had continued to bargain only to allay his suspicions that he might have done even better. In fact, I'd have been delighted to pay him 10 percent, or even 50.

But half an hour after I reached the office, he telephoned. "George here, old man," he said, the combination of a husky voice and a conspiratorial whisper making it difficult to understand what he was saying. "Listen, there's just one thing. I assume that when you see the Chief, you won't mention the, uh, the commission, will you?"

"See the Chief? What Chief? Of Air Staff? Why would I want to see him, George?" I asked, my voice becoming positively eunuchlike.

"Well, as long as he's round, old man, I'd better put him in the picture. I couldn't really arrange a business transaction on this scale without informing him, you see, if only as a matter of courtesy."

After a bit of a pause, during which he called down the line several times to see if I was there, I replied in smooth, reasonable tones, "Oh, I don't think we need bother the Chief about a few rotten old planes, George."

"I'm afraid I must, old man."

"But why? Aren't you in proper charge of your department?"

"Yes, of course," he said stiffly. "It's just that, after that ruckus I told you about—you know, the cabinet work for Hendon—it had better be cleared through his office."

"But—"

"No, that's definite, Bandy. I must inform him, the moment you're ready to hand over the check."

I flung myself to the floor and screamed and screamed, raining blows on the carpet and employing several fundamental Saxon phrases; but fortunately nobody noticed.

On the following morning I came into the office looking, everybody except Derby said, dazed with shock. Derby thought that it was just a variation on my usual expression.

Actually it was the result of my having had an idea. And I had been up all night, planning how to put it into practice.

Mays, Hibbert, Derby and Brashman were at a desk on the ground floor of the building, huddled round masses of charts and timetables. I checked to make sure that Khooshie's office was empty, then gestured the four of them inside.

"It occurs to me," quoth I, suppressing a yawn that might otherwise have turned me inside out, "that the answer is simple."

"Good," Mays said blandly. "Now all we need is the question."

"Right. Well, Group Captain Kempt indicated, did he not, that the CAS would have to be apprised of a deal as important as ours, not necessarily because he would have to okay it, but as a gesture of respect. Keeping the boss informed, and all that."

"Obviously. He is, after all, head of the air force."

"But what if he wasn't there?"

They gazed at me blankly.

"I checked with Kempt first thing this morning. I asked what would happen if by any chance the CAS was not available to be apprised. To account for the query, I pretended to be concerned—anxious in case the absence of the Chief held up the purchase of our Snipes.

"He reassured me. He said that in that case, he would just be informed when he returned."

They were still gazing at me blankly.

"Well, don't you see?" I hissed with rising enthusiasm. "All we have to do is remove him from the scene."

"You mean. . . ."

"You don't mean. . . ?"

"You can't mean. . . ?"

"Yes! We must get him away from the Air Ministry for the requisite period of time!"

Hibbert thought about it for a moment, then said in that hatefully calm way of his, "Roland and I have worked it out that it will take at least a month to complete the paperwork, take possession of the aircraft, pack them on site and deliver them FOB."

"That's just what I estimate," I cried; then hurriedly admonished myself with a "Shhh!"

"Well, in that case," I whispered, "we'll just have to keep him out of the way for a month."

"Splendid," Mays said. "How?"

"Well. . . ." I couldn't suppress a manic titter. The others looked quite alarmed. "I wonder if you remember the shockingly slanderous thing he said about me? What he said was that any course of action that I favored would be immediately suspect, as far as he was concerned."

"I remember," Derby said. "I remember he put it a good deal more strongly than that."

"Well, that was the gist of it."

"So?"

"Well," I said, almost frightening them out of their wits when a slow, mean smile began to steal over my face, "it's obvious. I must send him abroad for a month."

"How?"

"By," I said, "doing my very best to persuade him *not* to go abroad."

Various Shots

Unless the weather was particularly foul, the Chief of Staff of the Royal Air Force bicycled to work; or at least he bicycled as far as the nearest railway station. With his fierce face below a slightly mildewed bowler hat and his briefcase precariously balanced on the handlebars, he was a sight greatly appreciated by the locals. If they had dared to ask why such an important man as he should stoop, literally and figuratively, to such a lowly form of transport, he might have replied, were he in the mood for speech, that in a time of service austerity he was setting an example of thriftiness to his senior officers. Actually the real reason was that car travel made him feel sick, though there were only a couple of miles of country roadway to negotiate between his house on Dancer's Hill and the railway station at Potter's Bar. Feeling sick, he had found, made it hard for him to think; whereas a rhythmic pedaling freed his mind to contemplate the coming day's activities. It also gave him time to decide on whom to blame, disparage or disconcert. He considered himself a fair, evenhanded man: he was quite prepared to castigate subordinates and equals alike. Though to be fair, he was also capable of dispensing praise to his superiors; and sometimes even to his inferiors, on the rare occasions when he felt it was warranted. Besides, praise was part of his patented softening-up process. It made the recipients all the more susceptible to future criticism and thus encouraged them to try harder.

On this particular November morning, however, his pleasure in the contemplation of the discomfiture of others was sorely diminished by what he had just read at the breakfast table: a highly disturbing letter in *The Times*. It was from a Foreign Office official—possibly retired, though the position was not entirely clear—and concerned the Royal Air Force in Iraq.

It was not that the letter had been critical of his beloved RAF, as were most of the comments in the press these days. Quite the opposite. The theme of the letter was that the RAF had grounds for complacency, as the situation in Iraq was under complete control.

As for the concern that had been expressed in some quarters over the possibility of an attack on northern Iraq from the direction of Turkey, the letter had continued, the writer, W.D. Lewis, had it on the most reliable authority that there was absolutely no risk of such an eventuality, nor was there justification for any anxiety on the part of the Royal Air Force, which, of course, was responsible for military operations in that part of the world.

The writer had then gone into the usual wearying detail to be found in *Times* letters on Turkish ambitions in that region, based on their determination to reclaim territory lost in the war.

What disturbed the CAS so profoundly was not so much the content of the letter—though it contained a shock in that he had not been aware of any rumors of a Turkish attack—but that the reliable authority quoted was Major General B.W. Bandy, CBE, DSO, MC, DFC, Croix de Guerre, Legion of Honor.

Though the CAS found it hard to believe that there could be two Bandys, initially he dismissed the idea utterly that the Foreign Office man was referring to the Bandy he knew: that opportunist scoundrel—there was no other word for the fellow, except villain, blackguard, reprobate, ruffian, traitor, renegade and degenerate—who had been stopped only just in time from creating a disturbance in India. No, it was ridiculous. B. Bandy, an authority on Middle East politics and military strategy? It was arrant nonsense. It couldn't be the same man. Apart from anything else, the Bandy he knew had never been near the Middle East. If he had, the CAS would certainly have known about it. He had quite a voluminous dossier on that Bandy, by now.

Yet. . .certain details did fit—the decorations, some biographical detail and even, God help us, the fellow's rank, an extremely temporary wartime appointment that, through a criminal oversight on the part of the Canadian Ministry of Militia and Defence, had not been revoked by the time he was due for demobilization, so that the swine was now genuinely entitled to call himself Major General—though not even that insufferable knave had the gall actually to do so.

It was all highly perplexing as well as enraging. It made the chief feel quite disoriented to read all about a denial that the Turks were preparing to support the Iraqi rebels in the north with units of the Turkish army, when he, ultimately the man responsible for military operations in the area, had not even been aware that there was anything to be denied. It also made him wonder if there might not be something to the rumors. Turkish involvement was by no means beyond the bounds of possibility. The dictator Kemal Atatürk had caused a great deal of unexpected trouble two years previously when his revolutionary army had marched on Constantinople after trouncing the Greeks. His progress to political supremacy was barred only by detachments of Allied troops at a place called Chanak. Kemal had threatened to drive the Allies into the sea if they refused to let him pass. The confrontation had rapidly deteriorated into an international crisis. For a while it had looked as if the British government would drag the empire into another war. The conflict had been quite narrowly averted and only because the Chief's friend General Harington had personally visited the scene of the crime and had subdued the Turks by the force of his personality.

Further, the CAS knew that Kemal was indeed supplying rebel Iraqi tribesmen in the north with arms and ammunition. All the same, there had been no reports of direct Turkish intervention; which surely made superfluous the reassurance from Lewis's "incontrovertible source" Bandy—God, it was true, the letter writer really was referring to *his* Bandy—that the Turkish attack would not materialize. How the hell could it materialize if the threat didn't exist?

The CAS decided grimly that as soon as he reached the office he would get Marson onto it. As for Bandy's claim to be an authoritative source, by God, he would demolish that foolishness right at the outset by establishing that Bandy had never even been to Iraq, let alone become an authority on it. After that he would check up on this letter writer, Lewis, and ascertain if he was involved in some Foreign Office ruse or stratagem. In common with most people in other government departments, the CAS despised and distrusted the FO as a nest of perverts and Arabists.

Finally he would check with military intelligence to find out what they knew about it.

The Chief was to find out one or two things about it even before he arrived at the office. When he climbed into the first-class compartment of the train from Potter's Bar, he was followed into it by an impressive-looking gentleman with a white mustache who looked like a cabinet minister but who was actually an actor. This traveler, after studying his *Times* with increasing incredulity finally burst out, " 'Straordinary assessment, this letter about Iraq."

When the ferocious-looking gent next to him looked up sharply: "Sorry," he said with an apologetic smile. "Just couldn't help speaking aloud." And he buried his face in the newspaper again.

"Is it that Iraq letter?" the Chief asked.

"Oh, you've read it, have you? Well, you see, this chap they're quoting, Bandy—I don't see how on earth he's arrived at the conclusion that the Turks will never attack. I mean, I was there, I should know."

Again the gentleman smiled apologetically. "But please forgive me for disturbing you. I know you can't possibly be interested in—"

"I'm interested," the Chief said sharply; then, attempting to moderate his tone: "You're acquainted with this—Bandy?"

"I didn't actually meet him, of course, as I was on the Turkish side of the frontier, while he was on the Iraqi side. But—"

"He was in Iraq?"

"Oh, yes—last month. I understand he was investigating the situation out there for the Prime Minister."

"The Prime Minister?"

"Yes, I see what you mean," the gentleman chuckled.

Actually the Chief hadn't meant anything. He was still trying to frame a query that would enable him to find out what he had meant, when the impeccable gent went on to explain gratuitously. "It's typical of Bandy that he would back the wrong man, isn't it? It was the outgoing PM he was working for — the loser, Ramsay MacDonald."

"You seem to know a good deal about Bandy."

"Only what everybody says of him — that he's always uncannily wrong."

The Chief could barely restrain himself from bellowing, "By God, you're right there." Instead he asked, "How?"

"I don't know if that's strictly true, but certainly in this case, Bandy's findings are quite at variance with my own observations."

"What observations?"

"That Turkey *is* preparing an attack on Iraq."

"It is?"

"And that the hierarchy of the RAF has genuine cause for concern, rather than complacency, as Bandy would have it."

The CAS scored his fellow traveler with the diamonds of his eyes, but remained silent.

"I had business in that area, you see," the other continued, sweating surreptitiously. "I work for the FBDB — RMJ Division — international banking, you know . . . and, well, I'm no military expert, but even I could see that the Turks were up to something. Moving troops up to the frontier at night and establishing supply dumps and — "

"Let me get this straight," the Chief interrupted rudely. "Where were you exactly, in Turkey?"

"I was visiting sites in the area where the river Tigris flows from Turkey to Iraq."

"And that's where you saw these troop movements?"

"That general area, yes," said the actor, who had never been farther than Boulogne.

"Have you told anyone about this — the British government, for instance?"

"Well, naturally," the other said, looking offended, as if his patriotism had been impugned. "I felt it my duty to pass it on to the Foreign Office as soon as I got back."

Too anxious even to take the trouble to soothe the other's apparently ruffled feelings, the CAS leaned forward urgently and snapped, "Then why is this Foreign Office man saying the opposite?" And he rapped the other's copy of *The Times* with his blunt forefinger so forcefully that the paper tore.

"Obviously," said the other coldly, starting to collect his things together, "they prefer to believe General Bandy, rather than take the word of a mere banker."

"Look, could I have your name—"

"Excuse me, this is where I get out."

"Wait, wait—"

"Sorry, this is my station," the other said stiffly, and he slammed the carriage door and hurried off down the platform before the CAS had the chance even to open his mouth again.

The moment he pounded into his office on the sixth floor of the Air Ministry, the CAS jabbed the bell push, pressing it as if trying to crush a snail with a particularly callous shell.

When his secretary and military aide appeared, the Chief shouted, "Get onto 10 Downing Street. See if they'll confirm that Bandy was recently in the Middle East on behalf of Ramsay MacDonald. I don't care how difficult it is, but you find out, understand?"

"General Bandy, sir?"

"Don't call him that," the Chief shrieked. "Don't dare call him that. I won't have it, I just won't have it."

"Actually I can confirm part of it now, sir. Gen—er, Mr. Bandy *was* in the Middle East recently."

"How the devil," the CAS demanded, very loudly indeed, "do you know that when I don't? Why the hell didn't you tell me?"

"Well, I know how upset you get whenever his name is mentioned."

"And you chose to deny me the information because of that?"

"It didn't seem important, sir. I just picked it up in a routine signal from an outlying squadron to Hinaidi that they had spent two pounds two shillings and ninepence on entertaining Mr. Bandy in the mess. HQ had apparently queried the expense, you see, and. . . ." He dribbled to a halt.

The CAS sat behind his desk, lowering himself with painful slowness, his ferocious eyes fixed on the quaking officer.

"What mess was Bandy in?"

"Well, he's always in so many, that—"

"What squadron mess, you fool!"

"Oh. Mosul, sir."

The air marshal seemed to shrink to half his usual size. "Mosul," he muttered. "That's near the Turkish frontier, isn't it?"

"Yes, sir," Marson said, watching in alarm as the Chief's iron face, violent black eyebrows and armor-piercing eyes sank lower and lower over the bright green leather of the desk, coming so close to the surface that the secretary thought for a deranged moment that it would burst into flames at the pinpoint focus of the Chief's eyes.

However, nobody could deny that the Chief of Air Staff was a man of courage who, Marson loyally believed, could take even a Bandy in his stride. After no more than a few minutes, the Chief raised his head again and almost calmly asked Marson to get onto HQ Hinaidi immediately—copy to AOC Cairo—for a full report on Bandy's movements in the area. He would also appreciate an explanation as to why Mideast had not reported on the possibility of direct Turkish support for the unruly sheiks of Iraq.

It had been a long, tedious and risky wait, but finally the moment came: the Chief of Air Staff finally went to the bathroom. He came striding along the corridor and entered the washroom, the one for officers of the rank of group captain and above.

After he had ensconced himself in one of the cubicles and the aural evidence suggested that he was not in a position to emerge in a hurry, two men entered into conversation as they stood at the urinals. Judging by their speech they were senior officers; an obvious assumption, for surely no junior officer would have had the temerity to use a senior washroom, however tempting the inducements, such as the high-quality toilet paper, so much superior to the shiny stuff that was considered good enough for junior officers. Admittedly they sounded rather youthful for senior officers; but then the Royal Air Force was a youthful organization, with some quite young men in the higher echelons; so the timbre of their voices did not rouse suspicion.

Said the first: "I see you've made AVM at last, Lofty."

"Just thought the old fat stripe needed a spot of company, you know."

There then followed some gossip about people they knew in common, including Old Tobyjugs of Transcat 1084. Then there was the sound of footsteps, followed by the swish of water into separate basins.

"By the by," the second voice said, "Seen the report from SMIT(n) about the Turkish plan of attack?"

"My dear old chap," replied the other, speaking with unusual clarity and at greater volume than seemed necessary in the ceramic sanctum, "I don't even think the Chief of Air Staff himself would be allowed to see reports from that intelligence outfit, so they certainly wouldn't put me on the old mailing list."

There was a slight rustling as they turned the pages of their scripts. "Vaguely no, I suppose not," said the first; then made a face as he realized he should not have pronounced the direction "(vaguely)."

"What's it all about, anyway? They really are going to attack, are they?"

"Seems so, SMIT(n) has somehow acquired the operational orders of the Turkish Forty-first Division, the Salahaddin Division. I only hope . . . ?"

"What?"

"Well, I'm really praying that the CAS doesn't find out how desperately they need him in Iraq. What with all the problems over the new auxiliary squadron budgeting, we need him here."

"Yes, that's very true," said the other, and Derby and his friend, an officer who had also served at the Air Ministry, made their exits, a departure considerably speeded up when they heard somebody scrabbling as frantically at the lock of the cubicle inside to get out as some people suffering from, say, dysentery, might have scrabbled from the outside to get in.

* * *

Two minutes later the CAS stormed into his secretary's office, shouting, "There were two officers in the lavatory just now. Find out who they were!"

"Sir?"

"Well, get on with it, it shouldn't be difficult! One of them's just been promoted to air vice marshal. I want them in my office within the next ten minutes, understand?"

"But sir—"

"And another thing—they referred to an intelligence group called Smitten. Find out about it right now."

"Smitten?"

"That's what it sounded like. Well, get onto it, man, don't stand there gaping!"

But it was hours before Marson finally summoned up courage to enter the great man's office and report that nobody had been seen to enter or leave the senior lavatory except the CAS himself.

However, making things a little easier on himself, Marson was able to report that he had found out a little about an intelligence unit that was actually called SMIT(n). During the war, it had operated above a fish-and-chip shop in a side street off Charing Cross Road. After the armistice, most of the personnel had been released, and the core of the unit had moved to other quarters. But though SMIT(n) had vague FO connections, nobody knew where it was presently located; or if they did, they weren't telling.

When he arrived at the ministry on the following morning, somewhat sunken-eyed after a sleepless night, the Chief found a high-priority signal waiting for him. He swore aloud when he saw that it was from the air officer commanding at Hinaidi and read that photo reconnaissance had revealed the presence of Turkish troops and equipment, including armored cars, in northern Iraq territory partly controlled by Sheik Majed. HQ had also received reports that Turkish limited support for Majed would include Turkish infantry when Majed next raised a revolt against King Feisal. Such a revolt was expected at any moment. Ordinarily he, the AOC, would take care of a revolt in the usual way, by a bombing campaign aimed at hurting the rebels economically. Unfortunately, experience had shown that Majed needed a much sharper lesson to bring him to heel. The only thing that seemed to chasten him, temporarily at least, was the loss of a few men as well as the destruction of a few villages. But the AOC felt that he could not risk a bombing offensive against Majed if there was a risk of Turkish troops being killed. This was a distinct possibility, as they would almost certainly be intermingled with Sheik Majed's men. Even if Turkish casualties were inflicted on Iraqi soil, establishing that the Turks were invaders, the repercussions could be serious for the air force. It was well known that Kemal Atatürk was determined to regain at least some of the territory his country had lost during the war. He could seize on the death of his soldiers as an excuse to intervene in Iraq on a large scale. To repeat, there were reports of troop movements on the other side of Iraq's northern border. In fact the writer's CSO, Air Commodore Greaves, suspected that that was what it was all about. Atatürk was deliberately creating the conditions that would justify a major intervention by Turkey. To summarize: the dilemma was that if the RAF attacked Majed's columns they might kill Turkish soldiers. But if they refrained from such attacks, Majed's rebellion, with help from Turkey and possibly other warring tribes, could become extremely serious. The AOC needed the CAS's guidance in this matter, preferably on the spot. The CSO concurred.

All morning the Chief dithered and prevaricated in a most uncharacteristic fashion over what appeared to be a growing emergency. An atmosphere of crisis was enveloping him, and it seemed to be growing more poisonous every hour, yet at the same time anesthetizing. He felt as if he had hardly a will of his own anymore. In the train from Potter's Bar that morning yet another first-class passenger, obviously a man of authority, had expressed concern over the Iraq "crisis," portraying it as quite possibly the cause of another world conflict. The situation was serious for the RAF, which was in charge out there, and which would bear the brunt of the fighting and the major share of the blame if the situation were allowed to deteriorate further. The speaker thought that the crisis called for someone in authority to leave for Iraq forthwith, without a moment's delay. It would obviously have to be a military man rather than a politician or a diplomat, as the new government had not officially taken over yet.

"You look like a man who knows how to get things done," said the speaker, addressing the CAS. "What is your opinion, sir?"

"Personally, if there's one thing I hate, it's traveling, especially abroad," the CAS muttered; a response that, to the other passengers in the compartment, seemed a distinct *non sequitur*. The original speaker however, was observed to lapse into a state of gloom rather than perplexity.

Marson, the secretary and military aide, was in a state of gloom *and* perplexity. For three days he had been bombarded with a series of instructions from the CAS, almost every one of which seemed to be impossible to carry out. How on earth was he to investigate a train passenger from Potter's Bar to some intermediate halt on the line when the fellow had never reappeared, had no name—and hardly even a face, considering the Chief's inadequate description. All Marson had to go on was that the man was, "About fifty or sixty—use your initiative, Marson!"

Further, the air marshal had sent off so many signals to Hinaidi and to HQ, Mideast that it was almost impossible to tell which were the replies to what questions. As for SMIT(n), that intelligence organization was so secret it was almost as if it didn't exist. Still further, Marson was supposed to have interviewed *The Times* letter writer, W.D. Lewis, but he was not to be found. The CAS had wished to see the evidence cited by Lewis on which Bandy had based his opinion that there was absolutely no cause for alarm; but while the FO had received his, Marson's, queries with flattering affability, they hadn't actually replied to any of those queries—a typical response from that pansy bunch, Marson thought.

Then there was the problem of the conversation overheard in the washroom. Marson had established that there was only one air vice marshal in the building at the time. He had denied all knowledge of the incident. Even so, the CAS had had the AVM on the MAT and had bellowed at him for ten minutes before the air vice marshal had the temerity to answer back. "As far as I'm concerned, you can go to Iraq and stay there until doomsday," he shouted back, and marched out, leaving the Chief still uncertain as to whether he had been blaming the right man or not; though that parting shot had suggested to him that the man was culpable. In which case there was a conspiracy afoot.

"Nonsense," his wife said that evening over the mince and potatoes. "Conspiracy indeed. You're just tired, dear. Why don't you take a holiday, somewhere nice and hot? The change would do you a world of good, you know."

Me, Upside Down

It was a disheartened group that assembled in my office at the end of another day of maneuvering, fibbing, imposture, trespass, creative writing, obfuscation and split-second timing.

"The campaign's obviously not working," I said, picking dejectedly at a tiny splinter of wood at the edge of my desk. "He's showing not the slightest sign of leaving for the Middle East."

Hibbert suggested that it was perhaps too early to tell; but I was enjoying my gloom and pessimism too much. "I told you it was essential to keep piling it on like incidents in an Aldwych play, to give him no time to think or recover from the last revelation — to keep him pothered and flustered so he wouldn't know where his day ended and senility began. It's this slackening of the pace that's ruined it all," I said, glaring around for a moment, to see whom I could blame, before resuming the attack on the splinter. I was attempting to wrench it free so that it wouldn't catch on my new gray suit. "Didn't I say it was essential to pile on the agony without giving him a moment to receive an emergency injection of common sense? Well, didn't I?"

"Yes, Bartholomew, that's what you said," Derby replied, with the kind of patience you used on a fretful child. "And if you don't stop picking at that wood, you'll soon have no desk left in which to keep your pens, pencils, choccy bars, cream buns and hair restorer."

"I don't see what else we can do," Mays said, smoothing the distinguished gray hair at his temples with an exquisitely manicured hand. "We've had people whispering to him in corridors, and when he turns around there's nobody there. We've sent him *billets-doux* from the anarchists threatening him with bombs if he goes to Iraq, and from little old ladies threatening him with umbrellas if he doesn't. We've arranged for him to see the fake battle orders that you purchased in Cairo, convincing him they've come from SMIT(n). My God, we've even had somebody dress up in fez, pantaloons and curly slippers and sidle up to him, and—"

"Yes, yes, we know all that," I snapped distractedly. I was becoming uneasy at the way the splinter was refusing to separate from the main body of the desk. Already it was four inches long and lengthening every minute. At the same time it was veering deeper into the woodwork.

With characteristic strength of will, I desisted from these efforts, smoothed down the splinter, and said curtly, "Anyway, what d'you mean, *fake* battle orders? We won't know they're fake until the day the Turks are supposed to attack—December the first."

"That was two days ago," Mays said.

"What?"

"December the first was two days ago."

"What?"

Mays turned away impatiently.

"Well, anyway," I mumbled, "it could have been a genuine document."

"Come, sir, how could it have been genuine? We've had our experts examine it—"

"That Turkish bath attendant, you mean?"

"Others agree with his assessment."

"Well, it could have been genuine. There *is* a genuine Salahaddin Division."

"Naturally they'd use the names of real units," Mays said patiently, obviously feeling that *he* should be behind the important desk, not me, even if it was splintering. "Probably the names on the list of battalion commanders are genuine, too."

"For verisimilitude," Hibbert put in.

They all nodded as if they knew what the word meant. I'd have nodded too, if I hadn't been feeling mulish.

"All right, all right," I conceded peevishly, discovering that I had resumed the obsessive picking at the splinter. Actually it was more like a stick of kindling at the moment. "I'm well aware that I exceeded my common sense in Cairo, buying those five pages of toilet paper. You don't have to rub it in."

"I suppose it was a tactical error, fixing it for the Chief of Air Staff to see that rubbish you bought from Kekevi," Hibbert said, watching me pick at the desk. "It should have occurred to us that the RAF might have access to expert evaluation. Experts who were bound to establish that Kekevi's material was fake. It'll make the CAS more inclined than ever to stay put."

"And we know now he doesn't need much of an excuse. He hates traveling."

I mumbled to myself, as I yanked and peeled, "Well, it could have been authentic."

"You know," said Derby after a moment, "I'm getting nearly as confused as the old Chief must surely be by now."

"How?"

"All these signals they're getting, about Turkish intervention and Sheik Majed and all that stuff—I don't remember us planning any of that."

"It's perfectly simple," I muttered. "The RAF out there has found out about the Turkish troop movements across the border, and they've established some sort of connection with this Sheik Majed, that's all."

"Yes, but there *aren't* any troop movements."

"What?"

"There aren't any Turkish troop movements. We all know now that Kekevi's information was false."

"What?"

"We've been building on your friend Kekevi's fake plans, inventing all that stuff about the Turkish menace."

"Mm, so we have."

"There is absolutely no Turkish threat. Now have you got that, sir?"

"But if it's all made up," Derby said, "then what's all this anxiety from the Middle East?"

"It's simple enough," I said, perhaps with slightly less conviction than before. "Greaves adores me so much he's decided to help us bamboozle the CAS."

"But damn it, they're talking about evidence of Turkish troop movements from photo reconnaissance."

"Oh, that's probably just old Greaves with a Brownie camera."

"I don't know. I think the situation's getting out of hand," Derby said. "Between us and Kekevi, we invent Turkish invaders, and Middle East Command starts to see them."

"As I said, it's all perfectly simple, John," I replied. "Greaves's troop movements will turn out to be a shot of a row of Turks moving their bowels in a ditch."

A low, dark voice said, "It's beginning to muddy the waters."

We all looked around to see who had said it. It turned out to be Philip Brashman. We hadn't realized he was at the meeting until then.

"All this stuff about Sheik Majed," he added darkly. "That wasn't in our plans."

"That's right," Derby said, encouraged. "Personally I'm beginning to think that the CAS had better go to Iraq after all."

"For God's sake," Mays said exasperatedly, "that's precisely what we're trying to achieve."

It was Derby's turn to falter. "Oh, yes," he murmured. But then, rallying: "See? I told you I was confused."

As he watched me wrenching away at the splinter—kindling, faggot, yule log, what you will—a muscle in Hibbert's cheek started twitching like mad. "We need a change of plan," he said in a tense way. "We've arranged for the Chief to lunch at Mays's club, but I think we need more drastic action—the ultimate step."

"What's that?"

"Sic Bandy onto him."

There was a silence. Mays started to speak, stopped. His eyes unfocused and he stared at the fancy cornice that ruled the office wall.

"No," I said.

"It may be our last chance," Hibbert said to Mays.

"No," I said. "That wasn't in the schedule."

But Mays was nodding thoughtfully. "It does seem logical," he murmured.

"No," I said. "I can't take any more confrontations with that man. I'm sure it's him that's driven me to drink."

"I can't understand why we didn't think of it before."

"Because our Mr. Bandy kept changing the subject every time it came up, that's why."

"For Christ's sake," Hibbert screamed suddenly.

We all started and gaped at him in absolute astonishment.

"Stop peeling your desk," Hibbert shrieked. "You're ruining it."

I stared at him open-mouthed, then muttered, "Well, I can't stop. I mean, I can't just leave the splinter sticking out like that. It could catch on my new suit."

"Look at it, for God's sake. It started out as a toothpick and it's ended up a bloody javelin."

"Steady on, Hib."

"Well. Seeing him sitting there—peeling."

"So—don't just stand there," I ordered. "Go and get a chisel so I can cut it off."

As Brashman led Hibbert to a chair and patted him on the shoulder, Derby said, "It's a bit late for a chisel. What about a bandsaw?"

"You're right," I said. "I'd better fetch the carpenters."

"You see?" Mays said. "He's doing it again—changing the subject."

"I yam not," I said, rising with dignity and forcing myself to leave the vicinity of the desk. "Very well, Hibbert, I shall take your advice and fetch the carpenters forthwith." And I made for the door.

Somehow Mays got in the way. "I know how you feel about the Chief, sir," he said, bland as curds. "But it's our last chance. If you can't drive him over the edge of sanity, who can?"

"Won't work."

"Yes, it will."

"No, it won't. 'Cos," I cried triumphantly, "there's no way he's going to stand still long enough for me even to wish him good day, let alone provide him with my analysis of the Iraq situation."

There was silence while they all reluctantly came to the same conclusion. "It's true," Mays said at length. "By now he'd prefer to practice the breast stroke in a sewage farm than talk to Bandy."

The gloomy silence returned. Derby got up and walked to the window, and stared down into Cannon Street.

"Unless," he said suddenly, "he had no alternative."

We all twisted round to look at him. "Well?" Mays asked impatiently.

"I was just remembering. . . . When we were skulking on the sixth floor waiting for the Chief to go to the lavatory, I was chatting to a maintenance man I knew when I was at the Air Ministry. He was fixing one of the lifts. They're his responsibility."

"Yes, so?"

"It occurred to me," Derby said, gazing up at the ceiling in a burlesque of the casual attitude, "that with a spot of encouragement, say twenty quid . . . ?"

It was fortunate that we had already arranged for the CAS to lunch with a friend of his at the Junior Carlton. So we knew to the nearest few minutes when he would arrive at the two elevators that served the east end of the Air Ministry building. The situation might otherwise have been impossible to manage. As it was, Derby had to make a frantic dash up the emergency stairs to signal the maintenance man, while Brashman, looking every inch an officer in mufti, held the elevator.

As the air marshal approached, wearing a bowler and a smart black overcoat that looked as heavy as lead and carrying his usual briefcase, Brashman departed smartly, as if he had just arrived at the sixth floor.

It was typical of the CAS that he made no effort to increase his pace to make sure he caught the elevator, like any normal per son. He assumed that even a mechanical contraption, let alone the people in it, would obey his orders, or at least would not dare to leave without being formally dismissed.

His confidence was justified. The elevator waited for him patiently, as did its occupant, a stalwart, dignified, smart-looking chap in a light gray suit of the latest cut and a matching overcoat. The man was busily reading an interesting framed notice on the shiny wooden wall.

The elevator was a modern, self-service contraption, which perhaps accounted for its unreliability. The walls were of inlaid woods, and there was a small window in the rear wall that enabled the passenger, if he were so inclined, to see into the shaft at the back and view the elevator counterweight as it glided up and down on its guide rails. The ministry happened to own this up-to-date piece of machinery because the building had started life as the up-to-date Hotel Cecil. The Air Board had taken over the hotel during the war and had never returned it to its owners. A list of rules for guests was still in evidence, albeit yellow with age and cigarette smoke. It was this list that I was reading when the Chief entered.

"Ground floor," he barked, without even glancing in my direction, though I was only four feet away. I suppose he assumed that, as he was the highest-ranking officer in the building, anybody else in the elevator was bound to be an inferior, so there was no point in glancing.

With my back turned to him as much as possible, I reached over and hauled shut the outer doors, then the inner doors. And turned to the controls. They were simple enough: a vertical arrangement of stout steel buttons with the floor number beside each, and one button for emergencies. I pressed the ground-floor button. The wooden room shuddered, then started down with a head-jolting jerk. Then, as instructed, I signaled with the emergency button.

Eighteen seconds later, as we were between the third and fourth floors, there was a distant bang, and the elevator came to so sudden a halt that our knees gave slightly, lowering us several inches simultaneously, like two comic policemen doing a music-hall turn. In fact I very nearly said, "Now then, now then, what's going on 'ere?"

Instead, after a moment of silence I said, "Hallo. The elevator appears to have stopped."

After I had uttered these immortal words, the silence resumed. Only now it seemed to have a different quality to it. Previously there had been a sort of official hush. Now, suddenly, there was a distinct air of tension. I could sense the Chief slowly turning in my direction.

With an effort, for I was nervous as Nellie at meeting the Chief again, I relaxed the old lineaments and turned to face him; and at the sight of him I started and leaped back several feet—perhaps just a shade exaggeratedly—and exclaimed: "Good heavens, it's you, sir. Fancy meeting you here."

For a moment he continued to shower me with shards from the broken bottles of his eyes, lacerating my face until the skin hung down like theater curtains and my eyes swung and dangled from their optic nerves below a dislocated jaw. Until, with a voice like sand in the gearbox, he enquired what the devil I was doing here.

"First things first, sir," quoth I. "We appear to have a slight emergency here. We seem to have stopped between floors."

"I want to know what the hell you're doing in this building, when I told you I never wished to set eyes on you again."

I made some hurried, rather incoherent excuse, adding quickly before he had a chance to analyze anything, "But anyway, now that we've met, sir, so fortuitously—I don't suppose you've changed your mind about helping us to solve our otherwise insurmountable equipment problems India-wise, have you, sir?"

He merely stared at me for a hideous moment with an expression that I can only describe (with some reluctance) as one of loathing and fury, before turning away and snapping, "Well get on with it, man. Press the button again."

"Which one, sir?"

"The ground-floor button, of course."

I did so. Nothing happened. "Well, try the emergency but

ton," he shouted, snatching open his coat in order to reach the watch in his waistcoat pocket. He clicked it open and glared at it.

"Well? Are you going to get this thing moving or not?"

"I've tried the emergency button, but nothing's happening."

"Here," he growled and, brushing me aside, started stabbing at one button after another, and several times at a large screw, apparently under the impression that it was another control.

"Looks as if we're going to be stuck in here for a while," I said conversationally.

He paid no attention, but next proceeded to bang on the door with his fist, and to enquire in a very loud voice if there was anyone there.

Then followed some more button grinding; a further burst of hollering; a ferocious kicking at the elevator door with a shiny black boot; a thump on the inlaid wood with a clenched fist and a further volley of shouts. At one point he held his large, tattered thumb on the emergency button for more than a minute; until finally, panting, flushed and in something of a snit, he gave up and glared at me again. "Well, don't just stand there," he bellowed. "Do something. I'm in a hurry."

"Nothing we can do but wait, I fear," quoth I in a soothing sort of voice. "Still, the time won't be all wasted. This will give us an opportunity to chat like civilized people, don't you think?"

"I have nothing to say to you. Nothing."

"We're likely to be here for an hour, Air Marshal," I said, giving myself a mental hug of congratulation at the success of our little plot to trap him in the elevator for just such a period as I had just prophesied, so as to give me the opportunity to onvince him that he should hurry off to Iraq by telling him that he shouldn't.

It was all working out better even than I had imagined. Or at east it would, as soon as he had calmed down sufficiently to llow me to stimulate his contrary impulses. At the moment he was glaring around, breathing heavily, his motivation to escape greatly enhanced by the discovery that he was to have me as ompany. He was looking quite desperately for a means of egress, but there was none that he could see. We had made sure of that. A previous inspection had confirmed that there was no obvious way out. There was an escape hatch, but it was concealed behind a decorative panel in the ceiling.

Now he was beating at the little window with his fist, though it was much too small to climb through, even had it been openable. And of course it led nowhere useful. As for the doors, they could be pried apart with difficulty, but as we had arranged for the elevator to stop opposite a brick wall, opening the doors would not accomplish all that much, unless the Chief had a pick and shovel in that valise of his, which he had placed against the rear wall when he first . . . entered . . . .

Valise? Why a valise? I had assumed that he was carrying his briefcase. Consequently a briefcase was what I had seen. But I now perceived that it was indeed a valise, a leather portmanteau, scuffed and scored, as if it were one of his inferiors. I wondered vaguely why he felt he needed to take a valise to lunch.

Meanwhile he was swearing again, referring repeatedly to his pocket watch, tramping up and down, two and a half steps each way, and breathing so agitatedly that I could see the hairs in his nostrils writhing, as if there were a couple of Medusas up there He was getting so steamed up about his predicament that I fel concerned that he might not calm down in time before the hou was up. I had estimated that I needed sixty minutes for a calm and irrational discussion on the Iraq situation. The elevator wa due to be revived at 1:35 P.M.

I glanced anxiously at my own watch and was relieved to se that only six minutes had elapsed. So that was all right. Plent of time to get a nice conversation going.

Mind you, it was going to take a certain amount of subtlety t initiate it. "I hear they're calling desperately for you to go t Iraq and take charge of the crisis, Air Marshal," I could say "Personally I think it's pure bunk, this emergency they're talk ing about." No, that would not do at all. It was a trifle too bald I thought, as I ran a hand over my topknot. But how else to g onto the subject when he was storming up and down the six-foo square elevator like that, panting and goggling at his watc

"Talking about Iraq, I think this appalling situation they're talking about has been greatly exaggerated," perhaps. Maybe he wouldn't notice that introductory "Talking about Iraq" when we weren't talking about it. Yes, maybe I should chance being bold and direct about it. "After all, I've been in Iraq quite recently," I could continue, drawing on a manly, unreliable expression. "I've seen for myself that there's nothing to be seen—even when I didn't have a hangover. Just because the Turks are bringing up several Kekevi—that's the technical Turkish term for a battalion, Air Marshal—at certain jump-off points close to the border on the most direct route to the vital Iraqi city of Mosul is not the slightest cause for concern. It's obvious that the Turks are just holding a series of Sports Days, not making troop movements. I myself have observed them running hundred-yard races—in full pack—and throwing the discus and then diving down behind parapets immediately afterwards. I mean," I would laugh, "do you think for one moment that the Turks, who are so renowned for their peaceful qualities, their exquisite, not to say foppish manners and their reputation for subtlety, sensitivity and love of wildflowers, not unmixed with that manly resolution that so distinguishes us from the brute beasts, as witness the recent massacres at Smyrna—do you think for one moment," I would reprise, in case he had forgotten how the sentence started, "that a people like that are capable of such fiendish ambition as to wish to fight for their former homeland in what is now Iraq? Absurd. So what if the diplomatic corps, the imperial general staff, the new government and the entire Royal Air Force are unanimous in their opinion that your presence is urgently required in order to avert a second world war? That's only their opinion. I mean—"

However, it was no good convincing him exclusively in my head. We had been stuck in the lift now for seven minutes. I had better join issue aloud.

The only trouble was, he still wasn't in the mood. Instead of adjusting himself philosophically to the situation like me, making the best of it and resigning himself to the inevitable, he was growing steadily more agitated, not less. Now he was pounding the sides of the elevator as well as the door, as if trying to find a weak spot so that he could break through, despite the drop of seventy feet on the other side, down to an oily pit filled with waste, concrete, dead rats, razor-edged scrap metal, plaster, paper and puddles of oil.

Now he was turning on me in a rage and demanding to know why I was leaning against the wall like a street-corner oaf, instead of making suggestions as to how we might escape.

"I'm thinking, Air Marshal, I'm thinking."

"Oh, yes? Thinking about what, may I ask?"

"That we can't escape. So we might as well wait patiently until they come to our rescue."

"I see. I see. And that's your contribution to the emergency, is it?"

"One must cultivate patience, detachment and serenity, my dear Air Marsh," I said with an airy smile. Still in a standing position, I crossed my legs at the ankles. On an afterthought I drew out my pipe, noticing complacently that it still contained a few strands of unburned tobacco among the blackened embers. "There's nothing we can do about it," I added, patting my person, "so we might as well relax, and have a nice chat."

"Chat? Chat? You expect me to chat when I've less than an hour to catch my plane?"

That straightened me up, all right. I was brought to the vertical with the kind of jar you experience when you've missed the bottom step. "What?" I asked, and only just in time restrained myself from blurting, "But you're going to lunch at the Junior Carlton with Sir Greensward Trumper, KCSI, DSO."

"If you must know," he raged, "I'm booked on the Imperial Airways inaugural flight from Croydon. And there isn't another flight until next week."

"Inaugural flight to where?"

"Egypt, damn you! It leaves at one-thirty."

"Oh, no."

"It's urgent I get to Baghdad."

"No, no."

"I tell you it is! And if I don't leave today, there will be no point in my going at all!"

"Oh, my land," I said with admirable restraint, considering that the blood was flowing down my neck as if draining from a hippo's bathtub, leaving my face ragged, haggard and the color of self-raising flour.

It appeared that the campaign had worked after all.

And I had stopped it dead in its tracks with a five-ton elevator.

I was still saying it a minute later. "Oh, my land," I was saying, as the CAS stared at me, surprised and perhaps faintly mollified by my evident concern for his travel arrangements.

Concern? I thought this might easily be the very worst moment of my life—and I'd had a great many worst moments, I can tell you.

The anguishing thing was, I was the architect of my own downfall. I had arranged for the elevator to break down and be restored to health exactly one hour after we entered it. Which would be at 1:35 P.M.—five minutes after his plane departed for the flight to Egypt.

It was more than just a shock. I had become convinced that 1924 was to be the most vital, the most critical year of my life, with fate offering me a choice of forking off either toward final obscurity or into the pages of history as one of its great men, along with Fred Hurwitz, Sir Hebrand Dilly and Cyrus Candrop, Jr. And this was the precise point at which I was to fork off.

Slowly the shock gave way to disgust, and then onward into indignation and fury—these emotions directed at the Chief of Air Staff. It was his fault, for not leaving for the new aerodrome with plenty of time to spare.

The rotten, filthy, selfish pigdog. If he had allowed himself enough time, as any normal person would, especially when the journey was urgent, this emergency would have been a good deal less acute. But no, *he* had to leave things to the last moment. *He* wasn't going to allow himself an extra hour just in case the official car that was waiting for him downstairs had a puncture, or it got stuck behind a manure cart or a rag and bone merchant on the Old Kent Road. No. *He* had to dawdle—to piss about in his office consummating affairs of state, or signing stupid international agreements, instead of leaving for the aerodrome in plenty of time, like any normal traveler.

However, I couldn't just stand here accepting God's will like some religious fanatic—as if God was ever on the side of the passive—without making some effort, however feeble, to release him from his predicament. And perhaps there was still a faint chance that he could catch his flight if I could release him within the next ten minutes or so.

So when he blared, "Well, you're supposed to be so handy, Bandy—do something, damn you," I replied, with a really impressive air of resolution, considering that I was feeling bloated with fury, frustration, despair, loathing, rage and desperation, "Air Marshal, I'll get you out of here and to the aerodrome on time if it's the last thing I do." And so saying, I leaped, hands raised, palms facing upward, and smashed the decorative panel overhead out of its slots with such force that the wood cracked like a rifle bullet and splintered into shrapnel. Inset screws flew about, ricocheting like anything. (The panel had been secured by screws, for God's sake, as if the manufacturer had assumed that anybody trapped in his stupid elevator was bound to have a screwdriver on him.)

As rusty screws and splinters of decorative wood flew about, the Chief ducked and covered his head. As he straightened, he gaped up at the metal hatch that was now visible through the ragged rectangular opening above. He stared at me with an expression almost of awe at my ability to act so fast, so powerfully and with such intuition in guessing that there might be an exit overhead.

Dragging over the valise—so *that* was why he had brought his luggage—I stood on it and started wrenching at the lever that secured the hatch.

Naturally it was rusted shut. It would not move a millimeter.

At frantic speed—which was poor physical economy, as desperate activity drained the energy at a high rate—I hauled on the lever until the muscles were practically bursting through my gray suit. Within seconds I was sodden with sweat. And the effort was quite wasted. The lever refused to budge.

I got down from the valise, panting like a donkey engine, snatched off my jacket, tie and collar and hurled them into a corner, then clawed off one shoe and climbed aboard the luggage again to use the shoe as a hammer. In the confined space up there I found myself hitting the back of my hand against some projection more often than I hit the lever. In any event the lever refused to turn.

Meanwhile my head was a bedlam of thoughts, calculations and cusswords. "If you miss the flight from Croydon, surely your own air force could fly you out," I gasped, streaking my face with rust and grease as I tried to wipe the sweat from my eyes. But he replied curtly that there was no way he was prepared to put the RAF to the expense of such a trip when even flying training had to be curtailed these days for lack of funds.

"Besides," he added, "all our long-distance transport is already in the Middle East on transport and bomber duty."

"Sir, we have a Vimy available. I was thinking that we could perhaps manage to . . . ?"

That was an error, born of thoughtless urgency. He looked as if he'd been keeping his face in the cold-storage locker. "Avail myself of any facility of yours? Never. If I cannot leave today by Imperial Airways—who are paying the fare because it's an inaugural route—I will not go at all."

So now there really was no alternative but to carry on vertically; and though it seemed hopeless, I redoubled my efforts to loosen the lever. To no avail. Its bolt seemed to be welded with rust.

"I don't suppose you have any oil on you?" I enquired in tones of drab futility.

There was a long silence from down there. I imagined him staring at me as if at a cretin. But then he spoke: "I have a little hair cream in the bag."

"You have? Quick, get it, get it!"

"I cannot."

"Why not, why not?"

"You are standing on the bag."

I got down and watched, panting, as he rummaged through his sordid duds and finally came up with a small jar containing a white cream.

I opened the lid and sniffed. "I haven't tried this before," I panted. "What's it like?"

"It's not bad. It doesn't leave your hair oily."

"I must try it some time. Usually I don't use hair oils or creams because my hair is quite manageable, what there is of it."

"I happen to have this because it's a free sample."

"It smells nice."

"Yes. My wife likes it."

"Maybe I'll try some after all."

"In the meantime, Bandy . . . ?"

"Pardon me?"

"Presumably you wanted some lubricant for the mechanism up there?"

"Yes. . . . Yes!" I cried and, leaping onto the bag again, I began to smear the hair cream lavishly on and around the bolt of the lever, deciding inconsequentially as I did so that I would not use it on my hair after all, as it felt quite sticky to me and not at all likely to dry quickly once applied to the hair.

A few seconds later as I banged again at the lever, I felt it give slightly. Redoubled efforts finally brought it around by ninety degrees; enough to allow the hatch to open fully onto the outside world.

By the time I had climbed onto the top of the elevator, I was quite exhausted. I had been working with far too much haste. But at least an enforced rest now gave me the opportunity to look around with a view to determining the best escape route. Fortunately the elevator well was adequately lit by means of naked light bulbs bracketed to the walls every dozen feet or so. Black metal, though, as well as black grime was doing its best to cancel the candlepower.

Not that it really mattered whether there was lots of light or little. There was enough to expose the fact that there was no escape. On the outside wall were the counterweight guide rails, but they led nowhere useful even if they had been climbable. The inside wall was the one I had been putting some faith in. I had hoped to find that the elevator had stopped within clawing distance of the next floor above, the fourth. And in fact the doors to that floor were only nine or ten feet up. But there were absolutely no footholds in the wall, or any other way to reach the doors, not even if I stood on the machinery that took up about half the roof of the elevator. This was the machinery into which the ropes led, that hauled the car from floor to floor, the ropes driven and controlled by the electic motor and other apparatus high above, under the roof of the former hotel.

As I sat there, gasping, the counterweight for the adjoining elevator glided past, heading downward. Which meant that our sister elevator was on its way up. I looked over the edge, and recoiled as the other elevator swept past only three feet away, and continued upward to the top floor.

Gingerly, still panting in lungfuls of stale, oily air, I peered over the edge again, but of course there was no way out in that direction either. Far below, a filthy, greasy shaft ended in a dreadful dark pit filled with debris.

I cursed the engineers for not putting an iron ladder into the shaft. Surely there was some maintenance to do that required workmen to move freely in this vertical space? But no, nothing but stretches of blackened brickwork, with crosspieces of various sorts at the floor levels and inset doorways with inch-wide ledges. Even if I could climb up there, I could never force open the doors, not with those footholds.

There was only one possible way out. The only trouble was that with every second's hesitation, the objections to such a course became steadily more pressing and convincing. I could think of so many objections that the other elevator had gone past twice before I called down to the Chief to tell him what I would try to do: jump onto the adjoining elevator when next it passed.

His answer rather surprised me. "No, no, you mustn't do that," he shouted back. "It's far too dangerous."

"It's only three feet to get across."

"Three feet onto a moving machine. One mistake and you could plunge all the way to the bottom, man."

I wished he hadn't used that word "plunge." It was a good job I'd moved my bowels recently.

"That's an order, Bandy," he called up, not making it entirely clear whether the order referred to the jump onto the other elevator or the plunge to the bottom.

"I've just got to get you out of there, sir, I've just got to," I whined through the hatch.

He must have climbed onto the valise. His granite face appeared only a few inches below the hatch. Good Lord. He was looking almost worried.

"Look here, Bandy," he said gruffly, "your concern is appreciated, but it's hardly a situation worth risking your life over."

"Oh yes, it is."

"Nonsense, man. Fact of the matter is, I don't entirely understand why I'm making this trip," the Chief said, passing a slightly shaky hand over a vaguely disoriented brow.

I had responded with, "Because they desperately need you out there, sir," before I could corral my wits.

Oh, God. I really was determined to undo all our intricate planning. Not content with placing him in solitary down there, now I was encouraging him to cancel his plans by exhorting him to fulfill them. I must be suffering from some sort of death wish. It was madness on my part to say such a thing. How often had he told me that whatever course I took was bound to be 180 degrees out?

He failed to hear me. I was flooded with relief. He had started to speak almost simultaneously. "If you will not obey my order, then at least heed a request," he said. "I ask you most sincerely not to try—you are quite obviously not a young man anymore."

I so far forgot myself as to glare down at him through the hatch. I stood up, mumbling huffily, now more than ever determined to effect egress.

All the same, I wished that I had written in an escape clause, in case I needed to get out of the elevator. It was exceedingly frustrating to think that Derby and his friend the maintenance man were only a hundred feet or so overhead, the latter working away like billy-ho on the motor until the hour was up. At the very least I should have arranged for emergency communication in case the Chief grew violent. Now I was faced with a jump across a gap of three feet onto a moving platform, which, like the one I was on, was cluttered with the metal framework that held the car together, and with the rope machinery, which left me with only a few square feet of clear space to land on. And as if to make it even harder, there were the car guide rails to avoid. A three-foot jump might not sound like much, but with seventy feet of nothing underneath, or the risk of snagging myself on some moving part—and practically the whole contraption was made of moving parts—it meant that I would have to summon up all my reserves of courage, reserves that I feared had become flabby with disuse.

There was no point in dwelling on it. Timing, reflex efficiency and judgment were all that were required. All. Ha. So I looked upward to see where the other elevator was; and once again just about suffered a heart attack as it swooshed up from below. I thought I had been keeping an account of its position, but it must have passed me on the way down without my noticing.

It stopped four floors up, at the top floor. Great loops of greasy cable hung from its grimy underside, which was crisscrossed with the frame that enclosed the car. I closed my eyes for a moment, trying to work out how to land on the top of that ominous black cube without whacking my head on an iron member or falling into the hauling-up-and-down mechanism or gashing a limb against the platform with the clamps that presumably braked the car to a halt. Think, think. To land as gently as possible, the car would have to be slowing down, to call at the floor immediately below. This, of course, assumed that I was going to make the jump while the other elevator was descending rather than when it was rising.

It was moving down. Now it was halting at the sixth floor, from where we had started days ago. Pause. Faint rattle and clump of doors. Now down to the fourth floor, just a few feet overhead. I tensed, ready to jump. The car started down. But either through good sense or cowardice, I failed to jump when the moment came. It had seemed to me that it was accelerating too fast.

When I shuffled to the edge, clinging to a guide rail, and peered down, I saw that the instinct had been right. The car had not halted at the floor below. It had been gathering speed for a trip all the way to the ground floor. If I had taken that car I might have been hurt. I saw myself leaping down onto it while it was descending and failing to catch up with it before it reached the bottom. There I was, hurtling down the shaft, trying to catch up with the elevator and reaching it just as it halted at the ground floor—me going through the roof at thirty-two feet per second per second, and then through the floor at a slightly reduced velocity.

No. I was glad I hadn't taken that elevator.

I looked at my wristwatch and moaned aloud. Four minutes to one. It was all so pointless. Even after the CAS was sprung from solitary, he had still to make the journey to the new airport, miles out of London. I remembered that when I had traveled to Croydon it had taken more than an hour.

God, it was hopeless. Well, after all, he'd advised me not to jump, so why should I? In fact he had ordered me not to. Don't do it, he'd ordered. It's too dangerous. I was aware of that, all right. I was putrid with funk. It was worse than my first parachute jump. At least then I'd had a few whiskies at the bar with Cyril Greaves. (Good Lord, old Greaves, an air commodore now.) Anyway, the risk wasn't worth taking. I wasn't likely to accomplish anything even if I landed safely. No, really, I ought to climb back through the hatch and wait patiently to be rescued. After all, there was only another half hour to go. I should wait patiently . . . and hopelessly.

The other elevator was rising again. I peered down at its roof, heart thumping with funk. It stopped, buzzing, at the second floor. Somehow I seemed to have decided to jump onto it as it rose rather than as it fell, even though I didn't at all fancy thus increasing the landing impact.

Get ready. It was rising again. Now slowing. Stopping at the floor below. The roof was about twelve feet away. Over a vertical distance of twelve feet it would surely not be traveling too fast as it drew level.

There was the faint sound of the doors being closed manually. A pause. Imagining myself plummeting had not raised my confidence all that much. Again I ordered myself not to think but to act. That was what I usually did—whether appropriate or not. Rely on timing, reflexes and judgment. Unfortunately my judgment was telling me that the three-foot gap between the elevators had widened to seven feet at the very least.

Still, I jumped.

I even managed to land where I was aiming, in the corner of the roof between the guide rails and the brick wall of the shaft. In retrospect I would marvel that I'd had the nerve, for I also had to avoid the steel platform that held the hoisting mechanism, pulleys, brakes and so forth. Bumping into any of them could have sent me staggering over the edge.

But I managed to land with hardly more of an impact than if I had jumped off a seawall onto the beach, and the worst that happened was that I whacked a set of already bleeding knuckles—I couldn't remember how they had come to be bleeding—on the iron frame that held the car together.

So the next moment I was riding upward on top of the other elevator, smirking weakly to myself and muttering aloud, "See? I *am* as young as I used to be." And as the cage halted two floors farther up, I danced happily on the metal roof, to attract the attention of those inside.

Minutes later I was still dancing, but now with fury and frustration. Nobody inside the elevator was taking a blind bit of notice.

I was really banging on the roof, and also doing a sort of rhumba, in the diminishing hope that the movement thus imparted to the car might be communicated to the occupants and alert them to my presence. But of course the car was much too heavy to jiggle. Nevertheless, I kept on and on, hollering and dancing with fury. Every time the elevator halted at a floor I would wait for the sound of the doors and then bellow like mad. I could hear both sets of doors quite clearly, whining and clumping. I could even see movement down there. In the fraction-of-an-inch gap between the top of the elevator and the brick wall, I could just make out faint variations of light that suggested the movement of people as they shuffled in and out of the car. But there was not the slightest indication that my furious cries were being noted.

I gave up when, at one point, the elevator started off unexpectedly and I lurched against the moving wall of the shaft. Scraped by the brickwork, I staggered, tripped over an obstruction and very nearly pitched down the shaft. I received such a fright my legs gave way. I crouched down, shaking and clinging onto a steel bar so tightly that when I came to let go, I had to pry my fingers loose with the other hand.

After a while, I started thumping on the roof again, but feebly, and no longer with any faith in a response. Then I looked at my watch again, and screamed silently. Ten minutes past one. Impossible for the Chief to reach Croydon within the next twenty minutes. So after getting this far, aging myself with fright and fury, I had achieved nothing. Our last opportunity to complete the formation of the Royal Jhamjarh Air Force had been irretrievably lost through incompetence. There was now not a hope in hell. Fate had decided the course. Toward oblivion. I had become, at best, a footnote.

And yet, despite the logic, and the fever that seemed to be consuming me as I crouched there, shivering and sweating at the same time, despite the suspicion that the Chief was right, that I was getting too old for this sort of thing because the adrenaline was thinning down, some swine having topped it up with water—despite fate and common sense, I was still searching for some way to attract the attention of the elevator occupants. It was plain from my demented behavior that I still believed there was a chance. I still hoped. It was ridiculous. Even if the Chief scrambled into the ministry car right this minute with a racing driver at the wheel and the kind of deserted streets that you got only on Sunday mornings, the Chief would never reach the Croydon Aerodrome by one-thirty. And come to think of it, there was no guarantee that the old fool had actually arranged for an official car. I had only assumed that he had arranged for one despite his tendency to carsickness, but for all I knew he had intended taking the bus, to set an example to his senior officers.

To continue cavorting like this in this grimy shaft was madness. So for Christ's sake, why was I still trying?

But I was. Besides, giving up meant that I would have to leap back onto the other elevator. I would have to go all through that again. No.

Anyhow, I couldn't just crouch here, begrimed and befilthed, quaking and dribbling until the hour was up. Despite the hopelessness of it all I would have to go on.

I noted that the arrangement of the steel members that held the car together were such that if I weaved my feet between two of them, they would grip my ankles if I hung upside down. That was the theory. To be on the safe side, however, I thought I'd test it first. Though the war's legacy—a secret despair—sometimes suffused me, I was not quite in the mood just at the moment for plunging headfirst down the shaft and killing myself that way. For one thing, the bottom of the shaft was so filthy.

So as the elevator rose and fell on its invisible errands, I maneuvered carefully over the side, holding onto the framework at the corner of the elevator, and wiggled slowly downward, head, as I said, first. I could feel my ankles sliding into position, though they were still not locked between the two lengths of metal. Meanwhile I was taking most of my weight through the vertical frame member.

On this side of the elevator the air seemed to rush past faster. Also the counterweight kept speeding past. Every time it did so I cringed, shutting my eyes, though there was no danger of being dislodged by it. There was ample space between the elevator and the counterweight guide rails. A further cause for discomfort was that every time the cage started upward, it increased the strain on my already creaking arm and shoulder muscles. But worst of all was the view downward. I tried hard not to look, especially when we reached the top of the shaft and the full depth of the shaft became apparent; but somehow it is difficult to avoid glancing down when you're clinging vertically to the side of an elevator head downward.

However, I finally reached my objective. This was the little window in the back of the elevator. Still hanging upside down, ankles now firmly locked in place and with a good grip on the vertical frame member, I peered inside.

At that moment there were just three occupants, a man in blue air force uniform, one in civvies and a girl, probably one of the clerks in the records department. Naturally they were all facing the door, and so presenting only the backs of their heads. And I was in no position to tap on the glass with my knuckles.

I did the next best thing. I tapped with my front teeth. It did the trick. The girl turned. Her eyes widened. So did her mouth. And presumably it emitted a piercing shriek at the sight of my face, a reaction that was not all that flattering, though I suppose the fact that the empurpled visage was upside down and the upper lip drawn back in a deathlike rictus in order to expose the front teeth that were being used as a door knocker accounted for some of her shock at seeing somebody where it was evidently impossible for him to be.

Working my way backward up the side of the elevator was the hardest work I had ever accomplished, and I was still lying on top exhausted and mentally in neutral when five minutes later the doors above, on the fourth-floor level, opened and the maintenance man let down a ladder. And after all, it turned out to be worthwhile because, just before he climbed into his car outside the Air Ministry, the Chief of Air Staff informed me almost emotionally that he would never forget what I had done for him—taking such incredible risks merely to enable him to catch a plane. He did, in fact, catch it when, alerted by a telephone call, Imperial Airways accommodated their honored guest by holding up their inaugural flight to Cairo for nearly an hour.

My selfless actions, the Chief continued, had quite altered his opinion of me, not as regards the Indian business—for that was quite plainly inimical to the interests of the state, and so he must regretfully continue to disrupt that misguided enterprise—but insofar as my character was concerned. He had been convinced years previously that I was a devious knave, but the reckless disregard for my own safety that he had just witnessed, my selfless exertions, my altruism on his behalf—and he must now confess his shame at having used his influence to damage my career purely out of spite—had made him realize that there were hitherto unsuspected elements of nobility to my character that, partially at least, solved the puzzlement he had always felt that a man whom so many others considered to be a hero and an original could to him appear to be so blank, enraging, buffoonish and utterly offensive.

"I'm just an ordinary chap doing my duty the best way I can," I said with overweening modesty, which went well with the fake English accent that I was working on; while at the same time thinking to myself how nice it was to be appreciated, and that I really hoped he would not change his mind when he returned from Iraq a month later to find that I had managed to acquire several dozen fighters from his own air force and to spirit them out of the country.

In the Rain

Though I had been living there for months, I'd had no inclination to furnish my flat on Ponsonby Terrace with anything other than the barest essentials: a kitchen table, a chair, a sofa and a bed. The floors were still uncarpeted, and only the bedroom window was curtained.

I believe that this was the only occasion when I ever looked out of that window.

I had just finished dressing for a night out, and had already switched off the bedroom light, intending to walk through into the living room. I was not even thinking about her. I was thinking about Khooshie. While the rest of us had split ourselves up into advance parties, main bodies and rear ends, Khooshie had announced his intention this afternoon of leaving for India as soon as possible, instead of waiting for his father's yacht to arrive in late January.

"You can't do that," I had protested, though even as I said it was beginning to think that it was a good idea from the standpoint of his personal safety.

"I have already done it," he said, and informed us that he had booked passage on the *Viceroy of India*, which was sailing for Bombay at the end of December.

"But I need you, Khooshie."

"You only need me to sign checks."

"It's not just that, Khooshie."

"No?"

"I also need you to sign contracts."

"You only love me for my money."

"Not at all, Khooshie."

"Now you are saying you don't love me at all?" snapped he, confirming that he had finally recovered from his attack of spirituality.

But a moment later he was all shiny-eyed again, as he confessed that he was leaving ahead of time because he had fallen in love with another girl. "Oh, Bartholomew," he sighed in a love-retching voice, "she is the most perfect English rose. I cannot sleep, I cannot read, I cannot write, I am positively aching all over for her."

"I see. You fall in love and immediately leave the country. That's love, all right."

"I am not leaving her," he explained. "By an amazing coincidence, she, too, is sailing on the *Viceroy of India*, with her father and mother."

"So *that*'s why you're leaving early—to be with her. But Khooshie," I cried, "what about dear Bubba? You can't just abandon the poor girl like that."

"Why not?"

"It's . . . it's just not done."

"But I have already done it," he replied in innocent surprise.

"I mean, she's so perfect. Interesting, witty, attractive, warm—ıot, in fact."

"Don't worry, she will get over me in time," he said sententiously. "She will recover in a few years, I expect, from the great ove of her life. Besides, I have not left her empty-handed. I am eaving her something."

"Money?"

"Muriel. I am giving her Muriel, as a memento of me."

Ie had dashed off to finish supervising the packing of his lephantine trunks without explaining what exactly he meant, ut certainly none of us ever saw Bubba or Muriel again. Anyay, at seven that night, I was still shaking my head over this evelopment, which is perhaps why, after switching off the bedroom light in my flat, I remained standing there in the semi-darkness, thinking about it.

And then, for no reason, I turned and walked to the bedroom window, drew back the curtain and peered into the darkness.

At first, all I could see were the great yellow haloes round the street lamps, and then the rain posing Euclidean problems in the black street puddles. Yet I continued to watch, and a few seconds later I saw somebody out there, walking slowly past and looking up at my windows.

She disappeared from view, but a moment later she reappeared. I wondered how long she had been walking up and down out there, poor child. She was wearing a sou'wester and a shiny black mac—just the way I had first seen her.

I draped a cloak over my white tie and tails—it was a chill evening as well as a wet one—and hurried downstairs, out the front door and across the road, slowing as I drew close.

"Hello."

"Hello."

"Come on up."

"It was a lovely letter that you sent."

"You look frozen."

"Nonsense. I am used to this sort of weather."

"The letter? Well, you wouldn't see me, so I was forced t write. Anyway, come on up."

"You are obviously going out on the town."

"The tails? No, I was going to a meeting at the Royal Aero-nautical Society. But I can give it a miss."

"Please. Do not alter your plans on my account," she sai haughtily; but I soon persuaded her to lead the way across th road, into the house, up the stairs and along to the door of m flat. She knew exactly which door to go to. I had to hurry t catch up.

I fumbled for the front-door key. I suppose I could have le the door open for a couple of minutes, but this was Chelsea, s it was better to lock up behind you. I'd been told there were lot of Bohemians about.

As she waited, Sigridur removed her sou'wester with a flouris that showered me with ice-cold rain and shook out her mop of golden hair almost as violently. "I wish to apologize," she said sternly.

"That's all right. My clothes will soon dry out."

"I wish to apologize for doubting you," she said firmly. "I now know from my reading that you were, indeed, a hero of the war. And also that you studied medicine, and it is said that you speak Russian fluently, though of course I have no proof of that. However, I have seen one of your films, which proves that you were a film actor. And I have made enquiries at Canada House and have been shown your name in a list of members of Parliament."

"Which of my hilarious films did you see?" I enquired.

"It was called *The Butler*."

"Oh, it would have to be that one. It's the worst of the lot."

"It was quite interesting."

"*Plane Crazy* is the one you should see. Or there's *Blenkinsop of the—*"

"It appears that everything you told me was true, and I thought I was being so modern and sophisticated in disbelieving you. I wanted to be thought sophisticated."

"My dear Sigga. That's quite all right."

"It is not all right. I behaved captiously and arrogantly. It is evident that you are an exceptional person, influential, respectable and rich," she said, just as I opened the door to expose an almost completely unfurnished flat.

"I see you were reading the newspaper," she said, gesturing at the pages that littered the sofa in the living room.

"Yes," I replied, gathering the paper together to give her room to sit down. Except that she continued to pace. "It's last Monday's paper."

"And it has been lying there for three days?" she asked, frowning, as if there was a risk that the newspaper might decompose.

Before I could answer she added quickly, "But that is all right. I will never again criticize. You are not married. It is perfectly all right for such a person to leave things lying around, and for him to live in empty rooms and encourage mold to grow on the dishes out there in the sink."

"Sigga, your English doesn't seem as easy as it used to be."

"It is because I am highly nervous. I sound like a schoolgirl when I am nervous."

"You are adorable. I know now more than ever that I love you."

"Go on."

"Go on what?"

"I am waiting for more compliments. You said so many lovely things in your letter, it quite melted my heart. It was as if I were falling from a great height, such was the sensation. I wept and wept with joy over the letter. It is almost illegible by now, it is so wet."

"Dearest Sigga, I was an idiot not to see that you were being loving in your own way."

Her face crumpled for a moment, but after turning away, she soon regained control and continued to walk up and down, the clack of her sensible shoes echoing in the bare room.

"Come and sit down, Sigga," I said. "It's hard to woo you when you're weaving back and forth like a target in a shooting gallery."

She approached and sat down heavily at the far end of the sofa. She must have come straight from work. There was a stain on the skirt of her gray cotton dress. She smelled of sweat and antiseptic. Somehow that made me feel all the more affectionate toward her.

"Was there anything interesting in the newspaper?"

"Pardon me?"

"I notice that you have folded the paper around some foreign news."

"So I have. Yes, it's about Iraq. It appears that the material Kekevi sold me in Cairo was genuine after all—except that it was amended and scaled down and the attack came on the fourth instead of the first of December and was more an infiltration than an attack."

"I have not the slightest idea what you are talking about."

"Well, you see, I happened to be in Cairo in October and met a spy named Kekevi who sold me a Turkish army document. Though I suspected it to be bogus, I was impelled for no logical reason to purchase it. Perhaps it was because it had to do with Iraq and I was preoccupied with Iraq at the time, and felt, perhaps intuitively or subconsciously, that it might come in handy, somehow.

"As things turned out, it did. We fed it to the head of the Royal Air Force, thinking it was all rubbish. Imagine our surprise when it turned out that it was genuine and that the Chief of Air Staff really *did* have a reason to take charge of things in the Middle East." I faltered and added, "I suppose this all sounds highly implausible. . . ."

"Not at all. I believe every word. I am sure you are not fibbing or exaggerating in the least. Your friend John Derby told me that you had been abroad since I last saw you, in Egypt and Iraq. I was surprised."

"You saw John?"

"I was at your headquarters today."

"You were? Why didn't you come up to my office?"

"You were not there. You were at the Tilbury docks."

"M'oh yes, so I was."

"You are greatly admired and loved at your headquarters."

"Oh, sure. By the way, Sigga, I would be overjoyed if you would consider marrying me."

After a kiss that lasted about ten minutes, Sigga said huskily, "I love you too, Bartholomew. That does not mean that I am entirely blind to your faults, of course, but. . . . Oh, Bartholomew," she said, tears in her eyes, "I have loved you from the very first moment you got lost in the harbor at Reykjavik. The experience of falling in love instantly was deeply disturbing. How can one possibly fall so instantaneously in love? It is quite inexplicable in physical or even psychological terms. I had no wish to love you. I did not know you, I had barely even seen you properly. How can one love before one knows what the other person is really like? Yet it is possible because it happened to me, and for the first time in my life, at the age of twenty-five. I found myself adoring you whether you were drunk or sober, sulky or elated, or indeed in any condition."

"I never suspected for a second that you loved me."

"It was such torture, thinking that you were unworthy of me."

"Eh?"

"After all, I was a doctor; I thought you were a nobody. That is why I was trying so hard to help, to improve you so that you would be worthy of me."

"I never knew that either."

"Now it turns out that you are not nobody, you are quite infamous in your own country. And soon you are to take up a position of great responsibility in India. Now you are too good for me."

"That's true. Still, I've always got on well with the lower orders."

"I have been miserable ever since I realized you were better than me. That you, who are so clever, would not want to hobnob with a simple country girl who only by desperately hard work—I am being stupidly frank, Bartholomew; I only just managed to scrape through medical school—a girl who—not even a woman, Bartholomew, I have not known a man, you know. Imagine, a virgin at the age of twenty-five, nearly twenty-six. In Iceland I was a national disgrace. They considered that I was letting the side down. Icelandic girls make love at the drop of a hat, or any other garment. Of course, one or two boys have felt my breasts, but that's about it. Where was I?"

"You were listing all the reasons why I shouldn't love you, in a way that makes me love you harder still."

"I have been so unhappy, Bartholomew, since you left, as if the world had become empty. And then I was so angry when you left, I just wanted to punish you. That is why I took off my clothes."

"Yes, that really hurt."

"I knew pride was stupid, but I couldn't help it."

"Sigga, I not only love you, I adore you."

"You cannot adore me as much as I adore you."

"Yes, I do."

"No, you don't. I adore you much, much more than you adore me. I feel that I want to do everything for you, to be your wife, mother, servant, slave. However, for the time being I will be only your MO."

"Eh?"

"I told Mr. Derby at your office that I intended to join your air force. I will be your senior medical officer."

"You mean you want to come to India with us?"

"Of course. John is very much in favor of the idea, you know. He said that if I was the MO he might quite enjoy having an FFI. What is that?"

"I think it's an RAF abbreviation. A VD inspection."

"Really? I say, isn't he awful?" Sigga said, chuckling.

"Now your English is getting *too* English."

"There is no pleasing some people, it seems. Anyway, what do you think of the idea, dearest, dearest Bartholomew darling?"

"It's shocking. A woman doctor looking after a thousand men? Facing all that danger, heat and dust? No gentleman with any sense of responsibility toward womanhood, or the fitness of things, would consider subjecting his loved one to such an experience. Personally, I think it's a splendid idea."

"Oh, Bartholomew," she said, and, after another course of osculation: "I will leave the pathology department. I'll try to get some experience in tropical medicine before we go, there is a hospital in London that specializes in it, I believe, and I shall do all the reading I can. I am glad to go, the chief pathologist is so mean, and besides, I am becoming disenchanted with corpses. My goodness, won't they be surprised at home when they hear I am going to India? John says that all the remaining officers are leaving as soon as your Maharajah's private yacht arrives at Portsmouth. Oh, isn't it exciting? I know! I shall buy a new frock!"

I suggested that we might mark the occasion by retiring forthwith to the bedroom, but old-fashioned fool that she was, she preferred to leave that sort of thing to the wedding night. Instead, we rushed back to her room, where she changed into her evening dress and her pearls, and we celebrated instead by going together to the dinner at the Royal Aeronautical Society, and to hear an interesting lecture on Load Grading Curves, Momentum Theory and the Effect of Wind Tunnel Interference on Airscrew and Tractor-Body Combination. Sigga thought it was quite interesting.

An Afterword from the Editor

In this latest account of the adventures of Bartholomew Bandy, the theme of the *Bandy Papers* as a whole has emerged most clearly yet: the devastating effect of World War I on Western society, as projected through the Bandy lens; a large theme, assuming that the war was perhaps the most critical turning point in history.

Throughout five volumes, Bandy has steadfastly refused to confess otherwise than that everything in the garden is lovely and all the weeds are comical. But the effect of the war on himself is increasingly evident, revelations escape like chinks of light from an absurdist blackout curtain. A suppressed fury is there in many a past chapter, and suggests the reason why he started to write his memoirs in the first place: to exorcise that most devilish and dishonorable of wars. But just as his inner life is a ridiculously unequal struggle between an overarmed ego and a conviction of his unworthiness, so his wooden stage is in conflict with the message. Following the publication of the first volume, *Time* magazine likened Bandy to "a clown tap-dancing on a coffin." Over five volumes, Bandy has been attempting to distract himself from the contemplation of what is in the coffin, and how it got there. Every now and then, he has failed. In *Me Too*, during a visit to Montreal, he observes: "I had seen a chauffeur shooing away a crippled, pencil-selling veteran so that the chauffeur's boss could march unobstructedly into his neoclassical head office, so that the boss need not be disturbed by the sight of one of those whose lost arm and leg had perhaps enabled him to become a millionaire." You can almost hear the vicious tone. Now, as his resistance has lessened, the truth has started to burn through. The cynicism that almost every participant in the war has confessed to is shared, after all, by him. He has begun to say it aloud, that the war was a false crusade that has damaged, perhaps permanently, the faith in others that is essential for the healthy functioning of society. Though even now he is still struggling against the truth. "I myself had come through the war unscathed," he says. "I had lost all belief in God, church and state, in the inherent goodness of man, in outwardly imposed discipline, in authority, even in virtue itself; but these were minor penalties compared with the furies and terrors that beset so many former fighting men." But the loss of those beliefs that he set out with so fervently, has, as we the discerning now suspect, produced furies and terrors every bit as intense as those suffered by others.

Yet for the sake of sanity, perhaps, after all, comedy is the best exorcist.